What

Napoleon

Could

Not Do

What
Napoleon
Could
Not Do

DK Nnuro

Riverhead Books   New York

RIVERHEAD BOOKS
An imprint of Penguin Random House LLC
penguinrandomhouse.com

Riverhead and the R colophon are registered
trademarks of Penguin Random House LLC.

The Library of Congress has catalogued the
Riverhead hardcover edition as follows:
Names: Nnuro, DK, author.
Title: What Napoleon could not do / DK Nnuro.
Identifiers: LCCN 2022042346 (print) | LCCN 2022042347 (ebook) |
ISBN 9780593420348 (hardcover) | ISBN 9780593420362 (ebook)
Subjects: LCGFT: Novels.
Classification: LCC PS3614.N87 W47 2023 (print) |
LCC PS3614.N87 (ebook) | DDC 813/.6—dc23/eng/20220915
LC record available at https://lccn.loc.gov/2022042346
LC ebook record available at https://lccn.loc.gov/2022042347

First Riverhead hardcover edition: February 2023
First Riverhead trade paperback edition: February 2024
Riverhead trade paperback ISBN: 9780593420355

Printed in the United States of America
1st Printing

BOOK DESIGN BY LUCIA BERNARD

For my mother,

Cecilia O. Gyamoh, who saw me through,

and for my maternal grandparents,

E.A. Ofori and Agnes Gyamo,

who never wavered in their belief in me.

Contents

BOOK 2

BOOK 3

Book 1

Worth

From where he was standing on the veranda, Mr. Nti watched as Patricia's people exited the pickup truck that held up two sedans behind it. On Saturday mornings stillness descended on Otumfuo, Deduako's busy main road, a stillness Mr. Nti surmised also infected the drivers. How else could he explain the Job-like patience of the people at the wheels of the stopped cars? Hardly a honk from either when they were both forced to idle, all while Patricia's people took a lifetime to cross Otumfuo for the clearing.

Otherwise bare, the clearing rose in several small sand mounds, making it feel like unsteady foam underfoot. Still this inconvenience did not disqualify the clearing as a favored football pitch. The usual footballers who assembled every Saturday at dawn had now dispersed; the dust they excited had dissipated. Mr. Nti had caught the conclusion of this morning's match, after which each side had brought down their collapsible goalposts. Today it had been skins versus shirts, with the skins coming out sand coated, some appearing as if a curious child had misconstrued sand for body paint; some as if a man had crept out of soot rubble. It was a shame that the dust they'd flared had cleared, Mr. Nti thought. A cloud of it would have precisely underscored the coming of Patricia's indecent lot.

Triggering the cloud would have been easy enough, except that Patricia's people were not heading for the house as he'd expected. Their pace matched the slowness with which they'd crossed the road, and in its current iteration it could even be mistaken for tenderness. He, of course, would not be mistaken; Patricia's people were the sort he knew to never accept at face value. When he couldn't see them under the shroud of bushes that was part of their trek to the house, he was able to focus on hardening his resolve. He took in the rainbow-like rooftops that his high-sitting house looked onto; he heard the hollow chirps of morning birds. In this respite of peacefulness, he lost track of Patricia's people, so that he almost missed it when Patricia's mother came to an instigating stop about thirty yards away from the house's front gate.

She held herself in place: one leg on the timber bridge that led to the house, the other on the ground behind her. It could have been a warm-up stretch in an aerobics class. But Patricia's mother, carelessly stout and in her sixties, had no use for aerobics. Maybe she stood wide legged to let whatever breeze was rising from the stream run up her thighs. Maybe she was savoring a secondary tickle: the dry weeds at the bridge's entry against her legs. Just as Mr. Nti was contemplating this, they locked eyes, the thirty yards between them contracting to a hair.

She smirked at him. She wobbled her raised leg. A taunt. That was it. She'd stopped only for that childish purpose.

It was just like her. Two days before, during a phone conversation to finalize today's plans, she'd predicted a quick divorce proceeding. "After all, it's not as if Jacob has anything of worth for us to fight over," she'd said.

Now, with her assessing leg, she was repeating herself. Such worthlessness in Mr. Nti's household. So much worthlessness that even the sturdiness of the bridge was now in doubt.

It was a mercy, Mr. Nti thought, that Patricia's mother would be out of their lives after today. All would be said and done. Why he hadn't followed his first instinct five years ago to thwart the marriage, only God knew. He'd done some investigating on Patricia's mother then. Someone had called her "a woman in charge." Another had said, "What father?" when he'd asked for the whereabouts of Patricia's father. That same person had mentioned that Patricia had a half sister whose father was also out of the picture. Worried about what might become of his son Jacob, Mr. Nti had sat him down to ask, "Are you prepared to marry into a home where men don't matter?"

Jacob had laughed off the concern, his eyelids flitting in that way of his. Patricia wasn't like her mother, he'd said. "Men matter to her."

How terribly Jacob had miscalculated, leading them to this point, with Patricia's mother enjoying her little taunt before marshaling onto the bridge the three men she'd brought with her to certify that if Jacob had ever mattered to her daughter, he no longer did.

On the bridge, they pushed on in single file. In front was Tot, Patricia's maternal uncle, in whose hand was a black polyethylene bag Mr. Nti presumed contained the bottle of aromatic schnapps they would present him to end the marriage. As for the two men behind Tot, also uncles, Mr. Nti knew them only by face, not name. Tot had stood in for the hypothetical father during the marriage ceremony five years ago, clutching absent Patricia's framed photograph to his chest—a forlorn beauty on some American pier seemingly awaiting her groom. Patricia's stare in the photograph had been fawning. It had added to the photo's backdrop of ceaselessness—the many birds dotting the sky, the rolling ocean waves—to speak of a forever for her and Jacob. At the marriage ceremony, Tot, wearing an amber organza number unseemly for a man, and speaking alongside the overhead whir of a snaking balloon arch, had sung Patricia's praises: a thick-and-thin warrior born to be devoted; a treasure. Obviously Patricia's readiness today to give up on the marriage spoke differently. She was not a thick-and-thin warrior. Devoted? Nonsense. A treasure? Even more nonsense.

Mr. Nti could not help returning to the one question that he had been asking himself for years: Had Patricia been at her own wedding, would he have been able to detect—from, say, the bunching of her face or the incessant pinching of her fingers—the untruths that came from her uncle's mouth?

An odd name, Tot. It was from his days as a drunkard—this according to one truth-teller from Mr. Nti's premarriage sleuthing. Even though Tot no longer frequented his neighborhood's teeming bars saying that a tot of liquor, any liquor, was all the pick-me-up he needed, the name had stuck. In her own efforts at a pick-me-up, Patricia had confirmed this piece of family lore to pry laughter out of Jacob. This was after Jacob's second visa rejection two years ago, when he'd told Patricia over the phone that he seriously doubted that the American embassy would ever favor him.

He'd called her from his cellular while on the bus from Accra to Kumasi. After finishing talking with her, he'd called the house to announce the disappointment and to say that he would not make it home in time for dinner. A truck carrying timber had toppled over in the road and he couldn't tell how long the typically four-hour journey would be prolonged. Mr. Nti listened on, hearing in the background the other passengers' intensifying murmurs of frustration. He believed their frustrations warranted. More than that, he believed that Jacob, a man who'd just been rejected by America for the second time—and who, to top it off, was facing an aggravating disruption on his journey back home—ought to have been leading them. Instead Jacob was unsettlingly composed.

"You sound well," Mr. Nti wondered aloud. "You don't have to."

"The hurt isn't so bad this time around, Pa. Patricia lifted my spirits."

Then on and on Jacob went, extolling *lively* Patricia, saying that she'd known just what to say to put him in a better mood after this second visa denial. "Tot was quite the drunk, you know?" Jacob offered.

"So I've heard."

Jacob laughed, adding, "The kind that ends up plastered on the floor."

Another chuckle followed—a vicious one. In an instant Mr. Nti gathered that Patricia had infected Jacob with her rancor. He saw his chance to help Jacob see who Patricia truly was. He decided to frame his point as a curiosity. "Is it a lively person or a cruel person who makes you laugh at someone's expense? Not to mention her own uncle?"

This rattled Jacob. He took a moment before replying. "It was the way she described Tot, Pa. That sometimes they would find him on the floor like a flopped rag doll."

Stepping down from the bridge now, Tot did not flop onto the ground. Nor did the other two men or Patricia's mother. They proceeded along the inclined grassy path to the gate. Scaling the low hill slowed them down again; this time, they had the manner of harried pilgrims.

It had been two days since their insufferable phone call, and yet Mr. Nti could still feel his tense grip on the receiver after Patricia's mother questioned Jacob's worth. In reply, Mr. Nti had demanded that Patricia's mother swiftly return the gold band Jacob had presented to the family at the marriage ceremony. How she was going to engineer the return, he harped, was her burden. The ring had reached Patricia's finger through one of her Virginia friends. This friend, unlike Patricia, possessed the papers required to move freely between America and Ghana. In the six years of Patricia's courtship and marriage, the friend had visited Ghana several times. Mr. Nti had taken to calling her Postwoman, for she'd delivered to Jacob clothing from Patricia, a cellular phone, a laptop, picture books of America that Patricia had wanted Jacob to study in preparation for his interviews at the embassy, in case the immigration officer sprang on him a particularly idiosyncratic question about American monuments. Mount Rushmore had been the one Jacob asked to be tested on most often, saying that it was a four-in-one monument; if an immigration officer truly wanted to trip him up, Patricia had told him, he'd ask about Mount Rushmore.

"There are others," Jacob anxiously announced to his father the night before his first appearance at the embassy. Standing in front of his wardrobe mirror, Jacob inspected his fifth blazer-and-trousers combo: ash against khakis, along with a cream shirt. He would go without a tie as not to appear too eager or overdone, he decided. Satisfied, he nodded at the reflection of himself in the mirror, capping off with, "According to Patricia there are other monuments all over Virginia but nowhere to be found in any of the books she sent me. That's because Americans in their right minds are ashamed of those ones. So no immigration officer is going to bring them up."

Patricia had also sent packs of white underwear and white singlets for Mr. Nti, and for Mrs. Nti she'd sent jewelry that, truth be told, quickly faded. Patricia's coordinated largesse wasn't endless. Over time it would lessen to trinkets, most notably in the way the Werther's Original toffees she sent went from five hundred-packs at a time to two ten-packs. Call that the point of no return. The last time Jacob had gone to meet Postwoman, he'd returned empty-handed.

What did it mean to dissolve a marriage when there'd been no *real* marriage? No embrace, no consummation, no sharing of a marital home. In all but name, "in absentia" described Patricia's role from the start. She'd been courted in absentia. Gotten married in absentia. It was, Mr. Nti thought, the perfect cap that in an hour she would finalize her divorce in absentia. The necessary rites of Jacob and Patricia's ending were straightforward enough: Mr. Nti and his delegation and Patricia's mother and her delegation would gather in the living room, grievances would be aired and exchanged, scores would be settled, the divorce eventually declared. A final act would follow: they would each take their turn drinking from the same quarter-filled glass of aromatic schnapps.

Mr. Nti understood that these customs were worthless in addressing his true grievance: What about Jacob? These customs were as worthless as he knew Postwoman's future delivery of the ring would be. True mollification had to come at the hands of something blisteringly unpleasant. Custom be damned! The ring be damned!

Last August, exactly a year and a month ago (how could he ever forget?), Jacob had learned that Patricia shared her two-bedroom flat in Virginia with a man. Over his cellular, Jacob had inquired about it and Patricia had responded in a roundabout way that the man was only her flatmate. For Jacob, that response had sufficed. But for Mr. Nti, it had demanded a deeper probing. He wondered aloud whether Virginia suffered from a scarcity of woman flatmates. Jacob had merely smiled. At any other time his flitting eyelids and his liquid smile would have effectively poured oil on the troubled waters. But Patricia had set in motion savage waves.

"Who told you about the man in the first place?" Mr. Nti asked him. "Why not ask that person who he *really* is to her?"

Jacob did not reveal his source, which Mr. Nti found a completely unnecessary commitment to discretion. Nobody but Postwoman could have told him; that much was clear. What was the danger in Jacob revealing to his own father that Postwoman had been kind enough to let him know the truth? Since childhood, Jacob had confounded him with his oddities—among them a seeming aversion to women, which had contributed to his younger sister, Belinda, essentially assigning him a wife he would never meet. Jacob had been fully grown by age fifteen—handsome, an enviable physique, a towering self that was rare among Ashanti men, who tended to be on the shorter side. Yet as much as these qualities promised a full life with women, his son spun through one lonely year after another. He was thirty-four when Belinda connected him with Patricia.

If Mr. Nti was being honest, Jacob's apparent glee over a life with Patricia was evidence that he did indeed like women, and that had encouraged him to support the union. In any case, such long-distance marriages were common and had been for some time, with so many young people in this country fixated on America. Yes, it was more often the case that the parties had been in each other's presence at least once, something that could not be said about Jacob and Patricia. That fret had received only brief attention from Mr. Nti, for Belinda, his only daughter, had repeatedly vouched for Patricia's decency. And for God's sake there was the fact of Jacob's glee over a woman. That glee! How vivid it was when Jacob showed him and Mrs. Nti the ring he would give Patricia, some of the cost of which Mr. Nti had covered. Mrs. Nti had held it up triumphantly. It was beautiful, but the triumph in her eyes was for the fact that Jacob—however convolutedly, however remotely—had finally solved his woman problem.

"Girls of today prefer white gold," Mrs. Nti said about the ring, "which has never made sense to me. Yellow gold is classic. Never goes out of style. You couldn't have made a better choice."

These days, whenever that memory of Sarah struck Mr. Nti, her enduring cynicism about the union reverberated. Sarah was wise. It was from her that Belinda had acquired her wisdom and startling intelligence, but Belinda had taken hers further: the Hotchkiss School in Connecticut, Williams College, George Washington Law, and magnificent wealth (even if that was the doing of Belinda's American husband, Wilder Thomas). A Sarah born in a different era—Belinda's era—would have charted a path of greatness like Belinda's, or even one outstripping hers. But in 1965, at fifteen, Sarah had been taken out of school and given to him for marriage. He was twenty-two.

Regarding Jacob and Patricia, Sarah had ultimately taken her cue from Belinda. During one of her calls home Belinda permanently subordinated Sarah's concerns when she said, "Ma, I want this marriage for you as much as I want it for Jacob. You will not live forever." A brash doctor had been direct with him and Sarah just weeks prior. He'd given Sarah three to four years, even with a pacemaker. Belinda was echoing the message more delicately.

"All right," Sarah said.

To Belinda's ears, Sarah had signed off on the marriage. But during moments when Sarah was certain of their privacy, she worried to her husband's hearing. Once, seated with him on this very veranda, she asked, "What if Jacob is doing this to hide?"

"Hide from what?"

"Himself."

Mr. Nti had needed a minute to settle on the right response. "Jacob is not duplicitous," he said.

Jacob. Good Jacob. A man of good conscience, Mr. Nti thought, courtesy of himself and Sarah. Jacob had remained faithful to his wife. The same could not be said, Mr. Nti was sure, about Patricia. The male flatmate was Patricia's true motivation for ending the marriage. Because Jacob's two visa denials did not seem like good reason. Nor were the two disappointing results from the American Green Card Lottery. Five months ago, Jacob had come home and reported that Patricia had asked him in their latest call, "How much longer can we hope that one day America will let you join me?"

The question had brought them to this moment when Mr. Nti, now in one of the veranda's cushioned cane chairs and feeling primed for battle, wished for lightning to strike Patricia's people dead. They banged on the high gate instead with a forcefulness he could have sworn shook the house.

From behind him he heard the kitchen door creak open. It let out to the left side of the house, where a strip of fertile land had been cultivated to grow red and green peppers, aubergines, and tomatoes. The rest of the walled compound was covered in cream ceramic tiling with a swirly rose-colored motif, against which he could hear his grandson's rubber sandals slapping. Alfred came into view in the front yard, dashing toward the gate.

Mr. Nti quickly got to his feet. "Alfred," he whispered.

Alfred stayed put at the large flowerpots that hemmed the veranda wall. He stood straight, as if, eight years ago, a midwife hadn't jerked him from his mother during delivery. The negligent woman had torn a crucial annular ligament in Alfred's right arm, leaving it to hang heavy at his side. It was rarely possible for Alfred to stand straight. Usually, he tipped to his right.

Mr. Nti leaned over the waist-high veranda wall. "Stay right there," he ordered. "I'm going inside. You can open the gate after."

From inside the house, he would give Patricia's mother a taste of her own medicine. Alfred could get them at the gate. He could offer them chairs on the veranda. But inviting them inside was beyond the bounds of his eight years on earth. Until an adult appeared—and Mr. Nti was the only capable adult available, as Jacob had fled the house before dawn and Robert and Martha,

Alfred's parents, were constrained by their inability to hear or speak—Patricia's people would be forced to wait outside.

Mr. Nti entered the house. He closed the door behind him and drew the drapes. Here was true taunting: invited guests made to feel uninvited upon arrival.

PATRICIA'S MOTHER'S TRADE as a distributor of organza had afforded her a mint-green two-story house. She'd found her relative success through pluck rather than education. This pluck should have mattered more to Mr. Nti, as should have Patricia's mother's impressive home, where the marriage ceremony, following tradition, had taken place. Without the financial assistance of his children—mostly without Belinda's husband, Wilder—Mr. Nti would have been unable to build his own, single-story home. He hadn't made it back to Patricia's mother's house since the marriage ceremony, as, apparently dedicated to the union as she was, she had made all the subsequent house calls. She was partial to holiday visits, though she hadn't made her annual pilgrimage during the most recent Christmas season, for reasons that were soon obvious. The Christmas before she'd come with her maid in tow. Atop the girl's head was an aluminum pan filled with two live chickens—immobilized by the string that tied their feet together—a fifteen-kilogram bag of rice, and two crates of eggs. That crisp afternoon had piqued Mr. Nti's awareness and he'd noted that the woman had a singular redeeming physical quality: a perfectly round face. Otherwise Patricia's mother's stoutness was unfortunate. Her triceps flapped. Her midsection, visible through her tightly fastened kabas, looked pleated. She must have refused

Alfred's offer of the veranda chairs, for Mr. Nti saw through the curtains that she stood by the flowerpots, taking them in as if she were seeing the red hibiscus and purple bougainvillea for the first time. Yet the flowers, like the bridge, were characteristic of Mr. Nti's home, and Patricia's mother couldn't claim to be unfamiliar with them. About the hibiscus she'd once asked, "What's your secret? Mine keep dying on me."

Was she wondering about his gardening competence now? Her eyes, as best as he could tell, observed the flowers like a flower show judge. It was unlikely that she was taking in the blooms in appreciation; most likely, she was finding fault, impossible as that was, with the hibiscus, or even the bougainvillea, despite their sensuous lushness. But fault she was to find: Divorce had a way of reversing one's perspective. Everything that had once been beautiful was now flawed.

Inside the kitchen, Yaa, the maid, sat on a low stool skinning and cutting cassava onto newspaper. Across from her, Alfred arranged the pieces into lines. He looked up at his grandfather when he came in.

"Did they say anything?" Mr. Nti asked.

"They are waiting."

"Where did you say I was?"

"In the toilet."

Mr. Nti smiled. Alfred had probably provided the quickest excuse that came to him, not knowing that he'd done his grandfather a favor: nothing was more needling than having to wait for someone to void his bowels. How perfect! Thinking to show a bit of graciousness, Mr. Nti asked Yaa to take some water out to their guests.

He looked back at Alfred, whose eyes had not left him. "Did you tell your parents that they are here?"

"I told them. They are putting on nicer clothes." He returned to his cassava and lined them up in columns with his useful arm without difficulty. That rare balance again.

"How about you?" Mr. Nti asked. Alfred was bare-chested. He wore a pair of mesh shorts, his orange rubber slippers paired at this side. "Won't you get ready?"

"Are we starting now?"

"Soon."

Without saying a word, Alfred rushed from the kitchen with characteristically right-leaning strides, forgetting his slippers. What Alfred suffered in smooth movement he made up for with a mature mind. He'd absorbed the role of interpreter between his parents and the rest of the household three years ago when Sarah at last succumbed to heart disease—she'd been the primary interpreter before Alfred showed early signs of his own capabilities. She'd mastered Robert's language not long after he started signing in boyhood, beating Mr. Nti to it. Mr. Nti had tried to learn but had soon given up because Sarah was always ready to pass on to Robert whatever her husband's message was. It hadn't helped that they'd sent Robert to a boarding school for the deaf when he'd turned six. Robert was gone nine months of the year, until he returned permanently at twenty-one. Belinda, being brilliant, had also picked up Robert's sign language, but by the time Robert came home for good, she was already abroad. Jacob was still around, but like his father he couldn't seem to master sign language. And so it was Sarah who burdened herself with the subtle bends in the fingers that differentiated "goat" from "sheep," "pear" from "aubergine," "red" from "violet." "Red, red," she'd once flicked her fingers in emphasis—they couldn't have Robert thinking that the blood drawn from her at the hospital was violet in color. This was during the latter part of her heart illness. By that time Robert was married to Martha and Alfred was five. Their little family made their home in the one-room guest quarters at the rear of the house. Sarah, relegated to the four-poster bed in the big bedroom in the main house, thanked the heavens for the gift of Alfred. "He will take my place when I'm gone. One-armed and all," she assured Mr. Nti after he tearfully confessed a diminished connection with Robert as one of his many grievances over losing her.

Alfred, despite his youth, would participate in today's divorce ceremony. Robert and Martha were the rightful participants, but they required a go-between to keep them abreast of what was happening.

By himself in the kitchen, Mr. Nti could feel its quiet thicken. Unnerved, he welcomed the faucet's aggravating drip. Before he could make his move to tighten it, he heard voices drifting into the house. His first thought boiled his blood: Patricia's people had let themselves in. He was in the throes of accepting that there might be no cordiality with which to begin when the rich alto of his younger brother's singsong speech patterns calmed him.

"Sorry we're late," Kwame Broni said.

Over the years, Kwame Broni's hair had stayed dark without ever being steeped in black coloring. This had always bothered Mr. Nti, whose own hair was spotted with gray.

"Not late enough," Mr. Nti said to his brother.

"I showed them to their seats."

"I heard." Sixty-eight years had made Mr. Nti lean. Kwame

Broni, on the other hand, only three years his junior, was sturdy.
One difference disturbed Mr. Nti most: his brother in more than
six decades hadn't contended with so much as a troublesome
tooth, while all four of Mr. Nti's back molars had been extracted,
which accentuated his jowls.

He could, however, take heart in his eyesight: he still saw significant distances without a blur while nearsighted Kwame Broni
had to wear tortoiseshell spectacles.

Mr. Nti peered past Kwame Broni's shoulder. "My plan was to
have them wait out there some more," he said. "Out of spite."

Kwame Broni giggled dismissively. "That's the best you could
come up with?"

"I'm not like you. I don't have a ready bone for cruelty."

Without a word they entered the storeroom of the kitchen for
some privacy. They stopped in the half dark amid a congregation
of pots and pans. "I came up with something," Kwame Broni said,
his voice low.

"As if that was ever in doubt."

"Do you want to hear it or not?" Kwame Broni asked. Mr. Nti
nodded apologetically. "Patricia's uncle," Kwame Broni said. "Tot.
When all is said and done, will he drink with us?"

"Not the schnapps." Mr. Nti had a sense of his brother's wicked
intent but he would not name it explicitly. "We don't want his
devil returning to him."

"We don't?"

"No. We don't."

"Not big on schadenfreude?"

"Not big on what?"

"Schadenfreude."

"Meaning?"

"Delighting in his misery," Kwame Broni said. "He's not innocent."

"Maybe. Or maybe not. Patricia's mother is his life support. You can't blame him for going with her will," Mr. Nti said. "Anyway, he's not our target."

Patricia's mother was. She was a proxy for Patricia, but also her aggressive instincts and attitudes deserved a proper reply. Mr. Nti and Kwame Broni had gotten together earlier in the week—after Jacob had confirmed Mr. Nti's suspicion that he would be a no-show at the divorce ceremony—and decided that Kwame Broni would speak on Jacob's behalf. They were certain that Tot, formerly a respected secondary school linguistics instructor at Kumasi's prestigious Prempeh College, would do the same for Patricia. It had been that way during the marriage ceremony: Tot was Patricia's spokesperson; Kwame Broni, Jacob's. This time, however, the two eloquent men would be pitted toe-to-toe to mold the situation's nuances in their respective faction's favor. The most successful working of these nuances would ultimately distinguish winner from loser, and the least of the wins that Mr. Nti was hoping for—achievable only through skillful use of language—was to reclaim some of the dignity that had been slowly sapped from his household over the past six years. There was no better man for the job than Kwame Broni, an economist and mathematician whose brilliance with numbers was matched by a silver tongue (owing to his voracious appetite for foreign novels). Previewing his plan for today, Kwame Broni had reframed the situation for his brother, introducing it as *symbolism*: it had been Patricia, Kwame Broni explained, who symbolized America, rejecting Jacob each time. He would launch his defense from there after Tot, per tradition, spoke first. He would place all the blame for the marriage's failure on Patricia. "Disgraceful people," Kwame Broni promised to call them. The look on their faces this would elicit, he said, would be worth everything!

TWO CEILING FANS whirred above them in the living room. Patricia's mother had stuffed herself into a flower-patterned armchair next to a maroon love seat with gold brocade, where Tot sat. Their two comrades perched on repurposed dining room chairs. One's feet touched the ground; the other's dangled.

Alfred occupied the seat at Tot's side. From there, his parents, in a matching love seat at Mr. Nti's left, could see him easily. Except for Alfred, everyone sat with kin. The table that had been in the center of the living room had been moved, the open space a no-man's-land between families.

Through her shadow on the curtain, Kwame Broni's wife, Afia, could be traced pacing the veranda. Why was she still outside? Mr. Nti wondered. He could use a woman like her to make Jacob's case. Afia frequently echoed Sarah's wisdom.

Mr. Nti nudged his brother's knee with his. "Is Afia not joining us?"

"She says this is family business."

"Isn't she family?"

"That was what I said."

Mr. Nti rose and shambled to the window. He pushed aside the peach linen and knocked on a glass louver twice. "Afia," he called through the parted louvers. "We are waiting for you."

She came quickly and sat on the ottoman next to her husband.

For a while, no one spoke. Patricia's mother scanned the room's clapboard ceiling, the forty-inch flat-screen TV in the corner, the large family portraits on the walls and the image of Jesus Christ ascending to heaven. She even looked behind her, at nothing but the closed door to the dining area. Next to Robert and Martha, two of the family portraits occupied their own dining chairs: one of Jacob by the front gate, another of Belinda and Wilder on their wedding day in front of a Houston courthouse. She'd planted her gaze on Belinda and Wilder.

"You didn't bring Patricia?" Mr. Nti asked.

"Pardon?"

He cocked his head toward the portraits. "You didn't bring Patricia?"

"No," she said.

He'd forgotten five years ago to take Belinda's portrait with him to the marriage ceremony. As the matchmaker, Belinda was an important player who'd deserved her own proxy participation. Mr. Nti wouldn't make the same mistake twice. This morning, as Yaa arranged the living room, he'd stressed that as she'd done with Jacob's picture, she should make a place for Belinda and Wilder's picture as well. The one with Wilder was the only framed photo he had of Belinda as an adult. As an added benefit, he would see Patricia's mother's one person—Patricia—and raise her three people: Jacob, Belinda, and Wilder. This, of course, was not coming to pass. Even better, he was seeing her zero and raising her three.

From nowhere Patricia's mother asked, "Do you have light?"

The question reformed as a repetition in Mr. Nti's head:

Nothing of worth. Nothing of worth. Were they able to afford something as ordinary as electricity?

He regarded her blankly.

"You haven't been having *light-off*?" she asked.

He still didn't understand.

Tot huffed. "The power outages, Mr. Nti," he said. "You look ignorant of them."

"I am."

Amazed, Tot asked, "Constant light? You have constant light?"

Mr. Nti nodded.

"Count yourself lucky, then."

Gray whiskers patched Tot's face from mid-cheek to the underpart of his jaw. An unkempt growth that called to mind a drunkard's neglectful grooming. "You will get to know soon," Tot continued. "They say that very soon every Ghanaian's power will be rationed."

Kwame Broni scoffed. "Who's they?"

"The dailies."

"I read them every day," Kwame Broni said. "I've seen no news of the sort."

"Which ones do you read?"

"Every last one of them."

With a hint of irritation, Tot gave up. He rested the back of his head on the love seat's upper padding. Next to him Alfred swirled his arm, presumably to relay to Robert and Martha what was being said: *Every last one of them, Kwame Broni had responded.*

After what seemed a needlessly long impasse, Kwame Broni jumped up. He said, "We Ashantis have a practice that should not be news to any of us." He spoke in English—a wily choice, as it excluded Patricia's unlearned mother. "When a guest comes into your home, you inquire about that guest's journey and about his or her purpose. We are not ignorant of your purpose. Still we must fulfill our tradition. As my brother's designated spokesman, I welcome you to our home. Most important, we ask about your journey. And, equally important, about your purpose."

Tot rose to his feet slowly. "Please, sit," he proposed in Twi.

Kwame Broni settled himself.

"On behalf of my sister and two cousins, who are really like brothers to us, I thank you." Tot was progressing in Twi, in clear condemnation of Kwame Broni's English. "Our journey here was rather smooth," he said. "We all know the unreliability of our roads. One day a surprise pothole the size of a basin. Another day a tree trunk falls from a tipper truck. Thankfully, we did not encounter anything of the sort. My sister's driver, Baafi, is an expert. But there was still the concern. After all, harm, when ready to befall, has no care for expertise."

He looked behind him at his sister, as if as a reminder. She encouraged him with two approving nods.

"Indeed, we know why we are here," Tot continued. "But as our elders say, 'Only a foolish man does not speak thinking he's been understood.' Five years ago, our daughter Patricia and your son Jacob decided to bring our families together. I can still remember that happy day and the joy I saw on everyone's faces has never left me. Patricia and her sister are more than my nieces. They are my children. I have no children of my own, which makes it easier for my nieces to occupy the place in my heart that the good Lord above had set aside for my own wards."

Tot's face turned sullen. "I never thought a day like this would come. Maybe we should have paid attention to the warning signs. After all, what were the prospects for a marriage between complete strangers? I must confess that I did wonder about this. But then I considered my own parents' marriage and the marriages of many of our elders. Even the marriages of some of our contemporaries." This mention of their contemporaries registered in Mr. Nti as a provocation from Tot that demanded a firm response. Tot, Mr. Nti thought, was criticizing his and Sarah's marriage. He would remain silent and respect tradition; otherwise he would have let Tot and the rest of them know that Sarah and he had never been strangers, that they'd grown up in the same compound. In fact, he had fallen in love with Sarah long before she had been given to him for marriage.

Tot kept on: "My mother was presented to my father on an especially hot day some seventy years ago. They were also complete strangers and yet their marriage lasted fifty-five years. Death was the only force powerful enough to part them. My parents are not unique. As I have already noted, the story of their marriage is the norm for most of our elders. Indeed it could be argued that in those days there was nothing like strangers getting married because nobody ventured into a neighboring village to find a wife for his son. Nothing like we have here in Kumasi, a global city that makes marriage across the Atlantic possible."

Tot paused, as if to take stock. Nobody delivered what he appeared to be waiting for—*You mean like Jacob and Patricia*, someone could have said—so he continued. "In any case, my parents hadn't known each other. They were strangers—because, honestly, same village or not, how well can you know someone foisted on you as a spouse? And yet they went on to enjoy a long-lasting marriage. If them, why not Jacob and Patricia? More so because in these global times the word *stranger*, thanks to technology, has been rendered meaningless. Familiarity can be cultivated through all kinds of devices. Patricia and Jacob had exchanged sweet nothings over their cellulars. Through photographs, they had updated each other on their physical changes. Last week I spoke to Patricia on a cellular she'd sent to her mother. Believe it or not I wasn't just listening to her voice. I could see her! My understanding is that she'd sent a similar phone to Jacob. Perhaps if Jacob were here, we could confirm?"

Tot gazed at Mr. Nti questioningly. In reply, Mr. Nti pressed his lips together and said nothing.

"Okay. Fine," Tot said. "I am confident that a time had come when Jacob had not simply listened to Patricia's voice, but seen her. How, then, could we call them strangers? Because they'd never had a face-to-face encounter? Rubbish." He cleared his throat. He did not ask for water. "I believed this five years ago and I continue to believe it today: there was great hope for Jacob and Patricia's marriage. What I had overlooked is what has ultimately led us here. Patricia, her own legal standing in America uncertain, was powerless in appealing for her husband to join her. How, then, was Jacob to get to her? I asked her this same question during our most recent conversation and she confessed that was the least of her worries. There are apparently many ways to skin that cat, ways her friends' husbands had utilized to join their wives. One way is the Green Card Lottery. Another is proving to the Americans that you have something *of worth* to return to in Ghana and will come back before your visitor's visa expires. That's what the husband of one of her friends did—he used a letter of support from his workplace to convince the American embassy of his high standing in Ghana. Acquiring the visitor's visa was painless for him. Of course, he has not returned home since he left many years ago. Another friend's husband, a low-level employee at the Agricultural Ministry, managed to secure an invitation to an agricultural conference in the American state named Iowa. Another had an affidavit of support from his bank. Showing the Americans that he had a lot of money in his bank account was all it took."

Tot sighed. "Patricia had expected more forcefulness from Jacob. Her friends' husbands had not required direction from their wives. But Jacob was timid, waiting for Patricia to direct him. The Green Card Lottery seemed the best option for Jacob—luck, after all, can be on anyone's side, timid or not. But twice he failed. Truth be told, we wonder whether he ever entered the lottery. That was his best bet. Otherwise what high standing in Ghana could Jacob have capitalized on? What reputable employment? What gleaming bank account?

"Our dear Patricia is out of options. And it doesn't look like Jacob will ever figure it out for himself. We have come here today after much soul-searching to finalize what has been brewing for a long time."

With that, Tot brought his speech to a close. He sat down again, clasping his hands around his right knee to conceal a noticeable jitter in his leg. His sister reached for his thigh, settling it, hushing it.

Mr. Nti squirmed. He desperately wished to move on from Tot's drivel but he could not get past it in his mind. At one point in Tot's speech, Alfred had brought his left fist to his chest and Mr. Nti hadn't understood the action's meaning, but he had been struck by the strong emotion that prompted his grandson's narrowing shoulders and closed eyes. A moment later, as if suddenly startled by an explosion, Alfred ripped the fist from his chest, opened his eyes, and straightened his shoulders. Mr. Nti began to understand: marriage, and its reverse, divorce. Sarah, with her two workable fists, might have joined them to indicate marriage and split them to indicate divorce. She would have been emphatic, but nothing like Alfred. She would have rightly reserved theatrics for when Tot called Jacob timid and when he questioned whether Jacob had even entered the lottery. These were the moments of highest tension, which Alfred had signed calmly without regard to their insults. These were the climaxes of their performance, their causes for agitation. Yet Robert and Martha had not so much as glared at Tot.

But Kwame Broni was agitated. The floor was now his. He stood up.

Which language would it be for him? From his brother's nebulous posture, Mr. Nti could not tell.

"We have heard all that has been said, and though we have tried for empathy, we will not force nature, which did not bestow upon us the flexibility needed to bend for the empathy we simply cannot muster."

Twi it would be. Which made sense—after all, Patricia's mother was his prime target.

"Indeed Jacob married your daughter Patricia on a *fine* day. Tot described the day as *happy*. I saw it as fine. Fine because the sun did not manifest its habit of beaming magnificently; it merely brought about a light sweat. In the pale blues and pinks of a rather wanting balloon arch, in the ill-advised sartorial choice of amber organza, we saw the wary glints of sunlight, which was just fine. Other aspects of that day might have been fine, but my memory no longer serves me well. However, I do recall that happiness stood no chance against my worries. There's a novel, *Pride and Prejudice*, by Jane Austen—I encourage all of you to read it if you haven't already. *Pride and Prejudice* begins: 'It is a truth universally acknowledged, that a single man in possession of a good fortune, must be in want of a wife.' *Pride and Prejudice* states the truth outright. Other novels have done clever things with this truth without resorting to Austen's overtness. I prefer Austen's overtness. In my view, it is, without exception, always best to call a spade a spade."

Patricia's mother appeared to be shriveling in her confusion: she didn't understand what Kwame Broni was saying. Kwame Broni noticed her bewilderment and smirked. "Other novels have considered the opposite: a woman in possession of a good fortune in want of a husband. The American Henry James is a master at this opposite truth. I recommend *The Portrait of a Lady*. Interestingly enough, Austen and James arrive at many of the same conclusions, one of which is that a man or a woman in possession of a good fortune is bound to have all kinds of suitors—good, bad, and ugly."

He paused and removed his spectacles, cleaning them with a handkerchief he'd pulled from his trouser pocket. He tucked the handkerchief in his breast pocket after he finished, then sat the spectacles on the bridge of his nose.

His tone changed. It was now accusing. "Patricia was in possession of a good fortune," he said. "Fortunes are not exclusively monetary. It is understandable and actually admirable—too many people leave home and refuse to look back—that Patricia wanted to marry a man from her home country. That said, she was positioned to have her pick of Ghanaian men because many of them think of America as the ultimate good fortune. Her suitors should have been uncountable! So why did she settle on a man she'd never met? Unlike my niece Belinda, who left for America at the age of sixteen, Patricia left for America in her late twenties. I refuse to believe that a woman of that age, who appears to be beautiful in her photographs, had known no man lovingly. She must have known a few lovingly. And knowing how young people think these days, I am certain that at least one, no matter how much things had soured between them, would have let bygones be bygones for the sake of America.

"Patricia was a hot ticket. So why hadn't anyone bitten? Because her standing in America was shaky? Nonsense. As Tot expressed so accurately, there are several ways to skin that cat, about which, again as Tot expressed, many young men are aware. What, then, had stopped them from biting? I could not be happy at the marriage ceremony because I could not avoid the answer. No matter how good Patricia's fortune, her bad character was impossible to overlook. A red flag! I am a man who prides himself in not prying into people's private lives, so I refrained from sharing my worries with my brother, or with Sarah—God rest her soul—or with Jacob. Only a few days ago did I find out that my brother had always shared my worries. Tot just referenced Jacob's timidity, his actions in contrast to the manners of other men, and his failure to seek his own pathways to America. We reject those characterizations of Jacob. More important, we know that this supposed weakness is a characteristic a woman with a bad character seeks in a man so that she can manipulate him. You've come to us today pretending to be aggrieved when your supposed reasons are the exact reasons disgraceful Patricia desired Jacob in the first place. But that's not Jacob. He's a man among men. Now that she knows this, she wants to rid herself of him. All of you. Disgraceful as you are. Want to rid yourselves of him."

Kwame Broni stopped there and scanned the room. Patricia's mother forced a smile without parting her lips. Tot sported the same look on his face. The two cousins stewed.

"We are all understandably frustrated," said the one whose feet feared ground, "but we must be careful not to make unfounded accusations."

"Moreover," said the other, "if we were to ask anyone who knows Patricia about her character, nobody would speak ill of her. Not a single soul."

Mr. Nti cleared his throat. Kwame Broni finally sat down.

"I would implore you to ask when you return home," Mr. Nti said. "Prior to the marriage, I spoke with several of your neighbors. Nobody outright said that Patricia's character was bad. Most, however, implied a possibly troubling character, owing to her mother."

"Then why did you proceed with the marriage?" asked the normal-legged one.

"Please pay attention: *owing to her mother*," Mr. Nti said. "Sometimes the apple does fall far from the tree. I was hoping—"

Patricia's mother parted her lips and clicked her tongue continuously. She shook her head. The loose skin of her upper arms jiggled like a rooster's wattle. "I'm successful, sir," she began. "Success comes with its list of enemies. Especially when the successful person is a woman. I suppose you have no enemies. Of course, neither does Jacob, if we are going by the standards of success."

She waited for her jab to find its mark. But Mr. Nti stared at her without expression.

"I also walked through this town in survey before they married," she said. "The reviews were positive. People were especially fond of you, Mr. Nti. But nobody allowed me to leave their house without expressing uncertainty about Jacob. He seemed to puzzle everyone. A puzzle we now know has to do with his shocking lack of drive."

She turned to Kwame Broni. "No, Patricia was not aware of Jacob's lack of ambition. Patricia did not desire Jacob because of a supposed preference for weak men. In fact, she thought him driven. A computer science degree from Tech is not earned through sleep. But as they say, 'Character is like pregnancy—you can only camouflage it for so long.' What is a woman to think when the man she is married to continues to live at home and requires financial assistance from her? Are you aware that Patricia funded all of Jacob's visa fees? And the Green Card Lottery fees—the question of whether he pursued that option notwithstanding? She even went as far as funding his trips to the embassy in Accra." Her round face glanced around the room and lingered on Alfred, whose animation appeared to melt her frown lines. "I will not belabor the point. But I'd be remiss not to point out that since childhood Patricia has dreamed of marriage. Dreamed of children. Marriage did not come to her as conveniently as she might have liked. But when it finally came to her, she was willing to do everything to make it last forever. That is Patricia. For her, marriage trumps all. Had Jacob had dependable employment and a home ready for a wife and family, Patricia would gladly have said good-bye to America. I assure you."

"What else can you assure us?" Kwame Broni asked.

"Nothing but this question: What kind of man requires his younger sister to find him a wife anyway?"

"A man among men," barked Kwame Broni.

"A failed man," replied Patricia's mother.

"You would know, wouldn't you?"

"What's that supposed to mean?"

"Aren't those the types of men you specialize in? Failed men you can turn into your puppets?" Kwame Broni said.

"Ha!" she exclaimed. "Hardly! Patricia's father owned two homes when I met him. Her sister's father was a successful merchant when I met him. Tell me, what does Jacob have?"

"Excellence."

She hmphed. "Even you can't possibly believe that." She gestured at the photo of Belinda and Wilder. "I think you mean to say a rich brother-in-law. And a sister shameless enough to marry a man as old as her father just for money."

Mr. Nti leapt out of his seat and pointed a finger at her. "You have no right to bring up Belinda and Wilder. You know nothing about them."

She pointed more forcefully at the image of Belinda and Wilder. "I know that that old man is the reason you have a roof over your head."

"Oh? That so?" Mr. Nti said. "Goes to show how much you know." With a sweep of his arms he added, "Jacob contributed handsomely to all of this."

"Handsomely? Eight bags of cement? Maybe ten?" She glanced

toward the ceiling, petting her chin with a finger. "Let's see. How much did Patricia say he came up with?"

Mr. Nti cackled with derision. "Yes, your harlot of a daughter. You believe your harlot of a daughter? Fine. Believe her. Go ahead. Tell us. What was the number? What was it according to the woman who shared her living space with another man while she was married? What's next for her? Bastards?"

Patricia's mother refused to take this invective lightly. She writhed in her seat. Tot and the cousins rushed to her and formed themselves into a crescent around her. They were mumbling what had to be consolations.

Prepared to keep the fight going, Mr. Nti felt breath on his ear. "Take a look at Alfred," Kwame Broni whispered, his voice even.

Alfred was sobbing, smearing his tears with his wrist.

"Martha is tearing up, too," Kwame Broni added.

Martha's eyes glossed. Rubbing her back, Robert appeared dumbfounded, his mouth a fixed oval.

"Maybe we should take our seats," Kwame Broni said to the room.

Everyone sat and worked to breathe normally. Patricia's mother, in contrast, was still panting when Yaa materialized. She handed Martha a roll of toilet paper for her tears, then swept Alfred up in a tight embrace. Alfred followed her to the kitchen and within a few minutes returned alone, smiling. Perhaps it was this smile that encouraged Afia to stand up and walk to the center of the room.

"Going back and forth in this way is getting us nowhere," she said. "It might feel good to assign blame. But it does no good.

Jacob and Patricia have decided to part ways. Our only goal here is to see it through without worsening the situation. Divorce is inherently unpleasant. Nobody comes out of it smiling from ear to ear. Find me a smiling fresh divorcée and I will show you someone masking intense pain."

She addressed Patricia's family with a smile. "It was said that Jacob and Patricia were not strangers to each other. I beg to differ. They were. All couples inherently are." Nobody disagreed. Turning to Jacob's side, she continued. "I do think there is a big elephant we are ignoring: America. Perhaps it's the real culprit? Perhaps it's the entity deserving of blame?" she said, eyeing her husband. "Maybe meditating on that might help arouse some empathy."

Afia permitted them some meditating time before facing Tot. "You and your family have something for us?" she asked.

"We do," Tot replied. "I set it on one of the veranda chairs. It would have been inappropriate for me to bring it inside."

"I understand," Afia said. "You didn't want to discount the chance of a miraculous reconciliation that would have voided the schnapps." She got closer and put her hand on Tot's shoulder. "I appreciate your gesture of hopefulness. It is a lovely note on which to initiate our ending."

"I can fetch it," Tot offered.

"Please."

They left in opposite directions—Tot for the veranda, Afia for the kitchen. Tot returned through the drapes toting a rectangular black box streaked with gold paint. Afia returned carrying an empty, squat glass in one hand; in her other hand was a glass half filled with water.

Tot knelt and held out the box toward Mr. Nti. "Life has a curious way about it," he said. "On behalf of my family, I return your generous offering of aromatic schnapps when you came for our daughter."

"What about the ring?" Kwame Broni snapped.

"Patricia is making arrangements for that," Tot replied.

Mr. Nti took the box from Tot. Opening it, he extracted an emerald bottle. "As is tradition," he said, "we will drink from the same cup."

Before directing the empty glass for Mr. Nti's pour, Afia offered the other to Tot. "Some water for you, Mr. Tot."

"No!" exclaimed Patricia's mother, her arm raised in objection. The silence that followed extended too long for Mr. Nti, as though Patricia's mother were a queen who'd brought her fearful subjects to a stop. He was readying himself to take charge of the moment when she said: "My brother doesn't need water. We came to do things right. As they are supposed to be done. My brother is a strong man. He can handle a little sip."

And so everyone sipped, even Alfred, whose twisting lips and scrunched face Mr. Nti had anticipated. But he had not anticipated Tot's sip. What an excitement it was to observe that on this day, in his house, Tot's devil would return. How prescient Kwame Broni had been to determine that this outcome would delight him. What was the foreign word? *Schadenfreude.*

"A little sip," that foolish woman had said. "He can handle a little sip." Didn't she know that even the tiniest drop can cause one to fall off the wagon? She deserved what was coming to her— the days-on-days requests for pick-me-ups, the drain on her finances. And to think that she could have avoided all of it by forgetting her pride—nobody was requesting proof of her claim that she exclusively associated with men of great strength and worth, men immune to failure. What good did it do her to sit and watch Tot shivering as he drew the glass closer to his mouth? What good did it do her to deem his first sip insufficient, tilting the glass from the bottom so that he could take a bigger one?

Tot coughed after she took the glass from him, beating his chest with his palm. It was a telling beating. Not the kind a fallen teetotaler might employ to emphasize his repulsion, but a seasoned drunkard's kind in appreciation of the pleasant burn.

WITH EVERYONE GONE—KWAME Broni and Afia had followed Patricia's family through the gate because Kwame Broni was scheduled to give one of his Economics Society speeches at their annual gala in Accra—Mr. Nti could finally let loose the boisterous laughter he'd kept inside. In his glee, he could barely hang Belinda and Wilder's picture back on the wall. He eventually managed to snag it on the nail, moving it to perfectly align it with Jacob's.

He rested his gaze on Jacob's photograph. Filled with pride that he'd represented his son well, he remembered Afia's mention of America. He could understand America in symbolic terms, being that his mind worked in symbols—why he'd quickly grasped Kwame Broni's symbolic rendering of America as a stand-in for Patricia. But Afia was referring to America as more than a metaphor. Rather, she was saying that America, like a living, breathing thing, was responsible for the dissolution of Jacob's marriage.

If there was anything he agreed with Patricia's mother on, it was that Jacob was a puzzle that America, truth be told, had only made worse. Now that he did not have to be in a battle mindset, now that he was released from blind allegiance to his son, he could say it: Jacob was exasperating.

Another thought was also worth considering: America was responsible for not only the odd love life of his younger son but also that of his daughter. He hadn't had the chance to witness the ebbs and flows of Belinda's as he'd done with Jacob's. In fact, he had not laid eyes on Belinda in twenty-two years and had never met her husband. The picture of her and Wilder on his wall was now ten years old. America had made it so that this singular vision he had of his daughter as an adult was outdated. Belinda had left Ghana at sixteen. Then a girl, now a woman.

And what did he know of her husband? What could he possibly know of Wilder? Besides the fact that Wilder had agreed to marry Belinda so that she could secure a green card—which was yet to materialize, he well knew—still they'd fallen in love. He owed so much to Wilder, this wealthy older man with a white beard like Abraham's. Without Wilder, Mr. Nti would not have a roof over his head. Without Wilder, their household would not enjoy their quarterly excesses shipped from America: three thirty-kilogram bags of rice, two jugs of canola oil, cans of tomato puree, powdered milk, oatmeal, cornflakes, the requisite condiments (they were using pink Himalayan salt before the world got a clue).

Wilder, he also knew, had fought in Vietnam. Three years ago, when he was finally able to pull himself together after the days he'd spent mourning Sarah, he got on the phone with Belinda to find out whether she could come home to Ghana for the funeral. He was about to ask but she did not give him time. "I can count on two fingers the times Wilder has spoken about Vietnam," she said to him out of the blue. "Hell, if you can even fucking count those as saying something."

Belinda had never been that unfiltered with him. He forgave her; she was in mourning, too. More than that, it was clear that she blamed Wilder and Vietnam for the delay in getting her green card, which meant that she wouldn't be able to come to Ghana for her mother's funeral, as there was no guarantee that INS would let her back into the United States. Belinda was beside herself; not knowing more about Wilder's past angered and exhausted her, and on that call, without having to say it, she was trying to mitigate her exhaustion by placing a gag order on the issue. Whenever Mr. Nti found himself wondering about Wilder's past, as he did yesterday on another call with Belinda to discuss the prospects of Jacob's divorce, he shoved it way back into a deep crevice of his mind.

Well, he was free to wonder now: What was it about Wilder and Vietnam? Why wouldn't he speak about it? How bad had he had it there?

Something else Mr. Nti had held back from mentioning to Belinda yesterday: Edith's wedding six weeks from now in Washington, D.C. Edith was Belinda's oldest friend, a spoiled rich girl Belinda had met during O levels at Wesley Girls' High School in Cape Coast. They were both twelve then, best friends until Belinda left for America at sixteen. A year later, they would be reunited in America at the Hotchkiss School in Connecticut, only for them to become estranged for reasons Mr. Nti didn't know. Belinda had been invited to the wedding and had come around to the idea of attending. While Mr. Nti had encouraged her to go and was glad she'd agreed to, he wouldn't have gone, envious as he was of Edith's good fortune. To avoid these feelings, he discussed the wedding with Belinda only when she brought it up. She hadn't mentioned it in her call yesterday, so he hadn't had to confront his own envy. But here it was now, as painful as ever. Why did Edith, a spoiled rich girl, deserve a genuine marriage with a real wedding and his two other children didn't? Why was Edith's father, Mr. Hyde, more deserving than him?

He heard something bang viciously and for a second he thought that one of the portraits had fallen from the wall. With more presence of mind he recognized the sound as the clap gate's bang. He hurried to the front door and opened it to check outside. His nerves heightened when he saw the gate swinging without a visitor to account for it. In the distance a figure sped through the clearing for Otumfuo Road. Alfred. Where was he going? Why hadn't he said anything?

"Alfred! Alfred!" Mr. Nti called out.

Alfred had almost reached the road. Mr. Nti's command for him to stop, loud as it had been, was sure to be just feathery vibrations in his ears. A thought occurred to him: he had always wondered whether his son Robert at least sensed the insides of his ears tickling when people around him were talking. Oh, to have been consigned to soundlessness each time Patricia's people opened their mouths. What grace that would have been! And who could blame Jacob for fleeing the house before dawn to find this sought-after grace?

Jacob

One

The day before his divorce, Jacob sat at his desk in the office and stared at the monitor. The columns of numbers on the screen appeared to be rushing down, like waterfalls. This effect was made more confusing by the raucous car horns that spilled into the office from the street outside. As the noise was the background music of his work life, he was accustomed to ignoring it. But not today.

He'd resolved to escape work early. He looked at the time in the lower right corner of the computer screen. Noon. Lunchtime. He would leave for lunch, then make his way home after. He would think of an explanation for his absence later.

Azar & Co., where he worked, was a boutique software firm. His title at the eight-person operation: data entry specialist. It was owned and run by two second-generation Lebanese brothers, Nabil Azar and his younger brother, Mamoud. Nabil and Mamoud were by no means unique or special, as much as they liked to think they were, for the Lebanese had a long history in Ghana, especially in Kumasi, where many of them had first launched their nationwide family-business dynasties.

There was one Ghanaian in Azar & Co.'s upper management,

Festus Ntiamoah. Festus occupied the large corner office because Nabil and Mamoud preferred the two that looked into the lobby of the five-story building. They claimed that being able to see their customers entering the building motivated them, even if they were mere errand boys. The truth was that Nabil and Mamoud were overbearing and they watched the four employee cubicles at the center of the office, one of which Jacob occupied, like security guards monitoring a CCTV camera feed.

Jacob's cubicle was closest to Festus's office and farthest from Nabil's and Mamoud's views. With Festus out of the office today and the hope (empty as that was) that Nabil and Mamoud would be too distracted by work to notice his post-lunch truancy, he might not need to come up with an excuse for his absence after all.

He shut down his HP computer and grabbed his brown canvas workbag. He turned to find Mamoud standing outside his office and flipping through documents, the office secretary standing with him. She was the eighth member of their small work family, a petite woman of Lebanese and Ghanaian descent everyone suspected had been hired for her looks but who had quickly—and surprisingly—proven invaluable.

Jacob was almost to the exit when Mamoud called for him. He stopped as Mamoud, often mistaken for Nabil's twin—they were both squat with mops of bountiful black hair suggesting toupees—came up to him.

"Lunch?" Mamoud asked.

"Yes."

"What will it be today?"

"Whatever's on the fire."

Mamoud smiled knowingly: if you were not careful, the chop

bars would serve you day-old food heated by the scorching sun. He peered at Jacob. "Your eyes, they are red," he said.

"Four hours straight at the computer will do that, sir."

"No," Mamoud said. "Yours are very red. If I didn't know better, I would say that you should see someone about them."

The only better informed Mamoud could have been was if he knew about tomorrow's divorce ceremony. Everyone at the office knew that Jacob's wife lived abroad, but nobody knew that after tomorrow there would be no abroad wife to speak about. Knowing better would have also meant this: Jacob's deeply reddened eyes were the consequence of an earlier surge of his routinely flitting eyelids, this time the flitting having to do with his attempts to hide the involuntary tears he'd been shedding.

It occurred to Jacob that Mamoud had given him the excuse he needed. "I will make sure to see someone immediately, sir," he said.

Outside, the heat spun him into a fiercer daze than the one he'd suffered at his desk. He undid the top three buttons of his white shirt. Irritability made him more critical of his surroundings; he concluded again that Kejetia, Kumasi's downtown, was coming apart. More and more its business district was overlapping with its market district. Traders lined their goods along the footpaths that fronted the mid-rises. Azar & Co. occupied the ground floor of one such mid-rise. Jacob took note of the offerings before he crossed the street: tomatoes, okra, onions, dried herring, smoked catfish, smoked salmon, fresh snails and crabs. The early afternoon gave off a miasma that he was desperate to escape.

On the other side of the street, he winnowed through throngs of people. There was a new scent here, a stale scent: day laborers, hawkers, wheelbarrow pushers. Everybody's goal was to make enough to stay alive, evidently at the cost of proper hygiene. The stench consumed his senses. He no longer had a taste for food. The thought of it, in fact, sickened him.

He had decided weeks ago to sit out the divorce hubbub. What good would it do for him to be involved? It made sense to head home now, take care of whatever required his attention, get to bed early, and be fully rested before dawn tomorrow, when he planned on leaving the house.

At the lorry park, a few taxis waited. There was no trotro in sight, those passenger vans that were the much cheaper option to get to Deduako, where he needed to go, a distance of thirty-five miles.

He walked up to a Toyota sedan with a red-and-green exterior and stripes of gold. Crouched next to the car with a yellow rag in hand, the driver vigorously wiped the vehicle.

"How much to Deduako?" Jacob asked.

"Hundred cedis."

The man did not look up; he continued wiping. His outlandish quote was an intentional invitation for Jacob to barter, so why break from his work when bartering took time?

They went back and forth for a while. "Thirty cedis," Jacob said, pretending to leave in order to emphasize this was his very last offer.

"No problem, thirty cedis." The driver relented, tossing the rag over his shoulder.

It didn't take long after settling in for Jacob to doze off in the passenger's seat. When the driver got to Deduako he shook Jacob awake, and Jacob directed him to a stopping point on Otumfuo

Road, where he could take a straight shot home through the clearing. Jacob paid the driver and got out of the taxi, groggily making it to the house and through the kitchen door. He was only a few feet from the phone in the living room, yet his presence had not distracted his father from his phone conversation.

The old man was talking with Belinda in America. Realizing this, Jacob paused to listen.

"You did what Napoleon could not do, Belinda," the old man said. "You achieved the unachievable." He took a breath. Then he said, "You don't know that."

Jacob imagined a quick response from Belinda. Although he hadn't spoken to her in three years, he was confident that she could still be abrupt.

Yet his father was quiet for longer than Jacob expected. Jacob thought the silence meant he'd been found out. He took two delicate steps away before the old man said into the phone, "I'm here . . . right here." And then he went on to talk about his own death.

"Belinda. Listen. It is something I have been wondering about. There are only three of us in the house now. Jacob is at work. Alfred is at school. Yaa is at the market. I'm here with Martha and Robert. Let's say that I am choking on something or having a heart attack. Who will hear me when I call out for help?"

Jacob was thinking that he might have asked the same question when the old man moved on to the divorce. "By this time tomorrow we will have settled things with Patricia's family," he said. "I will give Jacob the time he needs to recuperate. Personally, I don't see why he will need the time—this marriage was a sham. But I will give him the time because you can't be too careful with these matters. At some point, however, either you or me . . . well, best it be me since a face-to-face would be more appropriate. And since . . . well, you and Jacob, you know . . . Anyway . . . at some point I am going to sit him down and give it to him straight: he better find someone for himself. If not for love, then to prevent the kind of aloneness that breeds death. A man needs someone at his side. Preferably a woman. What is wrong with him, Belinda?"

That was enough for Jacob. He headed to his room.

JACOB WENT TO BED early enough to witness through his louvers the daylight vanishing. He'd been waiting for the sky to go dark before drawing the curtains over the louvers. He pulled himself out of bed to bring down the brown cotton, finally achieving the decisive seclusion he wanted, like a child finding refuge inside a cherished hiding place. He got back into bed, this time lying on his stomach, and gave himself fully to reflection.

On the day of the marriage ceremony five years ago, Patricia's people had offered him and his family an excessive welcome. In the front yard of Patricia's mother's home, a pink-and-blue balloon arch wiggled over Patricia's relatives, spread seven rows deep. Jacob and his clan, dressed in simple whites, were directed to the white plastic chairs arranged under a tent. Tot and Patricia's mother sat across in matching amber organza, an eccentric choice for a man. They beamed like proud parents. It was a hot day. As they weren't protected from the sun under the tent, Tot and Patricia's mother were drenched in sweat, and they passed the same white handkerchief between them to wipe their foreheads. The same attentiveness to foreheads could be seen in the rows behind them, the guests' grins seemingly intended to demonstrate the threat of heatstroke as nothing worrisome. It was a preview of what they'd willingly endure for Jacob, with other inconveniences soon following: waiting until Jacob's people had filled their plates before proceeding to the buffet table themselves; Patricia's mother taking Jacob's hands in hers and washing them in a basin of warm water. She'd done the same for his father and mother. Her willingness to be accommodating seemed limitless when in response to learning that one of Jacob's distant relatives was allergic to tomatoes, she rushed to the kitchen and whipped up an aubergine sauce to go with the yams.

"Humility, servitude, overextension of self—these are the ideal traits of a wife," his father announced at the close of the day. A long, happy marriage depended on the wife's character, he added, and Jacob's prospects, burnished by the magnificence of Patricia's family's decency, heralded only good. Belinda had chosen well for her brother.

Yet five years on, things had changed. These days his father would not even dream of associating Patricia and her people with anything resembling decency. But instead of questioning Belinda's shrewdness during the phone call Jacob had eavesdropped on, their father had asked her, "What is wrong with him, Belinda? What?" This reminded Jacob of his suspicion that his family members wondered whether he was a homosexual.

He had wondered himself when he was fifteen because he was not finding the girls at Kumasi High School's sister school, Kumasi Girls' Senior High School, enticing. His mates would gawk at them in their knee-length skirts, the most daring among the giggly girls rolling up their hems to expose an inch or two more of their thighs. There'd been rumors of his mates putting some of the girls on their backs, but the conquest registered in him without thrill. This was in 1986, and one of the spreading international news items was that a name had just been given to the disease that was killing American men who preferred men. Perhaps, Jacob thought, he was one of them. And despite that preference being a death sentence, he would have at least identified his condition. He eyed the boys in the shower stalls, awaiting an evasive arousal. Gratifyingly (for he was not a homosexual destined for death) and disappointingly (for his condition remained unidentified), he never stiffened. He stayed flaccid even when the boys slapped his manhood so that it whirled, for it was something to behold.

Maybe it was meekness. Despite the obvious bounty below his waist, Jacob wondered if he was just too shy. As the years progressed, Belinda, two years his junior, clocked more and more achievements, making the lack he sensed in himself even more stark. Belinda could even speak to Robert without trouble.

Jacob was nine when Robert, recently back from his boarding school, dragged Belinda to him. Robert took her arm and, signing to her, dug his fingers into her flesh.

"Is he angry?" Jacob asked. Robert's fingers were going like stomps.

"A little," Belinda said.

"What did you do?"

"Nothing. It's you."

"What did I do?"

"Look at me and look at you, that's what he's saying. I'm only seven. But I can talk to him. But you, you're nine. And you can't. Fool."

Robert had his eye on a neighborhood girl, who was neither deaf nor mute. "He doesn't want me to talk to her for him," Belinda said. "He wants you to do it."

Jacob was not going to pass up a chance to collude with Robert and exclude Belinda. It was enough that Belinda's signing, in addition to her being a girl, had forged an enviable closeness with their mother. Belinda could have that.

So he took more concentrated stabs at learning sign language. Robert, rarely seen without a book, taught Jacob by pointing at words on the page and signing them for him. *The Vicar of Wakefield*, Robert's favorite, introduced to the Nti children by their uncle Kwame Broni, served a secondary purpose. Whenever Robert thought Jacob needed to be reminded of their primary goal of setting him up with a girl, he opened to the novel's opening line: *I was ever of opinion, that the honest man who married and brought up a large family, did more service than he who continued single and only talked of population.*

But try as they might, Jacob's fingers made too many mistakes. In the end, he gave up. How many times was Robert at home to be spoken to anyway? And wasn't it best for him to stick with girls who neither heard nor spoke?

Jacob was entering his final year at Kumasi High when Belinda left for America. She'd already excelled at Wesley Girls', Ghana's most prestigious girls' school. Her exceptional score on the American exam, the Preliminary Scholastic Aptitude Test (PSAT), was no surprise, which resulted in a full scholarship to the Hotchkiss School in Connecticut, where she would complete her secondary education. The man who'd made Belinda's American future possible, Mr. Hyde, was the father of Edith, Belinda's best friend at Wesley Girls'. He worked at the American embassy in Accra as their top educational counselor.

After A levels, on which Jacob scored passably but without distinction, he forced his father to take him to Accra. Mr. Hyde had done wonders for Belinda. And though Jacob's own abilities paled in comparison to hers, Mr. Hyde seemed to have power to move American mountains.

In Mr. Hyde's office, Jacob sat across from this miracle worker, Mr. Nti to Jacob's left. Speaking on Jacob's behalf, with everyone pitching their voices over the din of the air-conditioning, Mr. Nti inquired about the possibility of an American destiny for his son.

"You can take the test, too," Mr. Hyde said to Jacob.

"But I've finished with secondary school."

"There's another one for universities. SAT." Mr. Hyde retrieved the SAT registration documents from his desk and handed them to Jacob. "Schools in America really like it if you play a sport. Do you play a sport?"

He remembered the conversation his father had had with Mr. Hyde. "You put down volleyball for Belinda, didn't you?" Jacob said.

"Yes," Mr. Hyde said. "And looking at your physique, Jacob, yours would be an even easier case to make."

Jacob glanced at his father, who looked him over with an appraising eye. "Jacob has the build of a sportsman," Mr. Nti said. "I don't know about the temperament."

After they filled out the forms, Mr. Nti refused Mr. Hyde's invitation to lunch; he did not want any part of the four-hour drive back to Kumasi to be in darkness. At the embassy's canteen, they purchased two loaves of bread (one sliced, one not), two bottles of Fanta, and two large bottles of water for the trip home.

The start of the drive was jerky. Unnerved by Accra's bustle, Mr. Nti drove with a counterintuitive offensiveness, leaving gaps in front of him that cars zoomed in and out of, prompting him to hit the brakes repeatedly.

At Nsawam, with Accra behind them, he drove with more ease. Ahead, drivers drove with a sense of order. Mr. Nti reached for the back seat and retrieved the sliced loaf of bread. He held it up so that Jacob could pull two slices from the plastic bag. Jacob handed him one.

"Too bad Robert is not the sprinter he used to be," Mr. Nti said between bites. "One of the American schools would have otherwise scooped him up."

At the school for the deaf, the Lutheran missionaries who had founded it had singled out Robert—who was an inch taller and even more muscular than Jacob—and groomed him to be a sprinter. They even trained him to watch for the gunshot so that his starts were comparable to those of other runners. They had big ambitions for him: "Imagine him leaving his competitors at the Olympics in the dust," they said, despite the extra second he took to drop his head.

But Robert's training had been poorly handled. By the age of eighteen the wear on his knees was so great that it excluded him from serious competition anywhere in Ghana and definitely the Olympics.

"I can be more serious about football," Jacob said to his father, suggesting a new commitment beyond the pickup games that he sometimes joined.

"Maybe," Mr. Nti said.

Ultimately, Jacob did not make the cut to be an athlete at an American university: there was no quickness of feet to be exploited, no innate wiliness on the field. He did not make the cut academically, either: his SAT scores were unimpressive. As the rejections from the three American universities that Mr. Hyde said were "fifty-fifty" were no surprise, they did not hurt. As for the three that Mr. Hyde said were "safeties," sure bets, Mr. Hyde made sense of their painful rejections by saying that the college application season in America had been "odd." He reminded them that his own daughter, Edith, hadn't gotten into Hotchkiss the first time she'd applied along with Belinda. Another odd year that had been. But Edith had gotten in the following year. Jacob could give it another try.

Jacob refused to try again. At Tech—the Kwame Nkrumah University of Science and Technology—he was admitted to study computer science, an unpopular major perceived to be for secretaries (Ghana had been slow to enter the Computer Age). After he graduated, the jobs he'd found had paid a pittance; he could never dream of renting, let alone building, a home of his own.

In December 1999, four years before he reached the official retirement age of sixty, Mr. Nti left the brewery where he'd started on the assembly line and had risen to supervisor. He'd decided that the pending new century required new beginnings: a house of their own. He set aside a percentage of his lump sum retirement package and purchased land in Deduako, a hamlet that was fast folding into Kumasi. Working with a contractor, he settled on a three-bedroom house with a one-room guest quarters.

It was understood that the three Nti children would contribute to the building costs. Over the years Robert had proven himself highly industrious. With a diversified portfolio of micro-investments he'd made on his own, he delivered when his father asked for financial help. It made sense for Robert to give half of his investments for the house. By then he had a woman in his life and was on the threshold of marriage. Together, they would make a life for themselves in the new semidetached guest quarters.

Jacob was unable to provide at Robert's level, only rustling up enough money for eight bags of cement. But compared to Belinda's nothing—she told her family she was financially strapped in America, despite having an economics degree from Williams College and a law degree from a university named after the country's first president, George Washington—Jacob's eight bags might as well have been one hundred.

And then Wilder appeared in Belinda's life. A Black American who'd fought in Vietnam but never said a thing about it. More important, Wilder was rich.

Nearly two years after work on the house had begun and had progressed in only occasional spurts, Wilder's generosity made it possible for the house to be finished quickly. In 2003, the Nti family moved into their new and fully furnished home.

There, they lived a life of surplus. No longer short of money, Belinda delighted in replenishing the family's food supply quarterly, even introducing them to pink Himalayan salt, which she said would be kinder on their mother's weak heart.

Belinda also showed off beyond food. Alfred soon evolved into something like a small-time Nike collector, having acquired a new pair with each growth spurt, Belinda delivering the sneakers like clockwork. Over the years Robert's reading preferences had expanded to include works by Black American writers. When Alfred relayed this information to Belinda on his father's behalf, she started sending stacks of books. The gifts Jacob received from Belinda—he especially loved the fragrances: Davidoff Cool Water, L'Eau d'Issey—prompted muttered thank-yous to her over the phone.

Belinda's call to Jacob about Patricia was unexpected. He had listened partly out of curiosity and partly because it fed the small place in his mind devoted to American fantasies. Maybe he would find in Patricia what Belinda had found in Wilder: financial freedom.

"She's very hardworking," Belinda assured him.

What Belinda never made clear to Jacob or to the rest of the family was that Patricia, like Belinda, lived a tenuous life in America: even if they married, Patricia would not be able to bring Jacob to America. When Jacob came to realize this a year into the marriage, the jealousy he'd long felt for Belinda grew into something like hatred, expanding so much that he felt it press onto his rib cage.

He did not talk to his sister for a year after his first visa rejection. When their mother died and his father asked him to break the news to her, Jacob wiped his tears as he began to sense the gentle blossoming of satisfaction within. It was attributable to two reasons. The first was that he was being entrusted with an important responsibility. The second, and maybe more appealing, was that he could hurt Belinda. But after getting off the phone with her, he felt nothing. His assumptions had been wrong. His father had been too heartbroken to speak and had passed on the duty out of necessity. And Belinda, without sorrow, abruptly made it clear that she was committed to getting her green card over returning to Ghana for their mother's funeral.

"I cannot come, Jacob. I'm not going to fuck things up for myself."

SO ON THE DAY of the divorce, Jacob headed for By His Grace Internet Café before dawn with his laptop. Benjamin, the owner, was waiting in front wearing only his boxer shorts and house slippers. He'd come to let Jacob in and lock him inside before returning to bed.

The internet café—its pompous name scrawled on a rectangle of cardboard tacked to the door—sat along Otumfuo Road. A narrow space, it was equipped with two long desks facing each other on which sat four thick-butted machines whose heads had to be struck sometimes to turn on. Under the desks snored the hard drives. Tattered desk chairs with screechy wheels accommodated customers at the computers—if the chairs were pushed too far out, they collided like bumper cars.

The café was next to Ohemaa's Provisions, a store that doubled, after sundown, as a bar. Ohemaa, with her overpainted face that looked more clownish under bright orange bulbs, ensured that her establishment romped until three a.m. She stocked her large freezer with Star and Gulder, favorites of patrons whose conception of Ohemaa's Provisions was neither bodega nor mart but an outdoor bar. Every night as the daylight faded—some said at seven, some said at eight—she would bring out plastic chairs onto the pavement in front of the place and blast slow love songs through her speakers.

It was long past three a.m., Ohemaa's supposed closing time, when Benjamin locked Jacob inside the café. It was nearly a fully formed new day. Still there were stragglers next door hoping to prolong their revelry. Jacob could hear someone bellowing into the night.

"Take me, life! Sweet, sweet surrender!"

He wondered who it might be. He should know: Deduako was the kind of town where everyone knew everyone. But try as he might, he could not identify the voice hoarsened by inebriation.

It was his first time inside the café by himself. The place fit ten people comfortably, including Benjamin, who always kept watch from the doorway, unbothered by the standing fan that gusted in his face. Truth be told, the place was just big enough for five (excluding Benjamin), but Benjamin, who levied both an entrance and a computer-use fee, wanted to maximize his profits. He argued that fifteen- and thirty-minute sessions at the computer were not smart buys and instead would guide patrons toward buying hourly blocks. If they had only enough money for fifteen- or thirty-minute sessions, he encouraged them to leave and come back with a friend or two. The two of them (or three of them), their pooled funds meeting the price for a one-hour session, would crowd at one of the Dells.

At forty, Jacob may have been the only person to pass through the door alone. The explanation people gave was his relative means—after all, he always arrived with his own laptop. His sister's rich American husband was common knowledge, so it was to Wilder that everyone attributed Jacob's laptop.

But unbeknownst to the café's patrons, Benjamin also contributed to Jacob's uniqueness among them: Jacob could come on his own because he did not have to pay. Their friendship began eight years ago, when Benjamin hawked secondhand kitchen utensils from a small kiosk farther up Otumfuo Road. Knives and spoons and pots covered the kiosk's walls like an old soldier's exhibition of the armor he used to wear. Ever the businessman, when electricity came to Deduako, Benjamin had gone to Ghana Telecom and filled out paperwork to have a phone installed. The telecoms men came a week later to set up the phone at the kiosk's entrance. When they were finished, Benjamin set the white Nortel phone on the floor by the entrance and posted a sign outside the kiosk's wall: MAKE YOUR INTERNATIONAL CALLS HERE.

The phone's arrival coincided with the Nti family's move to Deduako in 2003. Two years later, when Jacob started his long-distance courtship of Patricia, he began to confide to Benjamin tales of Patricia, the woman on the other end of the phone. The Nti house had a phone, but to avoid his father, Jacob used the phone at the kiosk almost daily after work to recite the events of his day to Patricia. She would listen and ask questions. On Saturday and Sunday afternoons, Jacob was a mainstay at the kiosk. As Jacob talked, Benjamin would make crude gestures that Jacob laughed at. In solidarity, he reduced Jacob's phone fee to a flat insignificance they kept to themselves. Benjamin called it a "blue balls discount."

By the time of Benjamin's ascent to internet café owner, Jacob

DK NNURO

owned a cellular and visited Benjamin just to chat. Further advancement had come by way of a laptop, underscoring the fact that Jacob had no need for Benjamin besides friendship. But Benjamin still wanted to help. His advice about proper conduct at the American embassy, even though Jacob followed it, did not bear fruit. Don't wear a suit, Benjamin directed, you will appear too eager. Don't try to make your English sound like theirs, they will think you are a charlatan. Sometimes play dumb because Americans want to feel they are saving you from ignorance. Don't smile, don't frown, keep somewhere in between.

Benjamin eventually found his chance to be more helpful when Jacob turned his attention to the American Green Card Lottery, which could be entered online. For free, he let Jacob unplug an ethernet cable from one of the computers at the café and pop it into his laptop. The waking of the internet on his device, they agreed, recalled the cry of the kiosk phone.

Business at By His Grace invariably peaked during the lottery's open periods. Customers journeyed from beyond Deduako to join the long lines outside seeking the blessed computers' life-altering destinies. Paying customers who'd come on the days Jacob tested his luck on the laptop would inquire about the idle desktop that sat in front of him and Benjamin. "I decide which computers are in use and which aren't," Benjamin would bark. Nobody argued with him.

In four years, Jacob had entered the lottery twice. In 2009, the second time he'd entered, everyone had done so with enlarged expectation because four months before, Barack Obama, America's new African president, had come to Ghana. People were sure that great favor was to descend upon them. In the swirling line stringing

62

toward By His Grace Internet Café, everyone believed they were setting sail for America.

Disappointment struck once more for Jacob. When the lottery results were posted online and he repeatedly searched in vain for his name on the list of winners, hopelessness engulfed him, prompting him to question how much Patricia truly yearned for him. Why had she wanted him to memorize all of those American monuments for his embassy interviews? The immigration officers had never asked about any monuments, a fact that now made Jacob feel like Patricia had been intentionally distracting him. Was she in cahoots with America to keep him from seeing the country for himself? He was beginning to think that she did not wish him to join her as much as she claimed.

He regretted this reasoning the following day. It was the kind of irrationality that his hopelessness fostered. Truth was, Patricia, in her desperation for him to succeed, had gotten him to overprepare. At least he'd learned more about America than ever, able to make this connection: Mount Rushmore featured George Washington, after whom Belinda's law school was named.

But he was still stuck in Ghana. He was numb with disappointment and despair. Benjamin viewed his numbness as too much insouciance. He wanted Jacob to express his feelings by breaking something or spending his nights next door at Ohemaa's, reaching Tot's level of inebriation.

But Jacob did none of this. As a result, Benjamin concluded, "You only wanted to win. I don't think you really cared about what winning meant."

"You're saying you don't think I loved Patricia?"

"I'm saying you wanted to win."

Of course Jacob wanted to win. For the thrill of it and for what it meant: being with Patricia in America. Jacob could hardly blame Benjamin for the difficulty he found in imagining the latter as a possibility. He'd been tepid, after all, about his honest want of Patricia. The reason was so embarrassing, so dirty, that confessing it was not worth the awkwardness and shame. Perhaps one day he would explain it to Benjamin. But not now.

AMONG THE PARTICIPANTS in the divorce ceremony, only Alfred knew of Jacob's whereabouts. They had agreed to this: promptly after Patricia's family departed, Alfred would hurry to the café and deliver his version of events. Later, when Jacob returned home, Mr. Nti's rundown would follow. Jacob wanted both perspectives: that of a disinterested child and that of a prejudiced old man. There was also this: Alfred's would have him in stitches.

A short stack of twelve pirated CDs stood next to his laptop. Jacob had not wanted to add to Benjamin's electricity bill, so he'd asked Benjamin to switch off the lights. In the darkness, he aimed the laptop screen at the CDs, finding in its glow the seventh in the twelve-part series on coding. His last promotion at Azar & Co. had been eight years ago, and for nearly a year he'd been using the CD tutorials to learn to code computer software independently, the key to professional advancement. Festus Ntiamoah, he'd been told, had been made his direct superior at work because Festus's computer science education was better suited to the Information Age. Festus was only twenty-five years old.

Starting the lesson, Jacob followed as best he could as the

man on the screen droned through his revolving slides describing C, C++, COBOL. Especially at this hour, with first light dozily emerging, the man's languorous voice was more conducive to daydreaming than learning. And there was something else this moment was probably most conducive to. Jacob could not resist the bare truth of that something: checking on Hotch'91.

He was by himself in the café, alone in the semidarkness. Since committing to Patricia, Jacob had stopped visiting a certain website where he'd found a virtual community of men like him and women with the brutish sensibility that, in the words of Hotch'91, "drove him wild." He liked that American idiom. He'd even said it to Patricia once: "You drive me wild, Patricia." She sure did. Patricia surely drove him wild.

His last log-in had been nearly six years ago. As should be expected, the website had changed. He recognized only the blackness of it all, like seedy nighttime. The colors, once flecking the page like beckoning light, now shone as if reflected through gauze. Leather whips and metal chains now bordered the home page; previously, they had been scattered all over.

It took him some time to find the spaces for his username and password. He remembered both. How could he ever forget? Username: WeakLongDon. Password: PainGlut30.

His in-box held one message. The message, from Hotch'91, indicated her last visit to the site as almost two years ago, on December 31, 2009, at 1:45 a.m.:

> I know it's been a while. And I get it. You probably
> decided this thing is not for you. It's pretty nuts,
> right? I don't even know why I like making men feel

like shit. Well, I guess it's not making them feel like shit if they like it, right? In any case, it's not like I had an abusive father or brother or uncle or someone like that who touched me. Nothing like that. I'm a rich, white chick from Greenwich, Connecticut. Who knows why I like this shit? I just do. And that's what I wanted to say to you, Jacob. I can't imagine you are not struggling. I imagine that giving it up has not been easy. It's ok if it hasn't been. What you like is what you like. Nothing wrong with that. But honestly that's not why I'm reaching out. I'm reaching out to say I'm sorry. I have realized that the fantasy with you was different. I was on some Massa's-wife-and-the-slave-type shit. I'm sorry, Jacob. Entering 2010, I want to do better. I'm evolving. I thought it was important for me to share this with you, whether you ever see it or not. Happy New Year!

Massa's-wife-and-the-slave-type shit? What was wrong with that? Yes, him, a slave. Wasn't that the point? For him to be in servitude? Whipped when he erred?

He did not get much time to think about it; full dawn was spreading through the café and someone was thumping on the door.

He slammed the laptop shut.

He thought it was Benjamin. He went to the door and tried to turn the knob. While fidgeting with it, he remembered that Benjamin had locked him in. It couldn't be Benjamin on the other side.

"Who's there?" he asked.

"Are you open?"

"No."

"Then what are you doing in there?"

"Waiting for Benjamin."

"He opened it for you?"

"Yes."

"Did he also give you one of his women to sleep with?"

Irritated, Jacob didn't reply and went back to the coding lesson on the laptop. He ignored other knocks on the door.

At eight a.m. Benjamin arrived and unlocked the door, letting it hang ajar to signal the official start of the day's business. The place quickly filled to capacity. Jacob sat at Benjamin's side; the laptop sat on his lap. The standing fan's turbine-like swivel started to distract him. He closed the laptop again.

"What do you think your family is talking about now?" Benjamin asked.

"What a wonderful husband I was."

"You're making light of it, but I know for sure that you would have been a perfect husband," Benjamin said. He signaled for the laptop. Jacob passed it to him and Benjamin stuffed it into a black leather satchel at his side. "You are one of the good ones. Not like the rest of us. Look at me. Two children with one woman. Another two with another woman. A fifth on the way with a new mistress."

"Don't sell yourself short," Jacob said as he tried not to reflect on his own shame. "At least you did the right thing. You married them."

Benjamin heaved a sigh. "I will have to do something about the new woman."

DK NNURO

"You won't marry her?"

"Three wives?" Benjamin said. "No."

"Won't change a thing," Jacob said. "Won't make you less of a good man."

Benjamin's nostrils flared. "Yes. That's me. A real saint." He raised his arms and leaned back. "Deduako's Jesus," he pronounced.

Afriyie, a teenager who came to the café regularly, construed Benjamin's declaration as an invitation to join the conversation. "Does that mean this café is by *your* grace?" he asked.

Facing him, Benjamin said, "Who owns it?"

"You."

"Who takes your money?"

"You."

"You just answered your own question." Benjamin leaned closer to the boy. "But don't go telling people. Let them keep thinking Jesus. He's a lot better for business than I could ever be."

Afriyie didn't know how to respond. Benjamin pointed at the monitor facing Afriyie and his two friends. "I know you and your friends come here to chat up some white woman. You are not exactly the brightest bulbs when it comes to being discreet. Who is she?"

"She's my friend," Afriyie said.

"Friend? What kind of friend?"

"The normal kind."

"We all should be so lucky to have a normal friend like her. We wouldn't need to work." Benjamin's voice turned stern. "You come here every day, pay for two hours, then plop yourselves down. You get on Facebook and type nice things to that lonely woman. You know she's foolish enough to believe you, so you type whatever

68

nice thing pops into your empty heads. Every few weeks, you ask her for money, and like the foolish woman she is, she sends it. That's your grace. That's why you keep coming here."

Benjamin's words crystallized something in Jacob. Hotch'91, her real name Sims, thought she had taken advantage of Jacob. But what had he sent her? Nothing. Nothing but the fantasy she was reciprocating. Moreover, for a while he'd believed that she might be his ticket to America. If someone was taking advantage of someone, it had been him working her with the intensifying language of submission—*spit on me harder, Madam*; *whip my ass harder, Madam*—until Patricia came into his life.

Alfred burst through the doorway. Jacob got up. "Are they gone?" Jacob asked.

It took Alfred a minute to understand the question. "Oh. Yes," he said. "That's why I came."

"Did anyone see you leaving?"

"Like Grandpa?"

Jacob nodded.

"No," Alfred said. "I was quick."

Jacob gestured toward Benjamin. "You didn't greet Uncle Benjamin."

Alfred acknowledged Benjamin with a salute. He stuck out his chest.

"At ease!" Benjamin ordered.

Alfred relaxed. "How was that?"

"Very good," Benjamin said. "Just like Rambo."

Jacob gripped Alfred's shoulder. "All right, Rambo," he said, nudging him. "Outside."

Outside, Alfred balanced himself step-by-step along the low

roadside curb, stabilizing himself with his extended arm. It was Saturday early afternoon, and despite the uptick in the number of cars on Otumfuo since morning, it was nothing compared to the weekday rush. Had it been a weekday, Jacob would have shooed Alfred from the curb. The risk of dan- ger would have been high. Other risks to Alfred's well-being, particularly the unreasonable ones that heightened Mr. Nti's anxiety, had always struck Jacob as a waste of energy. What great danger was there in an impromptu football game on the clearing? Or a mad dash with friends on that same tract of woolly sand? His father's fears that Alfred was destined to fall and hurt himself from his lack of balance were ri- diculous. All children fell. If anything, a fall would help Alfred's striving to be normal.

They walked along the dirt path that separated the row of ven- dors from the curb. He'd promised Alfred a reward of something sweet for bringing him the news, and they were headed to the end of the row where the sweets seller sat. A thought had sat at the top of Jacob's mind as he'd made his promise to Alfred: Had he pur- chased toffees for Alfred since Patricia stopped sending Werther's Original?

"How many of them came to the house?" Jacob asked.

"A lot." Alfred reviewed with his fingers. "Aunty Patricia's mother. An old man called Tot. And two other old men. The old man called Tot said that the two men were their cousins. And then he said that they were their brothers. That confused me. I don't know who they were." He stared at his fingers as if they would reveal the men's true identities.

"Don't worry, I know who they are," Jacob said. "Keep going."

"They sat by the kitchen. I sat over there, too. Grandpa and

Grandpa Broni and Grandma Afia sat by the door. And my father and my mother, too—"

The fishmonger interrupted Alfred with her call. "Mr. Jacob, Alfred, how is it today?" She sat behind a display of glinting whole fish.

Jacob paused. "We are alive," he said.

"We are alive," Alfred parroted.

"We thank God," the fishmonger said. She focused on Alfred. "Tell your mother I have fresh supply. Won't last long."

"I will," Alfred promised.

They moved on. "And then what happened?" Jacob asked.

"Grandpa Broni got up and said welcome. I didn't listen because it is the same every time." Mimicking the familiar drumbeat of adults, he said, *"Ashantis say welcome. Ashantis ask about your journey. Ashantis ask about your purpose."* He stopped with his little sway. "I know all of that so I don't listen anymore. I just signed for Ma and Da," he said. "Grandpa Broni talked in English. So it was hard to sign. His English is different. . . .

"Then the old man called Tot got up. He talked in Twi. He said they didn't get into an accident. He said every day there is an accident. But they didn't get into an accident. And then he said that Aunty Patricia's mother was his sister. That was also when he said that the two men were their cousins. And their brothers, too." Alfred shook his head. "No. Wait," he said. "I got it wrong. First, he said she was his sister and the men were their cousins and brothers. Then he said they didn't get into an accident. Yes. I remember. That's how it went."

He took a moment to gather his thoughts. He looked up regretfully. "Uncle Jacob?"

"Yes?"

"The old man called Tot said something I didn't understand. I made it into a song in my head so that I could remember. But now I can't." His eyes rolled back as he attempted to retrieve the song from his memory. "A foolish man . . ." he crooned. "A foolish man . . ." He tried once more. "A foolish man . . ." Relenting, he admitted, "Okay, I forgot. It wasn't important anyway. It sounded like one of the things old people say."

"Probably," Jacob said, hanging on to the word *foolish* in his mind. The *-ish* dropped off, reminding Jacob of the time Robert called him a fool through Belinda when they were children.

Alfred said, "Then the old man called Tot talked about when you went to marry Aunty Patricia at her mother's house. My mother said I went, too, but that was too long ago, so I don't remember." He crouched on the raised pavement, then sprang to his feet, then crouched again. He stood up. "The old man called Tot said that the day you went to marry Aunty Patricia at her mother's house was a happy day for him because Aunty Patricia and her sister are his nieces and daughters." He rolled his eyes. "I didn't know somebody could be your niece and daughter."

"It's a figure of speech."

"What is figure of speech?"

"It means what you say can have more than one meaning. Take me and you. Sometimes I tell people that you are like a son to me. But you are not really my son, are you?"

"No."

"But I can say that. Did Tot say anything about me and Aunty Patricia?"

"He said you were strangers."

"How do you mean?"

"Strangers don't get married. That's what he was saying," replied Alfred. "He said that his father and mother were strangers, too. But they got married. That's because in the old days strangers could get married." Gently, he asked, "Uncle Jacob, can you see Aunty Patricia on your cellular?"

"I've tried, but it's not very clear. Why do you want to know?"

"Because the old man called Tot said that you saw Aunty Patricia on your cellular. He said that's why you could get married. Because you saw each other on your cellular. I remember he said 'Rubbish' but I don't know what was rubbish." He thought for a moment, then added, "Maybe it was the lotto for the Green Card. That was what was rubbish." He giggled. "My mother and father didn't understand when I signed the lotto for the Green Card. They thought I meant the real lotto at the store. So I did my fingers like this." He fluttered his fingers. "Like an airplane."

Jacob smiled. He watched Alfred expectantly.

"At the end the old man called Tot said they came to the house so that you and Aunty Patricia could go your separate ways. It was the first time I heard *separate ways*. You want to see how I did it for my mother and father?"

Jacob motioned with interest and Alfred delivered: fist on chest, eyes shut, shoulders curved. Then, rapidly, the harmoniousness was torn asunder. Jacob snickered inwardly: Alfred had a flare for theatrics. He couldn't fully bask in his amusement, however. A troubling thought occurred to him: Alfred's rendition of Tot had been unbelievably tame, even equable. "Are you sure about the *rubbish* part?" he asked. "Oh, and the *foolish* part. Do you remember the song now?"

Stammering, Alfred said, "I am sure about the rubbish part but I don't remember the song." He stared at the ground. "Uncle Jacob," he said to the earth, "please don't be angry. What I said is not true. I am not sure about the rubbish part."

Jacob smiled. "It's all right," he said. "It's all right." He spotted a lanky ice cream hawker on the other side of the road and signaled for him. The hawker noticed Jacob and with both hands secured the Styrofoam cooler to keep it from toppling off his head. "You want yogurt?"

Without looking up at Jacob, Alfred nodded. His dismay over not remembering what was rubbish still weighed on him. But by the time the hawker crossed the road and Jacob had helped him set the cooler on the ground, the dismay had fled.

"Want two?" Jacob asked him. Alfred nodded vigorously.

The man untwisted the polyethylene casing and brought out two plastic pouches of strawberry-flavored yogurt. They were frozen into perfect rectangles, the plastic covered in thin films of ice. The hawker wrapped each in newspaper and passed them to Jacob, who paid for them. With his free hand, Jacob helped the hawker return the load onto his head, stopping a car so that the man could cross back to the other side of the road.

Alfred gaped at Jacob's filled hand. He snatched one treasure when Jacob offered both. Save for shaking the yogurt out of its newspaper wrapping so that it dropped on the ground, there was no easy way for him to access it with his one hand. He let it drop onto the curb and Jacob retrieved it, wiping it clean with his white polo before handing it back to Alfred.

Alfred bit into the plastic and spat out the scrap and sucked the sweetness into his mouth.

"Do you want me to hold on to the other one for you?" Jacob asked.

Without pulling the pouch from his mouth, Alfred angled the edge of his shorts toward Jacob.

"Your pocket? Won't it melt?"

Alfred broke from his delight. Barely pulling the yogurt from his mouth, he said, "It won't. I will finish this one very soon. Then I will have the other one."

Jacob removed the newspaper covering and sank the frozen yogurt into the pocket. He got just about three-quarters of it in there; Alfred's leg shivered. "Too cold?" Jacob asked.

"A little." He shook out the leg. "But I'm strong. Nothing is too cold for me."

He sucked for more sugar until he needed to come up for breath. "I wanted to tell you about Grandpa Broni," he said.

"What about him?"

"When he got up again, he talked in Twi," he said. "And he was angry. Very angry."

"Why?"

"I don't know," he said. "Nobody did anything to him."

Jacob thought the contrary was likelier: Somebody had done something to Kwame Broni. That something lay in the undercurrent of Tot's *foolish*, Tot's *rubbish*, an ugliness that Alfred hadn't caught. "What did Grandpa Broni say?"

"A lot of things," Alfred said. "He talked about the sun and organza and the balloons when you went to marry Aunty Patricia at her mother's house. He said that it was a *fine* day. And then he talked about a book. And then he talked about another book. Every time he sees me, he tells me to read. Sometimes I run away but he catches me and gives me a book. I give it to my father. Da will read anything.

"But I don't know why Grandpa Broni was angry. And then he made everybody angry when he said that Aunty Patricia is bad."

"Bad?"

"He said that she has *bad character*."

Alfred delivered this news nervously, apparently aiming to soften the blow, but Jacob was aware of his uncle's opinions. Yet the specifics of tone and delivery remained to be seen. Having denied himself a front-row view of Kwame Broni's indignation, Jacob realized that his appetite had been whetted for its ramifications. "Who was angry?" he said.

"The old man called Tot. And the other men," Alfred said. "And Grandpa, too. I didn't even know Grandpa got angry in that way."

"Did he do anything?"

"He got up. Because Aunty Patricia's mother said Aunty Belinda and Uncle Wilder built our house. Aunty Patricia's mother was really angry, too."

"Did they fight?"

"They were yelling. I thought they were going to fight. That was when I started crying."

"You cried? Did they see you crying?"

"Grandma Afia saw me. She saw my mother crying, too. She told Grandpa Broni and Grandpa Broni told Grandpa," he said. "And then they stopped."

"They left?"

"No. They stopped yelling and we drank schnapps."

"All of you? Even Tot?"

"Yes." Alfred peered at his uncle. "I heard Grandpa telling Grandpa Broni that the old man Tot wouldn't drink but he did. Why did they think he won't drink?"

"Well . . ." Jacob tried to come up with an uncomplicated explanation and gave up. "Did you like the taste of the schnapps?" he asked.

"I didn't drink it. I just pretended. It smelled like Dettol."

Jacob saw from Alfred's smile that he was supposed to laugh. But he couldn't bring himself to do it. In fact, Alfred's account hadn't gotten him to laugh as much as he'd anticipated. "Do you still want the toffees?" he asked.

With the yogurt in Alfred's pocket melting, the brown cotton had been steadily dampening into a perfectly rectangular imprint. Alfred had devoured the pouch in his hand up to a thin wedge of ice at the bottom. "No toffees today," he said. "But can I get it tomorrow?"

"Okay," Jacob said.

Alfred mashed the last bit of the frozen yogurt with his fingers and sucked on the plastic to complete collapse. He bunched up the plastic and fisted it.

"Don't you want the other one now?" asked Jacob.

"I'm full. I will put it in the freezer."

"You should get going, then." Jacob motioned toward the house among the colorful roofs in the distance. "It tastes different when you freeze it after it completely melts."

"That's true," Alfred admitted. "I don't like it that way." He readied himself to head back, monitoring the road in both directions. He glanced behind at Jacob. "What should I say to Grandpa if I find him on the veranda? He will ask me where I went."

"Tell him you came to see me."

The coast was clear, but Alfred stayed put. "I almost forgot, Uncle Jacob," he said. "Aunty Patricia's mother said something very strange." He waited for Jacob's show of interest. "She asked Grandpa, *Do you have light?*"

"I don't understand."

"At first, I didn't understand," Alfred said. "But then I got it. They said everybody in Ghana is going to have light-off."

"When?"

"I don't know," he said. "But that's what they said. Everybody in Ghana is going to have light-off."

THE CLICK-CLACK OF KEYBOARDS was the café's indisputable soundtrack, the whoosh of the standing fan its undergirding harmony. During the short time Jacob had spent outside with Alfred, the place had forgotten about him. No chair was open.

He checked the wall clock and confirmed that about five hours remained until seven, when he hoped Ohemaa would open for tonight's business. He was an infrequent patron and couldn't be certain of her start time. The last time he'd gone was the previous year, when Benjamin had asked him to have a drink and help him think through his girlfriend's—who would become his second wife—unexpected pregnancy. Tonight it would be Benjamin helping Jacob do his own thinking.

Benjamin noticed him and got out of his chair and nudged it at Jacob.

"Where will you sit?" Jacob asked.

"I'll stand. Why? How long are you thinking of staying?"

"I was hoping we could stop by Ohemaa's later."

Benjamin squinted. "Oh. You are reacting. Good. I thought I was going to have to slap you into it."

"I sat out the divorce show. Doesn't that count as reacting?"

"A smidgen," Benjamin said. "You have a lot more sitting out to do if the plan is to catch up to all of Patricia's sitting out."

"You know I'm not boisterous."

"Please," Benjamin said. "Even Jesus pulled out a switch when he had to."

"Then consider the drink the beginnings of me pulling mine out."

"Fine," Benjamin said. "Baby steps."

For the hours that remained until they headed to Ohemaa's, Jacob fell into a deep sleep in the chair, coming to only when Benjamin rocked him awake.

"Seven o'clock," Benjamin announced.

Jacob rubbed his eyes and looked around. "Where's everyone?" On Saturdays, Benjamin stayed open until ten.

"Closing early," Benjamin said. "You are reacting, remember?"

They were at the door when Jacob realized that he'd forgotten his laptop. He turned back to retrieve it but Benjamin said, "Leave it. You can come for it tomorrow. No telling what's going to become of you later."

Jacob lingered out front as Benjamin closed up. He admired the clear evening sky, the stars spectacularly shining and dimming seemingly in sync with the ups and downs vibrating from Ohemaa's loudspeakers next door. A few quick steps got them to Ohemaa's front pavement. She was inside the store attending to customers, not quite ready to transition to nighttime business.

She gestured for them to find a place for themselves at one of the tables she'd set out on the pavement, then pointed above to the top floor of the two-story building, where she lived with her family.

"She says to give her a minute to freshen up," Benjamin explained to Jacob.

They were first to arrive and had their choice of seating. They turned a table for four into a table for two by setting aside two plastic white chairs. When Ohemaa returned she groused about the rearrangement. She softened—Jacob could have sworn he saw the makeup caked on her forehead crack—after they promised to buy several bottles of Gulder.

The place was packed in no time; the girl who assisted Ohemaa at the store was now doing serving duties. By Jacob's and Benjamin's fifth drinks, large Gulders, Ohemaa reported to the crowd that only Guinness remained.

"Did we say we were allergic to Guinness?" slurred Benjamin over the music.

"Yes, Ohemaa," echoed Jacob, "did we say we were allergic to Guinness?"

Their chorus infected the others, and their voices whirled into a commotion of repetition. After it died down, the boom of the music took hold again and Jacob rocked his shoulders to the rhythm.

After a time, he said, "I don't think I know the kind of music Patricia likes."

"Do you know anything she likes?"

"Yes! We talked about many things she likes."

"Those are things she told you," Benjamin said. "They could have been lies."

Jacob poured the rest of his Gulder into his glass and shook the empty bottle in the server's view.

"What is Belinda saying about all of this?" Benjamin asked. "Have you talked to her?"

Jacob grunted. "I see she's done it to you, too—without ever meeting her. You think everything starts and stops with her."

"Didn't it start with her?"

"Fine. Let's give her that. Give her that power, Benjamin. But the buck stops with me."

"Which buck?"

"Her. Patricia."

Benjamin clinked his glass against Jacob's. "Let's move on," he said. "How about that woman who brings the things? Post-woman."

"Philomena," Jacob barked over the music.

"Oh." Surprised, Benjamin backed off.

"Oh what?"

"You're annoyed I didn't use her real name?" Benjamin said. "Something you forgot to tell me?"

"What would I have to tell you?"

"A man only fights for a woman to get her due if she's special," Benjamin said. "I was only teasing about you and her. But maybe I'm onto something."

Jacob downed his drink. "It's just right, Benjamin, to call her by her name."

The server came with two bottles of Guinness. Jacob took both and set them closer to himself. He poured one into his empty glass. Benjamin still had half a glass of his Gulder. He took a sip and then pointed out two girls in shimmery minidresses standing next to the strobe light pole, which flashed them like grand prizes. "They are prostitutes. The cheapest kind, too."

Jacob took note. "How old are they?"

"Eighteen? Nineteen? Who cares?"

"Which one?"

"One? Both!" Benjamin tapped his fingers on the table. "Really make up for lost time. I don't know how you did it, Jacob. Five years? Dry? Completely dry?"

"I was married."

"But you were not dead," Benjamin said. "And if we are being technical, you were not *technically* married. Married people have sex. When they go dry it's because they've exhausted the fun. You, on the other hand, started without fun. And have ended without fun. Christ!"

Jacob observed the girls. One was slightly shorter, her dress hiked up a little higher than the other's. They danced crotch-to-crotch, teasing each other's spaghetti straps. "How do you know them?"

"They are here every Friday and Saturday night." Sweeping his tongue over his upper lip, Benjamin added, "I've never tasted. But I can give you names of people who swear by them."

Jacob mulled the offer. Raising his glass, he said, "This thing is starting to get to me." He gulped the rest of the dark stout. A crescent of foam hooked onto his upper lip, which he licked off. "About those girls," he said. "Where?"

"My place."

The place Benjamin was referring to was the wood shack behind his main house. For privacy, he'd constructed it about forty feet from the three-bedroom home he lived in with his family. His first wife and the children he'd had with her had their streaks of rowdiness. With nowhere to turn for peace and quiet, certainly not the café, he'd hired a carpenter and together they built the simple structure in a week.

Jacob could count on one hand the number of times he'd been to Benjamin's house, a quick two-hundred-yard walk from the café. He had never seen the shack.

"About the same size as the kiosk," Benjamin explained as they closed in on the girls. Jacob could not walk straight; for support, he rested his hand on Benjamin's shoulder. "But no kitchen utensils," Benjamin continued. "No phone. And no floor tiling like I had inside the kiosk. Just a concrete floor. With a mattress, a radio, and an ice chest for when I am in there for long. You get me?"

It couldn't be that Benjamin was sleeping with other women forty feet from his wife and children, Jacob thought. "I don't get you."

"Yes you do."

The girls had eyes only for Benjamin. They rushed to hook arms with him, pushing Jacob to the side. Jacob stood with his legs spread apart, gripping the ground through his shoes.

"Finally, you are minding us," one girl said to Benjamin.

"We were starting to wonder," added the other.

Benjamin extracted himself from their clutches. "Maybe next time," he said. He got behind Jacob and squeezed his shoulders. "This is Jacob. He is your guy."

The girls smiled at each other, then at Jacob.

"Even better," one said.

"No problem at all," said the other.

BENJAMIN'S HOUSE was brightly lit and his family could be heard watching TV inside. All along the girls had been competing to wrap their arms around Jacob's waist—"He's mine," "No, he's mine." They had also had a few drinks, and together with Jacob they staggered behind Benjamin. Pushing on each other for ownership of Jacob hadn't helped, and they'd each fallen once, taking him with them.

Benjamin gestured for them to stop. With a finger to his lips, he instructed the girls to be quiet as he led the three of them around the house and toward the shack. When they got there Benjamin fanned them in as he held the door open from inside. "Hey, you," he said from the doorway to the girl with the lesser grip on Jacob. "Let him go. Wait until you get him on the mattress. You see how tall he is? There will be enough of him to go around when he's on his back."

The world escalated to a frantic spin as the girls lowered Jacob onto the floor mattress. Though hazed by alcohol, he was fully conscious. Nibbled by the springs of the old mattress, he awaited the girls' commands, imagining Hotch'91's directives. The commands did come, but disappointingly in Benjamin's voice. "Take good care of him, got it?" he said. "Don't be too rough with him. Give him a good time." Benjamin lit a lantern before adding, "Otherwise I won't pay you." He slammed the rickety door.

One girl undid Jacob's belt and the other removed his shoes. Together they slipped his trousers from him.

"Oh, wow," one said, and the other snickered.

But Jacob was not erect. He sensed a typical coursing of blood below his waist. If they wanted him to "get hard"—another of Hotch'91's sayings—they would need to take charge of him.

Instead, submitting to him, one said, "Mr. Jacob, how do you want me?"

The other, not to be outdone, said, "No, Mr. Jacob, how do you want *me*?"

Night crickets thrashed like floggings. "I want you like that," he said.

"Like what, Mr. Jacob?" The one who said this rushed to hover in his view. She bunched up her dress and moved her panties so that Jacob could see all that she was ready to give him.

"You know nothing, Rosebella," said the other. "You know nothing."

"And you do, Christabel?" Rosebella said. "Do you know something?" She turned her focus to Christabel. Her dress dropped back to her knees.

"A lot more than you," Christabel said. "The man doesn't want to see that. Not right now." Jacob kept track of her in his periphery. "Look into his eyes. Do you see how they are dreaming?"

Rosebella looked closer at him.

"He doesn't want quick-quick, go-go," Christabel continued. "He wants soft. Romance. Gentle. Not quick-quick, go-go."

"Is that right, Mr. Jacob?" asked Rosebella. She knelt to roll up his polo. Noticing that Rosebella was following her advice with her gentle rolling, Christabel also got to her knees and stroked Rosebella's arm while simultaneously stroking Jacob's cheek with the back of her other hand.

His torso was now completely bare.

"You like that, Mr. Jacob?"

"He likes that."

Rosebella kissed the middle of his chest. "How about that?"

"He likes that."

Then Rosebella pulled aside to give Christabel her chance. Christabel kissed her way down. She halted. "See?" she said. Jacob was hard now. "He likes it."

Jacob did. But not what they were presently engaged in. He'd gotten hard thanks to one event and one event only: Rosebella's thinning of her panties, her jabbing her vagina into his line of vision. It was a hint of possibility, a hint of the initiation of his preferred way of brute intercourse. Despite Rosebella and Christabel's shift to softness, Rosebella had excited him enough for him to latch onto visions of floggings that the night crickets inspired. His eyes were not dreaming. They were hasped in willful imagination, in which Rosebella, in Hotch'91's words, dug her acrylic nails into his chest and spat into the scratches. In those same words, Rosebella wrapped half his leather belt in her hand and slapped him with the other half. Hotch'91 had once fashioned a threesome during one of their conversations. Now he witnessed her and the woman she had typed to life transfigured into Rosebella and Christabel. They fed him to each other. They lashed his buttocks when he disobeyed. There on that screen of his mind, right there, were all the necessary stings.

Two

Reluctant to give up on Robert after his dashed athletic hopes, the Lutherans still saw in him the gold nuggets that had made them starry-eyed in the first place. This was after they'd obliged his request to pursue a dream he had: a sprinting camp for deaf children. The venture failed. After a year, Robert hadn't been able to attract more students and lost the ones he had. He came to accept that the children's parents, all of whom could hear and speak, had never completely bought into the idea of the camp.

The Lutherans happily welcomed Robert back. They tasked him with recruiting the city of Kumasi's deaf population to the Lutheran cause. His efforts ballooned the congregation of the one Lutheran church in Kumasi devoted to the deaf, Martha among the new recruits. When Robert mentioned that his family had moved to Deduako, the Lutherans secured land for another church building and enrolled Robert in an informal pastoral training program. They sold parts of the land to three other Christian denominations: Apostolic, Presbyterian, and Catholic. When the circle of four church buildings was put up, that part of town came to be known as Church Wheel.

Steeped in Lutheran teachings from childhood, Robert was a

quick study, and he proved to be a natural at the altar. He resigned from the Kumasi secretariat so he could commit fully to church work. At the celebration of the church's first anniversary, the Lutherans presented him with two Ford passenger vans. One would belong to the church. The other would be all his. He could do with it as he saw fit. Which he did.

At the body shop, Robert directed the mechanics to strip the van of its twenty-two seats, turning the twenty-four-seater into a cargo two-seater. He planned to rent it out at competitive prices to businesspeople, especially wholesalers of canned foods, who were always looking for affordable ways to distribute to smaller provisions stores. He could beat other transporters' prices because he had no start-up capital to recoup. The Lutherans were still his avenue to wealth, Robert realized, Olympics or not.

Church Wheel was within walking distance of the Nti home. The four buildings were close together—too close, some people thought, but each congregation learned to accommodate the interruptions of one's prayer by another's chimes, or one's sermon by another's rowdy praise. In truth, one of the four had not needed to learn to accommodate anything. Nobody wished for deafness or muteness, but everyone agreed that the Lutherans had it best: eternal silence to commune with God.

Yaa, who kept house for Mr. Nti, worshipped at the Apostolic church. Alfred preferred a church where people spoke, so he went with Yaa after his grandmother's death, which freed his grandfather to stay home on Sundays. As for his uncle Jacob, he was anything but a churchgoer. And as far as his father, Robert, was concerned, Robert believed that God was everywhere if only one had an open heart, so he permitted Alfred's turn to Apostolicism.

With his own open heart, Robert had signed for Alfred, he'd found God through the Lutherans. Where would he have been without those innovators who had the foresight to set up a school for the deaf?

So it was on the Sunday after the divorce ceremony that Yaa and Alfred waited out the rain at the Apostolic church. The rain poured from the sky like water from a basin, thumping on the aluminum roof. They stared through the cascade vaguely. Yaa was leaning into the window from one of the church benches, Alfred at her side. He wriggled for more room on the windowsill.

"Stop it," demanded Yaa. She squished him further against the jamb.

Alfred shrieked. "You are hurting me," he said.

She slanted to the right so that he could slide out of the window. He sat more comfortably on the bench and groused: "You promised that it was going to stop raining. Now look. We are stuck."

After the service, as others wrapped their heads with black polyethylene bags and sprinted for home, the pastor had shaken two bags in their faces before leaving. Yaa had refused them, claiming that the rain would soon slow to a drizzle. She couldn't have been more wrong. And now, to Alfred's irritation, she was humming the service's closing song, salting the injury of the terrible choice she'd made for him. He retaliated by singing the lyrics out of tune.

"Alfred!" Yaa said as she came out of the window to cup her hand over his mouth. "Your parents are still at church."

"They won't hear me," he yelled into the cavern her hand made over his mouth. "Remember?"

Yaa chuckled at her own forgetfulness. "This rain will never stop," she said as she removed her hand.

"It will," he said. "Something is telling me that it will stop soon."

"What?"

"I don't know," he said. "Just something."

He shot from the bench and stomped toward the altar. "Look," he called out to her. He flexed his arm, then rolled on the ground like Rambo on a covert mission. On his knees, he made a gun out of two fingers and pointed at Yaa. "Boom. Got you. Just like Rambo."

Yaa clutched her chest and pretended to catch her last breath. "I think I like the first Rambo more than the second one," she said.

"I like the second one more. It has action."

"So does the first one."

"But not more than the second one. If I was like Rambo, I would tell everyone. I don't know why Uncle Wilder doesn't want to tell everyone about being in Vietnam. Every time I talk to Aunty Belinda I want to ask. Then I remember how hard Grandpa warned me not to. I just don't understand. Why doesn't Uncle Wilder want to tell everyone?"

"Maybe because Uncle Wilder's not like Rambo."

"He fought the same war Rambo fought."

"I know, Alfred, but you've seen Uncle Wilder's picture. That white beard. Does Rambo have a white beard?"

"Uncle Wilder is old," Alfred admitted. "Old Rambo." He'd never made this comparison. Usually the white beard meant

Abraham. The Bible. Church. He hurried back to Yaa. He stood in front of her. "Let's go and wait at my father's church."

"Why?"

Alfred had never actually observed his father deliver a sermon. "It will be fun."

"Fuuun?" Yaa said in disbelief. "Maybe for you. Not me. I won't understand a thing."

"I will explain." He tried to smooth the creases in his shorts to prepare to head next door. His father would want him to look presentable. "And if the rain doesn't stop, they will take us home in their church van."

"Okay, but don't think I am doing what a little boy like you is telling me to do. I don't want to walk home in the rain. That's the only reason I'm coming along."

Outside, they pressed their backs along the church walls and shuffled to the side where a bit of open air separated the Apostolics' building from the Lutherans'. They held hands and closed their eyes before plunging into the chilly downpour. It took all of three plods through the rain for them to get under the roofed pavement that fronted his father's church. Still they needed a minute to shake off rainwater, and Alfred had to stamp his black Oxfords to dislodge the wet mud that clung to them.

From the doorway, Alfred saw Robert, robed in white, at the altar three steps above the front pews. A cross was carved into the wooden podium that plateaued at Robert's chest. Alfred locked eyes with him and waved. But Robert, signing God's word with an orchestral leader's fervor, ignored him.

He tiptoed in with Yaa. The building was about the size of

theirs—a compact space with two sets of pews separated by a narrow aisle. Alfred counted six rows in each section. He followed Yaa into the nearest pew, where she slid all the way to the wall. She rubbed her palm across it and checked it. "Nothing," she whispered, showing him her palm's cleanliness. "Nothing." Needlessly, she wiped her hand on her dress and then scanned the pale yellow walls. "So many times I have peeked in here and wondered if the walls were painted with yellow powder. Doesn't it look like powder?"

Alfred stretched over her and rubbed the wall with his fingertip.

"I wonder what kind of paint it is," Yaa said.

"Special paint. My father always says that Lutherans are special."

Special, too, was another feature in the church: the piercing quiet. Alfred was used to a preacher who roared into a microphone. *Amen*, the preacher would say. *Amen*, the congregation would respond. *The Lord is good*, the preacher would say. *All the time*, they would respond. He was also used to the thirty minutes reserved for Sunday prayer when the preacher sparked them off, summoning the Holy Ghost with *Fire!* Everyone in turn shook in prayer. *Fire! Fire! Fire!* Overcome with shakes, Alfred always watched Yaa, whose shakes he could not allow to outlast his. She exhausted herself before he did every time.

"What is your father saying?" she asked, her voice still low.

He felt the urge to shush her, then recalled that they could speak at the top of their voices if they wanted. "Somebody is going to get married," he said.

"Who?"

"I don't know. Somebody in this church. Oh, I know." He

pointed at the front pew. "You see those two sitting next to my mother?" Next to Martha was a woman with a pink feather hat angled on her head. The man next to her was dressed in a suit. Her soon-to-be husband. "Them. They are the ones getting married."

"Because of what they are wearing? Couldn't they just be celebrating a special occasion?"

"Look how my father is looking at them," Alfred said. Up on the altar, Robert was beaming. "He's advising them. About what married people do."

"Oh, wow!" Yaa's giddiness was youthful, childish. "So we're at a wedding?"

Alfred's attention was pulled by another figure, whose presence threw him for a real loop. How was he only now seeing him?

Before he could say anything, Yaa asked, "Is that Uncle Jacob?"

It was. And he could call out to him without disrupting a thing. "Uncle Jacob!"

His uncle turned around, a finger to his lips.

"Why do we have to be quiet?" Alfred whispered to Yaa.

"He's listening," Yaa said.

"To what? He doesn't even know what my father is saying."

To his surprise, some of his father's congregants had turned back to look at him as if his call had startled them. Everything, Alfred thought, was off course. First off, these deaf people acted as if they could hear him. Not to mention his own Uncle Jacob had gone to church. Not just any church, but his father's church for the deaf. There was this strangeness, too: Uncle Jacob was wearing the same clothes from yesterday. His white polo was crumpled and dirtier.

"Is he all right?" Yaa asked.

Whatever Uncle Jacob was suddenly made Alfred sad. Uncle Jacob almost resembled one of those messy madmen on the streets. Alfred tried to suppress his sadness by focusing on his father. The Word of God was invariably replenishing.

Yet another unsettling issue came to his attention: he realized he'd misdiagnosed the couple sitting next to his mother. In a low voice, seeking to shift responsibility for the misdiagnosis, he said, "Why would you say we stumbled on a wedding? Do you see any flower girls? Do you see a page boy?" He watched Yaa as she took stock of the congregation. "They already got married. They have just come for my father's advice."

"I see," Yaa said. "So what is he telling them?"

"Give me a second." He squinted to follow what his father was signing. After a moment, he said, "'If you don't know your wife you will be in trouble.... If you don't know your husband you will be in trouble.... I know somebody who didn't know his wife.... I told him he shouldn't do it.... He's a talking person.... Talking people don't listen to us.... I wrote him a long letter.... Careful, danger ... careful, danger ... Keep learning about her, keep learning about him.... Many changes, many changes...'" He turned to Yaa. "That's all."

"Many changes?" Yaa asked.

"Yes. That's his main advice."

"Who's the person who didn't know his wife?"

"Didn't you hear me?" Alfred said. "Some talking person."

For a moment, Yaa stared at him. She was fond of lording their seven-year age gap over him. "You know something?" she said, a condescending smile on her face. "Because of all the grown-up things we make you interpret, I sometimes forget that you are still a child."

"What does that mean?"

"Some talking person?" Yaa said. "Alfred, think! The talking person is Uncle Jacob."

"Oh," he said, confused. Uncle Jacob had walked out a few minutes ago. Alfred had seen him leave as he was translating for Yaa. "Then why didn't my father say Uncle Jacob? Or, *my brother*?"

"Let me tell you a secret about grown-ups. When they don't want people to know their family business, especially embarrassing family business like ours, they pretend that they are talking about other people. The whole situation is even more embarrassing for your father. He's a pastor and he couldn't advise his own brother to marry wisely."

"That's because Uncle Jacob can talk."

"And that's the most embarrassing part of all," Yaa said. "Your father doesn't want these people to know that because he can't talk, nobody listens to him, even in his own family. It's actually very sad."

Alfred realized that this was true. He'd once seen Robert and Martha discuss that his arm was the result of talking people not listening to deaf people. Had the midwife cared about Martha, she would have pulled him out of her more gently.

"The rain stopped," Yaa said.

Alfred glanced outside and was heartened that the sky was bruised gold. The brightness reminded him of the light-off that Aunty Patricia's mother and the old man Tot said was coming. "Is it true?"

"Is what true?"

"The light-off."

"People have been talking about it. I think it's true."

Around them, the congregation stood. "They are about to close," Alfred said.

"Perfect. That means we won't have to walk."

After the service, as the church members filed outside, Alfred could feel under his Oxfords the mushiness of the grass within Church Wheel's center, but the ground had dried enough so that nothing was sticking to his shoes.

Robert and Martha were the last people to come out of the church. Not too far from where he stood with Yaa, his parents moved among clusters of people, saying their farewells. Out of his pastoral robe, Robert was wearing a black suit, the collar of his red shirt complementing Martha's dress.

Several feet away, a queue was forming parallel to the church van. The driver rounded the van's front. Tugging on the door handle, he slid it open.

Alfred hurried over.

"Alfred! Where are your manners?" Yaa shouted. "Let the others get in first."

Alfred stopped and slumped his shoulders, watching the van windows fill with heads. Soon only the two front seats were empty. Of the two, Martha took the one closest to the driver. She patted her thigh at Alfred, who winked at Yaa and bounded forward. Robert seized him by the waist and lifted him into the van. He settled on his mother's lap and looked on as Robert searched for a place for Yaa in the back. The other riders did their best to make space, but as hard as they squirmed, they simply couldn't make enough room. That Yaa would have to walk home amused Alfred—had she followed his instinct to run for the van, she would have found a seat. He was prepared to order her to get to trotting when a woman readjusted herself further by half sitting on her husband's lap.

Robert fanned his hands to get Yaa's attention, but she was too focused on pressing out the wrinkles in her dress to notice.

"Yaa!" Alfred barked. "Get in. They have made room for you."

She looked up, startled; she hadn't expected to hear anything but the van's engine starting. Whether from euphoria or shock, Yaa, like an Olympic athlete that Robert might have become, leapt across puddles and climbed into the van.

AFTER LEAVING CHURCH, Jacob walked home and got into bed. He had no idea how long he'd been asleep when he heard a bewildering noise. Forcing his eyes open, he identified it as knocks on his bedroom door. He tried to ignore it.

"Jacob, Jacob," his father called, his voice insistent.

He sounded like a man on a mission, a person who refused to be ignored. Jacob got out of bed and opened the door. His father stood there, looking smaller than usual.

"You are not dead," the old man said, sounding surprised.

"No," Jacob said.

Mr. Nti squeezed his nose. "But you are drunk."

"Am I blowing fumes?" His throat split dry, and his tongue tasted rotten.

"That. And your eyes look like you have Apollo."

From nowhere, Yaa appeared with ice water. She handed the glass to Mr. Nti, who handed it to Jacob. "Here."

Jacob accepted it. Downing it in large gulps, he sat back down on his bed.

Mr. Nti stood looking at him, his gaze resolute.

"You're not sitting?" Jacob asked.

"I only came to check on you," Mr. Nti said. "But if you want me to stay . . ."

Before Jacob could answer, his father sat down next to him on the bed. Jacob set his glass by his feet on the terrazzo. He tugged on his white boxer shorts, which were riding up his thighs. He rubbed his chest, working his way up to his face.

"You and Robert are lucky," Mr. Nti said, looking him over. "You take after the men in your mother's family. Chiseled like hunters."

"The men in yours are not so bad."

"Exactly," Mr. Nti said. "Not so bad."

Jacob bent for the glass on the floor, expertly tipping it into his hand so that the water skirted the ice floating at the top. A small puddle collected in his hand. He replaced the glass on the floor and spread the liquid onto both palms like ointment, then moved his hands over his face to soothe—and maybe obstruct—his distress.

"Alfred came to see you yesterday?" his father asked.

Jacob kneaded his cheekbones with his fingertips. "You didn't punish him, did you?"

"So you know he snuck out?"

"I made him do it," Jacob said. "What excuse did he give you?"

"None. I ignored him when he returned. It was the best recourse. The best way to punish Alfred is not giving him a chance to explain himself."

"So how did you determine that he came to see me?" Jacob said.

"I decided that I'd punished him enough so I asked him when he came home from church. He also said he saw you at his father's church."

"I was there."

"What for?"

"A change of pace."

They sat quietly for some time. In the silence, Jacob thought he observed a sudden vulnerability in his father's inquisitiveness; the old man's mouth trembled with self-consciousness.

"It was not my plan for Tot to drink," Mr. Nti said. "I'm not cruel."

The admission threw off Jacob; he had almost forgotten that part of Alfred's rundown. "Tot said something was *rubbish*?" Jacob said. "Also, *foolish*? Did that drive him to drink?"

Mr. Nti shook his head. "All sorts of words were used," he said. "*Rubbish* and *foolish* were probably the kindest among them."

Jacob stretched for the door of the built-in wardrobe at the foot of his bed. He pulled it open and removed a pair of shorts from a folded pile. Without standing, he pulled them over his boxer shorts. "Such as?"

Avoiding Jacob's gaze, Mr. Nti answered, "Timid."

"To describe me?" Jacob asked.

Mr. Nti nodded.

"That's nothing new," Jacob said. "Weren't we expecting that?"

"Not to the extent—"

"To what extent?"

"Of questioning your manhood," Mr. Nti said quietly.

Jacob flicked his hand to dismiss the accusation. He was ready to move away from the topic. His father, however, stretched his legs out in front of him. Jacob recognized the action. It was the posture of a person preparing to address a difficult subject head-on.

"Jacob," Mr. Nti said, "what kind of man requires his younger sister to find him a wife?"

"A disturbed one," Jacob said.

"I'm serious."

"As am I," Jacob said. "I went to church, Pa. Me, of all people. I went to church."

"For the deaf."

"Church, all the same."

"Fair enough," Mr. Nti said. "But what did it get you?"

"Forgiveness," he said. "I went for Robert's forgiveness. Turns out he's the most sensible one in this family." In many ways, Jacob thought, Robert had been right when he called him a fool decades ago, which Robert had indirectly underscored in his letter concerning Jacob and Patricia's prospects.

"Robert is well read," Mr. Nti admitted.

"He has common sense. Nothing you can get from books." Jacob paused because he sensed anger rising in himself. "He's the only person in this family who never came around to the idea of the marriage."

"Your mother, too," Mr. Nti said. "She never came around. She just had her own way of showing it. You missed it."

"So just you and Belinda, then."

"I thought you wanted it," Mr. Nti said. "And it's not as if you ever stopped wanting it. Never giving up on joining her in America. Not giving up on her even after you found out from Postwoman that she was living with a man."

"I did want it."

"So how was I wrong?" his father asked.

"You weren't," Jacob said. "But I wonder what convinced you more. My wanting it. Or Belinda's orchestration of it."

"Does it matter?"

"It does," Jacob said. "If we are going to mend things, it does."

"Belinda feels terrible," Mr. Nti said.

"What Napoleon could not do, right? She found me a wife. Hurrah!" Jacob leaned back into the wardrobe for a black T-shirt. "How terrible?"

"What do you mean?"

"How terrible does she feel about the divorce? I imagine Wilder's money is quite the antidote to terrible."

"You know she has her headache," Mr. Nti said.

"She's been fighting for a green card for ten years," Jacob said. "That's a headache of choice for someone like her. She has access to that old man's money. She has all those fancy degrees. She doesn't need America."

"Who doesn't need America?"

Jacob pulled the T-shirt over his head carefully. It had been part of the most recent—and probably last—package that Patricia had sent through Postwoman. On the front of the T-shirt was a photograph of Mount Rushmore, which Patricia said she hoped would help him keep the faith.

"Belinda is disturbed, Pa," Jacob said. "Who doesn't come home for their own mother's funeral? Especially someone with the means she has? It looks to me like she's lost her mind trying to make sure that nobody can ever say there was something she could not achieve." He shook his head. "So there you go, Pa. Three children. Two disturbed. One a deaf-mute," he said. "If not for that, Robert would be perfect. You can't have it all, I guess."

His bluntness startled his father. After a long moment Mr. Nti said, "I want to understand something. What was it about Patricia?"

"Someone said you can't explain love, Pa," Jacob replied, though he could perfectly explain what it was about Patricia.

"Well, it was something. For God's sake, Jacob, you told her everything. Which a good husband should do. But your situation was different. Still you went as far as even telling her what you contributed to build this house?"

Jacob shrugged and looked at his father more closely. There was pain and sorrow in the old man's face; his eyes welled up. Catching himself, he blinked a few times to dry his eyes and restore their usual whiteness, which he credited for his perfect vision even at age sixty-eight. He asked, "So how much time are you going to need to move forward?"

"You're asking if I'm going to be able to find someone else."

"Yes," he said. "She's the only woman you've ever been serious about. And you were thirty-four when she came into your life. I would say I'm entitled to my concern."

"That's all you are concerned about? My finding another woman?"

"There's a way Patricia pushed you, Jacob," Mr. Nti admitted.

"Her people were not privy to how she pushed you, so they came here and spewed unfounded claims. But I had a front-row seat. The many trips to Accra. How badly you wanted her. Or should I say America. There's no denying that they are one and the same."

"Hardly."

"Not hardly. Because legally or illegally, she's still there. In America."

Jacob smiled. "There's something I never shared with you."

"What?"

"Patricia told me she would have come back to Ghana to be with me if I had something for her to come back to."

"Her mother made that claim, too," Mr. Nti said. "You believed her?"

"Yes."

"And?"

"And I would have liked that."

"I see," Mr. Nti said quietly. "All this time I have been waiting for you to confirm my suspicion that it was always about America. Nothing to do with her."

Jacob brought up his legs and set his feet on the bed. He hunched over to touch his chin to his knees. "Belinda's friend. Mr. Hyde's daughter . . ."

"Edith? What about her? Why are you bringing her up?"

"She's marrying a white man."

"According to Belinda, yes," Mr. Nti said.

"I see," Jacob said. He leaned back onto the bed and propped himself up on his arms. "Maybe that's what Belinda should have done. Better yet, maybe she should have found me a white woman." He dropped onto his back. Looking up at the ceiling, he said,

"Belinda might not be so smart after all, Pa. She may have gotten into Hotchkiss before Edith did, but if you ask me, Edith has proven herself smarter. Smart enough to know to go with white."

Mr. Nti stood up. "Jacob, black or white, pink or green, any woman would want you to have a life. A life befitting a man. Frankly, that's my real concern."

Three

Over the next month, Jacob made significant strides. More and more he moved on from Patricia, finally confronting the likelihood that she had been having an affair with her male roommate while they'd been married.

"Roommate." That was how Patricia referred to him. The American way. Here in Ghana, it was "flatmate," which implied separate rooms. Flatmate was how Jacob had described the man to his father—Patricia's male flatmate—and yet his father had determined it to mean that they were sharing a bed.

But Patricia and the potential of a new man in her life were hardly Jacob's current worry. Nor was it the possibility of another woman for himself. He was more occupied with concerns about his life—his inability, at forty years of age, to provide for himself or anyone else.

He was about to turn the page on that. After weeks of research and planning, he had put together a business proposal he knew would afford Nabil and Mamoud Azar an opportunity to grow their business. Maybe even expand into Accra.

In a few hours he would pitch his idea to Mamoud, who exhibited a youthful penchant for risk. Mamoud, as everyone at

Azar & Co. knew, arrived at the office with his own key to the building's front doors and unlocked them at least an hour before the building manager did so for the official start of business. It was said that Jacob's boss, Festus Ntiamoah, had sealed his promotion by catching Mamoud early one morning and making a case for himself. When Nabil later showed up at the office, Mamoud had already come up with responses to his brother's objections and natural caution and Festus was promoted.

On any other day, the collar of Jacob's work shirt would have stayed unbuttoned and limp. Today, however, required a sartorial shift. As Jacob stood at the wardrobe mirror fussing with the ends of a striped tie, he took note of the morning's darkness through the louvers. After several failed attempts at winding the tie into a clean knot, he finally got it; he tugged on it to make sure it lay straight down his chest. He twisted his neck to the left and then to the right. The tie pressed his Adam's apple uncomfortably but there was also a fine slash of ecstasy. Pain and pleasure. Pleasure. Pain.

Physically, Jacob never looked as if he had a meek temperament. The mirror said as much, especially when he was dressed this way: a man of decisiveness. White business shirt and starched beige trousers, a blue-black striped necktie precisely tied; spotless black Oxfords. Other than Robert's and Benjamin's, no other man's height came close to his. How many Ashanti men—for that matter, how many Ghanaian men—were six foot three? The teenage girl from his Tech days, who was his roommate's sister and the first of the women he'd had sex with, had said that men like him, with long arms and long legs and long fingers, were long everywhere. He'd pointed to his round head. Kittenish, she'd responded with a wink at his crotch.

There'd been two other women over the years, even though he'd never had a steady girlfriend. That was because, ashamed of the kind of women he was drawn to, he'd gone with his lovers covertly. There was Pearl, ten years his senior and a client of Azar & Co., who'd spent most of her life in Berlin and who oozed sexual deviance. After Pearl there was Merya, who at twenty-seven was only three years older than he was but who was already a married mother of five. He'd met Merya at the Kumasi sports stadium, across the street from the last house his parents had rented. Merya had come to register her deaf son for Robert's sprinting camp, where Jacob worked as registrar since all of the parents could hear and speak.

Pearl, he remembered, had employed a rubber whip; Merya, her husband's leather belt, which inflicted a more wicked burn.

"Do you have a stopping point? A ceiling?" Merya once asked him.

"Whatever you decide you don't like," Jacob answered.

The belt was enough for her, Merya confided, but she set Jacob to thinking. What was his ceiling? Years later, through a discussion board on the website where he'd met Hotch'91, Sims, he identified where it stopped for him: he couldn't see himself getting defecated on.

Jacob plucked from his bedside table the final touch to his outfit: the watch with the scratched-up tan leather strap, courtesy of Patricia early in their marriage. If all went well today, perhaps it would soon be replaced by an entirely different watch, made of gold. And he would also stop using the imitation fragrance he was now reaching for, which required too many pumps. Eventually, Belinda had had enough of his half thank-yous and stopped sending the authentic kind, and he didn't have the heart to ask Patricia for either of his two favorites, Cool Water or L'Eau d'Issey. He grabbed his wallet, which he'd bought himself. It was fine for him today, but for his future self it would have to be replaced by one made from more durable leather.

He wondered whether he should wear a blazer. Last night, he'd decided against it and tucked the blue-black flannel, which would have nicely matched his tie, behind the shirts hanging in the wardrobe. Now he wasn't so sure about going without it. As he contemplated further, he soon recognized this resurgence of uncertainty as nothing but anxiety, which he had read was the enemy of success, and which he couldn't allow to get the best of him on a day as important as this. Anxiety was a feeling he knew well: it had contributed to his two visa rejections; it had spurred his incoherent answers to variations of the same question, *Why do you want to travel to the US?* The one time he'd spoken with certainty—"I am going for love"—the immigration officer responded with a question that insinuated that Jacob was a homosexual—"You are not able to live as your full self here in Ghana?"—to which Jacob had answered, again with confidence, yes. He suspected that the empathetic immigration officer, while stamping DENIED on his application, had quietly bemoaned Jacob's opportunism: a straight man claiming homosexuality to bolster his application for an American visa. But Jacob wasn't being duplicitous; he was telling the truth, albeit another truth regarding his sexual preference.

And yes, Patricia had already made him certain that he could live out loud with her in America.

He felt his pocket for his phone. It was there. Instead of his work satchel, he snatched the leather one that Benjamin had given him—black, not brown, was the color of executives—and hung it from his shoulder. The laptop was inside, bobbing against his thigh with every step.

He walked toward the trotro lot in atypical darkness and quiet. He checked his watch—five a.m. To catch Mamoud Azar before the workday started, he'd set off an hour ahead of his habitual time.

At the lot, a small group of commuters were climbing into the trotro van to Adum. At the center of the queue of vans sat the gray van to Jacob's destination, Kejetia. Scrawled on the van's side in red was *Jesus Is Lord*.

The bony mate, who was in charge of shepherding passengers in and out of the van, bounced on his toes and heels, chanting his marketing wail, which soared higher and higher as it dominated the competing wails. His oversize yellow T-shirt was spotted with oil stains, insignias of his daily labor. It was a humid morning; his forehead already leaked sweat.

"Boss. Very early today," he said upon sighting Jacob. He scurried out of Jacob's way and held the door as Jacob climbed into the van. Jacob set the satchel on a two-seater and slid to the window. "Boss. Any minute from now," the mate said, his voice steely. "We will leave any minute from now."

"No problem," Jacob said. He laid the satchel on his lap, feeling certain that the van would pull out in reasonable time.

A woman wearing too many layers of clothes got into the van and sat next to him. Her head was wrapped in a black scarf, signifying that she was somewhere in a period of mourning. Over a black Lycra top that reached down her arms to her wrists and up her neck to her chin, she wore a Pepsi-Cola T-shirt. A piece of dark cloth was wrapped around her waist. It cut off at her knees, where Jacob spied that she also wore loose plaid trousers that looked like pajama bottoms. On her feet were white athletic socks notched by the thongs on each of her rubber slippers; in her fist was a wad of money. She unwrapped a small section of her cloth and shoved the money into it before tying a fat knot she secured at her waist.

"Morning, morning," she said. A tinge of warning stiffened her greeting.

"Good morning."

"Your car not working?"

"My car?"

"I've never seen you on here before." She dropped her voice. "You probably don't need this advice. I'm sure your car will be fixed soon. But in case you take this trotro again, don't trust these people." She eyed the satchel on his lap. "Hold your bag tight. They will smile in your face but they are all thieves."

Humoring her, Jacob widened his eyes to feign shock. He couldn't imagine these passengers being more morally compromised than those on his established route, only an hour later. But he retrieved his wallet from his pocket and dropped it into the bag. Closing it, he pulled the bag closer to him.

When the van filled up, the mate took his seat by the door and closed it. He squawked for the driver to start, which he did. Inch by inch, the van's wheels crept toward the main road.

Minutes into the journey, Jacob noticed that children out-numbered adults in the van. They wore checkered brown school uniforms. "Are the children thieves, too?" he asked.

Whispering, the woman said, "Thieves in training."

Jacob laughed. "They are schoolchildren."

"The school is where they get their training. It doesn't have a start time or end time." She took in the trotro's passengers with condescension. "The school is someone's house. You can drop off your child at any time you want and pick up your child at any time you want."

"Sounds like a holding pen."

"Exactly what it is," she said. "Their parents are market people. They need a place to send their children early in the morning and pick them up in the late evening. It's no school. No school at all. Don't let their uniforms fool you."

The trotro wobbled, diving into one pothole after another. The woman quickly fixed her eyes on the peeling metal ceiling. "Mate!" she yelped. "I hope you tied my sacks well."

"You don't trust me?" the mate said, staring forward.

"This is not about trust," she said. "It has happened before."

"And I learned my lesson."

"I hope you did. For your sake. I really hope you did." She turned to Jacob with a glint of mischief to her. "Nobody wants to go toe-to-toe with a crazy woman."

Jacob knew he didn't but didn't tell her that. "You have some-thing up top?"

"Five sacks of beans," she said. "Maybe you've heard of me. Maame Beans? I supply beans to the chop bar owners in Kejetia."

"I eat lunch at Bujumbura."

"Then you've had my beans."

The van pulled off the road to let out a passenger. The driver turned off the engine and hopped out to relieve himself. He returned to the driver's seat and restarted the engine. Still they waited to get back on the road as the mate banged on the passenger door from outside, drumming along to his repetition of their ultimate destination: *Kejetia, Kejetia, Kejetia*. He was looking to replace the passenger they'd just dropped off. When at last a young man got on, their journey continued.

Maame Beans crossed her arms and sighed. "If I had my own van I wouldn't have to deal with these people. And all the stops. Where do you work?"

"Azar & Co. Do you know it?"

"Is it where people wear ties?"

Jacob smiled. "Not all the time."

"But sometimes?"

Jacob nodded.

"Then I don't know it."

"I'm a computer scientist."

"Computers? Amazing," Maame Beans said. "As soon as I saw you, I knew you didn't fit in with us."

"Because of the tie."

"That," she said, "and you look noble. Like a gentleman."

Her commendation frightened Jacob: Was she aware of his lie? Could she tell he just entered data and didn't write software?

"Maybe I can help you," he said.

"With what?"

"With getting your beans to the market. My brother has a van. He helps businesspeople move their things."

"Can the van go anywhere?"

"It goes everywhere."

"Wonderful. Excellent." Maame Beans's face brightened. "It is God that has led me to you. He knows how much I'm suffering."

Jacob felt himself twitch in his uncertainty. He didn't know the confident language of faith, and his most recent visit to church hadn't helped.

To his relief, Maame Beans dozed off without warning or shame, clutching the waist of her cloth like a tool belt. Her message was clear: she didn't trust him enough to sleep with her hands free, despite bestowing on him the honor of looking *noble*. And why should she? Jacob guessed her to be in her late forties, wrinkled by life's struggles so that she appeared older than she probably was. She knew not to judge a book by its cover. Whatever superior occupation he might have, however fine his clothes, she knew not to let her guard down even in sleep.

The van tossed him violently when it plunged into another pothole, and his head struck the window when the driver made a sharp turn to avoid another. Neither woke Maame Beans.

After settling more comfortably into his seat, Jacob dug out from his bag his presentation note cards. He read through them and soon decided that he already knew by heart what he wanted to say to Mamoud: for the local market, and in multiple languages, Azar & Co. would produce its own CD tutorials on software design and development, setting up a computer school where after purchasing the educational CDs, students could pay for guidance or general computer training. An idea, truth be told, that sold itself.

His thoughts drifted before landing on Patricia, recalling her outsize joy for everything. That had been his first impression of her, her voice bursting with excitement at the most humdrum aspects of his day: the pile of receipts that had been placed on his desk, his five rotating lunch options. His morning and evening commutes had been fantasies to her: what she wouldn't give to spend an hour in a trotro feasting on Kumasi's sights from the window. Trotros, in her American mind, had become limousines, no longer hazardous transportation with peeling paint and terrible shock absorbers. When she asked him to describe the ring he would be presenting to her family, he lied that he'd only been able to afford a yellow gold band with a central faux crystal stud; she'd squealed, admitting that though white gold was in vogue, it had never appealed to her. He hadn't believed her echo of his mother's sentiments about yellow gold but had gone with it, holding out for the moment of surprise.

When he and Patricia next spoke after she received the ring, she squealed again. "Jacob, you sly guy," she said. "It's a real stone."

Ironically—at least if what he'd learned from his father was any indication—it was his mother's joyful sentiments about the ring he should have always doubted, for she had never fully come around to the idea of the marriage. His mother had been present when, without Jacob asking, his father had given him some money to add to his savings for the ring. "Get her something that would really excite her," he had said, clutching his wife's hand in what Jacob at the time thought was a gesture uniting their respective pride.

He would keep a close ear on the excitement in Patricia's voice over the years, enough that he knew things were not right before Philomena mentioned Patricia's roommate, and before she later confirmed that Patricia had sent Jacob nothing, even though Philomena had called him to let him know of her arrival in Ghana and that he should stop by. "Stop by" was how she communicated that Patricia had sent something. "As soon as you can," she would add. "Otherwise I will mix up the money Patricia has sent for you with my own."

Patricia had always tittered over the label she'd given to the money—"discretionary upkeep"—belittling the large sum that was often twice his monthly salary and driving out the thoughts of inadequacy she correctly presumed her assistance prompted in him. He knew they were near the end when once, out of context, she enumerated the total she'd sent him over the years, without even rounding to the nearest tenth of a cedi after calculating the exchange rate.

Long before Jacob knew it was over, he'd asked himself why she'd still not questioned him about his past sexual partners—though it was a reticence that he welcomed and reciprocated. His past was too strange a history to go into. After reaching the certainty of his undoubtable liking of girls, he'd secured a number of them easily, his looks making his case before he even opened his mouth. But there was effort. Too much effort. The night-with-the-prostitutes kind of effort to become aroused in the moment. In the most perfect sense of virginity—in which both parties happily consented to the act of losing it—he'd remained a virgin until Tech, at the age of twenty. All his roommate's sister had required were his quick erections and even quicker thrusts, as, she said, her brother had a sneaky way of interrupting her enjoyment. He'd never needed to dive into his mind with her; she took command of him and it was as though he had no mind. Her name escaped him now, which would never be the case with Pearl, because Pearl, Berlin Pearl, had lashed her name out of him with a rubber whip. Nobody had to tell you that Pearl did not suffer fools; it was obvious in her sharp features, as if whoever had created her had gone about it with a fierce focus: her jawline and her pitched shoulders, tossing in her quick temper for good measure. She worked for Azar & Co.'s biggest client and had made her intentions known to him the first time she saw him, going so far as to emphasize that she would tire of him in no time. For Jacob it was a titillating proposition of indentured servitude. Not even six months elapsed before she threw him over, leaving him to seek the delicious sting across his buttocks elsewhere. In Merya, he lucked into a dual vulnerability: with her need for touch and a deep resentment of men—owing to her philandering husband—she worked out on him with her husband's leather belt. When she arrived to register her son for Robert's sprinting camp, they chatted innocently enough. She left without registering the boy and Jacob racked his mind for what mistake he'd made to change her mind. To his relief she returned two days later, but on her own. She'd switched out her dowdy housedress for a pair of jeans and a white men's shirt she'd tied to show her flat stomach. Seduction marked her calculated presentation of herself. She asked Jacob whether he believed that she was a mother of five, to which he responded that he believed whatever she wanted him to believe. Their five-year affair lasted until she relocated to Accra with her husband, which coincided with the dawn of the new century and Jacob's own wish for new beginnings.

It was Berlin Pearl who later told him about the website when they reconnected for three months in 2001. He didn't have a primary person he connected with then; he simply read the stories people posted, often doubting the outlandish experiences that some members claimed to have had, and decided that some of the extremes were not for him.

Without Merya or Pearl and with his career going nowhere, the world reached peak bleakness for Jacob. And with Belinda's new life thanks to Wilder, his jealousy ballooned. Good things were happening for Belinda in America. Perhaps America was the answer after all.

But going back to Mr. Hyde was out of the question. Belinda and Edith no longer got along, and everyone was supposed to be keeping their distance from the Hydes. He briefly explored the idea of going to him anyway, out of the spite he had for Belinda, but decided the risk outweighed the reward.

Channeling his spite, he searched for a companion on the site by restricting the parameters to the state of Connecticut, where Hotchkiss was. It was where it had all begun for Belinda; it felt right for him to begin there, too. He further restricted his search to citizens of Greenwich, where, he knew, some of the state's wealthiest people lived.

It didn't take long for him to find the right person.

For three years, they stuck to their screen names: WeakLong-Don, Hotch'91. And their conversations ranged widely.

"Ghana is very difficult," he admitted in one chat. "Very few jobs. I'm lucky to even have employment."

Later he typed, "I wish I was there with you."

In response to one of her questions, he said, "Yes, I still live at home with my family. Goes to show you how desperate my situation is."

Hotch'91 never sent money. Which was fine; it was not money he wanted from her. He sought intimacy, an intimacy that might compel her to send for him.

But she never did.

Eventually, he came out with the detail he thought would force the closeness he wanted: "Did you go to Hotchkiss?" He'd been drawn to her by the five letters of her screen name.

"OMG," she typed. "Oh my god. Do you know me? Oh my god."

"No. Please. Don't be nervous. I don't know you. It's just that it's a very famous school in Ghana." Nobody had ever heard of Hotchkiss until Belinda.

"Oh my god. Oh my god."

He waited, considering that this might be it for them.

"Yes," she finally typed.

He didn't bother asking the year she graduated—'91 said it all. The same year as Belinda.

"I guess I wanted to be found, right? Otherwise, why choose the screen name I did? My name is Sims."

"Okay. My name is Jacob."

It became too much. Too much time in front of the screen—so much that a condition had even come out of it: flitting eyelids. He even chatted with her when he was at work. Perhaps this had contributed to his lack of promotion. Maybe he'd been found out and out of sympathy he'd been intentionally overlooked rather than fired outright.

Still he kept in touch with Sims. Frantically pursuing America. But Sims never asked if he was even interested in a one-week American getaway. With Patricia, he had a seemingly certain entrée to America. With Sims, Jacob met a dead end. He stopped with Sims.

Yet the more he heard from Patricia and the more she hinted that she would submit to him, the more he wanted to recant his declarations of attraction. He was about to break up with her when one of Philomena's deliveries arrived with a surprise: nude photographs of Patricia standing with one leg on a pedestal, hands on her waist, ready to whip him into shape if he erred. That was all he needed. Here was wildness! At the marriage ceremony he smiled wryly at the contrasting photo of his soon-to-be wife in Tot's hand. Patricia was far from the shy person Tot held up. Jacob knew better. Jacob had proof.

"What are you learning?"

The question jolted him back to the present. Maame Beans was gazing at the note cards in his hands.

"It's for work," he said.

"I see."

She knew the appropriate protocol and looked away. He put the cards back into his satchel and looked out the window. The trotro crawled steadily forward.

Before long, Maame Beans grazed his thigh with her fingertips. "Last stop," she said.

When the trotro came to a final stop, he followed her out, going behind the van, where five men with their shirts bunched on their heads waited in a line. With care, the driver and mate untied

Maame Beans's sacks from the top of the van. One by one the men propped them on their heads, speeding off into the market crowd.

"They know where to go?" Jacob asked.

"Yes," she said. "They work for me."

The mate spread his palm at her, but she was already in the middle of refastening her money knot in its place around her waist. She pressed her balled hand onto the mate's palm. "Here," she said, releasing the wad. "It's for the two of us."

Jacob rummaged through his satchel, feeling for his wallet. "Please, no," he said. "You don't have to do that."

She grasped his elbow. "It's the least I could do."

He stopped, letting the satchel swing from his shoulder. "Thank you," he said.

"I should be the one thanking you. You are about to change my life."

"Not me. My brother."

She motioned to a place opposite the horde, where a few people were lingering beside colorful wooden kiosks. Next to a purple one she dug into her stretchy undergarment and pulled out a small cell phone. "The day is fast moving. I can't talk much." She flipped the phone open. "Let me have your brother's number."

"Let me have yours instead."

"Why?"

"He's deaf. I'll give him your number. He'll text you."

"Okay," she said. "Still, give me yours. I'll call you for mine."

Jacob gave her his telephone number. She made him repeat it for confirmation. He felt the vibration of her confirming call deep in his quadriceps. When he retrieved the phone from his pocket, she said, "Wow." She leaned closer to look it over. Bright sunlight twinkled the glass screen. "It is the iPhone, is it not?"

"It is."

He stored her number under her name, capitalizing each letter. She was a purposeful woman and deserved the emphasis.

"I look forward to hearing from him," she said, stepping back.

Jacob said nothing in reply. Instead he waved his phone as she retreated into the crowd; he proceeded on his own trek to the office.

Nearing the traders who assembled in front of his office building, he considered that Maame Beans need only witness the encroaching might of her vocation to realize the irrelevance of status. There was no difference between them; attire was cosmetic, meaningless. The laptop and phone he had were evidence of one woman's efforts to help him rise. That woman had left him in this dreadful place at the bottom. That was the heart of the matter, despite his father's desperation to paint Patricia as a slut who was moving on because she'd found another man. He was stuck—marooned. Still, he could take heart in the effort he was making to untether himself from the bottom. He knew he was helpless to change his carnal desires—what he thought of as his blight—but he was determined to succeed at work. And he would. It was a wonder to him that management hadn't already put this idea into practice. It was so simple, so sensible. CD tutorials on software design and development produced in several Ghanaian languages by Azar & Co. Focused on the local market. An attached school for computer training. He would spearhead and manage the initiative. He'd been unknowingly laying the groundwork with his year of self-study at the café. He only required the go-ahead and infrastructure.

Closing in on his office building, he noticed a peddler he didn't recognize, a boy positioned at the foot of the office steps. He may have been six or seven, selling an assortment of wrapped round toffees fanned out across the surface of a flat pan. Jacob had intended to pass the boy, but something about him—maybe his age and that he was selling toffees—reminded him of Alfred. The Werther's Original toffees Patricia used to send through Philomena had helped Jacob compete favorably with Belinda for Alfred's awe. In Alfred's eyes, Belinda's Nikes and the sweet stuff ranked equally, and by extension, his uncle and aunt were of equal rank. Admittedly, he'd been trying to climb back to that high place of Alfred's wonderment ever since Philomena handed him Patricia's final consignment of Werther's Original toffees: two ten-packs that paled in comparison to the five hundred-packs of their early years. Two ten-packs that drove Alfred to ask, "Uncle Jacob, are you angry with me?"

"Give me two cedis," Jacob said to the boy, who scooped two handfuls of toffees into a black polyethylene bag. The purchase barely made a dent in the bag, and about four additional handfuls remained on the pan. "Give me everything," Jacob ordered, and he held the bag open as the boy drizzled the bright colors into it. Without inquiring about the cost, Jacob retrieved a twenty-cedi bill from his wallet. "This is for you," he said. The boy shyly accepted the money and stumbled between a curtsy and a bow in appreciation. He withdrew with little steps while Jacob, bag in hand, made his way up the steps.

He had overpaid and hadn't even batted an eye. He relished

this spirit of self-determination. He'd set his price based on two factors: admiration for the boy's entrepreneurial drive and worry about the poverty that had brought him to the street before seven a.m. Twenty cedis was not going to uproot him from poverty, but that was practical thinking, and practical thinking had its limitations. Had Jacob been thinking practically he would have paid the appropriate price, perhaps six or seven cedis. Yes, the extra money would do nothing to change the lives of the boy and his family, but wasn't an extra meal worth the impracticality?

Of course, it was practicality that Jacob feared would come from the mouth of Nabil Azar, who, when Jacob entered the building, was the one he saw through the glass window at his desk twiddling a pen as he went through documents. Where was Mamoud? Standing in the lobby, Jacob scanned the windows, trying to locate an absent Mamoud Azar. He watched as Nabil continued to spin his pen between his fingertips perfectly. Nabil was an expert at keeping things in circles in one place.

Would Nabil Azar's pen drop? Would it spin free from his fingertips?

The answer, Jacob knew, was no. It was an answer that charged him anew.

The decision to escape was easy. He turned around, rushed out of the lobby, and plunged into the open air.

JACOB PASSED the day in contemplation of the days and months—and dare he think, years—ahead. At Bujumbura chop bar, he feasted on bean fritters and eggs for breakfast. "What the eye *can* see, the eye *should* see," he thought, for he had concluded that the answer for him had been right there all along. He could launch a school with just his laptop and have one-on-one meetings with clients. His study CDs had been pirated anyway; why couldn't he produce his own copies to start, then after he saved enough capital, launch his own locally focused product? He had some money in the bank—not enough to have convinced the people at the American embassy to give him a visa, but enough nonetheless. For much of their five years of marriage, Patricia's "discretionary upkeep" had made it possible for him to save half his monthly salary.

At noon he was still plotting. Still seated at his table at Bujumbura, he hadn't even taken a break to use the toilet. The waitress now set his lunch plate of fried plantains and fish in front of him. Before reaching for the fork, he flicked residual scales from the fried fish head. They scattered like glass shards. Their multitude was revelatory. He realized he had more than one computer at his disposal—he had access to four others. The idea of partnering with Benjamin settled on him like a second skin—at first awkward, but soon natural. It was high time they took their friendship to the next level and monetized it. Benjamin had helped him with his pitch for Mamoud Azar; it was just a matter of telling him that the idea was now theirs to take by the horns.

It helped that Benjamin was ambitious. Like any successful businessman, he knew how to cut corners to get ahead, what he called "maximizing opportunities," which was a skill he was ready to deploy for not only his own benefit but Jacob's, too. As a last-ditch effort to help Jacob achieve America, Benjamin had offered to create a fraudulent deed to the café in Jacob's name. "Show them that you have something in Ghana to come back to," Benjamin said.

Jacob refused but the offer made him wonder. He asked Benjamin why he'd shown him so much kindness over the years.

"Because you are a real-life good person," Benjamin said. "If there is a heaven, maybe they will let me in because I was good to you."

His own goodness, Jacob thought, was doubtful. And he did not know how much the heavenly gates welcomed those who solicited prostitutes or engaged in fraud.

But together, he and Benjamin could build something if not good, then successful. Several times people at the café had approached him for help with their computer problems, which he was able to solve. The opportunity was there.

In the past month, ideas like this—revelations, really—had been coming to him. One had to do with Sims, to whom he'd ultimately decided to not write back, a decision made easier by her expressed intent to sign off forever. Yet her message—*Massa's-wife-and-the-slave-type shit*—would not leave him. It lingered like a pinprick, and, reading dozens of websites, he'd worked hard to understand what Sims had meant. He finally put the pieces together.

Sims was invoking American slavery, expressing that with him she'd been living out a fantasy of that dark and horrible era of American history. Naturally, he'd thought of Wilder, who was Black American, a descendant of slaves. He had never spoken to Wilder beyond pleasantries delivered over the phone. The little he knew of him he knew through Belinda, and the two peculiarities about Wilder were that he did not like whites and that he hated his own country of America.

"How is that possible?" Jacob once asked his sister. "The place has made him so rich!"

"Well, with what I'm going through with my papers, sometimes I can see where Wilder's coming from," Belinda said.

Belinda. He'd thought of her, too. And somehow, he was even starting to feel compassion for her, going as far as regretting the ways he'd tried to hurt her in the past. Principally he was ashamed of how far he'd gone three years ago.

Philomena, after handing him Patricia's gifts, had surprised him with her own: a stack of DVDs. "For you," she said. "But mostly for your nephew."

At home, he looked through the titles, none of which was appropriate for a child: American films depicting wartime, romance, and sex, of course. There was one he had never heard of, *9½ Weeks*, with a cover showing a man and woman touching lips intimately. Philomena surely had known that the film was unsuitable for a child. In fact, not just *9½ Weeks*, but all of them. He quickly recognized that she had, which was the point. Philomena had never intended the films for Alfred's viewing pleasure and had said that only because she was uncertain of how direct she could be with Jacob. This thought scandalized Jacob. He wondered what Philomena's love life was like.

Two months later his mother died. His father had needed some time to speak to Belinda after she refused to return to Ghana for the funeral, and Jacob had thought that maybe the old man was starting to see things his way, that Belinda might not be the golden child after all. Yet within a few weeks, the old man was back on the phone with her. After one call, he came to Jacob's room and announced, "She's suffering so much."

What suffering? At least she was over there, in America, across a whole ocean. He was still at home, weighted down by real suffering. Wasn't it easier to bear loss from far away than to do so in the middle of it?

His father confessed days later that a major part of Belinda's suffering had to do with her ignorance about Wilder and Vietnam; she felt it was a critical part of him that she knew nothing about. Moreover, more than the suspicion she now had that Vietnam had something to do with her stalled green card, her not knowing, she thought, was proof that Wilder did not love her as much as she loved him. Jacob was already not talking to Belinda, so what his father said—"Let's not bring the topic up with her"—did not pertain to him.

But it could pertain to Alfred. One of Philomena's DVDs was a special box set, *First Blood* and *Rambo: First Blood Part II*, both of which Jacob, like every other Ghanaian he knew, had already watched. He knew Vietnam to be at the heart of both films' story lines.

He broke his conviction to keep all of the films from Alfred. He rationalized that he could make an exception for the Rambo series—viewing them, after all, was like a rite of passage for a Ghanaian boy. Also Alfred, delicately handled as he was by the family, particularly by Mr. Nti, could use some grit.

Jacob waited until a quiet Saturday at the house when Mr. Nti was gone for the weekend settling a land dispute in his hometown and Robert and Martha were at a weeklong church retreat. That morning, Jacob announced to Alfred that there would be a back-to-back "matinee."

"What is *matin-ay*?" Alfred asked, sounding the word out in two parts.

"It means we will watch the films this afternoon."

They took their places in the living room at one o'clock. Jacob put the disc for *First Blood* into the DVD player but it didn't start. He called for Yaa, who came from the kitchen and helped Jacob untangle the web of wires behind the TV. She connected the right wires and successfully fiddled with the remote. At the opening credits, she drew the curtains to block sunlight and took up a seat next to Alfred.

As Alfred watched, he began to mimic Rambo's movements. Jacob noticed Alfred kicking his legs during the action sequences. When Rambo was being taken away in the final scene, Alfred scurried to the louvers and drew back a curtain. "Good, it is still afternoon. We can watch the second one."

Yaa got up to swap out the DVDs. "Alfred, won't you have nightmares?" she asked before pressing play.

"Why? It is not horror," he said.

A few minutes into the opening scene of *Rambo*, Jacob leaned over to Alfred's ear. "Uncle Wilder fought in Rambo's war. Vietnam."

He hoped that during one of Alfred's chats with Belinda, thinking of *Rambo*, he might slip and unwittingly mock her with a comment about Uncle Wilder and Vietnam. Yet he never did.

Now, with his newfound feeling for Belinda, Jacob was pleased that the scheme hadn't worked. He took heart in another positive outcome: he observed a new confidence in Alfred when he acted out Rambo's missions. Alfred bent and twisted his body as if it were perfectly balanced.

Balanced was how Jacob was beginning to feel about the three of them. Belinda, Wilder, and himself. They each had their share of financial success (his soon to come), yet each was plagued by America and what it demanded from them. Wilder's American woe, Jacob reasoned, was likely more brutal than his and Belinda's. He couldn't blame Wilder for his silence on Vietnam. Why relive pain? Lucky that Wilder had been transformed into just a silent hating man and not a killer like Rambo.

He would call Belinda when his financial security was assured. He wasn't crazy enough to think that the business would succeed within a few months; a year or two was more realistic. Enough time for him to find the right words for Belinda, and maybe for Wilder.

From the corner of his eye, he saw the waitress drawing near. "Mr. Jacob," she said. "We are closing."

Four soft drinks and two meals had brought him to five p.m., the end of the workday. He dug into his pocket and retrieved a ball of cash, leaving the payment on the table with a meaty sense of completeness. He did not know when next he might return.

For the evening trotro, the mate blocked a young man at the front of the line and waved for Jacob to get on. Jacob hurried inside, targeting the perfect seat one row from the rear. The driver appeared to be in a rush—he set off so soon that the last person to get into the van was dropped into his seat as the trotro lurched forward.

At the roundabout with the statue of an Ashanti warrior, with two more stops to go before Deduako, the trotro stalled in traffic. Unease rose in Jacob. It was getting dark and the streetlights were out, the only illumination the white beams that streamed from the car headlights and crisscrossed like clashing swords.

"What happened to the streetlights?" Jacob asked loudly.

"Light-off," the driver yelled from the front.

"It's our turn," said the mate who sat closer to Jacob. The mate had morphed into a silhouette. "You missed the announcements, Mr. Jacob?"

"The power rationing," Jacob remembered.

Soon the van's meager headlights were all that lit a short stretch of the narrow road and its edging thickets. Yet Jacob could see the path ahead unfurling in his memory. In no time the van would have to slow for a speed bump, then another, after which it would have to prepare for the broad curve ahead.

It all played out exactly as Jacob had mapped it in his mind. He even envisioned Deduako exactly as it was before actually seeing its new nighttime normal: house after house was hollowed out by glowing orange flames, as though each family had been ordered to partake in a candlelight vigil.

He was as well as he'd ever been with remaining in Ghana, for success was on the horizon. Yet he couldn't help contemplating the obvious, especially under these circumstances: in America, everywhere shone with light.

Belinda

Ballads

One

The day before Jacob's divorce, Belinda got on the phone with her father. Early in their conversation, she sensed his need to hear and identify anger in her voice, but she simply did not have it in her. She spoke in an even tone, and because he determined this evenness to be evidence of her guilt over Jacob and Patricia, he said, "You did what Napoleon could not do, Belinda. You achieved the unachievable."

She chuckled. "Pa, matchmaking is hardly what Napoleon could not do."

The sudden silence from the other end of the line sat on her ear like earmuffs. "Are you there? Pa? Pa?"

He finally exhaled, sounding like a resuscitated man's newly caught breath. "I'm here. Right here," he said.

"Good. I thought I'd lost you."

"You thought I'd died?"

"Not died. Thought I'd lost the connection."

"What if I had died?"

"That's not funny, Pa. Stop. Please."

"No, Belinda," he said. "Listen. Who will hear me when I call out for help?"

"That's what you've been thinking about?"

"There are only three of us in the house now. Jacob is at work. Alfred is at school. Yaa is at the market. I'm here with Martha and Robert. Let's say that I am choking on something or having a heart attack. Who will hear me when I call out for help?"

"What are you suggesting?" she asked.

"Not suggesting anything. I'm saying it."

"That you are lonely?"

"Alone. Not lonely. Alone."

Belinda glanced at the clock on her nightstand. Nine thirty a.m. in Houston. Which meant it was two thirty p.m. in Ghana. "Pa, they will all be home soon."

"That's not the point. Don't ignore the point."

"I'm sorry. I guess I missed it."

"You didn't miss it. You just don't want to confront it, which I understand," he said. "By this time tomorrow we will have settled things with Patricia's family," he said. "I will give Jacob the time he needs to recuperate. Personally, I don't see why he will need the time—this marriage was a sham. But I will give him the time because you can't be too careful in these matters. At some point, however, either you or me . . . well, best it be me since a face-to-face would be more appropriate. And since . . . well, you and Jacob, you know?" She did: Jacob hadn't spoken to her since they last got on the phone three years ago to discuss their mother's passing. "Anyway . . . at some point I am going to sit him down and give it to him straight: he better find someone for himself. If not for love, then to prevent the kind of aloneness that breeds death. A man needs someone at his side. Preferably a woman. . . ."

He said something else but Belinda was too consumed by the question his comment provoked. "What about women, Pa? Do we need someone at our sides?"

"Women, too. You need men," he said. "But you are more self-sufficient. I wouldn't put it past a woman to reach into her own throat to pull out whatever she's choking on."

She laughed quietly. "How progressive of you, Pa."

"Progressive? See? There you go again. You Americans always want to put a difficult name to everything."

Next to her, Wilder, still sleeping, rolled over, pulling the covers from her legs. She tugged them back forcefully; he mumbled but faced away from her.

"Is that Wilder I hear?" her father asked.

"Yes."

"Please greet him for me," he said. "And Belinda? Thank him for me."

"I will."

"You will? Really? You won't say something snide?"

"No, Pa, nothing snide. Wilder knows. You appreciate what he's done for us. He knows a million times over. But if you want me to tell him a million and one more time, I will."

"It won't hurt. Thank you."

A LITTLE MORE probing from her father and Belinda would have had to confess she was of two minds. The first had to do with Jacob, whose marriage would end tomorrow. She had made her peace with that, having forgiven herself. She was sorry about the marriage but not angry. Whatever anger there was had blended with her fury over America's singular skill at simultaneously engendering and dashing hopes. The hand that giveth did so to take back what it had offered.

Her second mind had to do with Edith's imminent wedding. The invitation had arrived a year ago, and she'd informed her father as soon as she'd received the silver-trimmed envelope.

"She's your longtime friend," he'd said. "You should go."

It had taken months, but eventually she had RSVP'd yes. It had been a while since her father brought up Edith or her wedding, which was to be in Washington, D.C., and now was exactly six weeks away. To Belinda's surprise, Edith had decided on a Friday wedding. Belinda had chosen not to remind her father about the wedding because she did not want to live through another rehashing of memories about Edith and her, their friendship long destroyed.

She had decided to attend the wedding for several reasons. Perhaps chief among them was that it had been Edith's father, Mr. Hyde, who'd made America possible for her. It was the right gesture of appreciation to give Mr. Hyde the opportunity to see her again. How long had it been since he'd visited Wesley Girls' in Cape Coast, treated her and Edith to lunch at the nicest restaurant in town, the table cleared when he'd said on a whim, "Belinda, Edith will be taking the PSAT during vacation. You should take it, too"?

It was clear that Mr. Hyde liked her when they'd first met. Belinda was brilliant, he'd said. His daughter, who was naturally competitive, needed a brilliant friend like Belinda to compel her to aim higher, he had added. He'd persuaded the American embassy, where he worked as its top educational counselor, to pay Belinda's fees for the PSAT, the entrance exam American boarding schools used for students.

On the day of the test, which was to be given in Accra, Belinda's mother handed her a tall flask with fresh porridge. "You can have it in the car," she signed, so as not to wake Jacob.

Belinda set off in the early morning gloom with her father. An hour into the journey, the sky cracked with a thin orange beam. She unscrewed the flask. The steam bathed her face and cooked off her nervousness.

The exam was administered in a room inside a high-rise in downtown Accra. With an empty cubicle between them, she and Edith sat for the nearly three-hour test.

When they finished, Edith was confident.

"Was it easy for you?" Belinda asked.

"It was not hard," Edith said as she squatted on the building's front steps.

Despite Edith's confidence, Hotchkiss took Belinda and not her, even in the face of Mr. Hyde's influence. Edith did not speak to her—the first crack in their friendship—until she arrived at Hotchkiss herself a year after Belinda started.

Before Edith arrived at Hotchkiss's campus in Connecticut, Belinda's father asked, "You think Edith will talk to you now?"

Belinda had to admit that she didn't know. When Edith and Mr. Hyde arrived on campus the next fall, they came to Belinda's door, onto which she'd taped an artistic rendering of her name—large bubbles capturing her childlike zeal at acquiring her own room for senior year. She'd prepared herself for the worst from Edith, who would be entering as a junior. Edith's aggravation at not being admitted when Belinda was would have hardened, and Belinda wasn't expecting her to thaw.

When Belinda opened the door to her dorm room, Mr. Hyde embraced her first. "My dear," he said. Soon Edith patted his back for her chance. She put an arm around Belinda's shoulders as if they had just seen each other yesterday. "I am happy we are friends again," Edith said.

As term began, Edith would not explain what her father had done differently to get her into Hotchkiss this time, confessing only that she hadn't retaken the PSAT. When one afternoon Belinda saw her wielding a field hockey stick, she knew. But she wondered why Edith had elected to advance the charade. One of the early realizations Belinda had come to about Hotchkiss was that nobody expected the person in the application to be a replica in real life. If she were ever asked for directions to the gymnasium where volleyball—her supposed sport—took place, Belinda would gesture toward the science building, behind which she knew the gymnasium stood. On paper a girl could present herself as a woman of the people—a standing volunteership at a Latin American orphanage every summer, for example—but prove herself at Hotchkiss to be wickedly self-absorbed. That was the case for Emmy Coddington, who lived across the hall from Belinda. There was Lindsay Viktorin, their proctor, who in her personal statement wrote about a long-running internship at her uncle's firm only to later admit, as she pulled a small bottle of tequila out of her pocket, that she'd only seen her uncle's office building from the inside of a town car. Nobody actually believed that Edith had the talent or skills to play field hockey, did they? As clueless as everybody in America was about Ghana, the Hotchkiss admissions people had to have known that field hockey, if added to Ghana's stew, would not mix well. Edith, as far as Belinda was concerned, could have let field hockey go.

Belinda once asked Kara, who had been her roommate the previous year and lived next door their senior year, what she thought of Edith. Kara was light-skinned with long black hair but always shut down speculation about her probable Caucasian heritage. "I am as Black as anyone," she would say.

"Edith is so different from you," Kara said in response to Belinda's curiosity. "She's effectively white."

"Her father is rich."

"And?"

"That's why you think she's a white girl," Belinda said.

"Is it?" Kara asked. "Where did you pick that shit up?"

"I know her well. I know why she's the way she is."

Kara frowned in confusion. "Belinda, are you hearing yourself?"

"Which part?"

"All of it. Your unfounded rationale."

"What's unfounded about it?"

"By your rationale I'm poor. And every Black person is poor. Right?"

Belinda shriveled in disappointment with herself. "That's not even close to what I mean," she said.

In Ghana, she'd watched Black American films (she would learn in America that her favorite, *Petey Wheatstraw*, was of a genre termed "blaxploitation") and thought that their English translated to a most acute poverty. At Hotchkiss, the English of a Black American played like rich music. Kara spoke with the eloquence of a seasoned orator, like Belinda's own uncle Kwame Broni, who claimed to have acquired his lyrical gab through books. Kara also loved books. For as long as she could remember, Kara said, she'd read. Reading above her age had nourished in her what Belinda saw as an infinite depth to Kara's language skills. But she never read an author who was white or male. Kara once asked Belinda to select a book from the stack of six in her hands. Belinda could not decide, and in the first of the many generosities Kara would show her for years to come, she gave Belinda her personal favorite, *The Bluest Eye*. It was a book by Toni Morrison. Who was Black American. Who was a woman. Who, Kara said, was brilliant.

Belinda read the book during her first American Christmas, which she spent with Kara's family. The book, about suffering Pecola Breedlove, had ended satisfyingly for her. But, according to Kara, Belinda had misinterpreted Pecola's attainment of blue eyes as a happy ending, and Kara challenged her with another interpretation. She characterized the novel as a cautionary tale. There was nothing *feel-good* about Pecola's story, Kara warned. Nothing *feel-good* about desiring stunning whiteness and all that went with it. After all, hadn't Pecola become blind to reality?

The following fall, Edith arrived at Hotchkiss. Before long, Belinda started to notice parallels between the novel and Edith's own story. In Ghana, Edith had yearned for Pete, a white boy. It was the reason a lot had gone wrong for her, blinding her to excellence.

Pete had been a Peace Corps volunteer whom Edith's father had brought to their house in Accra the day he picked him up from the airport. Pete was going to be stationed in Cape Coast, where Wesley Girls' was, close enough for Edith to see him while she was in school. It was Edith who suggested at the dining table that she and Pete meet up when they were both in Cape Coast.

"How old are you?" Pete asked.

"Twelve," Edith said. "How old are you?"

"Twenty-two."

Edith convinced Belinda to join her the first time she went to see Pete. They slipped away from their school group during a holiday excursion and took a cab to the beach, where Pete was waiting with Mike.

Mike was also a white Peace Corps volunteer stationed in Cape Coast. Mike was more handsome—he had a neat goatee, his eyes were like a cat's, and his skin was perfect, like a half-caste boy's, not too black, not too white.

Pete, on the other hand, sported a ramshackle collection of dots on his face and arms, which Edith later told her were called freckles. He had frizzy hair and whiskers on his chin. Belinda did not have the right vocabulary for Pete's red-orange coloring, most vivid in the color of his mop of hair. Many years later, she would think back and smile at the thought of his being a ginger.

She didn't understand why Edith preferred Pete over Mike. The two of them rode off on one of the horses the boys had hired. Belinda had refused to get on the other horse with Mike because she harbored a fear of falling off and going mute like her brother Robert. Some American film, the title of which she did not remember, had planted this fear in her. Unaware of this history, Mike pressed the issue of horseback riding along the beach.

"I hate horses!" Belinda said conclusively. The groom led the horse away.

Belinda plopped onto the sand. Mike sat beside her. They were watching the rippling of the low waves along the shore when she said, "Mike, what is Peace Corps?" Edith hadn't fully explained.

"After college—Ghanaians would say *university*—any American who's interested can take two years off to go help out in an another country," Mike explained.

"Anyone?" she said. "I thought it was only white people like you."

Mike laughed. "Wouldn't that be crazy?"

She did not know how to agree, despite Mike's stare suggesting that she should.

"Anyway, anybody can be a Peace Corps volunteer. Whites. Blacks. You just have to be an American. And up for an adventure."

Her inquisitiveness grew. "You said it would be crazy. Why?"

"Because it would be racist. *Whites only* all over again. Think about it."

She thought about it. She thought hard about it. There was no sense-making of it.

"You don't get it?" Mike asked.

Belinda shook her head.

"All right," he said. "We had something called segregation in America. Whites and Blacks were separated. And Blacks couldn't do everything whites could do just because they were Black. We are past that now. I don't think we want to go back."

She knew she wouldn't want to go back. She was grown, twelve years old, which she liked being. She said, "Blacks. They are the Black Americans."

"Yes. Same thing."

"They are different from white people."

"Skin color, yes."

"And the way they talk, too. In their films. They don't even sound like they are speaking proper English."

Her statement wasn't meant to be rude but Mike looked shocked. "You shouldn't say that."

"Why?"

"It's a terrible thing to say," he said. "And the accent only sounds odd to you because you are not used to it." She could almost feel his disappointment.

He went on, "We are sitting here watching the water and you are telling me you don't understand Black people when they talk. It's really heartbreaking. Because guess where Black Americans came from?" He motioned at the ocean. "Right here."

Edith and Pete returned to the beach only when darkness started to creep over the horizon. Edith and Belinda got back to school so late that they were punished with a week's worth of bathroom duty. It was punishment that was also exceedingly generous. Suspension was the retribution they feared when they found Mrs. Gyebi, their dorm mistress, waiting by their bunk beds. "I am forgiving the fact that you slipped away from us this afternoon," Mrs. Gyebi said.

For the two years he was in Ghana, Pete spent most holidays with Edith's family in Accra. After one Christmas, Edith told Belinda that Pete loved her.

"He told you he loves you?" Belinda asked.

"He didn't say he loves me," Edith said. "But he got me a lot of presents. More than my parents did." Edith heaved herself from the top of the bunk bed they shared at school. They'd climbed to the top bunk, where Belinda slept, to catch each other up on their Christmas activities. Edith pulled from her suitcase a T-shirt, which she spread out on her chest. Edith's breasts were the biggest among all the girls in Form-1.

"Washington, D.C. That's where he's from," Edith said. She balled the T-shirt and brought it to her nose. "It smells like him," she said.

That was the moment Belinda realized how uncomfortable she was with Edith and Pete. She would see it as more than that—madness, even—when, after Pete returned to America, Edith began to fail one exam after another and bumbled about Wesley Girls' as if she were lost. A greater madness soon followed. Edith did not score well on the PSAT, and the PSAT would have gotten her closer to Pete.

Indeed, in *The Bluest Eye*, Pecola had gone mad from pursuing whiteness, but she had also gone mad because her father, Cholly, had raped her. Perhaps it was an unfair conclusion. Perhaps it was the way the novel had lit Belinda's imagination and pointed her into uncharted territory. Whatever the reason, it made perfect sense to her that twenty-two-year-old Pete had had his way with twelve-year-old Edith that day at the beach and for two years thereafter, leaving Edith mad. Moreover, Edith's madness was graver than Pecola's because Edith's two sources of madness had been packaged in the same person.

But maybe there was nothing to worry about now that Edith had made it to Hotchkiss. Finding out that Edith hadn't retaken the PSAT made Belinda think twice. Had Edith done so and scored well, Belinda would have had evidence that she had gotten back on track. There was no such evidence. And now there was a new whiteness in the madness that Edith was pursuing: field hockey. With volleyball, at least Kara and Melody, a Black sophomore, could be pointed to on the varsity team: they were actual players, unlike Belinda. With field hockey, there wasn't a single Black girl to be pointed to on the freshman or junior varsity teams, let alone varsity.

Two

The day before Edith's wedding, Belinda flew from Houston to Washington, D.C. The flight arrived on time and she made it out of Reagan National Airport without delay. At the curb, she looked across the street at the row of waiting black town cars in search of hers. None of the suited men wielding white placards were moving toward her. She squinted to make out her name on one of them but didn't see it. She decided to get closer.

Before venturing forward, she gazed at her waist-high suitcase and regretted the decision to check a bag for the weekend stay. Wilder was to blame. He'd stressed that she give herself several clothing options, as, lest she forget, she was chiefly attending Edith's wedding to ground one point: that her life was now overflowing with choices.

She dragged the bag behind her. Twice the wheels locked and released. Finally, she spotted her driver—of course Wilder's driver would be Black and playing the part of town car driver to a T: he was the only one still wearing his black hat. In faded ink, her name was missing an *a*: *Belind Thomas*. She waved at him and he looked over both of his shoulders to confirm. He laid his placard on the car and hurried for her suitcase.

She waited as he loaded it into the trunk. She would open the passenger door herself, but minutes before, the driver's brow had wrinkled with disbelief—and something like disappointment—that his passenger was a Black woman who could afford a town car from the airport. It was always more painful when it was another Black person diminishing you, Belinda thought. She did not acknowledge him when he opened the door for her.

The air-conditioning whistled sonorously as they waited in the traffic departing the airport for the district.

"It's chilly, mind turning down the air?" Belinda asked.

He did as she asked, then peered at her in the rearview mirror. "Ma'am, first time in Washington, D.C.?"

"No."

"Where from?"

"Texas. Houston."

"I beg your pardon, ma'am, but I don't mean here in America." He peeked over his shoulder to say, "I mean back home. Where in Africa?"

It was the last question she'd expected to hear from him. She'd guessed him to be Black American. Now she studied his face in the mirror. With his hat sitting on the dashboard, his face was put to full view and she observed the luminousness of his black skin unique to East Africans. "Where are you from?" she asked brusquely.

"Congo."

"You don't have an accent."

"My *sista*," he said, beginning anew in grittier elocution, something more Congolese, she supposed. "You know how it is when you come to this country? Assimilation, my *sista*."

"That can be difficult."

"Yes *ooo*. But you have to." He pointed to the hat. "It's like my hat. You put it on when you need it. You take it off when you don't."

"You don't need it now?"

"Do I, my sista?"

"No," she said. "I'm from Ghana."

"Ah! I should have guessed. I couldn't tell when you were coming. Maybe that's why"—he stopped himself—"anyway, as soon as I looked closely, I knew you were one of us."

Had her hair, styled in locs for a decade now, been a different color, it might have more readily given her away as Ghanaian. Or maybe if they draped the sides of her face? They were collected in a formal updo, contrary to her first thought, which had been to set them free for the weekend. She envisioned herself shaking her head periodically, her locs slithering through the air and leaving a faint hiss to torment Edith's guests. But at the salon her hairdresser, Ramatou, had stressed an updo as more appropriate for weddings. Coiled snakes were as good as dead and made no show of themselves, Belinda immediately thought.

She agreed to the updo, on the condition that Ramatou dye her hair a different color.

"Deeper black?" Ramatou asked.

"Oh, no. Nothing safe," Belinda said.

Ramatou was not seeing things her way. Maybe, she suggested after a moment of contemplation, she could throw in a "tiny" streak of bronze. For Belinda, this was too small a compromise.

She stepped from the salon chair to call Wilder. After he did some thinking on the other end of the phone, he found the perfect compromise.

"Red," he said. "Pure red. Militant red."

Her high bloodred topknot had likely shaped her driver's impression of her: a Black American lowlife to be avoided. A refined driver of a town car who refused to have his brand tarnished, he had looked over his shoulder hoping that it wasn't him Belinda had waved at, and wrinkled his face with disappointment when it was. Ramatou, herself from Senegal, had effectively delivered the same message with her downcast gaze as Belinda admired her bloodred hair in the mirror. But Ramatou knew better. Belinda was kindred, in the same way she had just proven herself kindred to her driver. Whatever discomfort her appearance had spurred in him had been wiped away by his thirst for home. She knew that thirst.

"What's your name?" she asked.

"Laurent."

"Kabila?"

He brightened through the rearview mirror. "If only," he said. "I wouldn't be driving you around if that were the case. Even more strange, our former president is dead. So technically I'd be a ghost."

"You could be his long-lost son. Which would be in keeping with the seed-spreading habits of African presidents," she said. "Anyway, my name is Belinda."

"Belinda?" he asked. "That means I left out an *a*."

"You did."

"Forgive me."

"Forgiven," she said, feeling satisfied that he was embarrassed by his mistake.

Looking through the tinted passenger window, Belinda concluded that Washington, D.C., hadn't changed much in the years she'd been away since law school. She noted the usual monuments along the way from the airport to confirm that Laurent was taking the right route to her hotel. Ten years of not realizing her American dream of a green card had made her inner lens more critical of the monuments. Washington. Jefferson. A panoply of American virtuousness? Hardly. Originators of America's knack for false propaganda was more like it.

"When was the last time you were here?" Laurent asked.

"It's been a while," she said. "I went to law school here. GW. But I moved out of DC after my first year. I lived in Alexandria."

"No way!" He cast a succession of quick glances between her and the road ahead. She gestured forward. "I'm sorry, Belinda," he said. "It's just . . . that's where I live. I've lived there for twenty years. I don't know how I missed you."

"Alexandria is big. And I look very different now."

"Alexandria is not that big. And I never forget an African face."

"Maybe my African ship is the one yours passed in the night."

"I don't understand."

"It's a saying," she said, realizing that it took only a common American idiom to smear the gloss off Laurent's faux-American patina. "What I mean is I'm not surprised our paths never crossed. It was always school, work, and home for me."

"I see."

She felt the car turning. She sat up. They'd landed on a slim, residential road.

He said, "Almost there." He fiddled a bit with the radio, then gave up. "I have to say something."

"Go ahead."

"I have driven a lot of people to the Ritz-Carlton. Even eight years ago. When it opened in 2003," he said. "All these years. And this is my first time taking somebody who looks like me."

"Oh?"

"But it's our time, you know? Know what I mean?"

If she had a penny for every time a Black person said that to her.

With more rasp, he continued, "But sometimes I get scared. I fear I will wake up one day and say Obama and people will be like, *Obama who?* As if it had all been a dream. You ever feel that way?"

"No," she said. Her take on Obama was a lot more complex. A lot less exuberant, too. Wilder Thomas believed that Obama was a trick of white people, who always permitted Black highs before they descended to Black lows. Obama, the highest of highs, would inevitably be followed by Black Armageddon. On election night 2008, as a reminder of this, Wilder shattered the two bottles of champagne that Belinda had set out for celebration. For, as he put it to her before they went to bed, there was "nothing to celebrate."

Laurent had gone quiet for so long that Belinda wondered whether she'd drenched his joy. He was entitled to happiness wherever it came from; instances of joy, as she saw it, being too few and far between these days. She was readying to admit that she also cherished Obama, ready to set aside Wilder's legitimate argument that his presidency was a tool of white manipulation. Instead she heard herself say, "The birth certificate," then realized how much she'd come to view things through Wilder's eyes.

"That stupidity," Laurent said. "I just laugh at that stupidity. You know why?"

"No."

"Believe it or not, I was on this exact path to the Ritz-Carlton and Donald Trump was on the radio. I had a man in the car. Nobody needed to tell me he was rich; he smelled like money. I will never forget what he said about Trump: 'He is the purest form of an imbecile. Know why? He's an unintentional comedian.' What are we supposed to do with a comedian, my sista? We are supposed to laugh. So, I laugh. Laugh!"

But Belinda could not laugh. What Laurent saw as stupidity had succeeded. Obama had shown his birth certificate to the world. And anyone paying attention could tell that the forces that had driven him to reveal it were working their way down. They would get to her in no time.

"So you are a lawyer?" Laurent asked.

"I have a law degree. But I've never practiced law."

"A businesswoman."

Giving in, she said, "That's probably more appropriate."

He went quiet again, seemingly to give her field of work its proper due. "Well, congratulations, my sista," he said. "It's not easy. But you made it. You made it all the way to the Ritz-Carlton."

He was prompting her. Familiar with this banter of kinship, she responded with automatic humility. "Small, small, my *broda*," she said. "Small, small."

"No," Laurent exclaimed gutturally, more Congolese than ever. "Speak propa' about yourself, my sista. You are big, big. Real big."

How much she wanted to repeat and believe this affirmation to herself in the glare of her American insecurity, which had become a matter of serious concern after she'd graduated from Williams College sixteen years ago. In response, she'd enrolled at George Washington law school because in America foreigners could enroll in school to buy time for papers. She graduated and passed the DC bar exam, and yet even with two degrees she was back to where she'd started: insecure. Finding a job as an attorney without a green card had proven difficult. Only one firm had taken charity on her, offering paralegal work.

In the summer of '99, after two summers of declining an invitation from the Richardses, she returned to Oak Bluffs on Martha's Vineyard, where since arriving in America ten years prior she had vacationed with Kara's family.

Wilder often joined the family at their summer home in Oak Bluffs. He'd attended Princeton with Kara's father, Rutherford, which was how he'd come to be part of the family. He was older and seemed joyless, with a salt-and-pepper beard as if he were striving for Abraham's look, which made Belinda laugh. He was short, but everyone agreed that his beard made him seem taller. Over time Belinda came to look on him as a kind of uncle.

The house sat on a promontory. One day at breakfast Belinda sat at the kitchen table and stared out into the morning fog that enveloped the island. Her father had recently informed her of his plan to build a house of their own in Deduako, a hamlet fast folding into Kumasi, and she knew she couldn't possibly contribute to the construction. She sat at the kitchen table wallowing in her burdens.

"You hate your job," Wilder said quietly, pulling her out of her daze. They were alone in the kitchen.

She stiffened. "What makes you say that?"

"You look like someone who hates her job."

"It's not the job," she said. "It's the fact that it's my only option."

"Bullshit. You're sharp as all else. And you've got Rutherford and Suzette." Rutherford and Suzette treated her like another daughter. "They have all the right friends. Say the word. And poof. You have a new job."

Wilder waited for Belinda to say something.

"My student visa expired," she said after a long silence.

"And?"

"And I have to stick to where I am. Not only because the firm I work at was the only one that took pity on me. If I get another job, a new HR will go digging. When they dig, it will set off hazard lights."

Pondering this, Wilder sat silently, his eyes roaming the space. Then he stretched out his hand, beckoning for her plate. She handed him the beige porcelain, which he stacked on top of his.

"Only one solution now," he said, picking up the plates. "Marry me."

It was Patricia, at the time Belinda's roommate in Alexandria, who helped Belinda realize that she would have to relocate. "Whether it is a fake marriage or real marriage," Patricia said, "he can't be in one place and you in another. INS investigates these things. You need to make sure that you are in the same house when INS comes knocking."

Belinda knew she was out of options, but still a year elapsed before she accepted Wilder's proposal and agreed to move to Houston. In Houston, Wilder lived in a mansion. Eight thousand square feet, he announced when she arrived, at the center of which was a spiral staircase. She took in the marble floors, the high ceilings, the bay windows, the strong sunlight that one instantly noted thanks to the many windows. Downstairs were three sunrooms, one adjacent to the library with bookshelves to the ceiling, another opening to the casual dining room, the third a sectioned-off portion of the formal living room. The library and formal living room, with velvet wall coverings, were cast in indigo. There was an entire room—in which she thought she could do twenty continuous somersaults from end to end—dedicated to displaying Wilder's collections of guns in glass cases.

She shrieked. "All these guns!"

"Welcome to Texas."

"You're a Republican."

"I'm waiting for the right Black man to make me one."

Wasn't there already one? "No fan of Colin Powell?"

"The worst of them," he said. "Token. A nice face to put up about that war."

Among the stories that she'd heard told about Wilder Thomas was that he'd fought in Vietnam.

"I'm going to ask a stupid question," she said. "Did your paths cross in Vietnam?"

His answer was not to answer. Instead he pointed behind the house. In the distance was a wooden structure that appeared to be a stable.

"You have horses?" Belinda asked.

"I do."

"They frighten me."

"Then we're going to have to figure out something. Either I get rid of them or you fall in love with them."

That was the level of Wilder's care for her. Her father

understood the significance of Wilder's charity, which was why he, who had always thought Belinda's greatness was incomparable, now saw Wilder's as superior. A million-and-one thanks went to Wilder, never to her. Always it was *Thank you, Wilder*, never mind that after ten years the marriage had yet to produce a green card for Belinda.

A WHITE CLAW TUB with gold accents featured in the bathroom of Belinda's suite at the Ritz. She soaked in it for so long that the water turned chilly. She crept out and slipped into the waiting terry cloth robe, pressing every part of it onto her skin to dry off.

At the closet, she observed the three coats she'd hung up, each of which Wilder had stressed she bring with her. If she really wanted to make a show of herself, she would go with the cream cashmere with chinchilla trim, the closest thing to a fur coat that would fit into her bag.

"Take two bags, then," Wilder had said.

"I may not even wear a coat," she'd said. "DC isn't that cold in October."

And here she was, doing exactly that, forgoing a coat. She'd decided to wear the kente dress—a multicolored print. The vigorous reds would complement her hair color.

In bed she wondered how Edith hadn't come up all day. Oddly enough, Laurent hadn't asked why she was in town, and there hadn't been an opening for her to share. What would she have called Edith anyway? Her "longtime" friend? With whom she was hoping to make amends? And how ludicrous that it had all come down to field hockey.

Within days of being at Hotchkiss, Edith had started to sound different. High-pitched giggles punctuated her flat speech.

"Why do you keep doing that?" Belinda asked. "Giggle after everything you say."

"That's how Americans talk, Belinda. The first day me and my father came to your door, I couldn't believe my ears. I thought, 'Wow, she sounds so American now.' But you don't sound all-the-way American. When you say something, you don't do a quick laugh." Edith giggled again.

By "all-the-way American," Edith meant the field hockey girls. Now that she was more aware of them, Belinda picked up on their giggles, too. She herself tried, her own tee-hees sounding odd and artificial to her ear. She eventually accepted the truth: she didn't have the tee-hees in her. Simply, she was not entitled to them.

The field hockey girls moved in packs, their movement asserting entitlement. They were always putting their field hockey sticks to work. One girl might work hers like a whip, flirting unnervingly with self-flagellation. Another might rake the ground, as if apportioning a region to be worked by a laborer. Most emblematic, though, was the manner in which they stuck their sticks above their heads, gently rotating them and catching the fiery glow of sunlight—at least it seemed to Belinda—recalling fired-up protest torches.

By winter, Edith, a varsity walk-on, belonged to them. Her previous way with the stick had been uncoordinated. But with practice she'd learned, and Kara took to calling her and her pack "Edith and her White-ingales."

That was Kara: sardonic. Belinda, however, saw Edith's new distinction as advancement and encouraged Kara to view it that way, too. When was the last time Kara had seen a Black captain of a decidedly white ship? Belinda was proud of Edith. But unbeknownst to Belinda, Edith was readying to sacrifice her.

Classes had ended for the day when Belinda, seeing Edith across the quad, chased after her. Reaching Edith and her Whiteingales, Belinda managed to say hi before Edith, in a rush, grunted a greeting, underscoring it with her quick laugh and speeding off with her White-ingales in tow.

That evening, Belinda told Kara, "I think Edith thinks she's too good for me."

"It was bound to happen, Bels. What was it that you were saying? Advancement?"

It had not been long since Belinda had used wealth to rationalize Edith. She had regretted how she'd framed it for Kara. Wealth, however, had to be given its due, because Edith's winter boots were the same expensive hairy kind worn by the American girls in her pack. But because Ghanaian wealth was showy, much showier than American wealth, Edith owned multiple pairs in several colors, ignoring the school's unofficial dress code of subtlety that the students adopted. Edith's constantly switching pairs of boots manifested sensational excess. Aspirational excess as well, it seemed to Belinda. It was how Edith had climbed to the top of her pack in so little time.

Eventually, Belinda and Edith no longer spoke. On graduation day, Rutherford and Suzette arrived with two medium-size U-Haul trucks to load Belinda's and Kara's belongings for Oak Bluffs. Edith and a small sampling of her girls were nearby, watching as workmen carted another graduating senior's boxes out of the dorm and into a truck.

Belinda heard her name as she brought out the last of her boxes. After handing them to Rutherford, she approached Edith.

"Something wrong, Belinda?" Edith asked.

"You said my name."

"Did I?" Edith asked her White-ingales, not Belinda. "I didn't say anything," she said, giggling, "but now that you are here, I'm sorry that you have to move your own boxes yourself."

Belinda realized she was to be pitied. Edith pitied her. In Edith's giggle was something wounding, something potent in its haughty judgment of Belinda's poverty.

Stumped by the injury, Belinda said, "Good luck, Edith."

She got in the truck with Rutherford. It had never occurred to her that her own parents would come from Ghana for graduation or to help move her out of her dormitory. That was a pleasure as far off to her as a nonchalant tee-hee. Next year, Edith's father and mother would arrive from Ghana for her graduation, perhaps even hire workmen to pack and bring down her possessions.

Suzette drove her truck forward with Kara at her side. They waved.

"Oak Bluffs, here we come!" Rutherford bellowed.

On Belinda's lap were the black moon boots she needed to return to the financial aid office. Heavy winter socks from Kara had helped give them a snugger fit. Belinda gestured at them.

"I know," Rutherford said. "We'll stop there first."

That was in '91, the last time she saw Edith, the last time she let Edith affect her. Belinda had been updating her information in the alumni directory since then, so when she received a Christmas card from Edith in 2000, she guessed how Edith had gotten her information. Edith now lived in Boston. Before opening the card,

Belinda inhaled in preparation for Edith's apology. Edith, however, let the card's short message of printed holiday cheer speak for her, signing only, "Edith."

Belinda tossed the card into a half-filled packing box; she was leaving Alexandria to join Wilder in Houston. When she got there she updated her name and address on the Hotchkiss alumni website: *Belinda Thomas (née Nti)*. She hadn't considered that Edith might still be keeping tabs on her. She received another Christmas card that year. Less understated, it was dusted with a whimsical rendition of a powdery Santa Claus. Belinda did not reply with her own card, resolving that Edith's outreach amounted to a mere formality, as the card was once again simply signed, "Edith."

The most recent card, received two years ago, confirmed that a new Edith had emerged, one more given to whimsy. This card required a quick shake to jiggle Santa Claus's gyrating paunch. Belinda chuckled as she opened the card but was stunned by the card's longer valediction: "With love, Edith and Pete."

Belinda held the card for a while, pondering. Edith had found him. She was dating the man who had taken her virginity when she was a child. More accurately, the American man who had raped her.

Eventually, she received the wedding invitation. As she had done with all of the cards, she threw the invitation into a pile of other items, this time with more disgust. She could get over Hotchkiss. But she could not see herself applauding the abominable union.

Later, once she'd gotten used to the idea that Edith and Peter were getting married, she reminded herself: Who was she to judge?

She who had not returned to Ghana for her own mother's funeral. Worse, she'd trained herself against longing for home, to the extent that she did not even permit herself mourning tears. She could even gulp her surfacing tears whenever Alfred, a boy she viewed as hers, sweetly thanked her for his gifts and asked when he might ever see her.

"No problem, Aunty Belinda," he was fond of saying. "My father is praying for your green card. Me, too. I'm praying."

She did fully cry only once. Jacob had just been denied a visa for the second time and Alfred, anticipating her disappointment at the news, said, "My father and me pray for you and Uncle Jacob all the time. It will happen."

She held the phone at arm's length and cried—for herself, not for Jacob, who no longer spoke to her. When she regained control, she got back on with Alfred. "Tell your father I love him." Then she remembered that the deaf sometimes took a person's arm and signed into it for emphasis, like finger stabbings. "Alfred, sign it into his arm, okay?"

That evening, she checked her text messages for Robert's response. There was no message from him. Thinking that her request had slipped Alfred's mind, she texted Robert: *I love you. I miss you. One day.*

Robert replied as she was heading to bed: *I love you too. I miss you too. Not one day. Very soon by God's grace.*

On an impulse, Belinda retrieved the invitation to Edith's wedding. Inside the envelope was a scrap of paper she had not seen when she'd first opened it: *Mike will be there. We are expecting 350 people. Can you believe it?*

Everything was not to be believed, Belinda thought, and she

would look back with disappointment at where her mind had gone, the way she'd started to reframe Edith's marriage, this time contextualizing it as a love story. Worlds apart, separated by a mighty ocean, Edith and Pete had found their way back to each other. That sparkling tale would endure: a time-tested, distance-tested love that had survived. The sleazy preamble of statutory rape would be forgotten. Perhaps Belinda could learn from her friend and not suppress her own longings for Mike. She'd been fond of him during the two years he was in Ghana, but she'd controlled herself; it was made easier in that for a long stretch Mike stopped appearing at Wesley Girls' with Pete.

RSVP'ing for one—even though the invitation offered her a guest—Belinda fantasized herself single again, where she was able to marry Mike, who in make-believe made an easy path to a green card. It didn't take make-believe to recognize that Mike, being that most privileged of creatures, a straight white American man, was not complicated by Blackness. Wilder's Blackness was a sure, sure ticket to complication. If only she had understood that sooner.

After she mailed her RSVP, she had second thoughts about Wilder not coming with her. She informed him that Edith had given her a plus-one.

"Do you want me to come with you?" he asked.

She could easily call to make the change, she thought. "If you want to."

"Best I don't."

"Because she's marrying a white man?" she said. "You can't stomach it?"

"I can," he said. "I can stomach what is important to you."

"So you'll come."

"No," he said. "Go relive your innocence."

There was so much Wilder did not know. "Edith ditched me at Hotchkiss."

"What do you mean?"

"She found white people then said to hell with Blacks. Especially poor ones like me."

"That's terrible," he said solemnly.

His restraint surprised her, as he could be extreme, especially when it came to matters of race. A few days later, more characteristically, he deluged her with designer purses, couture dresses, ball gowns, high heels, diamond jewelry, fur coats, hats, gloves, and boots.

Perplexed, she held up one of the fur coats.

"DC gets cold in October," he said. "And we tryna show that friend o' yours you ain't nobody's po'."

This magnanimity made her feel worse about replacing him with a younger, white man, even if it had only been in her mind. The best contrition she devised was freeing her locs like a revolutionary Black Medusa. But real contrition would come by way of Ramatou, who compelled her to call Wilder about her hair color.

"Militant red, Bels! Won't that be something?" he said over the phone. "Show them white folks we onto them. Whatever they preparin' for us after Obama, we meetin' with equal fire."

Three

Quarantined from their guests somewhere inside the Corcoran Gallery of Art, Edith and Pete were exchanging vows with their respective parents as their only witnesses. This was an unforeseen turn of events. Belinda had expected that the wedding guests would witness Edith and Pete's exchanging of vows. But in keeping with the atypical approach to the wedding, the reception's cocktail hour was scheduled at the same time as Edith and Pete's actual ceremony.

The announcement about the quasi-elopement had been made by Edith's effective maid of honor, Sims, from Hotchkiss. One of Edith's White-ingales, Belinda remembered.

Pale and blond and very white, Sims had appeared at the top of the Corcoran atrium's marble staircase in a shimmering lilac sheet dress. Apologetic about the mix-up without fully explaining, but promising that the reception would begin soon, she invited them to start on the drinks and hors d'oeuvres. "And make sure to view the art on display," she said.

As Belinda joined the stampede to the bar, she felt a hand on her arm. She turned to find Sims.

"Your hair! Wow!" Sims said, moving toward Belinda in a delicate embrace. "So cool." She stared at Belinda's hair as if it were one of the pieces of art on display at the Corcoran.

"How did you know it was me?" Belinda asked.

"We went to school together, silly. I could just tell." Sims had expertly circumvented the trap of admitting that Belinda was the only Black guest at the reception.

"Can you believe this place?" Sims asked.

"I went to law school in this town and I never knew this museum existed," Belinda said.

Long rectangular tables were being arranged throughout the atrium. The ones closest were draped in cream tablecloths as a group of men hurriedly arranged fancy dinnerware on them. Farther down, playing out in the corners of Belinda's eyes, other cloths flapped like enormous cream wings. There were boxes of pink and white roses waiting along the marble floor's periphery. All signs pointed to a forthcoming coalescence of razzle-dazzle in this space already gleaming with white marble floors and walls.

"Want to know a secret?" Sims said.

Belinda was uncomfortable with this woman's easy manner. Old friends they were not. Over the years, however, she'd observed that a sense of fraternity was engendered by a shared boarding school experience. At Williams, she'd passed her first weeks of college among a coalition of first-years who had schools like Andover, Exeter, and Choate in common. She'd eventually made her home with a group of Black students, many of them products of these same schools.

Despite their Hotchkiss connection, Belinda was not interested in Sims's confidence. Yet she could not deny the lure of the woman's muckraking compulsion. Was Sims's secret the same as hers: the knowledge of Pete's predatory history?

"What secret?" she finally asked.

"Edith only realized last week that they couldn't have the ceremony the way she wanted it," Sims said. "She almost canceled everything."

"Why?"

"Oh, you know how much of an airhead Edith can be."

Belinda nodded. She knew.

"Pete left all of the planning to her. Maybe it just got too overwhelming. She assumed that the ceremony would happen right here, then cocktails in another space, in order to set this place up for the reception," Sims said. "That seems reasonable. But you can't just assume things," she added. "She should have asked."

Bit by bit, the space was accruing elegance. The florist was halfway through setting the arrangements for the tables. "Especially when you are insisting on a Friday wedding. The earliest they could make this space available was six o'clock. Which messed up Edith's plans," Sims said.

"Looks to me like everything is working out well."

"It is now," she said. "She called me frantic. I couldn't even get a word in. After she calmed down, we agreed on what we have now. A private ceremony while the guests have some appetizers and drinks, and also got a chance to enjoy the art, which we didn't think was going to be possible, but we worked that out. Then pictures. Then the reception." Sims recalled this period's purpose and her eyes lit up. "Let's get something to drink," she said.

Four large tubs of ice formed a crescent behind the bartender.

The bottles arranged on the square table teetered. Sims ordered a vodka tonic. Belinda requested a Perrier. "You don't drink?" Sims asked.

"I do. But I prefer to start with water," she said, wiping the wet bottle with a napkin.

Sims stirred her drink with a squat straw while taking in the bustle of activity. "You don't think it's gauche, do you?" she asked.

"The decorations?"

"Yes."

A collection of white statues—angels, goddesses—added to the sense of fantasy. "Maybe the naked statues," Belinda joked. But Sims did not smile. She froze as if caught. "That was a joke," Belinda said. "It's all very elegant."

"Oh, okay," Sims said, exhaling as she resumed her stirring. It was peculiar how personally she appeared to be taking Edith's wedding. "I can't tell you how happy Edith was when you RSVP'd that you were coming."

To this, Belinda offered a near smile. Sims held out for more. Belinda was not forthcoming.

"Anyway, she wants me to keep an eye on things," Sims said. "I should probably not be standing here chatting." She gave Belinda's arm a departing squeeze. "This fabric is so rich," she said. "Kente? Right?"

"Yes."

"Your brother—" Sims broke off. "Oh, wait," she said. "You are not the one with the brother who deals in kente."

"No."

"I guess I'm mixing up Edith's friends from Ghana."

"Edith still keeps in touch with people from Ghana?"

"You sound surprised."

"I am."

Sims took two steps. "See you in a few," she said. "Don't forget to check out the art. There's an excellent exhibit: the works of thirty-one Black artists. Really cool stuff."

IN ONE PAINTING was a rendition of Jesus Christ in the tomb: bare-chested, a torso with defined abs, his groin covered by a white cloth but otherwise naked. The same white cloth spread out to drape what Belinda presumed to be a stone slab, on which this Jesus lay. Black Jesus. A sultry Black Jesus—his shining glory, a backdrop of romantic flower petals. It was called *Sleep*. The artist, according to the inscription, Kehinde Wiley.

The painting towered over Belinda. In the secrecy of her imagination she wished for a peek at the man's back muscles, which she suspected were impressive. Then and there, she sensed her blasphemy.

She was not religious, but if ever she needed to be told to keep the faith that Wilder was the righteous path, the road to the promised land of American permanence, here it was. Ten years it had been. Ten years was nothing in terms of biblical plight. The Israelites had wandered the desert for forty years. She'd had it much easier.

Of course, Wilder was a lot lighter-skinned than this Jesus; he was the kind of light-skinned that made it possible for him to pass for a member of Kara's family. Belinda considered her two lovers prior to Wilder. Had she witnessed Christ in their nakedness?

She hadn't gone with any boy during her two years at Hotchkiss. At Williams, she met Elliot, a sophomore from Northern California to whom she'd lost her virginity during her freshman year. He was somewhere between light-skinned and this Christ's black; within him, though, was the black of Black radicals. Years would pass before Belinda realized that part of Elliot's attraction to her was the legitimacy she afforded him: Who better than a woman from the motherland to validate his penchant for "ethnic" attire? Who better than a stunningly dark woman at his side to cast him in his preferred glow?

After Elliot graduated from Williams and went on to pursue a doctorate in African American studies at Stanford, he called her to say that he couldn't keep things going, and she accepted it, herself having lost interest. The second man was closer to home: Malachi, a Ghanaian physicist she'd met during orientation week at GW. He had the same definition in his torso and striations in his back; he was this Christ's black. These were the days in '96 when rumors swirled of INS picking up one illegal African after another; it was an election year and Clinton wanted journalists to make noise about his zero-tolerance immigration policy, which he knew would win him more votes. One day the woman who used to wait on her at Alexandria's largest African store vanished.

Belinda was at the time protected within one of America's ivory towers and she knew it. But she did not have peace of mind. She'd once half joked about organizing multistate armies and committing to a day of prison burnings, about which Malachi had guffawed for far too long. If there was a moment to refer to as their point of no return, that was it.

Perhaps as a result of that disappointment, Belinda suffered through a stretch of celibacy, until Wilder, whom she'd been fiercely attracted to when she first met him at the age of seventeen, rediscovered her.

Fate, Belinda would come to accept, had destined her and Wilder to be together, her American fate having revealed itself in the tenor of Ghana. Back home, Edith, her closest friend, had been a stupendously rich girl. In America, her closest friend, Kara, was a stupendously rich girl. She had recognized her American classmates' appreciation of her intelligence, the same appreciation her classmates in Ghana had had. Further echoes would come and go.

It wasn't really an echo when she met Wilder in Oak Bluffs during her first summer in America; it was more like déjà vu. They headed off to the beach known as the Inkwell and made a place for themselves on the sand, despite the beach being closed after a near drowning that had shaken everyone. They were breaking the rules, united in mischief, much like the rule-breaking that had surrounded her day at the beach with Mike back home. And like that day, the tingle of attraction swirled through her, until it grew into an all-over heat.

The idea of Wilder and her was just as wrong as that of her and Mike. She was seventeen then, more mature, but it still felt as wrong as her being twelve at Mike's side.

At the beach Wilder had stared at the water and not at Belinda, which irritated her. After she glared at the side of his face for too long, her vision started to blur and his beard, which reached his chest, seemed to drain into the silvery water. Quickly, she took off her shorts and ran for the water in her threadbare two-piece, splashing into it. When she looked back at him, his eyes were somewhere else. She started humming Nina Simone's

"Four Women," which Kara had told her was his favorite song. She thought the song would lure him closer. But he stood up and walked away.

He was aloof and cool for the rest of the summer. He did not show up the following summer. That fall, her first semester at Williams, Elliot took her mind off him.

Many years later, as she descended the escalator at the Houston airport to begin her life with Wilder, she would forgive herself. Truth be told, she had no preference for older men. Mike had been a typical schoolgirl crush. It was fate, she thought when she saw Wilder at the bottom of the escalator, that made it easy to see herself at seventeen in bed with a nearly fifty-year-old Black man. So it came as no surprise that when it finally happened, she could be effusive with him in bed without effort. Wilder winnowed out her tendrils of sexual pleasure, caressing them better than any man ever had. One night, after they'd made love, he held her tight and said, "Did you ever think?"

Was there anything like the freedom to determine for yourself when fate was at work? The freedom to stop oneself? What had Wilder been thinking when he instantly proposed marriage on that fateful day they found themselves alone in the kitchen at Oak Bluffs? He never said it outright, but she knew that she was supposed to be his fuck-you to America. She could hear him now: *You don't want her here, whitey? You want to push her out? Well, fuck you. She here and she gon' stay here if it's the last thing I do.*

A voice buzzed in her ear. "Powerful. Right?"

She looked in the direction of the voice and placed it without hesitation. "Mike."

"I see you're still sharp," he said, stepping closer.

"You haven't changed much," she said. "And you sound the same."

"Can't take the New England out of the boy," he said. "The speech patterns might be the same, but I've changed. No?"

Perhaps he carried more girth around his waist. Perhaps the three-piece suit he was wearing was too tight. Perhaps unbuttoning the suit jacket would have done him some good. "Your face has held up," she said. "Which is what counts."

With both palms, he rubbed the skin surrounding his lips. "Good shaving cream and a daily regimen," he said. He lowered his hands. "Your hair!"

"And you thought *you*'d changed."

"Last time I saw you we had the same hair."

"Practically speaking," she said. In Ghanaian secondary schools, the girls were made to sport short-crop cuts like boys.

He watched her keenly for a moment, as if evaluating. Then he spread out his arms. "Are you going to let me hug you?"

"Only because you asked nicely," she said, stepping into him.

"I had to ask." He exhaled, heating her earlobe. "It's been so long."

After they released each other, she noticed how quiet the gallery was. The space they were in was devoted to five works. They shuffled closer to *Sleep*, which, Belinda thought, had to be the artist's—Wiley's—attempt at irony. *Gospel of Death* was more like it.

"Wild," Mike said.

"It's a lot of things," Belinda said. "Biblical. Poignant. Pointed, too."

"It is all of those things," he said, "but I was referring to Edith and Pete."

She'd almost forgotten. "Edith and Pete are something, all right," she said.

He went around her and she bent down to pick up the plastic Perrier bottle she'd set on the floor. She held it in the hand with her clutch as they strolled aimlessly through the museum. Her heels clicked against the marble floor.

"You know, I asked him about Edith when we were in Ghana," Mike began. "We were drinking and I'd found the liquid courage to ask."

"What did you say?"

"I asked if he was fucking her."

Horrified, she paused. "Just like that? In those exact words?"

He nodded. "Over twenty-five years later and the question still elicits the same response."

"I imagine you now understand why."

"I do," Mike said soberly. "And I knew the implications when I asked."

"And?"

"What did Pete say?"

"Yes."

"He didn't say anything. He stormed off and stopped talking to me," he said. "Remember when he was showing up to your school on his own? After the beach?"

"I do."

"I was in the doghouse then."

"I wasn't exactly up for seeing you myself," she said.

"No?"

"We got into trouble because we sneaked away to come see you two. Avoiding you was best," she said.

He frowned. "You ever ask her?"

"No," Belinda said. "But here we are."

Mike looked her straight in the eye. He said, "Belinda, what I'm gathering from you is fear. Were you afraid of me?"

"Not actively afraid. You'd already gotten me into trouble once. Who knew what else you were capable of?"

Whispering, he said, "Statutory rape?"

She eyed him.

"I don't find that funny," he said.

"Neither do I," Belinda said. "I have ships upon ships of historical precedent to not find it funny. You were the person who introduced me to that history. Remember?"

Mike frowned more deeply, marring the face that had held up so well. "Pete is Pete. I'm not Pete."

"What made you so different?" she asked.

A group of guests moved toward them. Mike backed up to make way. After the small batch of people passed and were beyond earshot, he filled the space he'd created. "Whatever happened, we can at least take heart in this happy ending," he said.

"I can't be sure. Life happened. We lost touch."

"Well, I can tell you Pete is very happy," he said. "His first wife was a real Lady Macbeth."

The empty bottle slipped out of Belinda's hand and bounced erratically on the floor. Mike caught it for her.

"Thanks." She took the bottle from him. "I assumed this was his first marriage."

"Why? He's no spring chicken." He held up two fingers. "Two kids."

Belinda did not react. Mike cast quick glances around them. "Where's everyone?" he asked.

"Probably time to head back," she said.

"After you," he agreed.

Before leaving the gallery, Belinda admired *Sleep* one last time. Because of its large size, she could still make out several of its details from this distance of about ten feet.

Standing next to her, Mike said, "You said it's biblical, which probably makes what I am about to say blasphemous. It's also supposed to be sexy. Right?"

She grinned without shifting her focus: he'd read her mind. Without replying, she started walking.

Before they joined the reception that was taking shape in the atrium with the soft sounds of the jazz quartet playing in a far corner, Mike stopped. "Not married?" he asked.

"I am," Belinda said.

"I didn't see a ring."

"We are nontraditional in that way."

"He here?"

"Home."

"Weddings not his thing?"

"Nothing like that." She was eager to move on from the topic of Wilder. "How about you? Married?"

"Nontraditional," he said. "Never have. Never will."

"Why not?"

"Not my thing," he said. "Or maybe I am one of those people who let the right one get away and doesn't know it."

He suddenly looked distant, and for a fleeting moment, it was as though the whites of his eyes were all there were.

AT THE START of the reception, Edith and Pete, newly married, their arms looped, appeared at the top of the staircase to applause. Edith let go of Pete to wave at Belinda below. Belinda flapped a hand in response.

During dinner, Mike, who was seated next to Belinda, knocked his fork against her plate. When she looked at him, he pointed out Edith's dimpled gaze on her. Over an ornate table-scape of crystal china and an elaborate centerpiece of fall flowers, Edith was waving a small Hotchkiss flag.

"There's a Hotchkiss picture scheduled for later," explained Mike. "I asked about Wesley Girls'. She acted as though she hadn't heard me."

Belinda felt the photo should have happened by now. The reception was well into the dancing, at the end of which Edith and Pete would cut their cake and bring the reception to a close.

After one dance with Mike, Belinda returned to her seat, and Pete's mother, Lois, followed her. "There's no part of the country we don't know," Lois said, standing in front of Belinda.

She was referring to Ghana, which she'd confessed a fondness for, and the ownership of a collection of kente from the north, which were more affordable but less bewitching. She'd managed to acquire a few of the Ashanti kind, Lois said, which she preferred, evidenced by her ogling of Belinda's outfit.

"We've been to places in Ghana many Ghanaians haven't even

heard of," Lois continued. "We love Kumasi. It's not as hot as other parts."

"It has to do with the ranges of elevation," Belinda said.

"The ranges of elevation?" Lois repeated. "You sound like a geographer."

"That would be Wilder," Belinda said. "My husband. He's an oil-and-gas guy. Come to our house and you'd think he's a geographer. We are swimming in maps."

"For his work?"

"Yes."

Smiling purposefully, Lois said, "Oh, I get it. He wants to play in Ghana. We were there in 2007, you know, when the oil was discovered."

"Funny enough, he's not much interested in the oil." Belinda took a bit of delight in correcting her. "He has his eye on natural gas."

"Interesting." Lois dragged a chair over and sat down next to Belinda. Without warning she changed the subject: "I turned seventy this year," she said, loosening her pumps.

"Could have fooled me." Belinda meant this; Lois had been flouncing about the reception like a younger woman who was coming into her own after a divorce.

"I'm a scrappy fighter," she said. "Old age has nothing on me." She made her hands into fists and threw two weak jabs. Belinda feigned fright. "We first went to Ghana in sixty-four. A year after we had Pete," she continued. "Who could have foreseen this outcome? Peace Corps? Finding the love of his life?"

"Edith."

"She had a crush on him back in the day, I hear."

"Some crush."

"I'll say."

"She was twelve," Belinda said bluntly. "Those crushes don't last. Had to be more than a crush, wouldn't you say?"

"Yes." Lois touched her chest with her palm. "They reconnected four years ago. It's such a heartwarming story. To find each other so many years later. And to think that his father's and my love for Ghana manifested in this way. It's all so heartwarming."

"Troubling," Belinda said, resorting to a bit of indirectness—bluntly stating Edith's age at the time didn't work—to send Lois the message of the inappropriateness of it all.

It was clear that Lois had missed the point entirely when she said, "No, I mean Pete and Edith."

Belinda gave up. She would accept that Pete, he of the white American pedigree, had a predisposition toward exploiting African girls, regardless of what Lois believed. Or chose not to believe.

The light over the dance floor was changing from maroon to soft peach. Two little girls in matching frilly dresses—clearly Pete's daughters—pirouetted across the floor.

"The girls love Edith," Lois said.

If Pete and Edith had daughters, Belinda thought, they would take after these two biracial girls, which confirmed for Belinda that Pete liked his berries black. Belinda fought a rising chortle to ask, "How old are they?"

"Sasha is ten," Lois said, pointing out the taller of the two. "Sophie is eight."

"They're beautiful."

"Blessings, in fact. Only bright spots of that marriage."

Skipping toward Belinda was an older, white-haired man whose arms were spread wide.

"Belinda, come, come," Mr. Hyde, Edith's father, urged.

She stood up to greet him as he gripped her shoulders. "Oh, my, Belinda. Let me have a good look at you." He turned her body in several directions. "How you have grown, my dear." To Lois, he added, "She doesn't even look like the same person."

"You still recognized her," Lois said.

"Well . . ." he said, making a face at Belinda with a clear meaning: there were only two of them here, not counting Edith and her mother. And, Belinda remembered, Edith's two stepdaughters.

"The kente gave her away," Lois suggested.

"Yes," he said. "That was it. The kente."

He was not ready to take his hands from Belinda's shoulders. When a woman appeared behind him, he was startled into letting go.

"Henrietta," he said to his wife. "You remember Belinda, don't you?"

"Yes, Edith's friend." Henrietta scanned Belinda with curiosity. "You've changed."

Before Belinda could respond, Edith's father added, "You remember Edith's mother, Henrietta, don't you?"

"I do." Belinda did, but not this way. Henrietta Hyde had aged into a disappointing sight. The skin on her face was charred and rubbery, like the flimsy layers of skin Belinda imagined keloids leave if they could be released of their juice. Henrietta's makeup, try as it might, failed to disguise the obvious: years of skin bleaching had caught up with her.

"I wanted to wear kente, too," Henrietta said, "but Edith wouldn't let me."

"Your dress is perfect," Belinda said. It was Henrietta's saving grace, a navy blue ball gown with a million bits of shimmer.

"This dress is fine," Henrietta agreed, "but these days, the mother of the bride wears kente. I'm sure you know."

"I wouldn't, actually."

"You haven't been back?"

"No."

"Well, you and Edith should think about going back," she said. "Then you'll find out for yourselves. Only kente for the bride's mother."

"Is that true?" asked Lois.

"Yes," replied Henrietta.

"No," her husband said.

"Oh no," Lois said. "A lover's spat." She slipped on her pumps and stood. "Have to find cover." She wandered back into the crowd.

Free of her, Henrietta said in Twi, "That woman is odd. Very odd."

"That woman is now your daughter's mother-in-law," replied her husband.

Belinda searched her mind for something to say to defuse the tension. It was not necessary, for Henrietta grabbed her by the elbow and said, "I'm happy I saw you, Belinda. I'm going to sit down. We will talk some more later." Turning to her husband, she said, "Something hasn't been paid for. They are looking for you." She sped off.

Mr. Hyde watched Henrietta make it to her seat. "You know one thing I don't like about this America of yours, Belinda?" He lowered his chin to his chest and moved his eyes side to side. "I am paying for all of this."

"It's the American way."

"A bad way, if you ask me." He looked her over again, then sighed. "Well, I have to go and see who wants more of my money," he said. "You've grown into a beautiful woman, Belinda. I am so proud." Before leaving, he asked, "How's your father?"

"He's doing well." Her response had been inordinately enthusiastic, as if to mask a bout with cancer. "He wanted me to greet you for him." It'd been decades since she'd had the taste of this Ghanaian conjugation on her tongue. She'd become accustomed to simply saying: *He says hi*. "Mr. Hyde," she said sincerely, "thank you."

"For?"

"Giving me the opportunity years ago."

"I did nothing, Belinda. Nothing I wouldn't do for anybody who deserves it," he said. "Anyway, I have to go and do my father-of-the-bride duties." He patted his breast pocket, which presumably held his wallet. "We'll talk some more later."

Sitting back down, Belinda considered the contents of that wallet. Her managing Wilder's oil and gas investments had inevitably reframed Mr. Hyde's wealth in relative terms: by her standards now, Mr. Hyde was definitely middle class. At Hotchkiss, Edith had proven herself a worthy competitor—and ultimate winner—in contests of wealth. But those had been superficial triumphs: boots, nothing to break the coffers of a family with only one child. Truth be told, Belinda didn't know how Mr. Hyde had paid Edith's way through Hotchkiss. It was safe to assume that the embassy had assisted in that.

Because Wilder had inherited the beginnings of his wealth, he once wondered to Belinda if that was a possible explanation for how Edith's father had come into money. Belinda doubted that was the case: she'd never heard anything about Edith's ancestors being well-off, and Edith was the type who would flaunt that heritage. Belinda believed that Mr. Hyde's riches were average. On some level, she held on to this belief to help compensate for her last day at Hotchkiss, when Edith had made her feel worthless— or at least worth less than Edith. Belinda had come to this wedding to avenge herself, to show Edith how far she'd come, to lap her in the American race for money. She turned the tennis bracelet around her wrist as her mind did the same. Whether Belinda liked it or not, Edith's father boasted real money, the kind of real money that can fund an elegant wedding at a fancy museum in Washington, D.C.

Few people were dancing now. The dance floor light had gone peach. Belinda went to find Edith, who had left the dance floor, and to look for Mike, who might lead her to Edith and could serve as a buffer if necessary. But here was Sims again, her arm raised, breezing close, as if volunteering herself for Mike's place.

"Having fun?" she asked, her white teeth looming large in the light.

"Yes. Have you seen Edith?"

"Wait!" Sims exclaimed. "You haven't seen her?"

"I have but I haven't gotten a chance to talk to her."

Sims snatched Belinda's wrist tight enough that Belinda thought her bracelet might leave a mark. "Come with me," she said.

Inside an alcove, Edith, Pete, and Mike were sharing a laugh. Edith and Pete were cuddled on a white stone bench, while Mike stood. The music was muffled in this section of the museum as the alcove boomed with their laughter.

Edith saw her before the men did. "My God," she said, abandoning Pete on the bench. "Belinda!"

"I know," Sims said. She stood in the space that kept the two women apart. "How good does she look?" she added.

"Your hair!" Edith said.

"That's what I said." Sims was slowly extricating herself. "I did my duty," she said loudly, projecting her farewell as she left the four.

Edith grinned. "You know what I can't get over?" The question was rhetorical. "How much after all these years neither of us has lost her free spirit. I mean, come on"—she gestured at her dress—"who wears something like this for their wedding?"

It was a fuchsia tulle tutu dress that Belinda had identified immediately as a Betsey Johnson design. She'd assumed that Edith had changed dresses between the ceremony and the reception, as most American brides seemed to do. On the contrary: Edith confessed it was the dress in which she'd said her vows.

"Everybody was going on and on about how I should wear white. Or at least something more traditional," she said. "Pete didn't care, so I said, 'What the heck?' If your hair's any indication, you have a wilder streak than I do."

"I would have worn white," Belinda said.

Edith looked surprised. "You would?"

Belinda nodded.

"Who would have ever predicted this reunion?" Pete said, interrupting.

His beard was untidy, Belinda noticed. Indeed, even on his

wedding day, he wore a general aura of dishevelment, like a tuxedo that didn't quite fit. Belinda wondered how his fancy for Black women—who were culturally adamant about style—hadn't shaped him to get himself together.

"Have you two had a chance to chat?" he asked Belinda, referring to Mike.

"We have," Mike said. "We had all the time in the world, Pete. I thought I was coming for a wedding. Turns out I was coming for cocktails and a reunion."

"You aren't upset, are you, Mike?" asked Edith.

"You know Mike, darling—a lovable dick." Pete snagged Mike in a friendly chokehold. "Excuse us, Belinda. I'm sure you and Edith have catching up to do."

At minimum, Belinda expected Pete to comment on her hair. His reticence annoyed her. Years ago, in Ghana, he'd acted without inhibition. She wasn't here to witness growth in him. She had come to confirm him a monster.

"Sit?" Edith suggested.

"Sure."

Above the bench was a painting, a large square canvas of framed splotches of red that presented, Belinda thought, like a threat.

Edith inclined her head toward it. "It's so strange," she said.

"Is it blood?" Belinda asked.

Edith nodded. "Mike said that the artist mixed some of his own blood with the paint, so take it with a grain of salt." She compressed her ballooned tutu. "Did he say anything to you?"

"Mike?"

"Yes."

"The thing about Pete raping you in Ghana?"

Edith gasped. "What?"

Belinda had uttered the words without thinking. After they came out of her, she surprised herself by how angry she still was. About their competing. About Hotchkiss. She kept going. "Oh, that's not what you meant?"

On her feet, Edith picked at the sides of her eyes, as if trying to remove something from her makeup. "What a fucking dick."

Belinda covered her mouth with her hand to conceal her laughter. "Of course he didn't say that."

Edith looked stunned and sat back on the bench. "That was a terrible thing to say, Belinda."

"Oh, come on. Lighten up. We were both feeling awkward. The first thing you did after you sat down was to look up at that weird painting. To avoid looking at me. I thought I'd break the tension with a little joke."

"That's not a joke."

"Whatever it is, I got you to look at me," Belinda said. "Now, let's talk."

"About?"

"Ghana," she said. "And Hotchkiss."

"Hotchkiss was childishness," Edith said. "Complete childishness. I resented you for getting there before I did. And I wanted to prove to you that it was more mine than it was yours." She leaned back against the wall. "I regretted it later. When it hit me that I might never see you again. That you would be angry at me for the rest of your life. And that was a terrible feeling."

"You could have reached out."

"My pride wouldn't let me," she said. "Having to say sorry felt like defeat."

"Is that why you still haven't said it?"

"You're here, Belinda. Isn't it obvious how sorry I am?"

"Far from it."

"Okay," Edith said. "But I don't know what would be best now. If I say it to you right now, it would be because you are making me say it. That's not a real apology, is it?"

Belinda thought for a moment. "Fair point. I'll wait for whenever you are ready."

Edith winced in jest. "Seriously, though, did Mike say anything to you?"

But Belinda didn't answer the question. Instead she said, "Part of my coming here was for confirmation. But now I don't even care."

"Care about what?"

"What went on between you and Pete in Ghana."

"Does it matter? We are here now."

"That's what Mike said."

"He said that?"

"More or less," Belinda said. "Sounds like you were expecting him to say something else."

"Pete has it in his mind that we—all of us—were meant to be. Me and him. You and Mike."

"That's ridiculous."

"Is it?" Edith said. "Remind me, did you ever admit to having a crush on Mike?"

"No."

"But you had a crush on him."

"I was twelve."

Edith smirked. "I learned recently that my maternal grand-mother married my grandfather when she was fourteen, and she was already pregnant."

"What are you getting at?"

"Do you know about yours? Your grandparents?"

Belinda did not need to go that far back: her mother had been fifteen when she'd married her father. "Get to the point, Edith."

"My point is we are Ghanaians."

Belinda rolled her eyes. "How convenient."

Edith caught Belinda's sarcasm. "So what if I deploy my cultural identity to defend myself? It's mine. I can do whatever I want with it."

"And what about Pete? What does he deploy to defend himself?"

"Nothing. Because he has nothing to defend himself against."

Unsettled, Belinda decided to relinquish the fight—perhaps it was indeed in everybody's best interests to arrive at this truce of an ostensibly happy ending.

Edith cocked her head at her. "What's your husband's name? Something Thomas, right?"

"Wilder," she said. "Wilder Thomas."

"Would I know him? Hotchkiss?"

"Not at all," Belinda said, giggling.

"Why do you laugh?"

"The idea of you knowing him."

"Because we haven't talked since school?"

"That. And also because he's older than us."

"Pete's older than us. The source of this moment's tension—not to put too fine a point on it."

"Our tension is multifaceted, Edith. In any case, Wilder is older than Pete," Belinda said.

"How old?"

"Old."

"Belinda?" purred Edith. "How old?"

"Sixty-six."

"Belinda!" Edith looked around to confirm their seclusion. "We're thirty-eight."

"And he's Black. So the chances of you knowing him are slim to none."

Edith frowned. "Is this one of your jokes or an insult?"

Belinda smiled but didn't answer.

Edith's face held an expression Belinda couldn't read. "You will never forgive me for Hotchkiss, will you?"

"I believe in letting bygones be bygones," Belinda said. "I'm here."

"Then where did your comment come from? If you are implying that I don't know any Black people, you are wrong."

"I'm sure they must all be at the same conference, then," Belinda said. "Which conference made it impossible for them to attend your wedding, Edith? NAACP? UNCF?"

"Fine, you caught me," she said. "Since you are not satisfied by the ones on the walls . . . The living ones here are acquaintances. Actually, the help."

And just like that, Belinda was out of biting witticisms.

"I take it you didn't come with him. Wilder?" Edith asked.

The tension had eased. "Weddings are not his thing," Belinda said, skirting the reasons for Wilder's absence.

"That's too bad," Edith said. "It would have been nice to meet him." She pulled back from the wall. "Anyway, how's your brother?"

"Robert?"

"Jacob," Edith said. "Your father went to see mine for help with his visa. Something about joining his wife?"

Belinda could have told her that Jacob was divorced, but the two women seemed to be at the embryonic stage of a new alliance. Years would need to progress before she could let Edith in like family. "What did my father want?"

"I told you. Help with your brother's visa. But Daddy couldn't do much," Edith said. "Your father didn't tell you?"

"Yours still works?"

"Till his dying day," Edith groaned. "I've been trying to convince him to retire."

Actually, Belinda cared little about Mr. Hyde's continued years of service at the embassy. She'd only asked to give herself time to rationalize her father's disloyalty. He was still in touch with the Hydes. Since Hotchkiss, Belinda had worked hard to turn her father against Edith and her family. She thought she'd succeeded and was comforted when her father once said of Edith, "The apple doesn't fall far from the tree."

It turned out her father had been putting on an act this whole time. He was keeping company with Edith's relations in Ghana and not telling her.

Belinda could feel bubbling outrage start to overtake her. She laid a hand on Edith's. "I'm glad I came," she said.

"Me, too." Edith brought her other hand and built a triple stack of their hands. "How about Sims?"

"Over-welcoming," Belinda said.

Edith squeezed her knuckles. "It's really not my place, but if we are going to rebuild our friendship, I have to be transparent," she said. She paused and took a breath.

Belinda did not speak.

"Sims knows your brother."

Belinda remembered Sims's earlier mischaracterization of Jacob. "No, she doesn't."

"What did she say?"

"That my brother sells kente," Belinda said. "She must have meant the brother of one of your other Ghanaian friends."

Edith rolled her eyes. "That would be you, Belinda. You're my only Ghanaian friend. It's been decades since I heard from anyone from Wesley Girls'."

"But Jacob is a computers guy."

"Exactly," Edith said. "That's how Sims knows him. She met him online. She was concerned that you knew. I guess she dropped the brother line to make sure."

"What would be wrong with me knowing?"

Edith swallowed. "They met on some S-and-M site." She paused. "She has it in her mind that he went on the site to live out a fantasy that has to do with you. Incest or something. She's ashamed of the fantasy she was fulfilling with him. Antebellum shit, you know?"

Belinda did not know. At this point, she didn't know anything.

"Sims has been working on herself," Edith continued, "but she's really freaked out about your brother. What are the odds that he would find someone who went to Hotchkiss on a site? Not to mention someone who graduated the same year you did. Like he was looking for a white version of you."

Belinda managed an awkward smile. "Sims is hardly a white version of me."

"No. Of course," Edith said. "But you know what I mean."

Belinda had not been after *this* certainty of sexual deviance. This kind of revelation was supposed to be about Pete, not Jacob. "Why would she tell you any of this? Seems like something to take to your grave," she said.

"We were working on the wedding list. And I noticed that whenever your name came up, she went white. I finally got it out of her."

Belinda latched onto the served-up witticism: How white? But before she could ask, she heard, "Eeediiith."

Edith pulled her hands out so quickly that Belinda's palm stamped the stone bench. A thin coolness shot through her nerves.

"Sasha, darling," Edith said.

Bounding for the middle of the bench, Sasha bumped Belinda. "So-reee," she said.

Belinda rotated her shoulder. "I can still move it," she said. "No harm done."

"So-reee," repeated Sasha. "Edith, it's time to cut the cake!"

"Are they waiting for me?" Edith asked.

"Yes," Sasha said, pushing on Edith's lower back.

Edith looked behind her. "Coming?"

Belinda pretended to dig in her clutch for an item—lipstick, she hoped Edith would think. "I am, but don't wait for me. You can't keep your guests waiting."

OUTSIDE, Belinda shivered in the crisp darkness. Deep night speckled from the amber ovals of streetlights and streaked from the white lines of car lights. Through her folded arms, her phone produced its own light and served to warm her fingers. She regretted not wearing a coat.

Shaken by learning of her father's evident betrayal and a new element of Jacob's odd personality, Belinda had sat through what remained of the reception—the cake cutting (which she'd actually missed), the bouquet toss, the final song—before making a quick exit. To her relief, there had not been a Hotchkiss photo.

Among the last to leave, Mike had found her waiting out front and offered her a ride to her hotel.

"I'm fine," Belinda said.

"I won't step out of the car when we get there, if that's what you are worried about."

"Whatever can happen inside a hotel room can happen inside a car, Mike," she said. "And I'm not worried about any of it happening. My ride should be here soon."

After Mike left, she grabbed her phone to call her father but couldn't decide what to say to him. Now she was strolling along the Corcoran's perimeter, dallying on her call log. Pete's name appeared at the top, which made sense, as he was the last person she'd exchanged phone numbers with, having simplified the process by calling him so he could store hers. Edith's name followed, then Mike's.

Belinda scanned Seventeenth Street, yearning for her car. She leaned into the street slightly, unafraid of what was to come in the glaring emptiness of the street and sidewalk. After a stretch of nothingness, she rounded a corner onto New York Avenue.

Her father's betrayal worried her more than Jacob's unexpected proclivity. Jacob was odd. He'd always been that way, but at least with this new revelation, she had indisputable evidence of his preference for women. She had wondered at times whether she'd been an accomplice in her brother's attempts to hide his sexual orientation, a collusion that she suspected fate would not reward, as it had blocked him from coming to America.

Such thoughts fled after she'd forgiven herself. The fact that Jacob had stopped talking to her since calling with the news about the death of their mother was him nursing his pain by himself; he could have all the time he needed.

But never had she considered the possibility that her father had held back information from her. He had always sought out her opinion on Jacob's prospects. Whether Jacob should arm himself with pictures of the marriage ceremony for his first interview at the embassy. (To that Belinda had answered with an emphatic no: it might do a lot of harm and little good, seeing as Patricia was in America illegally and ought to remain a phantom to authorities.) Admitting to knowing nothing about the Green Card Lottery advertised in the newspapers, her father had asked her about it. It had recently gone digital, she'd said, so Jacob could apply online at the internet café, if he hadn't already. He'd asked her whether she thought Jacob's applying was a waste of time. He let the first disappointing outcome of the lottery pass without comment, merely acknowledging that the results hadn't gone Jacob's

way. After the second disappointment, he spoke of his initial op-
position to the idea. "And to think that people were expecting the
American gates to be open to them because of Obama," he said.
Jacob, he had told her, was observably sad. Depleted of happiness.
She, on the other hand, had done what Napoleon could not, as her
father reminded her.

How many times had she heard this over the years? It was her
father's highest compliment. And despite absolving herself of the
demise of her brother's marriage, the tailwind of her father's praise
never ceased to comfort Belinda. It was a reminder that she still
had his confidence, even if he bestowed all his thanks for everything else at Wilder's feet.

Now she sensed the tailwind differently. What Napoleon
could not do was no longer for her. It was for himself, as a means
of deflecting from the confidence he'd lost in her. Why else had
he failed to tell her he had gone to see Mr. Hyde on Jacob's behalf? The next time she spoke to her father, she would remind him
that it was he who suggested that she set Jacob up with someone
in America in the first place. She remembered the conversation
clearly. He'd said, "Don't you have anyone for him in America?
He's here in Ghana without a wife. Without a meaningful job.
Stuck. Wasting away. Maybe a new air?"

Belinda hadn't worried about Patricia's lack of papers or the
challenges that Jacob would face trying to make his way to her.
She was primarily interested in Patricia being a good candidate.
Patricia would care for her brother, love him whole. Jacob, wasting
away in Ghana, could be resuscitated by love in America. She
hadn't been able to set up Robert successfully when they were

children. Perhaps the universe was giving her a redo through Jacob. A second chance at winning.

She stopped on the sidewalk and made the call to her father. A tired, muffled voice answered after four rings.

"Alfred?" she said.

The voice, finding verve, said, "Yes. This is Alfred."

"Did I wake you?"

"Aunty Belinda?" Without waiting for her answer he added, "My eyes were open."

"Why are you up? It's a Saturday."

"I know. But I am going somewhere with Uncle Benjamin so I had to wake early."

"Uncle Jacob?"

"No. Uncle Benjamin," Alfred repeated. "We are taking my father's van to pick up chairs. And then we will go for beans."

Alfred's delivery indicated that he had more to add. Belinda ignored it, narrowing in on her goal. "Where's Grandpa?"

"On the veranda. Do you want him?"

"Yes."

She paused, waiting for her father, but she could still hear Alfred's whistling breath.

"Alfred?"

"Yes?"

"What is it?"

"Please don't be angry," he said.

"What is it?" she repeated.

"Somebody stole the Nike shoes you bought for me," he said. "I looked everywhere, and I can't find them."

"Just that?"

"Yes," he said. "Please don't be angry. My mother said you will be angry."

Belinda smiled. "I'm not angry," she said. "Guess I will just have to buy you another pair."

He squealed—a joyous, continuous note that gradually thinned and eventually vanished into the whir of the ceiling fan she guessed to be above the phone. After a brief wait, she heard someone fumble for the receiver. "Belinda?"

"Did Alfred not say who was calling?" she asked her father.

"He did."

"You said my name as if you weren't sure."

"I guess one can never be too sure."

She was standing on the west side of the museum. With her free hand, she clutched the metal railing bordering the building.

"How was the wedding?" Mr. Nti asked.

"Good."

"You saw Edith?"

"Yes. We talked."

"Were you kind?"

"Were you concerned?"

"Just answer me. Were you kind?"

"Everything went smoothly."

The railing's chill burned her palm. She removed her hand and shook it out as she started walking.

"Why didn't you tell me you went to see her father?" Belinda asked.

"Whose father?"

"Edith's."

"When I went to talk to him about Jacob?"

"You didn't tell me."

"It was impromptu. I was in Accra and Jacob's problem was at a serious point," he said. "I planned on telling you."

"Why didn't you?"

"I've always hoped that you and Edith would get back on track. I didn't want anything to spoil it."

"Telling me her father was helping with Jacob would hardly have spoiled things."

"Helping?" he asked. "He didn't help."

"I know. Edith said that he couldn't."

"That's a lie!" her father barked. "That's why I didn't tell you. He could help. But he didn't. He wanted money."

"Visa fees?"

"I know about visa fees, Belinda. He wanted money to make it happen. You know how that man makes his money? By peddling his influence at the embassy. Pay him ten thousand dollars and he will make sure you get a visa. He asked me for eight. And had the nerve to call it a family discount." Her father went quiet, and she visualized him reviewing the events as he shook his head. "I don't know what it was about you, Belinda. But count yourself among the lucky few who didn't have to pay a pesewa. You remember those years ago, when Jacob and I went to see him?"

"Yes."

"I think he wanted money but just didn't have the heart to ask for it. Probably why things didn't work out for Jacob."

Finally, Belinda spotted her car. By the time it meandered to a stop, she was at the curb. The dark window lowered slowly, disappearing into the car door like a vanishing stage curtain, and as though written into the play to induce the audience's loudest gasps, it revealed Laurent. She was not expecting him. Another driver had picked her up from the hotel earlier in the day.

"Pa, my car is here. I will have to call you back."

"Your car? Where are you?"

"Outside."

"In Washington, D.C.? At night?"

"Don't worry. I'm safe." She looked across the street. "I can see the White House from where I'm standing."

"Really? And Obama?" He chuckled.

"Maybe if I get closer," she said.

She hadn't laid eyes on her father in twenty-two years. She imagined the muscles in his cheeks twitching in amusement. More realistically, she imagined his old-man jowls shimmying.

"Before you go, are you still going to see Patricia?"

"Tomorrow." The time on her phone caught her eye. Amending her response, she said, "Actually, later today. It's past midnight here."

"Ask about the ring," he said. "Put that at the top of your list. Please. The ring."

"Well noted," she said. "The ring. Top of the list."

She sidled past Laurent, who was holding the car door open. She acknowledged him with a wave of her elbow. "Is Jacob by you, Pa?"

"Asleep," he said.

He was too quick with his answer. She detected protectiveness—that thing about Jacob. Her father also seemed to be in on it.

"All right, Pa," she said. "Later, then."

He hung up before she did, denying her the chance to emphasize her dedication to getting the ring. What was left but that? And she supposed it was fair that she should be the one to face that music, considering she'd been the principal conductor.

Inside the car, she spread out on the back seat. Laurent, assuming from her silence that she'd gotten off the call, turned to ask, "Surprised?"

There was no one on the other end of the phone but Belinda held it to her ear, pretending.

"Sorry," Laurent mouthed. He turned to look forward.

She did not have it in her to engage with him, pulled by a disabling force as she was. How this intense recollection of the sultry Jesus had taken complete hold of her, as if come to life, she did not know. He was lifeless as ever, this Jesus, and yet successfully choking her into silence. The image reverberated more as *Gospel of Death* than before. It reflected Wilder even more.

At the George Bush Intercontinental Airport, when she'd arrived to begin her life with Wilder, he led her to the luggage carousel. She knew Wilder to be spry, yet she had no intention of having him, a man a lot more advanced in age, help her with her bags.

As soon as the conveyor belt got going, she felt its movement in her toes. He had his arm around her. When she spotted her suitcase, she jerked away from him. Yet he was quicker, seizing its heaviness like a strongman. She could have sworn that he grabbed the second, heavier bag with even more ease. She realized that she was marrying a man who had more power in him than other men his age.

So it was dumbfounding that only four years later, without any hint of forthcoming frailty, Wilder got so sick that she feared he would die. She first blamed stubbornness for his refusal to see a doctor. When he started speaking breathily, she thought his refusal was an acceptance of the inevitable.

He was clammy, pouring sweat. "Please, Wilder," she pleaded. "I'm scared."

"Don't be," he said. "It will pass."

She kept dabbing cold towels on his forehead and administering aspirin. He was right. The illness passed within a week, and she accepted that his familiarity with it had made him certain of its passing. Sometime in his past, or many times, Wilder had faced illness, maybe even death, and survived. She wanted to know about those times.

One afternoon, as he was upstairs in their room recovering, she stole into his library, where he worked and kept his important papers. Pulling out drawers, she looked through an endless legion of folders and pulled down stacks of books to shake them out. She came across nothing that was unfamiliar or surprising; Wilder Thomas had been demonstrably transparent. She could point out the subjects in the sepia wedding photo on the wall: his father, the groom, in a dark suit; the bride, his mother, in a white gown; uncles and aunts; two flower girls with crowns of autumn leaves who belonged to one of the uncles. He had two sisters he spoke to on occasion; over the phone, Belinda would periodically wish them holiday cheer. She was well versed in Mexia, the Texas city where Wilder had grown up and that he never wished to return to because of the unbridled injustice they meted out on Blacks, particularly on Juneteenth '81—Juneteenth the pinnacle of Black joy in Texas—when white cops did what they do in America: they killed three Black boys in Mexia. Wilder had learned from that experience. It was the main reason he was especially wary of Black joys, he'd told her.

She moved over to his desk, on which sat their own wedding photo. They were both in muted suits—fitting for a slapdash court wedding. From one drawer she pulled out a file that contained Wilder's medical records, and she flipped through the papers hungrily, as if she might have missed something. The worst of Wilder's chronic ailments was what she knew it to be: high blood pressure. This did not override her intuition, however. There was more to his weakness. More he was keeping from her.

She could just ask him. She could. If only for the purpose of understanding more for the next time, when he might not survive. But she did not ask. She realized that she could not. It felt like venturing into his memories of Vietnam, which was also something forbidden to speak of, a choked memory.

The rest of the day followed an unremarkable tune: As Belinda had long since overcome her aversion to horses, the two of them went riding across the ten-acre property of perfectly manicured grass, their usual course from the horse stable up to the low fence wall. During dinner they agreed that the chef, Simon, had outdone himself. After dinner, they shared another bottle of merlot. They made love and he dozed off before she did. As she prepared for bed, she found herself in the bathroom weeping like a captive at last out of earshot. She wept for feeling constrained by the sacrifices she needed to make to achieve what was rightfully hers, a green card, and that Wilder, with his furtiveness about his past, was not reciprocating her love for him. She was alone.

Four

Last night, when she was by herself in the alcove after Edith left to cut the wedding cake, Belinda almost called Wilder to tell him about what she'd learned about Mr. Nti's duplicity, but she quickly decided that a real-time conversation would be more appropriate. She instead messaged him about Jacob—*My brother is even stranger than I thought, more when I'm home*—and to inquire after Laurent, who she'd thought would pick her up for the wedding. Merely annoyed at having to acclimate herself to a new driver, she hadn't pressured Wilder to do anything. She should have predicted that he would call the car company to demand that Laurent be assigned to her for the remainder of her stay in Washington. The car company had lured Laurent to work during his time off with the assurance of double pay. He'd been late picking up Belinda from the Corcoran because he'd had plans arranged for his day off, some of which could not wait. The rest of his weekend, however, belonged to her, he assured her when he arrived for today's expedition. He would drive her to Timbuktu if that was her aim.

Instead she wanted to visit Patricia. She'd forgotten about Laurent's purported knowledge of Alexandria and was startled when he described Patricia's apartment building, which had once been her own, a tall beige building that was part of a development of multiunit high-rises. The one with the green awning over the front door, he said. "You can even see it from here."

He meant that she could see the litter of high-rises from the highway, which was not the case, as right now they were still in Arlington. As she stared through the town car's window, awaiting the moment when Alexandria would emerge, Laurent divulged that he, too, knew Patricia. They locked eyes in the rearview mirror and he winked at Belinda's alarmed expression.

Patricia stood about Belinda's height, he said. Five-two, five-three, give or take an inch. She kept her hair in braids; her eyes were slits, almost like a Chinese person's.

"Epicanthic folds," Belinda offered.

"Yes. That," Laurent noted.

Patricia's upper lip, he continued, displayed a unique dip in the middle. "I think of it like an upside-down *W*. She's always coming and going in those scrubs of hers. She works at Sun Life Nursing Home, off Cardinal Drive."

Slumped into the black leather, Belinda asked, "What don't you know?"

Playfully, he said, "Just call me Mayor of Alexandria. A good mayor knows his citizens. From the pauper to the prince."

"Where does Patricia fall?" she asked.

"We are all paupers," he said. "But maybe her child will be a prince. In my country, we say that the bigger the belly, the brighter the child's future."

For a second, she thought she'd identified trouble in Laurent's mayordom. Then she remembered the ten years she and Patricia had gone without seeing each other. She also remembered her father's claim that Patricia had a new man in her life.

"She's pregnant?" Belinda asked.

"Big as a balloon," Laurent said. "I don't know how those scrubs of hers are still holding on."

As this was her day off, Patricia was out of her scrubs. She wore a less restrictive polka-dotted caftan and was, as Laurent had indicated, big as a balloon. When she returned to the square dining table and set a glass of water in front of Belinda, her dress caught the table edge and Belinda got a peek at the outline of her belly.

"It's not why I decided to end the marriage," Patricia said, rubbing her belly, as if the soft caress would pardon the betrayal.

"Jacob doesn't know?" Belinda said.

"No, I don't think he does."

"Does anybody in Ghana know?"

"My mother, of course. And the rest of my family." Patricia sat down across from Belinda. In the fullness of her face was a dourness that looked like embarrassment.

Patricia sipped from her glass. When she brought it from her mouth, a tiny drop sat in the dip in her upper lip. She pressed on it with her thumb, lathering the tiny dot into her skin. "I wasn't getting any younger, Belinda," she said. "You know I always wanted a family."

The two-bedroom apartment's layout befitted an American working couple with children. The living room furniture was a full three-piece set, in dark gray fabric that would hide any spills from a toddler's cup. The flat-screen television sat on a decorative oak stand. The stand shone a cheap gloss, which Belinda supposed to be a protective layer for when Patricia's children inevitably scratched the wood.

Were there already other children? Belinda saw no faint squiggles evincing a child's exploration of the room's light cream walls. She asked, "This is going to be your first?"

"I admit that I betrayed your brother," Patricia said, not answering the question. "But I held on for many years. Until I was at my wit's end."

Belinda glanced at the open sliding glass doors. The air coming through them was cold and the room's temperature was dropping. She wanted the door shut.

Noticing, Patricia admitted, "I get hot so quickly these days but I can close it."

Belinda affected surprise. "How did you know?"

"You were looking at the sliding door," Patricia said. "Do you want me to close it?"

"No," Belinda said, deciding she would not make a pregnant woman more uncomfortable. "I was only daydreaming."

"Makes sense," Patricia said. "It was once your place."

"Doesn't feel like it anymore."

When she was in law school, Belinda had lived in an on-campus studio apartment her first year. By the end of that year she wanted more space and found this Alexandria apartment in the For Rent section of *The Washington Post*. Kara's parents, Rutherford and Suzette, had rejected the idea and had offered to assist her with paying for a larger place closer to campus.

She declined their offer but appealed to their charity when she proposed that they serve as cosigners on the lease. She mailed it to them. Two days later, they returned it in a larger brown envelope with the family crest—a somewhat tacky take on the Great Seal of the United States—in the upper left corner. Clipped to the signed documents were two flapping sheets: a five-thousand-dollar check and a congratulatory note on monogrammed stationery.

She used the money to minimally furnish the place: two discounted pullout sofas and a glass coffee table for the living room, and a mattress and box spring that she placed on the floor of the bigger bedroom. She collected kitchenware in bits—her first purchases were one frying pan, one saucepan, a wooden spoon, and a spatula. Her second included a cheap set of dishware and silverware. Her plan was to find a roommate for the other room.

Her first roommates, Lucretia and Musu, were two Liberian women with secondary-school haircuts who'd spotted her slapdash advertisement at the barbershop they frequented for their secondary-school haircuts. In orange marker on computer paper, it had read: *One bedroom available in two-bedroom apartment. $500. 145 Wrangler Ln. 571-336-8282.* Individually, they could afford half the amount; together, they could afford all of it, which was why they'd called Belinda as a pair.

Musu contributed the forty-inch television, a gift from the man with whom she spent most of her free time. Often coming home to find Lucretia alone in the pullout with the remote in hand, Belinda worried about an imminent marriage that would leave Lucretia on her own and unable to afford the rent. Except it was Lucretia who fled first to live with her new husband, only months after she moved in; it was Musu who was left to rattle on assurances of swiftly finding someone for the other side of her queen-size bed.

She proudly delivered Patricia, whom Musu knew from the nursing home where they both worked. Patricia had only been in America for a year, Musu said, but she was already bettering herself: she was enrolled in an accelerated program to become a licensed practical nurse. Right now, they were both certified nursing assistants. If she didn't get her own act together, Musu added, Patricia would become her boss in no time.

Nursing school was costly, and Patricia needed to cut costs. Paying only $250 a month in rent was just what the doctor ordered. And Patricia was a gift for which Belinda ought to have been doubly grateful, Musu stressed. Like Belinda, Patricia had grown up in Ghana, more specifically, in Kumasi. Yet in spite of Musu's desperation to force a friendship, their similarities stopped there. Patricia had attended government schools in Kumasi and a secondary school that Belinda had never heard of. After secondary school, Patricia had enrolled as a part-time student at the polytechnic while helping with her mother's business.

Eventually, Musu's man woke up and married her, so she moved out. Now officially a licensed practical nurse, Patricia was making enough to cover the entire five hundred dollars. She also put her paycheck to work in other ways; the kitchen cabinets soon overflowed with pots and pans. Whenever Patricia cooked, she assembled a family of pans on the counter in an intentional order of increasing concavity with the deepest pan always on the stove, its contents bubbling. She claimed not to know what it meant to cook for one or two and that she ached to cook for more, whether she could afford to or not. "I was put on this earth to be someone's wife. Preferably someone from Ghana," she said. "Oh, and I want at least five kids. Do you want kids?" she asked Belinda.

Belinda, possessing a law degree from GW and contending with all sorts of uncertainties, only said, "Maybe."

In the new century, Belinda also packed her bags. For Texas, a distance much farther than Lucretia or Musu had gone for their husbands. Patricia planned on moving into the larger room and finding someone for the other. A succession of someones would come over the years. Five years after moving to Texas, Belinda connected her with Jacob. In no time Patricia informed Belinda that she'd given her new roommate an ultimatum. "I told *her* that when Jacob comes, she would have to put on more clothes or move out."

It did not surprise Belinda that even though she was yet to be married to Jacob, Patricia was already operating with the image of his coming to America. When Patricia committed, she committed fully, which was part of the reason Belinda had chosen her for her brother.

Belinda knew the names of the succession of roommates Patricia had shuffled through. It had come to her as a surprise that the most recent one, according to her father, had been a man. At first she chose not to believe him, thinking of it as another one of the several unfounded accusations her father, in frustration, had been leveling. In the time before her brother married Patricia, Belinda would have called her to find out the truth. But over the years their friendship had withered due to distance and the wedge issue of Jacob, their last phone call a far-flung memory.

Now at the scene of the supposed adultery, with the evidence right before her eyes, Belinda searched for proof of the man with whom Patricia was supposed to be splitting the rent and with whom she'd begun an unfaithful life.

"Who's the father?" Belinda asked.

"You don't know him."

"Ghanaian?"

"Yes."

"You two live together?"

"We do. He's at work. Quantico," Patricia said. "Marine."

Instantly, Belinda juxtaposed Jacob's virility with that of Patricia's marine. Objectively speaking, Jacob was less manly. "A marine. Was that the appeal?"

"He's Ghanaian. And he has a green card. And he was even more ready than I was," Patricia said. "The military was the least of his appeals."

"I was thinking that maybe you were attracted to the contrast."

Patricia pouted knowingly. "I thought Jacob was soft, but I never thought him less of a man."

With her finger, Belinda traced a circle on the table.

"I must admit, there was something about Jacob I couldn't quite put my finger on," Patricia said.

"You thought he was gay?"

"I didn't give that serious thought." She stood up and squeezed behind two dining chairs to tug the sliding door shut. "Of course I wondered if I was going to be able to satisfy him. He was just different from any other man I've known. The men I know have been more outright about . . . you know?"

"And?"

"Oh, we overcame that. Your brother and I would have gotten on very well."

The sudden blush of mischief about Patricia's face sickened Belinda: Patricia appeared to be in cahoots with Jacob's perverse inclination. But then it warmed her—they were two peas in a pod after all, just as she'd predicted they would be. What further secrets lay in the pod?

"Jacob and I last spoke three years ago. When he called to tell me that my mother had died," Belinda said. "What did he say about me?"

Patricia wasn't forthcoming. "You left Ghana when you were young. I never expected you two to be close."

"But what has he said about me?"

"I'm not surprised you two haven't spoken. Frankly, I think you irritate him. And with how things went between him and me ... well—"

"He holds me responsible," Belinda said.

"I don't think so. He's reasonable," Patricia said. "But you've been lucky. He hasn't been." She pulled her phone from her dress pocket and tapped it. Handing it to Belinda, she said, "This is Reginald."

In Reginald's military portrait, his cap was slightly cocked. His eyes bulged and Belinda thought that the combination of their extreme eyes—Patricia's lost behind her epicanthic folds, Reginald's bulging—meant a perfect set for their children. On the left side of his uniform a thin red strip shone as its single decoration.

"How long has he been a marine?" Belinda asked.

"Getting to two years."

In the photo's background, an American flag hung partially in view. "You know, my husband, Wilder, was in the military, too," Belinda said.

"You never told me."

"That's because he doesn't talk about it. He's mentioned it what . . . twice? I remember each time. First was because I was bullshitting about Colin Powell, which I thought would get him to say something. The second was immediately after my mother died—" She stopped, having revealed too much to Patricia. If part of today's plan was for herself to crack, this was not the time. "You said Reginald has a green card?" she asked. "He's not yet a citizen?"

"No."

"So you are still waiting for your papers."

"I am," she said. "But I have the security of being married to an American military man."

"How long have you been married? Had to have been before your family went to see my father last month."

Patricia looked down at her stomach. "I'm in my eighth month, which means I've been married for about seven."

So she committed bigamy, Belinda thought. Instead of debating the legal ramifications of Patricia's behavior she asked, "When will he become a citizen?"

"By the end of the year. It is our plan to start the process for my green card first thing next year."

"That's encouraging."

"How long did yours take?" Patricia asked.

"That thing you were saying about luck? Believe it or not, I'm still waiting."

"Still?"

"One delay after another. I have a rising stack of immigration letters with all kinds of excuses," Belinda said, returning the phone to Patricia. "But soon. Do you love him?"

In response, Patricia opened her mouth in disbelief. "That's the very last question I'd expect from you." She pocketed the phone.

"Why?"

"Do you love Wilder?"

"I do."

"Did you love him from the start?"

"I didn't go into marriage looking for love."

Patricia smiled and snapped her fingers. She said, "What's the word that white people use when they agree? It's at the tip of my tongue. It starts with a *D* . . ."

"Ditto?"

"Yes," Patricia declared. "Ditto!"

As if she had been thrust into a heat wave, Patricia stood up and frantically fanned out her dress.

"Hot?" Belinda asked.

"Pregnancy is something else. I'm hot when it's cold. I'm cold when it's hot." She went into the kitchen to the refrigerator. Opening the freezer, she brought out an ice tray. Wiggling the tray proved ineffective at releasing the cubes, so she slammed it repeatedly against the counter. When the ice was freed, she dropped some into a glass and returned to the dining table. She sat down and started sucking on a cube. "I would have gone back to Ghana," she said. "I would have gone back to be with Jacob." Belinda doubted that but Patricia pressed on. "I fell madly in love with your brother, Belinda. I couldn't tell you what it was. One morning I woke up and I felt it: I had fallen head over heels in love with him. But my love has sense. I'm not like other women who love without sense. What would I have gone back to do? There's a reason I left, you know. Go back and help my mother with her business? Imagine what people would have said. She went to America and returned to square one. If Jacob had at least had a good job, something we could have both relied on, I would have gone back in a heartbeat."

"And leave your life here?"

"What life? Hiding from immigration? I don't even use my own name to work." Her voice broke. "I slipped a few times when I first started. Instead of Mavis Gyimah, I filled out some of my paperwork as Patricia Ofori. My managers believed me when I told them that I was still learning English. Never mind the fact that I had correctly spelled the other name. Or the fact that English is Ghana's official language." She stopped to wipe the drool worming down her chin. "That was no life worth living. With Reginald, things are changing for me. Before him I had my bags open, available for a good reason to pack."

"You didn't tell me any of this."

"Jacob's your brother. I couldn't tell you everything. And other than your call to tell me you were coming into town, we haven't talked in a long time. Years." Patricia flexed her fingers, presumably to relieve them of the tensing chill from the ice cubes. "See how fat they are?"

Belinda could only focus on one of the fingers. "You took a cue from me," Belinda said. "No ring."

"On the contrary," Patricia said, inspecting her own ringless finger. "I love rings." She rested her hand on the table and glided it closer to Belinda. "My fingers are just too fat for them now. Don't you see?"

They were stubby and pulsed faintly from the rush of blood.

This was Belinda's opening. "What did you do with Jacob's?" she asked.

"I sent it back."

"You did?"

"He didn't get it?"

"I'm sure he did. I only thought to ask," Belinda said. "You mailed it?"

"Philomena took it."

"Who?"

"Jacob never mentioned her?" Patricia asked. "She moved into town after you left. A very kind woman. She's always going to Ghana. And was always happy to take things for Jacob."

She was the mail woman, the one her father often spoke of. "Postwoman," Belinda said.

"Postwoman?"

"That's what my father calls her."

Patricia's face squeezed in laughter. "Clever," she said. "I might start calling her that."

"It wouldn't make sense now," Belinda said. "I can't imagine you'll be sending things to Jacob."

They were out of words for a moment, which permitted the slow rise of ghostly noise from the other apartments. Belinda pushed the conversation along. "What is Postwoman like?" she asked. "She seems mysterious. Even to my father."

Patricia said, "Let's see . . ." She gazed at the glass. "She's a bona fide businesswoman. You name it, she's shipped it to Ghana for sale."

"Explains the many trips."

"Yes, but I'm almost positive there's something else. Someone."

"She's not married?"

"At least not in this country," Patricia said coyly. "Who knows who she has in Ghana? I'm my own best reason to think she has someone there. Does that mean you still haven't gone back?"

"I haven't."

"Honestly, Belinda, I never understood your refusal to return. Mine makes sense. There was nothing for me to go back to. Nothing durable for me to take with me. And all those blackouts going on in the country? I would go back into literal darkness. But you, Belinda. All of Wilder's money. And all of your degrees. What difference would a green card make?"

"I said that Wilder had only discussed Vietnam twice. I lied," Belinda said by way of answering. "These days he's obsessed with the blackouts in Ghana. He says before he left for Vietnam he was studying ways to harness natural gas for electricity. He actually said *Vietnam*. So that makes it three times."

Patricia had no interest in her answer. "What difference would a green card make?" she repeated.

"A lot," Belinda said. "The green card is my something durable." She searched for the right words and was surprised at how fluidly they collected within her. "You spoke to your situation. Now let me speak to mine. America plucked me from Ghana because I was among the best. This country likes to have the best. And it kept reassuring me that I was among the best by giving me access to all of its privileged spaces. Then, suddenly, the punch line: 'We were only toying with you, Belinda; you are not one of us. No green card for you.' It feels like the cruelest joke."

"It's not you, Belinda. It's Wilder. He's the one appealing for the green card on your behalf. So he's the one they are denying."

"That's exactly what makes the joke so damn cruel," Belinda said. "Let's show you how much you are not one of us, Belinda. A full-fledged American can't even make it happen for you."

"Maybe Wilder is not so full-fledged. You thought about that? What do you really know about him?"

"I know all I need to know about Wilder. He's Black American. Not so full-fledged, then, right?"

"That's not what I meant, but I see your point," Patricia said. "But that's America's darkness, Belinda. Unlike Ghana's, it's not literal. You can't see it. You will lose your mind trying to defeat darkness you can't see."

"Like Wilder has lost his?" Belinda said.

"More or less. From the little you've told me, he hates this country very much. You want this country to embrace you just as much. Different manifestations. Same offender." Patricia leaned toward her. "That darkness can change you. Let me tell you a story. I bought Jacob some books to help him prepare for his interviews at the embassy. I studied them before sending them to him. For good karma, you know? Maybe if I studied America through and through, I would miraculously get my papers. Isn't that funny? Anyway, everything in Virginia is Robert E. Lee this, Robert E. Lee that, so I was surprised that he was not in any of the monuments books. I thought I would at least see the statue they have of him in Richmond. So I asked one of my patients at Sun Life. Sweetest old white lady. She told me Robert E. Lee was a shame. Not right for a book on monuments of pride. I had so many questions, but I left it there. She was uncomfortable talking about it and I wanted to make her comfortable. But the questions, Belinda, I kept asking myself. How is he a shame when everything is Robert E. Lee this and that? And that tall statue in Richmond? So I take it back: in the Robert E. Lee case you can actually see the darkness. And you have a white person telling you that yes, you are right, it is a darkness, and that's why America won't celebrate it in a book on monuments. But then why celebrate it with a statue? Why have thing after thing named after it? I had to stop trying to make sense of it, Belinda. Jesus. What a mindfuck!"

The real mindfuck was Wilder, Belinda thought—and the reasons he acted the way he did were traceable, she'd concluded, to Vietnam. So when her mother passed, she capitalized on the moment and Wilder's love for her and asked about Vietnam.

"The last nineteen years of my mother's life are impossible for me to understand because I wasn't there for them," she said to him. "I can't have parts of your life be like that to me. I feel like you're holding back, that you're not letting me know all of you. I can handle it. Whatever trauma you experienced during the war."

Wilder let out a long breath. "Yes, Belinda, the truth is a kind of trauma," he said.

He was toying with her, she knew, and it angered her deeply, because America had been toying with her all these years, too. She would hold back no more. "You're a hypocrite, Wilder. You go on and on about the wickedness of this country, but you are just as wicked, keeping things to yourself."

She stormed off, not caring if he had anything else to say. Her outrage lasted; for days, she kept her distance. Even when they got back on speaking terms, the outrage still burned in her and she found herself unloading on her widower father, likely worsening his still-fresh grief: "I can count on two fingers the times Wilder has spoken about Vietnam. Hell, if you can even fucking count those as saying something." Later, she regretted how she'd put it.

Yes, it was true that she and Wilder had never set terms to their relationship. Their marriage of convenience, despite its quick transformation into a real marriage, still had boundaries they'd never set. She'd known from the start—Kara had made it abundantly clear—not to press Wilder on Vietnam. But wasn't it also understood that part of being his real wife was letting her in? Into his past, his fears, his rage?

After all, he'd shown her his Black rage and welcomed her on that front. No philosophizing about truth and trauma. It was intelligible Black anger, testaments of which now made them butt heads.

"This country ain't worth it, Belinda," he'd commented about her patience for, as he put it, "the green card bull."

The last letter from the INS had caused her to start resenting Wilder's money. Wilder's *assets*, according to the letter, had prolonged an otherwise quick background check. Green card bull? "Easy for a rich man to say," she told him.

"You know damn well it ain't about my money," he snapped. "Rich nigger. Poor nigger. Ain't no difference to white folks."

"I've told you many times, Wilder, your Black is not my Black."

"I know that. Them fucked-up ancestors o' yours. Makin' cargo o' ma Black."

"You mad at me for that? That's what's behind your sabotage?"

"Sabotage?" he repeated in disbelief. "Some sabotage. Sabotage that come with a mansion and some good-ass money."

"All of which I would gladly give up."

"Me?" he asked. "Mean give me up?"

That was out of the question; she was in too deep with him. She knew that. He knew that, too. He'd asked, with softness, to bring down the dial.

After the time it took for both of them to calm down, he said, "It's not worth it, Bels. Beats me why your Black wants approval from people who've not come around to seeing my Black as more than cargo."

"But they've come around some, Wilder." His disappointment showed on his face, but she pressed on. "My Black only wants a piece."

That conversation was a climax to what had followed her second and final prodding about Vietnam in the wake of her mother's passing. To her relief, the agony of her mother's death was calibrated by Obama's triumph a while later. Wilder, on the other hand, was morose. He believed that after Obama white people would deliver the lowest of Black lows, and he began to preempt what he believed was to come.

He notified five hundred business associates by email of his lost appetite for white colleagues. One delegation of Black businessmen defied him, bringing one of their white counterparts to Wilder's office for a meeting. From his chair at the head of the conference room table, Wilder looked at Belinda, and she could see what he was plotting. Before she could stop him, he pitched a letter opener at the white man expertly enough that it whisked a breath past the man's right eye. Everyone stayed put in shock. He demanded that they all leave the room.

Belinda stayed. "Now they know I was not joking," he said to her.

Even driving, Wilder had the capacity to quickly spy a white person crossing the street. He would pounce on the gas but would ease his foot the moment the target ran to get out of the way. "Giving them a little bit of their medicine. Before they wreak it on us," he'd say.

One night last year, he'd shaken her out of sleep. "I have something to show you," he said. "It's important."

Outside, the night was pitch-black. Underneath her nightgown she felt her skin perspiring from the heat. He led her to the stable and aimed a flashlight behind the building. She saw the smoldering embers and smelled the burned leather. When they got closer a mound of ash and carcass greeted her.

"That horse got onto the property," Wilder said over the dead animal.

"So you burnt it?"

"Shot it down first," he said. "Now those white folks will know to keep their shit off my land." He dug into the remains with a stick. "And what do you care anyway? You hate horses. After all the time it took me to get you to feel comfortable around mine, then this shit comes onto the scene to fuck up my efforts? Nope!"

She ran back to bed. Wilder did not join her. Under the sheets, terror immobilized her, then, just as quickly, a second wave, of love, charged through her. It was impossible to confront a man willing to kill for her with the accusation that he might be her greatest obstacle to her heart's desire. And yet the question would not leave her: What had Wilder Thomas done in Vietnam that was standing in the way of her green card?

Perhaps, Belinda thought as she sat across the table from Patricia, she could lead her to some answers. Belinda would not go into specifics about Wilder's past actions, however. She would never go into detail about her husband, out of the duty that came with love—you were supposed to protect those you loved from judgment. In truth, there was another force behind her restraint: she did not want anyone to know that she sympathized with Wilder. There was sense to Wilder Thomas, so much so that she'd found herself once admitting to Jacob—she supposed she'd let him in because he'd recently agreed to Patricia—"With what I'm going through with my papers, sometimes I can see where Wilder's coming from."

What she could see was nothing compared to what the passing years with Wilder opened her eyes to. During the drive from Reagan National to the Ritz, Laurent had instructed her to laugh about the Obama birth certificate "stupidity." She had never been able to muster a blithe laugh like Edith. How could she now, when it was evident that if a Black American president had to prove himself American, then there was real sense to Wilder Thomas's beliefs?

To Wilder, it was abundantly clear that America was not going to budge in Belinda's favor; in time, she would be pushed out of the country, and Belinda herself had started quietly pondering how she might go out momentously. Privately, she delighted in Wilder's dramatic near homicides and in the horse-killing, which were enticing examples of what Americans called "going out with a bang." Now when the question arose—What had Wilder Thomas done in Vietnam that was standing in the way of her green card?—it was more out of curiosity about what had happened and less about the card itself. Perhaps the act was the secret to going out with a real bang.

"What are you driving at about Wilder?" Belinda asked Patricia.

"Forget Wilder. My concern is you," Patricia replied. "You are entitled to your fight. My American experience is different from yours. I came here for money. You came here for money, too. But yours involved books. You used the word *privilege*. That privilege gave you time to think about things theoretically, fight theoretical fights. Part of why I stopped thinking about Robert E. Lee is because I don't have time. I'm too busy chasing after just a little bit of what you have."

"It's not just theoretical, Pat. The green card is a real thing."

"For people like me it is," Patricia said. "I can't say that it is for people like you. You've been using parables to explain why it matters to you. You even have me speaking in parables. How real can it be?" Patricia poked the ice inside the glass. "Or is it just that you don't like to lose?"

Belinda heard the question but her attention narrowed on the ice cubes. Incredibly, they still piled jaggedly to the top of the glass. They had resisted losing their stickiness, instead fusing together in their stubborn chill.

"Can you call him?" Belinda said.

"Call who?"

"Jacob."

"Why?" And yet Patricia took out her phone.

"He will pick up a call from you. It's about time he and I spoke."

Patricia touched the screen and put the phone to her ear. She pulled it from her ear after listening for some time. "Nothing," she said. She tried again. "Nothing," she repeated. "It's dead."

Light

One

I n the tight grip of an expectant mood, Alfred slowly pushed
open the bedroom door. He tiptoed in. On the right edge of
the bed, his mother slept on her side with her hands clasped beneath her chin. Her head was half-propped on the pillow and her
body was curved. Robert faced her, the arch of his body more ex-
pressive, owing to the flexibility from his days as a sprinter. His
pillow ballooned into two halves between his legs. His arms, which
appeared abnormally long against the pale blue linen, reached out,
as if to catch a toss or to take his wife in his arms.

One of the American storybooks Aunty Belinda had sent
his father lay open on the bed: M-A-M-A D-A-Y. G-L-O-R-I-A
N-A-Y-L-O-R. Alfred pushed the book aside and crept between
his parents. He could not decide whom to shake awake and announce that he was about to leave for the day. Unexpectedly missing his morning run, his father, he thought, might want to be
rocked out of sleep. More and more the sky's blossoming orange
was staining the curtains, further highlighting his father's prolonged sleep. Maybe there was a sickness he needed to sleep away.
Alfred leaned closer to his father's lips and listened. The rasp from

Robert was a normal sound. His father's breath did not have the added odor typical of catarrh. So he reckoned him to have been overtaken by a powerful exhaustion. About time, he thought; his father was always on the move.

He turned to his mother and found her eyes on him. He tugged at the collar of his crisp shirt and the waist of his shorts to communicate his preparedness for the day. She took stock of him, starting with his hair, where she aimed her reach, gliding her arm to mimic a comb in her hand.

Alfred sat up with his thumb upright: he would certainly run a comb through his knobby hair before he left.

She felt his shirt fabric and mouthed, *Fine*, sounding the usual murmur that accompanied the only three words she ever mouthed: fine, no, yes. She mouthed *fine* about his shorts as well, then signed that their navy color was the perfect complement to the shirt's off-white.

She gestured at his feet.

"Socks?" Alfred signed.

She nodded.

He pulled a pair from his pocket and dangled them in front of her. She fanned for them.

"No," Alfred indicated with a shake of his head. "I can do it," he signed, slamming the socks against his chest.

She knew he could, and signed as much. However, in the interest of time—she pointed at the clock on the wall—he ought to allow her. She put on his socks in a fraction of the time it would have taken him to get to the end of the bed, set his feet on the floor, and bend to steadily pull on each sock with one hand.

She gestured again at his feet, tying an invisible shoelace.

"My old sneakers," he responded, brushing behind himself with a wave intended to convey a time long gone, when he'd first acquired the shoes from his aunt in America. He squeezed his face to emphasize the displeasure the shoes brought him: they smelled bad and they fit tight. "They are the only ones I have now," he signed.

Before he could stop her, his mother slipped on her sandals and went through the door. She was waiting in the living room with the impoverished sneakers.

He let her fasten them onto his feet. His toes glued together painfully and he tapped her on the shoulder to express that she'd laced them too tightly. Loosening the laces, she tried again, all while looking up at his face for a grimace.

"Fine?" she mouthed.

"Fine," he said, thinking he could survive the mild pinch of the shoes for another day.

He spied Yaa stuffing his lunch pail into his schoolbag.

"But I'm not going to school," he called out.

"I know that," she barked. "Where else do you expect me to put your lunch pail? In that one hand of yours?" She held the straps of the bag with curled fingers. "Come here so I can put it on your back."

When she put it on him, he moved his back and shoulders so the lopsided bag would settle more comfortably. "It's heavy," he said.

"That's because I gave you more food," Yaa said. "You will be long."

"Just chairs," he said. "And then we will go for the beans. We won't be long."

Yaa winced in doubt. "You will be lucky if you make it back with time for *Rambo*."

He felt a whirlpool of disappointment take him at the thought of missing the time he had to watch the latest version of *Rambo*. Aunty Postwoman—Uncle Jacob said her name was Aunty Philomena, but he preferred to call her Aunty Postwoman, it was more fun—Aunty Postwoman had given the DVD to Uncle Jacob last Sunday. Because of power rationing—off-and-on light; so much off, very little on—they hadn't yet watched it. Two days ago, Yaa had pretended to be Rambo. She'd tied a red bandanna around her head and strung oranges around her arms for bigger biceps. Against the shadows of the candlelit kitchen she made explosion sounds. She'd done her best, but her acting hadn't lifted his spirits. Noticing his glum face, Yaa recited some lines from his favorite, *First Blood Part II*, even managing a believable man's voice: *I want what they want and every other guy who came over here and spilled his guts and gave everything he had: for our country to love us as much as we love it. That's what I want.*

"That was really good!" exclaimed Alfred.

"I know," Yaa said.

"But that's not what I want."

"You don't want our country to love us?" Yaa giggled at her own cleverness.

"I want the new Rambo. Uncle Jacob said the new Rambo is old. I want to see old-man Rambo."

"Because you want to see if he looks like Uncle Wilder?"

Alfred had not been thinking that. But now that she mentioned it, yes, he did want to see if the new Rambo resembled

Uncle Wilder. The DVD case was white, no picture; and the disc was silver, no picture.

So the expectant mood in which he'd rolled out of bed was attributable to the six hours of uninterrupted electricity—from five p.m. to eleven p.m.—that had been assured by the Electricity Company of Ghana, ECG. He believed them because they'd stuck to their word this morning; he'd woken before six a.m. to find that, as they'd promised, there was light, and as they'd promised, it had gone out at seven a.m. Not before he'd gotten the opportunity to speak with Aunty Belinda and found the courage to ask her for a new pair of Nikes. Thank God she'd agreed to buy them for him.

Bedtime was ten p.m. Grandpa would be in his bedroom by eight p.m. He had more than enough time for Rambo with Uncle Jacob and Yaa; he could hardly wait to be awed. Before that, however, he would enjoy his day of adventure with Uncle Benjamin. In his father's van, they would drive to a place in Kejetia to pick up new chairs for the computer school Uncle Benjamin and Uncle Jacob were setting up at the café. After, they would travel for maybe an hour for beans, the kinds with the black eyes. They belonged to Maame Beans, a woman who had started bringing her business to his father. He liked her money and had at first refused Uncle Benjamin the use of the van. Eventually, he'd agreed to rent it out at a discount to the budding partnership between Uncle Jacob and Uncle Benjamin on the assurance that Uncle Benjamin would collect the beans after he attended to the chairs.

They would be back by three at the latest, at least two hours before ECG said they'd give them light. Nothing had struck him as portending a different outcome to the day. He wondered if Yaa had introduced the possibility of disappointment for an ulterior motive.

"Are you playing with me?" he asked.

"Why would I do that when I want to watch it with you?"

Rationing his words, he said, "But it's just the chairs. And the beans. It's not like we are traveling to Accra."

"Maybe you are right," she said as she trailed him and his mother toward the door. "Maybe."

On the veranda, his grandfather worked the pages of a newspaper as he would an accordion. "Off already?" he asked.

"Bright and early," Alfred said. "That's what Uncle Benjamin said."

It was indeed bright. But past early. As they stood waiting on Otumfuo along the dry gutter, he stood with Yaa on one side, his mother on the other. A passing gang of cocks scuffed the pebbled sand with their claws. They crowed in succession.

Uncle Benjamin was nowhere to be seen.

"Want to check the café?" Yaa asked. "He might be there."

"Okay," Alfred said.

He flitted his fingers to apprise his mother of what Yaa had suggested when they saw Benjamin bounding toward them. "Am I late?" he said.

"You said bright and early, Uncle Benjamin."

"I know." He blotted his greasy neck with a handkerchief. "Forgive me."

Alfred could see to immediate forgiveness. He was interested in a more pressing question. "Will we take long?"

"Not too long," Benjamin responded. "Why?"

"*Rambo.*"

"Tonight?"

"Yes."

"Don't worry," Benjamin said reassuringly, "we will be back in time."

Alfred promptly searched for Yaa's eyes but he saw they were focused elsewhere. Caught in a lie, he thought, she was averting judgment.

"Who has the key?" Benjamin asked.

In reply, Alfred raised his arm to his mother's face and jangled the air with his thumb and index finger. She retrieved the set of keys from her pocket and tossed them to Benjamin.

"Thank you," he said. "Tell her we should be back by three."

"You can tell her," Alfred said. "You can use your fingers. So, you say, *three*"—he put up three fingers—"then tap your watch."

Benjamin did as instructed. Martha demonstrated her understanding with a smile, then drummed on Alfred's schoolbag as a reminder for him to have his lunch. With that, they were off.

At Church Wheel, where Alfred's father's two vans were kept, there wasn't a sound. The quiet was haunting, as though Alfred had been propelled into an era with everyone who'd once enlivened the atmosphere dead. Where were the Presbyterians who rattled on their prayers in competition with the Apostolics? Several times he'd imagined God watching back and forth like a boxing judge, picking his side, the Apostolics, as the victor.

"Hop in." Benjamin motioned from the driver's seat.

Alfred turned to show him his schoolbag and Benjamin took

it, setting it in the space between the driver's and passenger's seats, behind a tall gearshift dressed from waist down in a tiered rubber pyramid. For balance as he got into the van, Alfred tucked his right side into the crease of the open door and worked on raising himself onto the passenger's seat.

"Need a hand?" Benjamin asked.

He hopped out of the van before Alfred could answer him. By the time he'd gotten to the opposite side, Alfred had successfully arranged himself.

"I'll get the door," Benjamin offered. "Watch your feet."

A heaviness rumbled in the rear of the van as they pulled out. Alfred looked through the rectangular opening to the cargo compartment and saw concrete blocks.

"What are the blocks for?"

"To keep the chairs in place," Benjamin said. "There's also rope."

He searched for something snakelike. "I don't see any rope," Alfred announced. "It's too dark."

Giving up, he turned forward and started humming.

"You want music?" asked Benjamin. "I can turn on the radio."

"I'm practicing. For Children's Day at church."

"You are singing?"

"All of us," Alfred replied. He sighed.

"You don't want to?"

"Not that," he said. "We have to sing five songs. I'm still memorizing some of the words."

"Well, let's hear one."

"Do you know 'Light of Our Lives'?"

"No," Benjamin said. "But maybe if you sing it?"

Alfred nodded. Gently, he progressed from an initiating hum.

> *Prepare ye, prepare ye,*
> *Prepare ye, prepare ye,*
> *He cometh with clouds*
> *And every eye shall see him*
> *He cometh with clouds*
> *And every eye shall see him*
> *With ten thousand Saints*
> *As a thief in the night*
> *With ten thousand Saints*
> *As a thief in the night*

> *When he comes, darkness will turn to light.*
> *When he comes, darkness will turn to light.*

> *Goodbye darkness.*
> *Hello light.*
> *Goodbye darkness.*
> *Hello light.*

"Do you like it?" Alfred asked.

"Not bad," Benjamin said.

"It's about the second coming."

"That so?"

Alfred stared in disbelief. "Uncle Benjamin, don't you know about the second coming?"

"What should I know about it?"

What should he know? Everything! How remarkably lost of him! His soul, it seemed, needed to be saved. Alfred wanted to do the saving, but undertaking it now would be impertinent, especially without the guiding presence of a superior in Christ. "I'm afraid of it," he admitted.

"Why?" Benjamin said. "Listen to your own song. Goodbye darkness. Hello light. So no more *light-off*. You can watch *Rambo* whenever you want. So why be afraid?"

"I'm still afraid of it," Alfred said. "Where will I go? Heaven? Hell?"

"What's the difference?"

"You don't know?" How could Uncle Benjamin be so clueless? After all, his café's name was "By His Grace." "Heaven is good. Hell is bad," Alfred said carefully, trying to keep the judgment out of his voice.

"Is that so?"

"Yes."

"How do you get into heaven?"

"You have to be good."

"That's all?" Benjamin asked, smiling. "You have nothing to worry about, then. You will be the first person in line."

Hearing this filled Alfred with a specific joy: the promise of eternal life. Yet he could not celebrate in good conscience, having been confronted with evidence that Uncle Benjamin's place in line was far from secure. He said a silent prayer for this man who'd always shown him kindness. He implored God to start showing Uncle Benjamin the wisdom of differentiating between heaven and hell.

In Kejetia, they stopped at an imposing brown gate. Without warning, Benjamin reversed the van to show the gate the vehicle's back. Alfred watched through the side mirror as the gate automatically split in two and Benjamin gently backed up.

A man appeared by Benjamin's side after the gate closed, and Benjamin turned off the engine. "Mister Jacob," he said, his tongue lodging and freeing itself from where his front teeth ought to have lived.

"Benjamin," Benjamin corrected. "Jacob is my partner."

"All right." The man turned aside to clear his throat and hack out phlegm. When he was finished he looked up and stared past Benjamin to assess Alfred. "Who's going to help you?"

"He will," Benjamin replied, gesturing absently at Alfred. "How many chairs are there?"

"Ten."

"We can handle it," he said. "Just show us the way."

Between them they came up with a plan: Benjamin would wait by the van to load while Alfred extracted the chairs one by one from the shed. Being that they were office chairs with wheels, Alfred had several options, like riding on them to the van as if they were convertibles or advancing them speedily with his arm.

Benjamin handed him a yellow rag. "Wipe them first," he said. "And remember to point your nose away."

"Do they smell?" Alfred asked.

"They are old. They got new chairs and now they have no use for ours."

Alfred motioned at the building behind them, a lofty five-story structure. "This is somebody's house?"

"Oh, no," Benjamin said. "It's an office building."

The shed where the chairs were stored sat separate from the main building. Alfred opened the squeaky wooden door, which stretched the cobwebs that covered them like elastic. With the dust rag, he scooped the fibers away and beat off the remnants that had turned to lint on his shirt and shorts.

It was a musty, airless place. Sunshine filmed through lines in the slabs, which provided insufficient light. He had to hold on to the door because it closed each time he let go. "Uncle Benjamin," he shouted, "can you bring one of the blocks?"

Benjamin came over and propped the door open with two blocks. "Since I'm already here," he said, "let me help you with these chairs."

"I can do it, Uncle Benjamin." Alfred flexed his arm. "I don't need help."

Benjamin left him to it. The chairs were scattered about, and Alfred began with the one closest to him. Caked onto it were the hardened carcasses of moths, which demanded intense scrubbing. In order to achieve the ideal stability for wiping, he leaned his back against the wall by the door and proceeded to clean the chair with the balled-up rag. The wheels of the chair slipped often, slowing his progress but not frustrating his commitment to presenting a clean, even shiny chair to Benjamin.

Alfred rode to the van in the first three chairs as if they were open-top, driverless cars. The concrete of the driveway was veined by ruptures and he bumped along like a car along potholed roads.

Pushing the next chair with his chin proved overambitious—he couldn't stop himself from staggering—so he pushed with his arm instead. He alternated between riding and pushing the others.

Sometimes he gave a chair a big shove and ran after it, fearful that his grandfather might appear and reprimand him for getting carried away.

In what seemed like quick work, only one chair remained. Being his last, he mused on how he should end. What hadn't he attempted? Standing on the chair? Too dangerous. Dancing it toward Uncle Benjamin? What fun was that? In the end he decided to tweak the manner in which he'd already been riding in the chairs. He sat in the chair and leaned the back of his head against the headrest so that he could look up at the sky as if he was flying upside down. It proved more difficult than he thought. Only for the quickest of seconds did he go fast enough to blur his vision.

"Spread out your arm," Benjamin suggested. "If you stick out your arm, it will give you better balance."

Alfred tried it three times and each time the sensation of flight eluded him. In frustration, he slipped out of the chair and kicked it forward. It spun toward Benjamin, who caught it.

"It's hard," Benjamin said, hoisting the chair into the van.

"I bet my father could do it."

"You think so?"

"Yes. He can do anything with his body. Somersaults. Climbing trees. Even swimming." Alfred watched as Benjamin secured the last chair. "At the university there's a basketball court," he continued. "I went there with my father. He can even play basketball."

Benjamin jumped out of the back of the van and said, "Basketball is not hard."

"It is for me."

"Only because of your arm. If not for your arm, you would

have been a better athlete than your father." He looked Alfred in the eye, then down at his legs. "Look at your strong legs. Ask Abedi Pele. Ask Anthony Yeboah. They would kill for strong legs like yours."

"I'm not bad at football, actually," Alfred admitted. "I just fall a lot."

"There you go. Your arm."

Back in the van, they waited just outside the gate for their chance to enter traffic. A driver honked to notify Benjamin of the gap he'd created for him and Benjamin strummed the accelerator before filling the gap with the van.

"We only need to get past this traffic," Benjamin said. "There's never traffic on the Kumasi-Tamale road."

Alfred gasped. "We are going to Tamale? Tamale is far!"

Benjamin cackled. "We are going nowhere near Tamale."

"So I will still be able to watch *Rambo*?"

"I promise," Benjamin said.

The Kumasi-Tamale road was narrow, and as Benjamin had promised, it had little traffic. It was further slimmed by its curves and encroaching forest on both sides. Looking as far down the road as he could see, Alfred hoped that something interesting would catch his eye. But the stretch of black road uncoiled forward, with nothing notable.

The boring talk program muttering on the radio lulled Alfred into reflection, and he recalled a lesson on selflessness he'd received from Yaa. If he wanted to be a good person, she had told him, he would need to put others before himself. All day he'd been doing the opposite, harping for Uncle Benjamin to get him home in time for *Rambo*, ignoring whatever other goals for the day Uncle Benjamin had. Something in him turned inside out. He had the urge to apologize.

"It's because of the light, Uncle Benjamin," Alfred said. "That's why."

"Why what?"

"Why I have been worrying you," Alfred said. "I have been waiting forever to watch the latest *Rambo*. But if you have something to do, I will go with you." He trailed off. With more certainty, he added, "Yaa will tell me everything. She will even dress up like old-man Rambo."

"It sounds like you don't believe that we will be home in time."

"I do," Alfred said. "It's just that this road looks like forever."

A red sedan suddenly appeared on the other side of the road. Other cars steadily followed, which beguiled Alfred into reflecting further. Wasn't it funny that his father owned two vans he'd never driven? And could never drive? Come to think of it, what made it vital that a driver should hear? The horns from oncoming cars? The shouts of drivers wanting to cut into traffic? Or did it have to do with the fact that policemen directed traffic with whistles in their mouths like pacifiers?

Anyway, what was Uncle Wilder like? Aunty Belinda used to sometimes let him greet him on the phone. But after Grandpa said Aunty Belinda didn't want to talk about Uncle Wilder and Vietnam, he stopped asking to greet him and Aunty Belinda also stopped offering. How many people did Uncle Wilder shoot? Was his machine gun like Rambo's? How he would have loved to be there with Uncle Wilder in Vietnam. Killing bad people. Killing bad people left and right. If it had been him, he would have bragged to everyone about all the bad people he'd killed and not kept quiet like Uncle Wilder.

The curves in the road had straightened out. Coming toward them in the left lane, a timber truck was hounding a sedan in front of it with loud honks.

"What does the big truck want?"

"For that car to get out of his way."

"But how?" There was only one lane going in each direction. There was no place on either side of the road for cars to pull over.

"Who knows?"

In a flash, the truck swerved into their lane. Alfred gripped the dash but had nothing to hold on to. He made do with pressing his hands onto it firmly, as if forcing breath from it. "What is he doing?"

"Overtaking."

"He's coming," shouted Alfred. "He's coming."

"He won't hit us." Benjamin flashed the headlights, slowing down some.

"He's coming, Uncle Benjamin."

"Don't worry, he will overtake the car," Benjamin said, yelling over the insistent bleat of the van's horn. "He will make it."

In the end, it was Benjamin who made a frantic swerve to avoid a head-on collision. The van veered into the trees along the road and Benjamin was not quick enough on the brakes to avoid plunging down the slope. They pummeled through the greenery. Alfred screamed. Something struck the windshield and sprayed glass shards into his mouth and a gust of alertness made him shut his mouth tight, but not for long because he screamed again when the van flipped. His head struck something hard. A balloon in his head popped. Just then he witnessed a hand reaching for a light switch. No, not another light-off. No, not again. His good arm was not working. He could not reach out to pull the hand away. Everything shut off in him.

Two

S mothered by guilt, Jacob confessed, "I don't feel right."

"Is it me?" Philomena asked.

"No."

"Then what?"

Most of it, Jacob knew, had to do with the white lie he'd told Benjamin. It was innocent, harmless. At least that was what he thought at the time. He couldn't go with him to get the chairs, he'd said. He had to meet with a prospective client in town. Alfred would go instead. What better time than now to begin training the boy for the small tasks they were planning on having him take on at the school?

Jacob's true intentions were an unsettling turn of events. He'd hidden what felt dishonorable: only one day of Philomena's stay in Ghana remained and he wanted more time with her.

The smut between him and her had been building over time, culminating last Sunday when flirtatiously she'd refused to hand over Patricia's ring. To the tune of a childhood lullaby, she'd held it up and said something about a *mistletoe* (an American tradition), daring him to kiss her or alternatively snatch it out of her hand. Each of his lunges had failed. She set the ring glistening on top of her head, then buried it deep within her hair extensions.

She invited him to have a go at the mesh, but by that point he'd tired of her game. He looked away, hoping he could jolt her out of her playfulness. A coolness arose between them as they stood inside Philomena's small living room. Somehow she ended up struggling with a white ironing board that Jacob hadn't noticed among the many items that filled the place. She wanted to fold the ironing board but the legs resisted. In a lurch of frustration, she threw it, and the board fell. He saw the problem and was certain she saw it, too, but was pretending not to.

He decided he would play along. He reached for the board. The cotton covering was hot to the touch and he dropped the board onto its face, its legs in the air like an overturned beetle. The stuck lever, the problem he'd spotted, was there for a quick jerk. She sidled up to him and slid her hand into his trouser pocket, Patricia's ring tickling as she moved it down his thigh. He was being dominated. By the time Philomena's hand reached the pocket's bottom, his penis was completely engorged. They did not proceed with it because he left soon after.

In truth, her seduction started the moment she'd clued him in on Patricia's male roommate. "You are free to do what you want," she said triumphantly.

What he should have wanted was her, which Philomena didn't express directly but exhibited. Her blouse was unbuttoned just enough to show the upper parts of her breasts, where tiny curls of hair resided in the cleavage. The unbuttoned blouse indicated a willingness that awaited his consent. Not one thrilled by gentility, he took his consent home with him. When he returned, she was more aggressive with her words. Patricia's breasts, she said, were not as plump as hers. Patricia's stomach, she added, was loosened by excess skin. But no. Nothing even close to sexual contact between them had transpired, she said, before confessing that she'd learned what Patricia looked like naked after she'd broken the seal of a brown envelope Patricia had handed her to be given to Jacob. She couldn't say what she'd been after in the documents. Perhaps the key to figuring him out? Unfortunately, she'd ended up finding out more about Patricia than she ever wanted to know. She would have never pegged her as the kind of woman who sent a nude photo of herself to her fiancé. An innocent girl like her. With those vanishing eyes. But you could never tell the predilections of man.

If only he had told Benjamin the truth, Jacob now thought, he might have already consummated what had been boiling between him and Philomena, instead of being riddled with disabling guilt.

He confessed to Philomena: "I told Benjamin that I had a business meeting."

"You were embarrassed to tell him that you were coming to see me?"

"A little. You're no longer simply Postwoman."

Six of Philomena's blue drums, which contained the items she'd shipped to Ghana to sell, were spread out in the room. The two in his way impeded movement. She went around the sofa to the drum closest to the door and rested her hand on it. "This one's for your nephew," she said.

"Alfred?"

"You mentioned that you wanted to get him new shoes," she

said. "There are a few in here. It's mostly clothes, though. Shirts. Shorts. Pants. Did he like the movie?"

"We are yet to watch it."

"Why?"

"The power rationing. But we will this evening." Jacob scanned the other drums. "So are these all clothes?"

"Mostly."

"I wasn't aware that you sold clothes, too."

"I sell everything," she said. "Take whatever Americans don't want. There's a market for them here."

"So, these things"—he pointed from drum to drum—"they are all *foose*?"

"I don't like that name," she said. "Call them vintage clothing."

The iPhone Patricia had purchased through Philomena was in his shirt pocket. It had come in a sealed box. "The phones, too?" he asked. "Are Americans getting rid of completely new iPhones?"

"The phones are different," she said. "And it's not only phones. Sometimes it's computers. Sometimes it's TVs. All kinds of electronics." She tapped on the drum a few times to ask Jacob how he would manage to get the heaviness home by himself.

"There are taxis all over. I will get one and the driver will help me get it into the car," he said.

"Okay," she said. "I might as well tell you," she continued, "especially if . . . you and me . . . you know?"

He knew.

"I get the phones and the computers and other things like that from some guys in New Jersey," Philomena said. "They are all stolen. It's some crazy operation that I don't really understand. I imagine a network of thieves working in the stores. Maybe the people that work in the stores are not the ones actually doing the stealing. Maybe they just help the people doing the stealing. Or it could be the people who deliver the things to the stores. Maybe they do the stealing. I don't know. And I don't ask. I just get the things for cheap and sell them for a good profit."

This was hardly the sensational story he was expecting to hear. "You said computers," he said.

"Yes."

"I may need some soon. For the computer school."

Philomena clutched her chest and panted theatrically. He almost laughed.

"An angel like you wants stolen goods?" she asked in mock surprise.

"I'm already knee-deep in them," he responded, waving his phone.

"You didn't know."

"And who says I know now?"

This banter, delicious as it was, had to be its own foreplay. He turned off the phone and the screen went dark. He gave the room another look, wondering where they would prop themselves to make love. She exited through the cane door. Following her, he swung the door out boldly. From the doorway, he saw the back of her head, where the silk of her black hair extensions stayed at her nape in a bun, gilded by a dazzling refraction of faint sunlight. Her thin-strapped, frail housedress was absorbing some of the sunshine.

She was standing atop the front steps of her future home between two concrete columns. Still under construction, her *manse*—she preferred the word because it connoted the house as her crowning achievement—would be one and a half floors, an optical illusion she'd seen in an American architectural magazine.

Jacob exited the two-bedroom wing Philomena was living in while her house was being built. As he came up the rough concrete steps, his shoes made crunching sounds on the dust. He reached her.

"Have I shown you around?" she asked.

"No," he said. "Whenever I'm here, the workers are always here."

"I hadn't realized." She sighed. "You know better how hard it is to get anything done on time in this country. One problem after another." She threw up her hands, as if bowing out. "The power is out so they took the day off."

This announcement contradicted what he'd experienced inside her temporary residence. "But you have light in there," he said, pointing at the powder-blue structure.

"I have a generator."

"You do? I don't hear it."

She pointed with her thumb at the half floor above. "Up there. It's one of the silent ones." She took a few steps inside. "So do you want to have a look around?"

The place felt like a cozy home, despite the absence of a roof. Neither did it matter that the floors were untidy: a mix of dried and fresh leaves blown in from outdoors on a carpet of sand. Buckets of muddy water sat in corners. In one section, wooden planks leaned on a worktable and a pile of wood shavings sat underneath like an unfortunate detail.

Philomena encouraged him to imagine a seventy-five-inch television mounted on a wall of what would become the main living room. Sofas would be positioned at the other end of the room. In America, she had little time to cook. Here, in her soon-to-be state-of-the-art kitchen, equipped with a six-burner range tinted blue (she liked the color), she could bake her specialty: plantain cake.

"Are you allergic to groundnuts?" Philomena asked.

"Is that something people are allergic to?"

She nodded. "It's very common in America."

He ate roasted groundnuts, he said, which paired perfectly with plantain cake.

The first bedroom she showed him was for her mother and father. At the moment, they were renting a cramped house in their hometown. "My father never had enough money to build us a house," she said.

Her brother and his wife and child, and her two unmarried sisters, lived with her parents in the rented house. They would assign themselves to the remaining three bedrooms however they saw fit, she said. She guessed that her youngest sister would be given the smallest room, at the end of the corridor.

The top half floor belonged to her—her own private apartment. A hidden staircase behind the house—it would be hidden from view after the wall was installed—wound up to it.

"I don't know what to do with these," she said of the two side-by-side bedrooms before the master.

Jacob heard it as a disclosure of barrenness. "For your children."

"Maybe," she said. "It needs to happen soon. Forty is not too far off."

"You have time."

She scoffed. "Don't let all of this fool you, Jacob." She meant the grandness of the building she was putting up. "I am still a woman. A woman nearing forty."

The yellow-and-black generator snored in the area she said would be the master suite's bathroom. He'd first heard the sound when they reached the frame built to fit the door to the bathroom.

"I keep seeing water coming from the shower and getting on the generator. How terrible is that?" he said.

"Awful," she said. "I rebuke it."

She was mocking Pentecostal preachers. He smiled. "Do you go to church?"

"When I can."

He noticed the long black electrical cord that extended from the generator to no clear destination. "What is it connected to?"

"The meter."

"Where is it?"

"You know what, I'm not even sure."

She wiggled next to him at a window frame and looked down with him, searching for the wire's end point. From their shoulders to their wrists, their arms skimmed and skimmed.

"It's down there somewhere," she said. "You can check later if you are that interested."

"Only curious," Jacob said.

"It's an odd thing to be curious about," she said, leaving his side. Her voice was out of the room when she called, "Jacob."

He followed the summons and found her in a part of the suite that appeared too small for the king-size bed she'd mentioned earlier. Based on its size, the best use Jacob could envision for it was as a dressing room, which her predilection for hair extensions and makeup underlined.

"When was the last time you and Patricia spoke?" she asked.

"I don't remember. Months."

"She doesn't know that you know?"

"That she's pregnant?" Jacob asked.

Philomena nodded.

"No. Unless you told her."

"Tell her that I let you in on her bad deeds?" she said. "Hardly." From behind one of the concrete walls she retrieved a large piece of cardboard. "It's not lost on me that I'm no saint, Jacob. When I say *bad deeds*, I'm not referring to her alone. I'm no saint," she repeated. "I don't know what came over me. Or when what came over me actually came over me." She laid the cardboard on the floor and proceeded to unfold it. "You are handsome. Very handsome, in fact. But there's something more. This world is full of handsome men. And many of them have come into my life. The problem with them was that they were all handsome in a common way. Handsomeness without particularity. Square jaw. A nice forehead. Chiseled this. Chiseled that. It's tiresome," she said. "Yours isn't. I immediately noticed what was special in those eyes of yours. They are a perfect set. And when they look at you ... my God, when they look at you . . ." She blew sand from the cardboard, skimming over the nooks in it with her mouth. "There was one man I thought I had figured out. Funny enough, he wasn't handsome. Not common. Not uncommon. You could say his looks were simply plain. But he had a way of making everyone around him comfortable. It probably doesn't sound like anything special because you've heard it said about a lot of people. But take it from me, I had never experienced it to that degree. I used to tell him that he could single-handedly convert the racists in America."

Jacob grunted, not quite the laugh her hyperbole had elicited from her. "I was sure we were going to get married," she said. "And guess what? He drove to my job one day to tell me that his family had found a wife for him here. And to add salt to the wound he asked if we could keep going," she said. "Can you believe that?"

"I'm sorry."

"See, there it is," she said. "Your kindness. That's the other thing. You are utterly kind." She tapped the cardboard to beckon him. He moved nearer, kneeling. He was face-to-face with her. She wheezed lightly onto him. "I could tell you were staying true to your marriage. But Patricia clearly wasn't." He'd inhaled her sour breath as she'd spoken and now noticed saliva collecting on the curved stretches of her rouged lips. He wanted to take his thumb to those edges and wipe them away. "I couldn't let a prize like you go to waste, Jacob," she said.

They broke from their first kiss to look into each other's eyes. He rubbed from his lips the smudge of rouge he predicted to be there. He took account of their kiss: It was dry, despite their tongues' fastidious poking. Yet he could taste her on his tongue, sensing her odor from the lows of his throat. Her taste was more deeply sour than her breath had first let on. But he was not repulsed. In fact, her vapors mingled nicely with his; he could do with a lot more.

When they kissed again, Philomena trapped his tongue between her front teeth and gradually sank them into his flesh. He groaned and she released him.

"You don't like that?"

"I do," he said. "Very much."

"That was you liking it?"

"Yes."

"What else?" she said, kneading his waist with her hands and massaging her way lower. "What else do you like?"

"To be honest, with you, anything. Everything," he said. "Philomena, I even like that you are asking. You've figured me out."

She rolled her eyes. "You're just being a Casanova. Saying what I want to hear."

"That's what you want to hear?"

"Isn't that what every woman wants to hear?" she asked.

"I have a lot to learn about women."

"Oh, come on." She rolled her eyes again. "I'm seasoned at this, Jacob," she said. "You can't fool me with this meekness." She'd been exploring his thigh with her hand. She paused, pressing hard. "Is that the ring?"

He realized that he'd forgotten to remove it. He'd not worn the khaki trousers since the day she'd pocketed it there. "I never took it out," he said. "I forgot."

"Goes to show you."

"What?"

"You two," she said. "Goes to show you what the two of you were. Forgettable."

He thought he detected a smile. "Does it make you feel better? That Patricia and I were what we were?" He flattened her hand on his lap. "You may not be a saint, Philomena, but you are not some Jezebel."

She freed her hand. "When I said I was no saint, I was referring to other things," she said. "It had nothing to do with us. When it comes to you and me, I am more than content with how I've behaved."

"Perfect, then."

"Perfect, then," she repeated.

"Am I funny?"

"Very," she said. "Such a typical man. Exactly why I saw through all that meek shit you were trying to pull. You assumed that my saying I was not a saint had to do with you. Men. Always thinking it's about them."

"I'm not like that, Philomena," he said. "You even said it yourself. I'm kind."

Philomena's gaze converted to something like sympathy. "You are, Jacob. But that doesn't mean you can't also be self-centered," she said. "Look, if things hadn't gone the way they went, I wouldn't have you now. So I couldn't care less about what I'm about to say. In any case, how hard did you try with Patricia?"

"I loved Patricia."

"How hard did you try with her?" she repeated. "As I see it, she was the one doing all the work. You know why? And this is not your fault, Jacob. Trust me, it's not your fault one bit." She took his face in her hands. "You're a product of this place. Of the world, really. Men are able to leave the labor of loving to women because they can."

She pulled him toward her and lay on her back with him.

"Right here?" he asked.

"Everything belongs to me," she said. "I can fuck wherever I want."

She brought down one of the thin straps of her dress, exposing her nipple. He was surprised that she wasn't wearing a brassiere and that the dark pearl had not poked through the light material, not even during the day's many breezes.

Taking a cue from her, he released the breast on his right, ignoring the uncharacteristically tender symphony playing in his head.

She guided his head to her freshly aired nipple. With his tongue, he drew circles around it, coaxed on by her pants. He noted a modification in her panting and kissed away his saliva. Her return to a more rhythmic craving registered in him: He'd begun to identify the code to satisfying her. He broke from his feasting to wipe off the saliva.

You don't have to do that, he heard her whisper after another sweep with his thumb.

Keep it there. It feels good.

Instead of shooting for the other breast, he detoured by hiding his face in the small hairs between her breasts and sniffed her perfume cut with the harshness of talcum powder. He was completely absorbed by each scent. He'd never considered what America might smell like. Here he had it, he thought: sweetness sliced with wickedness. Perfect it was.

He launched into a new movement. He bit the ringlet strands and tugged at them with his teeth. She whimpered and it sounded like displeasure. He paused to watch her face. "No?" he said.

She caressed the top of his head. "I'm a bit self-conscious about the hairs on my chest," she said. "I usually get them waxed but I don't know of any good places here."

In appreciation of them, he blew lovingly on them.

"You don't think it's manly?" she asked.

"No," he said. "Many women have it."

"Oh?" she said. "How many women exactly, Casanova?"

Pearl. Berlin Pearl. He said, "I've seen it on a few women who were nursing their babies."

She did not respond. After a while she fed him her finger, expertly poking in and out of his mouth. "Nursing?" she said. "Like this?"

He nodded yes. He mumbled yes. They had exhausted their endurance of the wait.

It turned out that he was not completely exorcised of ferocity. At her soft, girlish grunts, his erection softened some. Her huskier calls for him were better at keeping him hard. She kept them up, soon going a step further by suctioning his penis more tightly and wrapping her legs around his lower back. Hers was a gruff noise of exhilarated suffering, unlike anything he'd ever heard. In due time his own noise reached a happy medium with hers, and they went on in that way, like soldiers charging at their goal, racing for the reward ahead.

After, they hissed on their backs. In the fervor of anticipating their lovemaking, he'd forgotten to ask Philomena for business guidance.

"Philomena, if you were me, what packages would you offer prospective clients?"

"You want free advice?" she asked.

"Free?" he said, pitching his voice humorously. "Didn't I just pay for it?"

She smirked and sank her chin into his chest. "Jacob, my dear, I'm a lot more vicious than that. You've barely made five percent payment."

Three

Grief had already sunk them into darkness when ECG struck. Their hearts splintered. They hadn't even enjoyed a full hour of light.

By then they'd been steeling themselves for life ahead. Kwame Broni was gently stroking Yaa's head on his chest. Earlier Mr. Nti had sent for him and his wife, Afia, but Afia had not been available.

Yaa was wrestling with her tears, heaving rather than crying. "It will be well," Kwame Broni was saying. "It will be well."

But even he couldn't keep from his voice what was true: Alfred was gone. Benjamin, too.

Among them, the information had been first passed to Jacob. Returning from Philomena, he received the message on his cellular just as two teenage boys drew nearer to him on the side of Otumfuo Road. They were coming to help him carry Alfred's drum; Jacob had noticed them while turning his cellular back on—it had 10 percent life.

As Jacob read Maame Mina's text, he wished for the kind boys to be part of a bad joke. *I would have texted Robert*, Maame Mina had concluded. *But how can I text someone that his only child is dead?*

Jacob pleaded with the two boys to go to the house. Left alone, he shook with anguish, fiercely biting his hand to keep from wailing.

Inside, he joined his father and Kwame Broni to compose a sensitive letter for Robert and Martha. They didn't leave the task to Kwame Broni this time because Kwame Broni was wording matters too insensitively. He'd wanted to include the sentence: *Tomorrow is a new day.* Just like that. Without padding. *Tomorrow is a new day.* What good would those words do? As though Robert and Martha would awake tomorrow and be liberated of sorrow over the death of their son.

To fetch Robert and Martha, Yaa needed to clear the redness from her eyes. According to Kwame Broni, who was now approaching the situation more thoughtfully, Robert and Martha should be eased into learning the truth, not shoved into it. Yaa's clearer eyes were what all of them had been waiting for when the electricity went out.

Leaving his house in a panic, Kwame Broni had forgotten to grab his cellular. Jacob's cellular was dead. They were both without an immediate source of light.

Now Kwame Broni and Yaa could be heard shuffling around the living room feeling for places to sit. They found them, for the cushions sighed. "Well," Kwame Broni said. "There goes the letter."

"Maybe they will turn the power on soon," Mr. Nti said.

"When was the last time you saw the power return after a few minutes?" Kwame Broni asked.

"Fair enough," Mr. Nti said. "Wishful thinking. Yaa?"

"I'm here," she said.

"Can you find the lantern? Or some candles?"

"I don't know," she said. "I don't even know where I am sitting right now."

"Not too far from where you were standing, I'm sure. You know this living room better than anyone."

"That's true."

"So give it a try," Mr. Nti said. "If anyone can find her way, you can."

Yaa was pondering the challenge, which could be detected in her rapid breathing.

"Yaa?" Kwame Broni said.

"Yes?"

"If you don't think you can—"

"I can," she said. "I'm only trying to picture the way in my head."

They heard sniffles, which turned to waning whimpers, confirming that Yaa had set off for the kitchen.

"Is the plan to have them read the letter by candlelight?" Kwame Broni ventured.

"Not if Yaa finds the lantern," Mr. Nti said.

"Will it be bright enough?"

"It will have to do," Mr. Nti said. "This can't wait until tomorrow."

"Why not?" Jacob asked.

"Will you be able to sleep?"

"It won't make a difference for me," Jacob said. "Tell them or don't tell them. I won't be able to sleep either way." His voice, hoarse with grief, fractured, evaporating into the deepening evening.

Kwame Broni gasped. "Oh, Martha," he cried.

"She will be strong," said Mr. Nti in a low, breathy voice.

"Oh, Robert."

"He will be strong, too," Mr. Nti added.

But Mr. Nti hadn't spotted what had startled Kwame Broni. A flame burned and floated closer. At the widest casting of the flame's bright net, it was evident that it was not coasting on air but was anchored by a white stalk cupped by two hands. They were Martha's, whose face came into view, her husband's appearing swiftly after. Robert aimed the way forward with the light of his cellular.

Stunned, Mr. Nti echoed his brother, "Oh, Martha." Then, "Robert."

As though the two of them could hear.

Martha's bouncy flame would soon be extinguished. Kwame Broni handed the letter to Robert. Martha drew the candle close. As they read, Robert gasped, and then Martha. When the flame died, curling into a thin line of smoke, it was a result of Martha's strangled wail. All that burst from her was one stinging current of air.

Book 2

Wilder

One

Wilder Thomas's wealth was traceable to his grandfather, F. R. Stones. In 1923, Stones, a land overseer, was gifted a parcel of oil land in Mexia, Texas. His benefactor, the Reverend Lee Wilder Thomas, as if the rarity of his being a Negro oilman were not enough, was moving to Oklahoma, where he would expand his dealings in oil and make himself an even richer Negro by diversifying into real estate.

A week before leaving for Oklahoma, the reverend led Stones to his vast territory in the Mexia oil field, stopping by a rig that Stones, whose job entailed knowing exactly where the reverend's property started and stopped, knew all too well.

"The lawyers are working on the demarcation," the reverend said. Then with a sweep of his arm he added, "It's a healthy acreage. All yours."

Stones fell to his knees at the gift, pledging that his just-born son, who followed three girls, would become Wilder Thomas, dropping the Lee for simplicity. The reverend pointed out that this longed-for son might be the only one; naming him Wilder Thomas could mean an end to the Stones name.

"Other boys will come," Stones said. "An' if they don't, just as well. I reckon you made me who I am. And now you tellin' me my boys, my girls, they boys, they girls, and on and on and on, gon' have some real money? For life? Better your name live on than mine," Stones said.

When he was seven, Stones's boy, the original Wilder Thomas, drew a family tree on his wood-framed slate. Stones did his best to recall for Wilder names to fit above his. He remembered back to his own paternal great-grandfather, who had never smelled anything beyond the tobacco fields he'd worked his entire life and had developed asthma in his thirties—the result, he thought, of inhaling new odors upon freedom. Between that great-grandfather and Stones had lived two men who, all the days of their lives, had risen only for work and fallen only for sleep. It was Stones who had realigned the trajectory of his surname for the better.

Viola, Wilder's mother, had only wanted to become Stones's woman. And one of the consequences of this devotion was neglecting who she'd previously been. All she could remember for Wilder was that her maternal grandmother had been called Rebecca, and that she, hailing from New Orleans, had spoken better French than English. She provided the names of her mother and father, of course, but she was more interested in Wilder's generation. For some time she scrutinized the four branches that Wilder had drawn for himself and his three sisters. When she understood, she eased the white chalk out of his fingers and, her eyes welling up, drew a fifth segment. She wrote in unschooled penmanship: *Baby FR Stones.*

He had lived only two days after his birth, and despite Stones's wish to have that bygone be indeed a bygone, Viola kept alive the memory of the child. Stones would never say it, but Viola said if he'd received a premonition of a single male heir, he might have tacked *Stones* onto Wilder's name: Wilder Thomas Stones.

But Wilder Thomas was simply Wilder Thomas. When he followed the path of the reverend and enrolled at Wiley College in Marshall, Texas, this achievement was understood as a continuation of the sterling legacy of the Reverend Lee Wilder Thomas. Some even professed Wilder to be his grandson. And when Wilder left school, those connected to Wiley who'd heard of his successes chalked them up to good Thomas blood. After Stones died too young, in his fifties, Wilder officially took the reins of the regional conglomerate, now an oil and mineral rights royalty company. The solid foundation set for him—Stones had expertly weathered the Depression, threats from white folks, and other periods of terrible lows—was incorrectly ascribed to the reverend.

Oil remained the family's primary industry and what kept them in Mexia. Still, they could have moved to Atlanta, or even north to Philadelphia or Washington, D.C., where Negroes were known to be doing well. Wilder often admitted to an inability to recall the last time he'd been on an oil field, the company his father had founded, Primrose Energy, now part of a series of partnerships, quarter buyouts, quarter acquisitions, and further partnerships that had made it a force requiring visits to company boardrooms in Dallas, Houston, and New York. Meetings occurred in gleaming rooms at shining tables several stories aboveground. That was the Thomas family's literal place now—aboveground. They could have chosen to drop anywhere on earth. Inexplicably, they'd stayed inside earth's pits of Mexia—*pits*, or *shit*, the term Wilder's fair-skinned son used when he lost his patience for decorum.

He was also called Wilder Thomas, and he was fair-skinned

because Viola had chosen a colored girl damn near white for his father. Born in 1945, the younger Wilder Thomas had reached in his teenage years the epiphany that Mexia was indeed shit. Three years before he was born, the US government built a holding station for German prisoners of war close to everything that mattered in town—the post office, city hall, and Sardis Primitive Baptist Church (the church the Reverend Lee Wilder Thomas had built in Mexia). The facility's disbanding began in 1945, the year Wilder was born and the year the Second World War ended. It became a school for lunatics in 1946, overflowing with them. By the age of seventeen, when fair-skinned Wilder Thomas learned of this history, he stood on the fact that no other town in Texas had housed both German prisoners of war and maniacs to conclude that Mexia was shit.

He set his mind to escape. Never mind that he had been educated at home by tutors, rarely needing to venture out. Never mind that he'd left for a Negro boarding school in Atlanta at age ten. Along with his father and mother and two sisters (like his father, he was the only son), he enjoyed a property encompassing two hundred acres. Three orchards—apple, peach, and apricot—were pruned to coexist and bear fruit of the highest quality.

The time just before harvest always filled Wilder with joy. He would sit for hours admiring the exquisiteness of the ripened fruits' rainbow-like gathering. He would suspend his senses until he saw in his mind's eye the fruits exploding into multicellular components. Boom, they went. A louder and louder boom with each new harvest.

When Wilder arrived at his epiphany about Mexia being shit,

he determined that his visions of exploding fruits were not merely part of the innocuous escapism of youth but that his brain was rupturing. The mania this town had once housed was still around.

Fortunately, his mother and father were unscathed. Their youth had preceded the mania. He'd been reared in it, as had his two sisters. As the oldest of the children—and a man—he could wrest the girls from its hold by setting a good example. So he headed northeast to Princeton University.

But the mania had wings; it joined him at Princeton. When his eyes closed at night and he dreamed, he saw again the detonating fruits. A few times the peaches morphed into human heads that popped. Amid the campus's Gothic architecture, which for many of his classmates had just the right amount of melodrama, Wilder gained the reputation of being more than merely brushed by madness. Other students tensed in his company; his jitters were contagious. Only after a classmate noticed his own fingers tapping frantically, making keys of the air, did he realize that he'd absorbed Wilder's eccentricity.

People began to be concerned. That was why Rutherford Richards, Wilder's friend, once asked out of equal parts curiosity and genuine affection, "What devil is in you, Wilder?"

"No devil," Wilder said.

Rutherford and Wilder made up the two Negroes of their Princeton cohort. When you combined all four undergraduate classes, there were seven. Rutherford, who grew up in Newark, New Jersey, had taken Wilder home with him for Thanksgiving. There, too, Wilder had been agitated.

"Everywhere makes you uneasy, Wilder," Rutherford said.

"Not everywhere."

"Everywhere, Wilder. Everywhere. My grandmother says there's no place on earth for you when the devil is in you."

"Wouldn't I sense him in me?" Wilder asked.

"Not necessarily. The devil can be inconspicuous."

"Fair enough."

"Is that an admission?" Rutherford asked.

"No admission," Wilder said firmly. "Nothing to declare."

He told Rutherford nothing about the mania within him, how it tickled him even as he studied at Firestone Library and walked with him down Nassau Street. At some point the disturbance within seemed to ebb, and he connected its disappearance to his determination that he could dominate the mania by doing right. He held steadfastly to that belief.

Excelling at Princeton was doing right. Moving to New York after graduation and securing a junior management position at an oil company unrelated to his family's was doing right. He deserved the job on merit alone, but the influence of his name in that world could not be denied. Doing right now would involve putting questions about his skills to bed. To stand out, Wilder studied natural gas. The men of his family had only been interested in liquid hydrocarbons—oil. He saw more potential in the vapor form.

In 1939, the Swiss had been first to generate electricity for public consumption from natural gas turbines. Seven years later, the Canadians had been the first to attempt it in North America. Wilder prepared a presentation for his firm's board, a group of otherwise traditional oilmen. He was clear, well prepared, and persuasive, and they bought in, setting him up as the twenty-two-year-old head of a new department.

Fully immersed in trying to fill the wallets of gray white men as the Vietnam War raged, Wilder Thomas possessed the ultimate weapon against the draft: gray white men were not going to lose him when he was on his way to making them millions. It didn't matter that he was of draft age and colored, a point one of them underscored by saying that Wilder, being Wilder, had already uncolored himself. He added that by writing a letter to the right people within the federal government, emphasizing that it was vital that Wilder be kept out of harm's way, he could render Wilder purer than white. Wilder heard in those words the blessings of a life done right. Because of a life done right he could avoid the draft.

But Mexia's fruits-turned-heads returned. He woke in a panic at the foot of his bed and recalled the moments of his less-than-doing-right. It hit him: How could he have thought to dodge the draft?

To keep out of the military, Rutherford had enrolled in graduate school at Princeton. He did not know of the promise the gray white man had made to Wilder, so he encouraged Wilder to follow his example, as Wilder had no conditions like marriage or illness to keep him from serving. Well, Rutherford amended in jest, Wilder was mad in the head, an affliction that had gotten a few out of serving. Perhaps Wilder could appear at the draft board with his jitters dialed up to real shakes. To demonstrate, Rutherford staggered along the sidewalk and across the street to catch the bus that took him to Princeton. Wilder laughed. He waited for the bus to drive away and laughed all the way back to his apartment. But there he stopped laughing. He leaned against his front door and shut his eyes. He had made the decision to enlist voluntarily. In these times, it was the only *right* there was. The only antidote to his nightmares.

At work he showed his paperwork to the gray white man who had promised to render him purer than white.

"I took you for another kind of Negro, Wilder," the man said as he scanned the document that was requiring Wilder to serve for three years on active duty followed by three years as an active reservist.

"What kind, sir?"

"Lucky." The man signed some company papers, releasing Wilder for the destiny he'd chosen. "In any case, Wilder, what do you Negroes owe America?"

That was not the question Wilder pondered after taking a seat on the bus at the Port Authority Bus Terminal behind other Negroes, all of them about to be driven to a Fort Dix many had heard about only that day. Wilder, in fact, pondered nothing. His mother had traveled northeast to see him off. She stood outside the bus and waved at him as they drove away. She was Mexia, and with the distance between them lengthening, he witnessed her fade into the afternoon's pitch-whiteness.

Two

Apparently digging toward purgatory, PFC Hillard started flinging mud too close to where PFC Thomas was drawing red circles and connecting lines on a map. Thomas sat with his legs spread apart on the jungle floor, his legs firmly positioned to stamp the overgrowth from covering the paper. He'd removed his helmet and set it next to him, a rare event in the jungles of Southeast Asia, where he had learned to shield himself against the surprise of enemy bullets and land mines. But Hillard had assured him that this was a safe section of the jungle to wait for the rain to come.

Nothing had flung from Hillard's shovel in some time but Thomas heard the shovel still working. He stretched his neck. "Hillard?"

"Still here." From the foxhole he'd dug, Hillard sounded like an underground workman.

"You don't think it's deep enough?"

"Close. Almost."

"Aiming for six feet?"

"Might as well."

Thomas trusted that Hillard had dug deeper than required for their purpose of a jungle pool. Still he murmured supportive words.

He was seated on his green poncho. The topographic US Army map of Quang Ngai province that was between his legs had regions of green, as if leaching color from the poncho. Certain regions on the map were a lighter green than others, accounting for the muddy glory of paddy fields and bodies of water.

They had been stationed in the province for almost three months. Every day, PFC Wilder Thomas referred to the map, and every day he bemoaned the map's failure to accurately mark the mountains they marched through. Thomas had a knack for maps. Back in New York, his job had included inspecting topographic maps of North American natural gas deposits. Those maps were marvelously precise. He couldn't comprehend the military map's comparative lack of precision, considering that it was supposed to lead them to victory. Or at least to keep them from dying.

He'd been given the job of map reader almost as soon as he joined the platoon. Recognizing Thomas's keen eye, their lieutenant, a broad-shouldered former amateur boxer, had delegated part of his own portfolio to him: the maps, one of three compasses, the safekeeping of blocks of explosives. All these responsibilities entrusted to him, yet Thomas was still at the same rank as Hillard and the other Negroes. Enraged by this injustice, Hillard and the other Negroes thought that Thomas should be more vocal about rank.

At the beginning, they'd thought Thomas an uppity Negro. "He gon' try to pass," Hillard had said behind Thomas's back when they'd all first met. "Lookin' fair as day as he do. Probably been passin' all his life."

But Thomas made clear that he considered himself a Negro. He joined their pack—there were twenty Negroes in the platoon and their pack comprised seven—as seamlessly as they themselves had joined. Thomas, they eventually all agreed, was all right. It helped that like most of them he had Southern roots.

And soon they confessed their long-held suspicion of their white lieutenant: that he would come to his senses and stop letting Thomas rub shoulders with him. What they were witnessing between the lieutenant and Thomas was rare: a white man respecting a Negro's mind. While they were suspicious, they were also pleased that their expectation the lieutenant would come to his white-man senses had not been fulfilled. At least not yet.

With this fact about white folks not respecting a Negro's mind, they appeared to be educating Thomas. This Thomas, who was twenty-three, didn't seem to know that, while many of them were yet to hit twenty and knew all too well.

Which America did he live in? Hillard asked. One apparently without the need for something like the march on Selma?

He'd only half paid attention to Selma, Thomas admitted. He'd been in school, his head in books.

Fine, Hillard said. But where in America did Thomas live that his reaction to typical behavior of white folks—retarding the Black man everyhow—was that of a toddler aching from his first burn?

New York, Thomas said.

A Negro Mecca was how they had heard it described. Still, it was a white-majority Negro Mecca, no?

It was, Thomas agreed.

He worked with white folks?

He did, Thomas said.

Granted, he was as fair as day, but the white folks still knew he was a Negro, no?

They did. But he'd risen, he added. None of the white folks had sought to keep him squat. "If they had," he said, "they would have failed miserably. They didn't clip my wings."

Hillard clacked. Here in this godforsaken place, he warned, Thomas was going to lose those wings. Already he had been outstripped by white soldiers promoted above him to undeserved rank. "That don't piss you off?"

Thomas shrugged. All his life, he said, he'd regarded good work and excellence as adequate resistance to racism. "It's *spectral*. Racism. So you have to find your own spectral way of fighting it."

Nobody responded, and Thomas shared nothing about how his nightmares had once again been put on hold since landing in Vietnam. All he said was that his code of conduct was informed by an ethos to do right.

"Fuck that mean?" asked Conley, a young soldier from Mississippi.

"PFC Wilder Thomas tellin' us he a good nigger," Hillard said. Then, in a fancy voice, he corrected himself: "My mistake, boys . . . my mistake . . . PFC Wilder Thomas telling us he a good Negro."

The boys cackled and wiped their M16s with dust rags as though they were trophies. Soon enough, Hillard asked another question. "Why be a good Negro when you gon' die?"

They were aware of bad Negro behavior in places like Newark and Detroit, bad Negroes burning down houses. That kind of rebellion percolated through Hillard and Conley and the rest of the

Negro soldiers in the platoon because they couldn't imagine dying tomorrow without acting up.

"Ain't no use," Conley said.

He reached into one of the pockets of his rucksack and pulled out the few items he stored there: packs of cigarettes, two bundles of photographs—one batch of his family, and one of his little and big (denoting the sizes of their rears) ladies back home—colored pencils, and folded drawing paper. He'd told the others he had plans to go to art school before he got drafted and he was keeping the colored pencils and folded paper close so as to practice his craft.

"Sure 'bout that?" Hillard asked. "Nobody seen you makin' art."

Conley unfolded the paper and handed one end to Hillard. "Too much shootin' fuckin' with my motivation," he said as he and Hillard exhibited the blank canvas like a banner.

Two weeks passed before Conley completed what he'd been working on: a new flag to go with the American one that accompanied their daily marches. He announced that when one of the white boys led them with the American flag, the Negro closest to the front could raise this flag. He was yet to attach it to a wooden rod. It was tricolor, tri-striped. A top red stripe. A middle black stripe. A green bottom stripe. And dominating the three, a brown fist in the middle.

"How about that fist? We lookin' to knock the livin' daylights out of white folk?" asked Hillard.

"If they ain't careful."

Conley was a big man, the best candidate to fly his own flag closest to heaven. Two daily marches swept by before he found in himself the revolutionary's courage. "Needed the few days to quarrel with myself," he informed them the day prior to his display.

They were sprawled around a fire at camp, taking turns heating their cans of beans in a small pot of boiling water. Finished with warming his, Thomas ate and pondered a plant he saw at the edge of the flickering firelight. It reminded him of a Texas bull nettle.

"Came down to that same question again," he heard Conley say. "Which one I prefer to kill me: the Vietcong or the white man?"

"Are they analogous?" asked Thomas.

"You askin' if they the same?" asked Hillard.

"More or less."

"You big-worded, Thomas," Conley said. "Your words don't never stay in my brain. But one did. And I went searchin' for meanin' in my mind. Use what I learnt in school: context clues. *Spectral*. That your word. 'Member it?"

"Remind me."

"Racism. Spectral. You was sayin' white folks fightin' us like they ghosts?"

He stared at Thomas for verification.

"Yes," Thomas said. "More or less."

"The Vietcong," Conley said. "They also spectral. Ain't seen a gook close in my face yet. But we always shootin'. Haulin' them heavy-ass explosives lookin' to blow up they tunnels. Burnin' up they land, too. But I ain't yet seen one of those motherfuckers in my face. It don't matter, though. I keep fightin'. Keep tryin' to get them before they get me." He'd been flicking burns from his vanishing cigarette. He took a last drag, then flicked the stub into the dirt. "I needed two days to think on the question. Which one I prefer to kill me. The Vietcong or the white man? That wasn't the right question, though. Wasn't the right question one bit. Right question is why I'm fightin' one ghost but leavin' the other scot-free. Both got the same purpose. Both want me dead. Seem to me stupid to kill one then die at the hand of the other. Hillard, don't that seem stupid?"

"Real stupid," Hillard answered.

Hillard passed on the question to another soldier, Wilson, who lay outstretched on the grass with his head propped on his rucksack. Wilson's face was always marked with a scowl, as now, even with his eyes closed. His fist pummeled the soil. "Real stupid," he said.

He also passed on the question, calling out Johnson, who sat next to him. And it went on this way, one man asking the other, until Johnson, Banks, and Smith concurred. That left Thomas to complete the chain. "Thomas, don't that seem stupid?" Smith asked.

Thomas took a second to think. "Perhaps you are right, Conley," he said. "Perhaps there's something to what you're saying."

Conley's flag was seized from him by the lieutenant seconds after he raised it. Conley was not punished.

"I let everyone lose their minds once. Only once, though," the lieutenant said, warning Conley.

Conley had more paper. He designed another flag for the day after, a less striking rendition without a fist, which he handed to Smith. That found the same end as the first flag, the lieutenant repeating the warning he'd given Conley. Two other flags came into being, each requiring a quicker turnaround than the preceding one, and each duller as a result. Only after Johnson, who had raised his flag the day after Banks had, who had raised his flag the day after Smith had, who had raised his flag the day after Conley had, did Thomas recognize the oath he'd unknowingly taken. He had sworn to pick up the mantle when it was required. But that responsibility—at least in the form of the flag—wouldn't get to him because the lieutenant had had enough of the flag-raising after Johnson. He charged the four with treason. On one of the lieutenant's maps, this one of Saigon and the surrounding area, Thomas had been unable to locate Long Bình Jail, where Conley, Smith, Banks, and Johnson were being held after their arrests.

A combination of anger and a desire to avenge his brothers brought Wilson to raise his fist in solidarity. He held it up during marches through the jungle. He held it up during silences. This was a demonstration the lieutenant allowed—Thomas assumed because it wasn't in direct protest to anything like the American flag. When a newcomer to their platoon noticed Wilson's raised fist during a march, he said, "That nigger has got to be a halfwit."

Wilson brought down his arm and turned around. His forever-scowling face brightened so much that one could easily mistake his striking that white boy's cheek with his fist as the greatest joy of his life. And Wilson would soon confess—from the back of the truck that sent him off to get his head checked—that this very moment was his greatest joy. "Much rather a straitjacket than stickin' around," he said. "Keep me from killin' the ghosts I ain't suppose to kill."

The mantle now fell to Hillard and Thomas. Hillard was first to it; Thomas was still reading maps.

"Up to me to raise hell now," Hillard said.

To Thomas's surprise, Hillard was uncertain with the mantle. What had happened to the others in the platoon had put fear in him. Thomas welcomed the softness; he wanted an end to the chaos.

Yet revolution was still at the forefront of Hillard's mind. He organized the remaining Negroes into the Fists, a group that met three times a week under an umbrella of banana leaves inside the jungle. In a perfunctory spirit of brotherhood Thomas agreed to record the minutes. He did not have to write much down at first because Hillard, as the group's leader, adopted a slow, meandering, conversational style, often stopping for lengthy pauses. When the men grew tired of talk without action, they filled Hillard's pauses with complaints, and Thomas's fine handwriting ebbed into scribbling as he struggled to keep up. The men wanted revolt and wanted it fast—setting fire to their camp or beating up white soldiers or sabotaging a mission so that their white counterparts suffered most.

"I agree," Hillard said. However, they had to be careful, he added. He looked every man in the face and asked, "What do any of us have to go home to?" Nothing. But it could be something if they served dutifully. A high-school dropout like him could make a life on the monthly stipend the government would pay him.

He was not advocating for calm. Far from it. He was arguing for activism steeped in common sense. "And we gon' start with PFC Thomas," he capped off.

At the mention of his name, Thomas stopped mid-curlicue.

"We gon' assign PFC Thomas the title due him," Hillard said. "Lieutenant. If he a cracka, that mos' certain be his title."

———————

"ALL DONE, LIEUTENANT," said Hillard after he clambered out of the foxhole. "Gone as deep as I can and still keep from hittin' purgatory."

He grabbed the transistor radio that he'd sneaked from their actual lieutenant's tent. He dragged his poncho onto the grass, made a place for himself across from Thomas, and sat down. He fiddled with the dial. "Some music to wait for the rain? What you think?"

The radio's static hacked gutturally. Thomas wondered whether the hovering mist and thick leaves affected the airwaves.

"Turn it down some," Thomas said. "We can never be too careful."

"Gooks?"

"Anyone, really."

"You spooked?"

"Not anymore," Thomas said. "A little thing I got to thinking about. You are probably not the only person to have dug up a grave out here."

He capped the pen in his hand, folded the map around it, and pushed it into a compartment on his rucksack.

"You spooked of the buried?" asked Hillard.

"Just a thought that occurred to me."

"Better earth than water," Hillard said. "All them rivers we been crossin'. Barely gettin' through dead bodies."

Thunder drummed and they were suddenly swept up in darkness.

"Sounds like we gettin' close," Hillard said, still playing with the dial. He landed on a station snapping with background static but not enough to swallow the music. A choir sang a hymn. "Woulda never guess gooks to be Christians."

"I doubt it's a Vietnamese choir."

"What other choir gon' reach these parts?"

"It's a recording. It could be any choir. From anywhere."

The song pitched with revolving bouts of lament and exaltation.

"Sound like a death song, don't it?" Hillard said. "Like somethin' ma mama gon' make them sing at ma funeral."

"You're too young to be this morbid, Hillard. You will bury her. She won't bury you."

Hillard closed his eyes and moved his arms like an enchanted bandleader. "Tell me you ain't thought about your last breath every day since you dropped in these jungles and I will tell you you a lyin' lieutenant."

"Not a lieutenant."

"But a liar?"

"Not a lieutenant."

"Ain't no way of escapin' thought of death, Lieutenant. Best to get ready for it. Check boxes you yet to check."

"I'm here, aren't I?"

"Sure are." Hillard opened his eyes and uncrossed his legs. He brought down his arms. "I know you on my page. 'Preciate you followin' me in these jungles to help me check ma box without judgment. Ain't even bother to wonder why you couldn' just teach me to swim in one of them waters. Guess you know now. Or guess you knew already. Can't even go two feet in them waters without steppin' on a dead gook's head. Might think you safe because ain't no bodies floatin' for miles. Then you take a step and, *splat*, a gook head. *Splat*, gook arms. *Splat*, gook legs. We cold-blooded killers, Lieutenant. It ain't about bein' morbid. About knowin' that we some cold-blooded motherfuckers. And what that mean? What cold-blooded mean? It mean if you ain't dead, you at the doorstep. Knowin' don't make you morbid. It make you smart."

After successive rolls of thunder, a spate of rain promptly followed. Thomas had doubted Hillard's assurances that the rain would hold out until his hole was ready. Timing the rain was a skill Hillard claimed to have learned from the Vietnamese nurse he'd befriended in Saigon. Months ago, they were there awaiting their permanent posting. For five consecutive evenings Hillard had vanished for hours. He'd returned steeped in smoky lavender and skirted the men's questions with assertions of sex: "grade A cunt," "pussy juice." There was only so much of this hedging gutter talk the men would take and eventually they got the truth out of Hillard. The nurse's name was Vatsana, a fittingly mysterious name because, as Hillard explained, she doubled as a kind of conjure woman and had been blowing ashes in his face to ward off death.

Whatever peace Vatsana's rituals brought Hillard hadn't lasted long. Here he was angling himself in preparation for his own turn to dust. But the rain had waited, coming down just when Hillard said it would. Perhaps this was a reason to trust in the magic of Vatsana's ashes against death. She'd equipped Hillard with a celestial knack for rainfall.

Hillard stood to put on his poncho, covering his head with the hood. He turned up the radio, then secured it between the poncho and his heart, crossing his arms just beneath the heaviness. Thomas stood up to wait with an identical split-legged posture.

"Ain't have to be tunnel rat tomorrow if Wilson still around," Hillard yelled over the downpour. "Wilson's the shortest among us, you know? Sure as hell comin' back to this earth as a tall man if I get a chance."

"I only escaped by a hair."

"Still escaped."

Thomas was probably only an inch taller than Hillard. Truth be told, an inch was negligible. He could just as well have served as tunnel rat tomorrow, the man who conducted the search-and-destroy of one of the enemy's narrow underground tunnels by blowing it up.

Like soup on fire, the grave cooked, rising with floodwater.

"Don't it make sense why I was shootin' for six feet?" Hillard asked, craning his neck to take it in more closely. "Perfect deepness for a jungle pool. Perfect longness to fit me from head to toes. And bitty room for some paddlin'."

The rain had lessened. It needed to slow further before Hillard could float on his back in his foxhole without water pelleting his chest. "Let's give it a little more time before we start," Thomas said.

The chatter on the radio became more audible. Thomas discerned a frantic news report in English. "Listen." He pointed a wagging finger at Hillard's chest. "Hillard. Listen."

Hillard lowered his head. "King?" he said. "Martin Luther? King?"

He caught the radio from under and stuck the box between his and Thomas's ears.

"King," Hillard repeated.

Thomas heard Hillard as though Hillard were vanishing in his own hole.

Hillard said, "Memphis." Then:

"They been wantin' him dead."

Thomas said, "Shot. He was shot."

"They been wantin' him dead, Lieutenant. Dead."

As one, they fell to their knees as they followed the rest of the report. When he could no longer sustain the weight of his misery, Hillard yanked the radio from their ears and hurled it into the bush. He slumped to the ground. "Think he check his boxes?"

"People like him know they won't live long, Hillard."

"Think he check his boxes?"

"He was ready, Hillard," Thomas said.

HILLARD DID HAVE his swimming lesson after all, in King's honor. Thomas had required some convincing. After the news of King's death had fully sunk in, he gathered his pack to abandon the pool and was moving toward the path leading to camp when Hillard asked, "You runnin' off?" Hillard had undressed to his undershorts and a garment of chest hair.

"You still want to learn?"

"I ain't damn near naked for you, Lieutenant."

Thomas sought to make it quick. The other Fists needed their leader at this disturbed, terrible time.

Inside the muddy water Hillard was a child king, ready to be led. The gutted earth had risen with the rain to a point inches from the brim, so that Hillard could begin his lesson by clutching handfuls of wet grass and soil while he paddled his feet behind him. Keeping his head up proved challenging; he wheezed at the effort.

"In cleaner water I would have you put your face down," Thomas said. "But I'm worried you might catch something."

Before Thomas could say more, Hillard dunked his head. When he came up, he blew snot onto the mud syrup's surface and spat a few rounds of phlegm. "Ain't too bad," he said. "Don't smell rotten. Thing I hate most about this land is all they waters smell rotten."

Thomas bent to scoop up some of the water. Gingerly, he brought his palm to his nose. "There's no odor."

"That's right," Hillard said. "Not a thing of a smell. Might not look much like water, Lieutenant. But sure smell like what water oughta smell like. Not a damn thing."

Pool water back home, thought Thomas, had a scent. Pool water had the smell of chemicals—chlorine. But there was no way for Hillard to have known that, this being his first pool.

For the next part of the lesson, Thomas would have had to get into the water. But he couldn't bear to. Instead he announced that they didn't have time for him to disrobe, get in, and, cradling Hillard, guide him through the water.

"Time to go, Hillard," he said.

Hillard looked up at him. "You tellin' me all my diggin' gon' be for nothin', Lieutenant?"

"We will come back. You have my word."

At camp, the Fists convened in quiet and song. *Swing low, sweet chariot. Comin' for to carry me home.* In the dark from across the low fire, Hillard's eyes were on Thomas, who was not singing along. Hillard slowed the lyrics, stretching his mouth desperately, as if willing Thomas to join them.

But Thomas couldn't bring himself to join in. His mind was

fogged with guilt. He felt the Fists' sorrow palpably, but it should not have taken the death of Dr. King for him to finally feel a pain the Fists had been nursing for a long time. No, he did not deserve to participate in this tender brotherhood.

In Hillard's face Thomas saw disappointment. He almost explained himself but he did not want to disrupt a moment that he wasn't worthy to be present for in the first place. He decided to wait until the next day, after a night's rest. He would pull Hillard aside after tomorrow's mission and make his case. Hillard would understand.

The Fists scheduled time after tomorrow's mission to consider a proper response to King's assassination. Even better, Thomas thought. He would not only have an opportunity to explain himself to Hillard but also demonstrate his unwavering commitment to whatever response they settled on.

They disbanded to sleep, and Thomas, unable to shut his eyes to the skittering schools of mosquitoes, watched with envy as Hillard slept in the shell of his poncho.

When Thomas woke to dawn's lurk, he figured he'd only managed about an hour of shut-eye. A morning sun veiled in leaden clouds peeked through in patchy amber. As soon as he glimpsed the imprint of Hillard's air mattress in the ground, he knew: Hillard was gone.

The remaining Fists speculated about Hillard's whereabouts.

"Gone AWOL," one of them said.

"Reassignment," another suggested. "Maybe he figure he ain't nobody's fearless soldier. Best to push paper."

AWOL was more likely, this according to the white lieutenant. And there was no place for Hillard to go, he blustered as he paced up and down the line of men. He was saying this about Hillard more in warning to the remaining Negroes than in recitation of fact. "Soon be back," he added. "More than likely in a body bag."

He had organized the men for the tunnel mission, for which Hillard, being the shortest among them, was going to serve as tunnel rat. Now the lieutenant was rechecking the men for height. "Thomas," the lieutenant said.

At the tunnel's open mouth, Thomas received supportive pats on the back from the men. Private Bond, who was white and jocular and had a gasping laugh, attempted to lighten the mood. "Ought to learn to stuff your boots, Thomas," he said.

Four white boys were soon huddled to Thomas's left. Two Fists were at his right. Their lieutenant was sitting this one out and had put Bond in charge. Bond was stacking the blocks of explosives they would use to blast the tunnel.

"Them blocks suppos' to be your task, Lieutenant," said one of the two Fists.

"Crackers scared. That's why," another said.

"Of what?"

"They suspectin' we ready to blow them up instead of this here tunnel."

"For what?"

"You losin' the little sense you got? King, dummy. For King."

Thomas shook his rucksack from his back. He held it out.

"You ain't got to do it, Lieutenant," whispered the man who took it from him.

"That's right, Lieutenant. Ain't got to do the cracker's biddin'."

But they were always doing the cracker's bidding, here in the jungle. Where the ostensibly sweet chirping of birds instead compounded one's sorrows. The loudest chirps arrived in the early morning, unveiling a new day but auguring their own possible demise by day's end.

Perhaps the two men were right, Thomas thought. Why obey? He had just about convinced himself not to follow the cracker's order and made no attempt to dig from his rucksack the supplies he needed to inspect the tunnel: the flashlight, the Ka-Bar. Locked in a pouch at his thigh was his .38; in another was his M67 grenade. In two quick swoops, he could rip everything from his body. His hand made to release the pistol when he thought he heard Bond biting into fruit. He turned to find Bond sprawled against a tower of the explosives. Bond held nothing, he chewed nothing; just the timid pink of his tongue. No one was chomping on fruit, yet the noise grew. Thomas's legs shook when he understood: Mexia's orchards. He was hearing it, neither daydream nor hallucination, a warning so close that it slapped his hand from the gun he was reaching to tear from his thigh.

Instantly, he decided on doing right. And like vindication, the two Fists men became identifiable: Bryant and Winstock.

He opened the rucksack in Bryant's hand and pulled from it the flashlight and gloved Ka-Bar, snapping both onto his waist. Bryant handed him a gas mask in case the enemy knew he was coming and had prepared for him a chemical agent. Thomas snapped it in place; it dangled from his waist.

"Oughta be a quick trip in and out, Lieutenant," said Winstock, who had his ear to the ground, listening. "Ain't detectin' no sign of life."

"'Cause you ain't really listenin' for shit, fool," said Bryant.

"How you plan on givin' the lieutenant confidence when you scared yourself?"

"Ain't scared. Mighty careful, that's all."

"Careful and scared. Same thing."

Wordlessly, Thomas got down on his hands and knees. He twisted the flashlight and pointed it into the tunnel; its brightness shone on brown foliage ahead. He stuck the flashlight between his teeth and crawled in headfirst. When he fully entered the tunnel he paused, took a breath, then proceeded. The leaves crunched each time he moved. Nothing like the skittering of rats he'd anticipated. Not the threatening *woo* of the enemy. Instead, adamantly, everything crunched. He could see the noises' source. He could touch their source with his hands, the warning that had slapped his hand from the gun confirming that this was what he had been intended to see and touch.

And so it was that the rest of Thomas's senses were at their sharpest. He could parse the layers of the tunnel's awful scent: the bottom layer of fetid animal decay, the middle layer of the remains of human odor, and the top layer of the walls' aged rind. There was no aroma of chemical agents, but there were tastes that swept his tongue and then gagged his throat: insects and maggots disintegrating into a bitter dust, degraded urine mixed with the dust into a distinct sourness.

Before long the taste of salt overtook the others. Beads of sweat had been running down his face and pooling on his upper lip. To lick off the saltiness, which he hoped would overtake the awful tastes on his tongue, he'd removed the flashlight from his mouth and held it. He'd been licking continually as he progressed. When he curled his tongue to swipe at the most recent film, it lacked the acidity of perspiration. To be certain, he moved his tongue across the lip twice more. In the diminishing acidity, he determined, was the slow advance of human life. He cut the flashlight and froze in place, listening. He thought he breathed too loudly when he devoted himself to listening, so he focused on licking the liquid from his lip.

Without a doubt, he detected that only one had been sent to face him. Carefully and silently on the cave floor, he slithered his hand toward his pistol, released it, and aimed the gun into the darkness. When the salt was a wholly low-rung tang, he knew that it was time. He buried his face and pressed his body into the mildewed floor for cover, then fired several rounds. He dropped the gun and shielded the back of his helmet with his arms. Because the floor reeked of bird shit, he hoped that the gelatinous clumps dropping onto his arms were also excrement. That was wishful thinking, for he'd dreamed this exactly: fruits morphing into human heads and then shattering into globs of human flesh.

Three

Winstock found Thomas facedown. He held up Thomas's head and set a pocket mirror at his nose. At half-minute intervals, gray whorls of fog precipitated on the mirror. He slapped Thomas's cheeks, but Thomas did not respond.

After Winstock had hauled Thomas out of the tunnel, he laid him on the ground and he and the others dumped water from their canteens onto Thomas's face, which also failed to revive him. Out of options, four of them constructed a stretcher with their shirts and carted him through the jungle back to camp. Two left the stretcher when they rejoined the rest of their battalion. Winstock and Bryant stayed, gripping their sections of olive cotton tightly as they awaited the helicopter in the mowed grass. When it finally landed after nearly an hour, Bryant left and Winstock boarded the helicopter with Thomas.

When Thomas opened his eyes, he was swarmed by men and women working him over, injecting liquids into his arms, stabbing him in his behind, cajoling him to "stay with me," shining bright lights in his eyes. When his heartbeat finally steadied, the army medics left him alone with the shadows that had been clearing from his eyes. He was listening to the nurse's drawn-out

account of his journey to the hospital, which she'd heard from
Winstock during Winstock's overnight vigil. "They made him
leave," the nurse told Thomas. "I'm pretty sure he would have
waited for the three days that you were out."

The hospital was a sweltering place. The fans merely revolved
the damp, hot air. Humidity covered Thomas's face like a heated
rag, and to counteract it he blinked his eyes repeatedly. These attempts at coolness and stimulating the persistent shadows' demise
proved futile. He held his eyes wide open to test another approach.

Noticing what he was doing, the nurse held up two fingers.
"How many?"

"How long did you say I've been here?" asked Thomas, his
parched voice sounding like a stranger's.

"Three days," answered the nurse.

He stared at an empty cot next to him, where a white cup sat
on a tray. "Two."

"No. Three. Three days."

"You asked how many fingers. Two." Each word cut the insides of his throat. The pain in his groin kept him from lunging
for the cup.

"Of course," said the nurse. "You must be dying of thirst. I'll
get you some water."

With some struggle, he pushed himself up on his creaky cot.
She had taken the remaining shadows with her. Shapes advanced,
displaying the room's swarm of human activity and cots that
stretched the length of the place. He counted seven cots, the first
two to three steps from the billowing brown tarp that served as a
doorway, up to the end of the length, where the seventh cot was
shoved against the steadier tarp. They were inside a medical tent.

Gaps existed among the cots, through which medical staff moved. A man's leg, sheathed from thigh to ankle in a cast, hung in a sling. A nurse flexed his other leg in exercise. Behind her a soldier, whom Thomas determined from the insignia on his uniform to be of high rank, locked a patient upright with hands positioned at the groaning man's bare abdomen and back. A white bandage covered one of his eyes; the other increasingly looked lifeless. Another uniformed man listened to the man's chest with a stethoscope. He pulled away in obvious frustration, splitting the stethoscope's listening tips from his ears following a few seconds of consideration. He restored them to his ears, going under the man's arm for a second listen. Thomas conducted his own inspection, waiting for the man's fingers to move: the fading pupil had completely gone out. The nurse's return distracted him a bit. Looking past her, he saw the doctors' faces expand with consolation while they gently centered the man's head on his pillow. He would live to see another day, it looked like.

The nurse shook a filled canteen at him. She unscrewed it and put it close to his mouth. "Would you like some help?"

Reaching for the canteen increased the pain in his groin but he labored toward it. He spilled some of the water onto his nose before he could wrap his lips around the spout. He drank in gulps, first satisfying his thirst, then drawing the spout some to rinse off the joined bitterness of maggot dust and urine vapors, and then the standout bitterness of salt.

When he felt the weight of the canteen lessen, he let the last of the water gather in his mouth. He gargled, and the burbling transfigured into Hillard's water call. He swallowed and pushed the empty canteen into the nurse's hands.

To test his sense of smell, he inhaled the heavy air. Lightness entered his head. He'd come to know the two scents that swirled intimately around him. One was gunpowder's fieriness; the other was blood. Liquid or flaky or caked, blood always released a distinctive metal tang. Some of the metal was sweet, as some of it was now, in the manner of pain turning to comfort.

"You look well, Private Thomas," said the nurse. "Like you'd needed the rest."

"I'm Wilder."

"Wilder Thomas."

"Yes."

"Wilder Thomas," she repeated, regarding him courteously. "Nice name. Worth saying a few times. Wilder Thomas."

Rather than sensing the pleasure she claimed to find in his name, Wilder recognized uncertainty in her careful enunciation. She did not know what she was supposed to do with his "looking well" and had been buying time by repeating his name on her full lips. It was a strange attribute on a woman who was slim everywhere else. Had she been bitten by a bug? Stood too close to the trenches and been struck by a stray bullet?

"Anybody coming?" he asked, glancing at the empty cot at his side.

"In no time," she said. "They don't stay like this for long."

After she left, Wilder heard a whisper: "Private."

It came from the neighbor to his right, whose neck was wound in a sand-stained brace. He could hardly turn his head toward Wilder. He looked straight ahead.

"That nurse ought to call you Jesus, Private," the man said. "Was right here when they brought you. Was sure you were dead.

Now look at you. Risen on the third day." He attempted to laugh but coughed instead. His saggy cheeks were a deep red. "Whereabouts are you from?"

"New York. You?"

"Missouri," he said. "Chaffee, Missouri. Heard of it?"

"Never."

"Doesn't surprise me. Smallest of the smalls." He strained to turn his head as much as he could, without being able to show Wilder more than an inch of the side of his face. "Left for Saint Louis when I was eight. To be with my old man. But Chaffee is still home. The old lady's there. Never been to New York. Those bright lights. Sure would love to see them. You lived there all your life?"

"My work is there."

"Oh, you work there."

It was a question awaiting an answer. But Wilder thought if this man had a question, he ought to ask. As though there was no need to squander his breath on the lesser place that had raised Wilder, this man had implied a question—*Aaah, as I suspected. . . . So, where are you really from?* Wilder himself would not squander his breath on Mexia, but that was his right, not this cracker's.

"Any Negroes in Chaffee?" asked Wilder.

"No. Not in Chaffee," the man said. "Definitely not Chaffee."

"How about Saint Louis?"

"Yes," he said, adding, "but not by us. Nowhere by us." The white soldier must have felt the clammy suspicion of Wilder's frown. "Maybe just a few," he relented.

Wilder didn't want to talk anymore. He had no conversational itch to scratch. A new soul had made a home in him—a fiery one that had pushed his original one from its chair. The wrong comment could enrage him. Not engaging with the dubious man at his right was advisable. Persisting in quiet was best.

"Nothing like Kansas City," he heard the man say. "Lots more Negroes in Kansas City. Why I fear that place is next. Know what I mean, Private?"

Wilder did not know. "What do you mean?"

"Apologies," he said. "You been out for three days." He sighed regretfully. "Negroes been burning up cities because of King. Most recent was Baltimore. Bet my bottom dollar on Kansas City being next."

Not having set foot in Kansas City, Wilder was ill-equipped at approximating the fieriness of its Negroes. "Can't say about their light."

"Light?" asked the man. "What's light got to do with it?"

"Everything."

"Like?"

"Everything is all there is to know . . . Private?"

"Stanley's the name."

"Light is all, Stanley. Light is all there is to know." Abruptly, Wilder saw Stanley's brace set on the most vibrant fire. He felt a slash singe his own tongue. "You itchin' to see some bright lights, ain't that right?" Stanley did not answer. "Sound to me like you gettin' it."

WITHIN A MONTH of being back on his feet, Wilder received his official notice of discharge at the Tan Son Nhut Air Base near Saigon. The envelope felt empty in his hand. The army was letting him go, in truth, for insubordination. But the reason given in the letter was *Medical discharge*. An easy route to take, he supposed. Better than admitting that he'd risen after three days and, naturally, had no patience for the foolishness of misguided mortals.

He left the commander's office and walked into shimmering daylight. Proceeding, he considered the irony of the letter, which hadn't disclosed the medical reason—as if it was yet to be discovered—for which he had been judged incapable of continuing in the US Army. But for the first time in a very long time, Wilder Thomas wasn't contending with any unknown trouble, medical or otherwise. In a week, every pain he had woken with on the cot in the medical tent had disappeared. His mind was as clear as the sky overhead, and therein lay the greatest irony: all his life he had lived with a muddled mind, fighting a mania he couldn't name. He'd wanted the name to be Mexia, perhaps even America. But far from Mexia and America the mania had proven to be more virulent, revealing itself, luring him into a narrow tunnel, then asserting itself. It was no longer a dream.

It was this clarity he wished to share with Hillard. Wilder had come to realize that the men had started calling him Lieutenant not because of rank, but because of other attributes: his age, education, experience, and pedigree—in short, who he was. These attributes had kept him calm in the face of injustice. Perhaps Hillard had anticipated that when the injustices reached their zenith with King's killing, his calm would disintegrate. But he hadn't so much as hummed along to the mourning songs they'd sung by the fire.

If he could reverse time he would express to Hillard the guilt he'd been feeling at that moment and beg for Hillard's forgiveness. He would sing to Hillard at the top of his lungs. Wailing songs so piercing that the white boys who'd gone to sleep would have spent the night tossing and turning in their beds. But time was not going to reverse course; he had to make do with its onward thrust. Onward, he would still sing to Hillard. *Swing low, sweet chariot.* Would he even find Hillard? The most probable likelihood was that he was dead. Finding him, if he should be so lucky, was for the purpose of carrying him home.

But there was reason to be hopeful. Wilder had returned to camp after regaining his health and to the rumor that Hillard was living with Vatsana, the conjure woman who'd once blown ashes in his face. Before he got his discharge letter, Wilder had searched for her inside the base hospital. He'd combed through the wards because he knew that Vatsana worked as a nurse there. Yet all he'd gotten from people was confirmation that she'd once been there but wasn't now.

"How long ago?" Wilder asked.

"Some days gone."

He was talking to a nurse he'd mistaken for Vatsana. She fit the picture of Vatsana he had in mind: dainty.

"Did she go alone?" Wilder asked.

"Come again?"

"Did she take someone with her?"

"That, I cannot say," replied the nurse. "After work we walked to the point where she goes her way and I go mine. The next morning when I got back to that point she was not there. I waited. But I was late. I thought she had taken the lead. She was never late."

"She didn't show?"

"I am still waiting for her."

"Have you gone to her house?"

"She is not there."

"Do you think?"

"Dead? Never. She terrifies death." The nurse did not blink. "Vatsana went home. To Laos."

"Where?"

"Laos. She's from Laos."

"I thought she was from Vietnam."

"No," she stressed. "Hmong. Like me. But from Laos."

"How do I get there?" he asked and closed his eyes to picture the maps.

"Sir, are you not well?" the nurse asked.

"I'm fine," assured Wilder. "Please go ahead."

He would need to make his way to the bus station in Saigon, fifteen miles south.

"Will you go by foot?" she asked.

"I will go by foot."

In that case he would turn right at the base's barrier, then aim straight, always turning right whenever the opportunity presented itself. On his way, she warned, children would chase after him for alms, naively seeing in his army fatigues guarantees of gold, frankincense, and myrrh. She paused here. He opened his eyes.

"You won't ask how I know about gold, frankincense, and myrrh?" she said.

"Should I?"

"There are not many of us. Hmong Christians."

She dug into her robe pocket. She pulled out a fistful of hard candy. Seizing his hand, she put the candy into it and said, "Take this. Pass them out to the children. They will leave you alone."

Two small groups of children had come and gone. Wilder had

taken advantage of their appearances to rest. Now a boy appeared on his own. Only two of the sweets remained in Wilder's pocket. Wilder offered him one and rewarded himself with the other. As he took his break the child sat next to him.

"Your name?" Wilder asked.

Try as Wilder might, the boy could not understand his English. All that was possible were the faces of displeasure they made at each other as they sucked on the sourness in their mouths, though Wilder welcomed the way it quenched his dry mouth.

The boy left before Wilder resumed his journey. He put his rucksack back onto his back and proceeded, building up speed, his army boots feeling lighter. Soon enough he encountered brightly painted shacks. His gaze feasted on a mishmash of goods: toy replicas of coffins; long, tubular bread. At a magenta shack a pleading woman pointed to plastic flower wreaths hanging from a window door. Then, sensing his disinclination toward them, she stretched a bouquet of the same flowers toward him. He winced at her and moved along.

The bus station could be found in the center of Saigon, on the other side of a roundabout. After accepting his discharge letter, Wilder had checked a wall clock to note that he was setting off on his journey at eight a.m. He wasn't wearing a watch. From the rush hour traffic of cars and scooters, he guessed that it was now past four.

Within the bus station's disorder of buses and trucks stood a seedy bar with hookers. Wilder knew it well. Months ago, within less than a week of arriving in the area, the American servicemen had usurped the bar from the locals.

There, Wilder was confident that he would learn about the

network of trucks the nurse had promised could deposit him at Laos. He entered, and behind him the bottle-cap strings at the entryway gyrated. Music played from a small radio; the familiar pungency of grain alcohol greeted him. Four men were huddled around a small white folding table.

The barman was the one Wilder knew. He set his rucksack against the wall and headed for a stool.

"Been awhile," he said.

"Long?" the barman said.

"You don't remember me?"

The barman squinted. "You have hat? American soldiers. All have hat." He raised the edge of his palm to his creased forehead. "From here," he said, knocking against his forehead. "To here," he added, knocking against the end of his chin. "How I know who from who."

Wilder's cap was somewhere in his rucksack. He did not venture for it. He stared outside through the doorway. "Which of those trucks goes to Laos?"

"Fight moving to Laos?" The barman drained a bottle of Tennessee bourbon into a glass. "The war?"

Wilder nodded.

"Americans moving to Laos?"

"No," Wilder said. "Nothing of the sort."

"I see." He handed Wilder the half-filled glass. "Not too far, you know. Laos not far one bit."

"I'm looking for someone."

"Woman."

"Yes."

"You and her have baby?"

"No," he said. "We've never met."

"Not problem if you and her have baby. Not problem for me," the barman said. "I have two sisters. One sister have two babies with white American soldier. Other sister have one with Negro. White American soldier leave. Negro leave, too, but send money." He gestured for Wilder to drink. "So no problem for me if you have baby."

Wilder downed the drink. It prickled his throat. "Really. I don't know her."

"Laos."

"I hear she's there."

The man turned and dug through a drawer. He returned to Wilder with a piece of folded paper in his hand. "Map," he said, spreading the brown paper on the scratched wood of the bar. He settled a finger at a point. "Laos." Then, with his other hand, he settled another finger at a point farther below. "You. Me."

From the map's legend, Wilder estimated a distance of nine hundred kilometers. Slowly, the man moved the finger of their location along the coordinates. A few times he steadied it, each halt representing a switch in vehicles. At last the two fingers met.

"Take you whole day. Six trucks. Maybe five."

"You know someone who could take me?"

"Yes," he said. "Viet. He make delivery of fertilizer."

"He'll take me?"

"He get you started," he said. "He deliver people. Hide them in fertilizer. Take small money. You pay?"

Wilder nodded.

"Fertilizer smell. Not for me. But if for you, Viet your guy."

Four

Wilder knew Vietnam's waters to be spoiled by defecation. Spoiled, too, by people rinsing off dirt. But these could not compare to the worst of all spoilages: too many times he had encountered the greenish opacity of the water due to decaying human flesh, the very vision of which—it didn't matter that this was Laos—deterred his agreeing to the river for his bath.

It had been at Vatsana's suggestion. Vatsana, conjure woman, all-seeing, said, "There are no dead bodies, Lieutenant, if that's your worry."

By then a few hours had passed since magic had brought him to her after two days, a small woman who spoke with the breeze of authority. Her black hair cut off at the nape of her slender neck, and he swore to himself that both times he'd seen her from behind, she'd worn her hair to her shoulder blades. That was the way he'd taken her in upon first seeing her: wanting to establish familiarity, confirming that her oval eyes were just as Hillard had described them, that her face exhibited the cherry undertone he said had made him think she was going red with fear because he was a Negro, that she was two or three inches shy of Wilder's height, one or two shy of Hillard's. If he made himself believe that he knew her, he would not need to go through the awkward chitchat of first meetings but could get straight to the point. He succeeded in making himself believe.

No, he did not want to go inside, he told her. No, he did not want water. No, he did not need help with his bag. "Where's Hillard?" he asked.

"You came for him?" she asked.

"He's here?"

"Not right now." She climbed up the ladder to her hut set apart from the others within her mountain village. "He will come later." From her doorway she said, "Please come inside."

The air inside the hut was stale, dampened by the trapped vapor of cooked food. He dropped his bag on the hard floor and sat on it. He freed the first three buttons on his shirt, up to where his stomach started to roll.

Vatsana pushed the flimsy bamboo door fully open and revealed a gaping rectangular hole. She moved to his side and leaned over him, prying open a window. When it finally opened, he smelled fresher, denser air.

Red-checked blankets strung on clotheslines sectioned Vatsana's hut into three areas. On one clothesline at arm's reach from Wilder, two blankets were drawn apart. Behind them pots were piled messily in a large pan, a pair of wooden ladles sticking out of it. Four raffia baskets ranging in size were strewn about as if kicked apart. Food was arranged on the floor in portions; he noticed the colorful vegetables wearing green crowns of yarn just as Vatsana drew the sheets together. In the midmorning brightness, a faint strip of fuchsia hovered overhead.

In one hand Vatsana held a rolled-up straw mat, in another a wooden stool. "Which one do you want to sit on?" she asked.

The stool fascinated him with its precise arches. He struggled at placing its wood. "I'm fine. When will Hillard be back?"

"Soon," she said. "We will be together by nighttime. After you've bathed. And gotten some rest."

Wilder unlaced his boots. "I really can't believe it."

"Believe what?" she asked, as she added the stool and mat to a pile of items at the other end of the room. Two black travel trunks with metal latches caught Wilder's eye.

"I can't believe I found him. Here. Alive." His boots off, he flexed his toes. "He's talked about me, hasn't he?"

"Why do you ask?"

"You are too comfortable with me, that's why," he said. "A Negro American appears at your doorstep smelling like all of the world's shit. Tells you his name and nothing else. Then says he is after your man. You don't resist. You don't ask why. You say, 'Come on in.'" He stopped speaking to watch Vatsana slip through the sheets across from him. Without gaining a glimpse of anything on the other side of the sheet, he deduced that it was the part of the hut where she slept. "He's talked about me, all right. And I can predict all he's said. That's why I'm here. All the things he told you about me. King? I want to fix it. I'm a new person. Might even say possessed. Best kind of possession there is. And better for it, too."

Her movements on the other side were manifested through pokes in the fabric. From her bends and twists, he suspected she was changing her clothes.

"I know you," Vatsana said from the other side. "I knew about you even in Saigon. You and the rest. Conley. Wilson. Johnson. Banks. Smith."

"That about covers it."

"Which is why I am comfortable. I will be comfortable around any of you. No reason not to be."

She reappeared with a multicolored cloth wrapped around her, concealing her breasts and hemmed at the tops of her knees. Her shoulders exhibited soft curves, like a young girl's. "I will have my bath now, too."

This announcement to bathe perplexed Wilder. She was Hillard's woman. "You can go first."

"That won't be necessary," she said. "The river is big enough for the two of us. You won't see me. I won't see you."

"Nothing clean about the water in these parts. No," Wilder said, shaking his head.

That was when she responded by assuring him that there were no dead bodies to be found in the river. He still resisted. So she presented him with an alternative: shrouded by the small bush behind her hut, he could wash with a bucket of water and a bar of soap.

At the back he found a weedy clearing and stone steps into the bush. Soaped up, he rinsed himself with scoops of water. He broke from splashing to consider the insufficiency of the water left in the bucket. The ground under his feet frothed with suds and more remained on his skin. Yet he continued to believe that he was right to have turned down bathing in the river. The rivers of Vietnam and Laos couldn't be that different. Yet a two-day journey would suggest that the waters here began in different places than those in Vietnam. But the two days were the result of chaos. All things being as they should always be, it should have taken, at most, half a day. Which had not been the case.

Viet, the fertilizer man, had been as thoughtful as the conditions allowed, offering him a frozen plastic bottle of water. The condensation on the bottle diluted the stickiness of the candy Wilder had handed out to the children.

"Stay cold through journey," Viet said of the water. "I have more at front. You scream for more if you want."

In the back of the truck Wilder took little sips sitting atop the packaged manure. Viet had ushered him into darkness by dropping the back covering. In the darkness Wilder skittered from thought to thought until Viet swung open the covering, reminding him that daylight was not yet lost.

"Not too long. See?" said Viet. "Not have to be with smell too long."

"This is where I get out?"

"This my delivery point."

Viet passed Wilder off to a vendor who, every other week, met with him a few kilometers from Viet's actual delivery point to purchase fertilizer at below-wholesale price.

"Everyone try to thief you," said the old man. "Everyone charging big money."

He introduced himself as Thanh. Gray-haired and yet sinewy, Thanh steered his van wildly to avoid the deep ruts in the road as he announced that the war had turned all goods into hot commodities. Listening carefully, Wilder managed to unmuddy the older man's explanation: a shortage of supply while demand stayed the same meant monopoly-level pricing. Never had Thanh imagined that fertilizer would gain so much in value. "Me? Pay big money for cow shit?" he said, laughing. "No me."

He disclosed that Viet was a family member. But nepotism had nothing to do with it—only through conversations about their heritage had they learned what they shared. "Don't know who your family," Thanh stressed. "Don't ever know."

The truck's dashboard sat higher up than American dashboards. A sliver of glass constituted its windshield. Two pillows propped up Thanh. "Even you find family here," he said.

"I doubt that," Wilder said.

"In Laos?"

"No."

"But you want go there. For what?"

For Hillard. In fact, Thanh was right. For family. "My brother," admitted Wilder.

He described Hillard as much to Thanh as he did to the gloomy landscape he could observe through the window. A droopy sky fashioned the mountains in tiered shadows.

"Your brother, soldier like you?" Thanh asked.

"The best of them," replied Wilder.

They were driving into fog. The headlights shone on only about three feet of the road ahead. "No seeing road," Thanh proclaimed. "You sleep inside my house. Continue tomorrow."

In little time they swerved onto a dirt path that filled Wilder's ears with the grinding noise of a truck protesting the deep ruts and potholes. Thanh raised his voice to say, "Over there. My house."

The headlights barely illuminated a box bungalow with an

aluminum roof hovering under reptilian trees. They parked by a low wood fence, four quick steps from the front door.

Several candles lit the dark interior. When Thanh's wife appeared with a candle in hand, Wilder observed the delicate wrinkles of her face. She looked older than Thanh; as if imploring Wilder to make this judgment, Thanh had quickly taken off his shirt, revealing taut skin. Wilder took Thanh's bare chest as an opportunity to ask if he could also strip off his shirt. It desperately needed to be aired out.

The breeze swirling through the house felt good. When Wilder looked for a place to hang his shirt, Thanh pointed to the handlebars of a bicycle.

He joined Thanh and his wife on a mat for dinner. Wilder lacked the dexterity for chopsticks, so he opted for a spoon, with which he mashed up the long noodles to ensure that every bite of his soup included their meaty texture.

"You have money?" asked Thanh.

Wilder had been waiting for the question. About twenty minutes into their drive, he wondered when Thanh would ask for payment. He swallowed. "A bit." He touched his pants pocket.

"No for me."

"I am happy to pay."

"No for me. For next part. For Bao. Him take payment."

"How much?"

"Him take anything," Thanh said. "All him want is fair payment." He regarded his wife, speaking to her in their language. Then, for Wilder's sake, he added, "I tell her you have brother at Laos."

"I don't actually know where he is."

"Laos small. People no hard to find."

"All signs point to his being there," Wilder admitted, "but the signs are not concrete. All I have to go on is what people have said. And you can't always trust what people say. If I had pictures of him there, or something like a letter with an address . . ." He let his spoon sink into the soup. "I'm acting on feeling. But I don't care. I trust the feeling too much."

Thanh again turned to his wife. "Hon?" he said.

She responded with silence, her eyes beseeching his. He looked to be resisting whatever action she had asked him to take. "You have strong Hon," he said, giving in. "She know more about Hon than me. But she no confident about her English." Thanh's wife smiled, nodding him along. "Spirit inside you say you have brother at Laos," he said. "Spirit inside us never lie."

The following day Thanh rode his bike slowly while Wilder walked at his side down a steep slope. At the bottom, a line of men leaned against their scooters. Thanh pointed out Bao. When they reached him, Thanh set his bike aside and slumped over the seat of Bao's scooter.

"Laos. Take how much?" Thanh asked.

"All the way?" Bao said.

"All the way."

"No get all the way." Bao evaluated Wilder with trepidation. "I get him somewhere. Somebody else get him another where. Very soon, Laos."

"Fine. Somewhere," said Thanh. "How much?"

"Fair price," Bao said. He squinted. "Him and bag heavy. So more than fair." He brought a pointing finger close to his thumb. "But markup very small."

They agreed on a price and were soon on their way.

The scooter stalled and then jutted forward a few times, each time jolting Wilder out of his relish of the open air. Bao chalked the scooter's fits and starts up to their combined weight. But Bao was a fat man who clearly had been straining his scooter's engine with his own heft.

"Gasoline hard to find," Bao shouted over the noise of the scooter. Wilder aimed an ear closer to Bao's mouth. "Small markup for gasoline, too."

"I hadn't realized."

"You no drive car. You no drive scooter," Bao said. "No reason make you realize." Bao looked to his left, then to his right. "Watch road. You see gasoline?"

As both sides of the road were edged by farmland, Wilder doubted that gas stations had ever been ubiquitous.

"Black market," Bao continued. "Only how to get gasoline now."

It was another way the war had augmented life, including ending other forms of transportation, like the buses that had once taken people into all parts of Laos.

"Who in Laos?" Bao asked.

"My Hon tells me my brother."

Wilder sensed the scooter slowing down. "Oh," Bao said. "You must listen."

The rest of the journey required Wilder to change from one scooter to another—twelve in all—and ride behind his last two drivers through the gloomiest night he'd ever experienced. His last driver deduced from the information Wilder provided him about Vatsana—she was a Hmong from Laos, she was some kind of conjure woman—that she lived on a mountaintop.

His name was Augustine, and for a little extra he stayed with
Wilder for the night. They slept with their backs against a tree
just off the road. The next morning, when sunlight burned Wilder's eyes open, he found Augustine already on his scooter.

"Ready?" asked Augustine.

Wilder swallowed a meager supply of saliva to try to wet his
dry throat. "Will you show me the way?"

He took Wilder to the start of a mountain climb. There, he
moved his hand snakelike in the direction of a dirt path coiling
upward through sunburnt greenery. "Just follow." He executed
the sign of the cross. "God take you safe."

As Wilder started up the path, he wondered what he needed
divine protection from. Why was everyone so consumed with
the divine anyway? First, the nurse at the base outside Saigon had
invoked her Christianity: gold, frankincense, and myrrh. Next,
there'd been Thanh's wife and her glee at the lesson her husband
had provided about Hon. Bao and the other scooter men's interest
in him had increased each time he brought up his Hon, their tones
more deferential. And then there was Augustine, just moments
ago wishing him well by invoking his Catholic God. Without
God he'd made it out of Vietnam.

He remembered a question his philosophy professor at Princeton had posed: Why do human beings strive for the divine in
times of hopelessness? Well, as God was his witness, he would suc-
cumb to piety if he found that Hillard was still alive. For it would
mean that Hillard, who had so deeply believed in Vatsana's ashes,
who had so believed in the divine, had survived.

At the mountain's plateau, his legs felt stronger and he sloshed
through the muddy ground more confidently. He noticed one

gaping basin in the ground after another: Vatsana's mountaintop seemed strangely scooped out.

He stopped at a piglet farm between two huts and listened to the piglets' oinks. After several rounds of low-toned practice, he imitated their sound. He oinked on, disturbing a flock of duck-lings. Disturbing chickens. Disturbing stray dogs. At some of the dogs he even pitted his oinks against their barks, coming out on top.

"Vatsana," he said to the first sign of human life he saw since he'd begun his walk up the mountain. The young woman with a metal bucket in one hand ran from him, signaling helplessly with her free hand. He did not take offense. He was a strange Ameri-can soldier. Who knew what he was capable of?

"Vatsana?" This time he asked a group of children inside one of the basins. They were digging in mire with toy shovels, their faces dirtied. More interested in their game, they pointed impre-cisely. One of them was confident in his English. He said, "Right there."

Wilder didn't know where but kept on. He asked after Vatsana twice more before he realized that he'd found her. She stood in front of her hut like a marvel. "Welcome," she said.

He was speechless.

WILDER FELL INTO a long sleep after his bath. When he woke, he thought for a moment that he'd been transported back to Thanh's candlelit house. In his vision was a multitude of spher-ical flames suspended like stars. Fairylike, Vatsana dawned.

"Sleep well?" she asked from the corner of the room.

"I did," he said. "I've had lots of practice sit-sleeping."

"I understand."

A dot of candle wax landed on his chest. It stung like a quick inoculation. His Laotian prick of welcoming.

The raffia mat crackled when he rose from it. He tugged on the shorts Vatsana had given him because they were riding up his thighs. He suspected they were Hillard's. "Is he back?" he said.

"You see the candles?"

Wilder searched for Hillard. "Did he light them?"

"I did," Vatsana said. She stayed with her back to him. "One belongs to him."

The gathering embers of understanding slowed him. Stuttering, he said, "I'm not sure I'm clear on what you mean."

"You are clear, Lieutenant." She turned to face him. "You choked on your words. Which tells me that you know what I mean."

He was about to roll up the mat and return it to its place against the wall. Yet of their own accord, his knees buckled and he kneeled back on it. "When?"

"I don't have the exact day," she said. "Or the exact time."

"He died here?"

"I don't know where exactly."

"How did you find out?"

"I saw it happen."

"You were with him."

"I was here." She helped him up. "Come."

On one side of the drapes sectioning off her room, a lone red candle was fixed in a triangular stand. It was not lit. "It no longer lights," she said. "The first time he came to me, I had him light it.

It was how I kept watch over him," she added. "I hoped for him to be ill when I saw the flame dying. It went out in no time. I've tried several times to light it again."

"Can't you find out where he is?"

"How?"

Wilder looked around the room. "The candle. Can't it tell you?"

"It doesn't work like that, Lieutenant," Vatsana said. "I am not a sorceress."

"You've been calling me Lieutenant. They weren't calling me Lieutenant when he was coming to see you," Wilder said angrily. "So how did you know?"

"He sent me a photograph in the post. Of the Fists. You were Lieutenant," she said. "He didn't believe you were a Negro when he first met you."

Wilder lowered his head. "I don't know that he ever came around to believing that I was." He heard "Swing Low" in his head. "Probably contributed to why he left." A realization pinged in him. "That means you don't know he left."

"A second time?"

"Probably around the time his candle was going out," Wilder said. "I was told that he was living with you. And I don't doubt that the night he left, he was headed your way. To you."

"Maybe. I taught him how to find me."

"Not well enough, apparently." His tone scorched with indictment. "I'm sorry."

"No need to be," she said.

He stood still, letting his fury and hurt gel. When they became so dense, so overwhelming that they needed release, they poured out of him in streams. Vatsana rushed to him and he collapsed into her as he wept. She cradled him as both of them went down. His knees struck the floor but the sharpness was muted by the gentle way Vatsana laid his head across her thighs. She stroked his cheek and blew air onto his face.

"Did you really blow ashes into Hillard's face?"

"I did. For protection," Vatsana said. "I can do the same for you."

"I'm not going back."

"It will protect you."

"Will it?" asked Wilder. "Why didn't it work for Hillard, then?"

"We don't know that it didn't, Lieutenant," Vatsana said. "It doesn't work if you don't want it to."

His eyes were stinging.

"You think he killed himself," Wilder said.

"He didn't want it to work."

WILDER HADN'T REQUESTED that Vatsana give him space, but she understood.

Coaxed on by the candles, to break the uncomfortable quiet he announced his intent to sing. He hadn't sung along with Hillard and the rest of the Fists, he told her, which he believed had been the final straw for Hillard. Vatsana disagreed. His silence couldn't have been what set Hillard off. She empathized, though, with where his mind had carried him. Self-reproach was an instinctive response to misery.

She asked which song and then said, "Why am I even asking? I know." She sang the song, slow and rousing; it was not "Swing Low." Her voice was sleek.

It was an unusual name for a song, "Four Women," like the start of an enticing story: four women walked into a bar . . . four women reached for the same knife . . . four women longed for the same man . . . He listened attentively; he hadn't heard it before.

"It's repetitive," he said.

"Aren't all songs?"

"Their chorus, yes," Wilder said. "But there's no chorus. The whole song is a chorus."

She looked at him puzzled. "It is not the song you had in mind?" she said.

"Not even close."

"He never sang 'Four Women' around you? He sang it all the time."

"No. He never sung it in my hearing."

As Wilder saw it, he and Vatsana were no longer lending each other space for their respective sorrow. It felt as if their sequestration was over. Yet Vatsana kept her distance, while he wanted her on the ground beside him.

She was clearly biding her time to be fully certain of his desire for her. His patience for her was running thin. The orange flares licked hot in him. "Which one are you?" he asked.

"Pardon?"

"Which of the four women are you?" He went through the names he'd just heard. "Aunt Sarah. Saffronia. Sweet Thing. Peaches. Which one would you say is closest to you?"

She waded through the blaze, her silken robe winking in lacy swirls. "That's obvious, isn't it?"

"I didn't want to be presumptuous," he said. "The yellow one?"

"Her name's Saffronia." Vatsana smiled. "He said that about you once, you know. As yellow as Saffronia."

"Am I yellow?" Wilder asked.

Vatsana gripped his arm and brought it next to hers. She pulled a candle closer. "What do you see?" she said.

Wilder looked at their arms side by side. "You are more yellow," he said.

"Yes, Lieutenant," she said. "And you have less color."

He did have less color. Strikingly. Regretfully. Where was Hillard, who was supposed to tell him that he was on the right track to color? There was no Hillard. But it was the way of black, Hillard's kind of black, to leave a perpetual mark when it burst. Vatsana's yellow, as Wilder watched it, deepened from an overlay of shadow.

"Vatsana," he said.

"Lieutenant."

"Were you Hillard's girl?"

"I loved him very much."

"Can you love only him?" asked Wilder, pressing his arm closer to hers. "Is it only him you can love?"

"No," assured Vatsana. "I've let him go."

"Me, too," acknowledged Wilder. "I think me, too."

"And?"

"I love you."

"That can't be true, Lieutenant," Vatsana said, unbuttoning his shorts. "You want me. A feeling I share. But you need time to get to love."

"There's been time. All I've had is time." He removed his

shorts, then hiked up her robe. He put her flat on her back and mounted her, kissing her hungrily, every part of her that was within reach of his lips. "I love you," he said. "I love you." He continued professing his love for her over and over. Over and over. An overplayed ballad.

THEIR LOVEMAKING WAS ALWAYS lush, involved, passionate. In the afternoons, as daylight activities clattered outside, they erred on the side of timidity. How uninhibited could they be when a neighbor's innocent shriek easily slipped between one of theirs? At the turn of night, they were released of all causes for inhibition.

But Vatsana once warned that even at night there were other lives to be cautious of. Albeit more hedonistic ones, and he'd been responding to their appetite for show. She was referring to the candle flames. He drew closer to one; looking into the orange flame, he saw all that she meant for him to see. He'd understood early in their time together that the candles served a purpose. They were a memorial for everyone but Hillard, whose candle refused to light.

Why did everyone seemingly vanish at nighttime? he asked her days later. There was hardly ever a candle flame lighting the interiors of the nearby huts, hardly a sign of those who lived inside. He'd been in Laos for three weeks now and had already found ways to occupy himself during the day. When it wasn't raining—which seemed to be a daily occurrence—he assisted the pig farmer and helped in the rice fields and vegetable beds. He'd also taken up playing a bamboo flute that Vatsana had in the hut, becoming something like the Pied Piper of their mountaintop when he practiced outside: children came to him. He danced to his own imperfect music with them.

But it was the night that bewitched him when it fell into its silence. He was at the window. He said in a low and speculative voice, "You know what I've come to realize? You can even hear a pin drop the minute it starts going dark."

"They head to the shelter," Vatsana said. "The others."

"What shelter?"

"It's a cave," she said. "Away from the bombs."

"What bombs?"

"Your bombs. American bombs. They drop them at night. It's been awhile since the last rounds. But to be safe, everyone still heads for the cave." On the mat, she lay naked, posed in a stretch. "I hear there's even a new cave."

The candle flames, she told him, represented those who'd passed on inside and outside the caves. She'd left Saigon to make sure that the dead were ushered into the afterlife properly and kept alive still. Keeping them alive was a new component to her duties. It was tradition for the remaining family to extend the lives of their loved ones in flame. But as it was disrespectful to do so belowground, the duty had fallen on her shoulders aboveground.

"I don't need to hide," she said. Hearing this, Wilder remembered what the nurse at the base outside Saigon had said to him: she terrified death.

"How long has it been since the last bombs?"

"A month and some weeks."

"So they've stopped."

"We don't know."

He saw in his mind's eye two round fruits erupting. It was his first taste of the vision since he'd arrived on Vatsana's mountaintop. To defeat it, he rushed over to her and wrapped her in his arms. In the course of their lovemaking, he sensed out of the corner of his eye a figure standing amid the candle flames. It was a child with Vatsana's face, the high cheekbones that belonged to Vatsana set against the sparks. She looked on with gleaming teeth as he writhed in Vatsana's deliciousness. When the fires formed into a ring of burning bush around the girl, Wilder quickened his pace, escalating it when she floated toward them. He thought the quicker he went the sooner the girl would disappear. With her only inches from swamping them, he felt success rising in him. At last his groin clenched, then tore blisteringly. He fell onto Vatsana from satisfaction and felt that he'd bled into her. He wheezed. Looking up, he saw that the girl was no more.

"Vatsana," he said into her muffling breasts.

She exhaled.

"There was a girl."

"Yes."

"She had your face."

"Yes."

"You don't sound surprised."

She murmured something indecipherable. Then, she said, "About how old?"

"I couldn't tell you," he said. "Young."

It could be argued, she began, that she'd never been a child. She was mothered by her grandmother, for her birth had paralyzed her mother. She never saw her mother stand upright. Together she and her mother had been infants, kicking and screaming on their backs. When she'd started to crawl, she'd had to crawl over her mother as she would a permanent nuisance.

Indeed, Vatsana had this capacity for self-awareness and self-possession even as a toddler. When she began to walk, she tiptoed around her mother. At a young age her brain understood the relevance of men. She recognized mothers and fathers holding on to their children and determined that a man and woman were required to bring about a child. In her house of three generations of women she wrestled with the absence of men. At some point men had been part of the equation, she'd figured, but she knew better than to ask.

Eventually, the great snap occurred. She was feeding soup to her mother, easing small spoonfuls into the narrow crevice of her mouth, followed by a pause as her mother swallowed. One spoonful bubbled on her mother's lips and dribbled down the side of her mouth. A second faced the same outcome. Instantly, Vatsana understood. She removed the rag that supported her mother's head and used a small corner of it to dab her mother's mouth and cheeks. She fetched a bowl of water.

By the time her grandmother returned from the fields, Vatsana had cleaned her mother's body and clothed it in a burial dress and was sitting in front of it like a palace guard. Her grandmother went around them several times in inspection, her eyes obscured by the brim of her straw hat.

"I didn't train you on the shoes," her grandmother said, referring to the pair Vatsana had slipped onto her mother's feet. "How did you know?"

"Maybe she will walk where she's going," Vatsana said. "You said she will become different."

The old woman removed her hat and folded it, putting it into her farm basket. She joined Vatsana beside the body. She smelled of rain. "I haven't believed in much of anything lately," she said. "That's why I didn't bother to say anything about the shoes. I know I'm supposed to believe that she will become different. Cross the caterpillar river in the afterlife. But I also believed that I could make her better."

After her mother was put into the ground, her grandmother lit a candle and set it in a corner; as part of the memorial, she hung three chrysanthemum garlands on the wall. She was re-believing.

By the time Vatsana turned ten, Western medicine had come to their village and people now sought out her grandmother's remedies only as a last resort. The old woman wished to understand this foreign healing, but lacking English, there was no chance for her.

In Vatsana, she saw an opportunity. When she was young Vatsana showed an aptitude for languages. In Saigon, a British-American woman had started a school for girls, where the girls graduated to work in clinics. Her grandmother heard about the school from the man who showed up monthly to dispense syrups and tablets, and she asked whether her granddaughter could attend.

"She has foresight," said the man when he returned from his walk with Vatsana, during which he'd interviewed her.

Vatsana left for Saigon when she was sixteen, returning during breaks. She came with gifts and departed with additions to her lessons in spiriting. Eventually, her grandmother taught her how to be still for hours on a brown wooden bench and commune with spirits. When she graduated from the school into a nursing career, she found a bungalow for herself in Saigon and set up her own shrines of talismans and candles. Her grandmother blessed Vatsana's own bench, which four boys then tied to the roof of a chartered car destined for Saigon.

Sometimes Vatsana stole behind the red-checked drapes, where her small wooden bench sat. Curiosity once kept Wilder from stepping out after she excused herself and went behind the drapes. Pacing back and forth, he pondered whether he should defy her wishes and have a look. He heard her mumbling her incantations and a series of questions raced through his mind. Would he turn into a pillar of salt if he peeked at her? What if in these moments Vatsana turned reptilian? Or something worse? He wouldn't, he decided. He couldn't handle seeing her in a form other than the one he loved.

Now they lay still in the silence that followed Vatsana's story about her life. Wilder's head rested between her breasts. He relished the warmth on his cheek. He relished the way she snuggled him.

"I never thought I would be back to this village for good," said Vatsana.

"Yet here you are," replied Wilder.

"I had no choice. My grandmother passed. I needed to take on her role here."

"I presumed." He pulled himself from her arms and looked at her. "What is this thing about death fearing you? She passed. Shouldn't you be able to as well?"

"I can," she said. "And I will when it's the right time. That right time will be natural. Not at the hands of American bombs."

She stretched and reached for her robe, which was lying on the floor. "I will be old, Lieutenant. Very, very old."

"How old was your mother?"

"Thirty-four? Thirty-five?" Vatsana answered as she sat up to slip on the robe. "Somewhere around my age."

"I doubt thirty-five was your mother's time. But she passed."

Admiring his nakedness as she stood, she smiled. "Lieutenant, my mother was nothing like my grandmother and me."

He got to his feet. "What about the girl in the candles?" he said. "That was you."

"Yes, that was me. The only me susceptible to untimely death."

Five

What an unfounded assumption it was to believe that all would be well in Laos. Vatsana's mountaintop, Wilder would learn, had been blasted to look otherworldly. What he'd thought of as basins and had skirted as he'd searched for her, what those cavities were that children played in, were in fact craters made by American bombs.

In resistance, Vatsana's people returned to relying on her grandmother. Any flower she could offer—weedy, wispy, furry—and any invocation of her spirits would help. When her grandmother died, Vatsana replaced her. One evening Wilder lost the battle with his own curiosity when he heard Vatsana's low tones from the other side of the drapes. He took a look behind the curtain and saw her on her bench in a trance. She seemed to be floating on her back, as though gravity were irrelevant. The bench barely fit her small frame; her legs and head hung over the edges. He could only manage to be enthralled for a short while. The earlier fear that had made him refrain from looking returned and he quickly stepped away. Yet the image of her remained.

When she came out, she showed no sign that she'd seen him, only expressing her relief at the calming of the bombs.

"But the Americans will be back," she said. "This break is only temporary."

Wilder went to the doorway of the hut and looked up at the overcast sky. "That's not just fog, is it?" Fog had ushered him from Vietnam to Laos. "It's smoke from the bombs."

"Don't you think the smoke would be gone by now?" Vatsana asked.

"The smoke never really goes away."

The parts of a disassembled kerosene lantern lay on the floor in front of her and she was cleaning the glass globe with a rag. She was preparing for the transition to a new source of light—believing, Wilder sensed, that enough justice had been done to the dead. Moreover, two gallons of kerosene had been delivered to the village and distributed among the households, much of it going to Vatsana, who remained aboveground during nighttime.

She finished with the globe and flourished it at him to boast of its spotlessness. After setting it down, she began to clean the lantern's frame, digging into the corners with the rag. "Are you afraid?" she asked.

"Of the bombs?"

She nodded.

Wilder hesitated. "I was not expecting to make it out of Vietnam alive," he said slowly. "Since being here, I've thought about home only once. And that was to consider writing a letter to my folks, to let them know that I'm well and happy. I'll get around to doing that. I know it will disturb my happiness, so I've been putting it off. But I'll get around to doing it."

"You're telling me you are not afraid?"

"I'm telling you I'm happy."

"With dying?"

"With everything," he said.

The lantern was ready to be assembled. She passed him the base, which he held to the floor as she twisted on the ventilation cap. "I hate to ask because I know how difficult it is for you, but I want to know how I'll be sent off when I go," he said.

Vatsana looked at him with an expression he couldn't read. "You want to be buried like us?"

"Can't I?"

"You can," she said, "but don't you want to be with your people?"

He shook his head. "It's no safer back home. I've been dealing with my own bombs since I was a boy. Visions of exploding fruits and human heads. I thought I could escape them, but they followed me to New York. Even to Vietnam. Inside a goddamn tunnel. A fucking tunnel, Vatsana." She handed him the globe. "The worst part has always been the tease. How things explode in your head but you never explode with them." He twisted the globe into place. "I can understand how you feel. It's a miserable thing. That wicked tease."

"I would rather go."

"So would I," he said, tipping kerosene from an old water bottle into the lantern's spout. "I hope you understand why I say I'm happy. Most of it has to do with you. But to think that the bombs are finally going to stop teasing me. Actually kill me."

She did not look at him. She gazed at the kerosene.

"Tell me, how do you bury the dead?" he asked.

"The children of the deceased dress them for burial," she said. "Will you have any children?"

Where had her mind gone? "Children?"

She didn't reply.

He swirled the lantern to evenly coat the wick with kerosene. "I'm sure the bombs have killed kids. Who dressed them for burial?"

"Their mothers. If they could stand it."

"And if they couldn't?"

"I did."

"It would have to be the same for me, then," he said, setting down the lantern. "What happens after?"

He thought her prolonged stare was a cunning silence to bury his question. He was about to repeat himself when she said, "Our funerals used to be beautiful." Her voice scraped with unshed tears. "Everything has changed. Usually with children the funeral would last three days. With adults, six days. That gave enough time for viewing the body. And for family to travel from other villages. It used to be that people would gather every day until the burial to discuss the dead person's time on earth. They would cry but also laugh about the happy times. There would be a lot of food and music. There's none of that now. If you are lucky enough to find the body more or less intact, no amount of bathing and dressing will make it suitable for viewing. Body or no body, we do things more quickly now. Within hours of realizing that the person is dead. The whole process lasts minutes if we are burying one person, a few hours if it's a mass burial." Distress kept Wilder still, seated. "We were lucky with the last child I dressed. He'd only lost an arm and a leg." She looked up. "It was just him we buried that day."

She seized the lamp and gestured for the matchbox. He pointed behind her; she patted the space without looking until her fingers found the box. "My job is to lead everyone to the gravesite. In order to confuse evil spirits, I always switch up the route. I almost got us lost that day. A strip of farmland had been cleared and I mistook it for a path." She lit a match and held it to the wick. A flame whooshed into being. "I slit the necks of two chickens at the grave. Then I said a prayer while the dead boy's father and uncle bled out the chickens onto the earth. That's one of the rituals expected of me. A prayer to go with the animal sacrifices. Another uncle played the bamboo flute. It's not like the single-piped one you play for the children. The funeral flutes have six pipes," she said. "As he was playing, I tossed three bamboo sticks on the ground. All three landed correctly, so I knew that the spirits were ready for him. I could say a final prayer in thanks. I left after that prayer. I never stay for the body to be put into the ground."

"You're not supposed to?"

"I choose not to," she said, twisting the knob to adjust the flame. "These days much of the funeral is improvised to fit our situation. Why not do something for myself?"

She adjusted the flame to a perfect oval. Its brightness pushed through the glass and her face shone. On her cheeks were white streaks. He did not want to feel the sadness they represented. There was no fighting it, however. How hard had Vatsana wept that her tears had stained her cheeks in blistering chalky marks?

———

A SHIFT OCCURRED IN HIM. A rumbling. It all came to a head when one of the children confessed that Wilder's flute music sounded too much like the funeral kind.

"Didn't you say," he gently asked Vatsana, "that the funeral flutes had six pipes?"

"They do."

"So how can mine pack the same punch?"

The answer, which he'd been already feeling, had driven him to at last write a letter to his parents. He didn't want to sound as if he was writing a suicide note, but the only way he could conceive of opening a letter to his parents—*Dear Pa, Dear Ma, Forgive me*—was the classic salutation of those leaving deliberately. His passing, he knew, would reside in the hinterland between suicide and murder, coming at the hands of another but with his willful participation.

Constable, who had twice delivered goods to the village and had recently delivered the kerosene, arrived this time with a wealth of chewing gum, peppermint, pens, pencils, papers, envelopes, exercise books, reading books, rubbing alcohol, canned beans, lighters, pocketknives, razors, shaving cream, blankets (some of them the same picnic ones draping Vatsana's hut), white and red candles, military flasks, military helmets, military boots. The flasks and helmets and boots were permanent components nobody ever wanted. The first time Wilder saw those items, he figured out Constable's benefactors.

Constable looked uncharacteristically glum today. Wilder passed him an envelope.

"Letter to America?" Constable asked.

"Can you get it there for me?"

"Easy." But he winced.

"Everything all right?" asked Wilder.

"I won't come for a while," he said. "An answer, if you get one, will take long."

"Why?"

"You know."

Wilder raised a brow, waited.

"You people," Constable said. "Americans."

"Where you get your items."

"Yes," he said. "They give me stuff. Then they say, 'Wait, don't go now.' Sometimes I wait two months, three, before they say, 'Okay, you can go.'"

"They told you not to show up for a while?"

He nodded. "They think plenty Vietcong here now. They will bomb very soon," he said. "You go! Leave!"

"Me?" asked Wilder. "Go where?"

"Your home," said Constable. "America."

Instead Wilder plotted his ideal end. He wanted to be dressed from head to toe in his army uniform, a wish with which Vatsana promised to comply. No need, he said. There was no telling where the bombs would fling him, so he'd resolved to dress in wait. If the Americans ever found him, he wanted them to know that they'd killed one of their soldiers.

For three days he wore his hat, fatigues, and boots. Sometimes, in his sleep, he unwittingly kicked Vatsana's shin with his boots, waking her. After those three days, he began to smell of sweat. On the morning of the fourth day she helped him out of his clothes, reminding him that the bombs always dropped at night. She agreed to let him keep his cap and went to launder his sweaty shirt and trousers. That night, and each of the two nights after, she handed him his uniform cleaned and dried in daylight. "Maybe tonight," she always said.

She'd been increasingly avoiding his sight line, which he took as a sign of her increasing displeasure with his anticipation. One day he decided to provoke glee in her. He stepped out of the hut with flute in hand and in search of her.

Beside her small vegetable garden, she washed his uniform in a pan of soapy water. Next to the pan was another with clear water for rinsing.

"Vatsana."

She peered at him through the fierce sunlight.

"You never taught me the song. 'Four Women,'" he said.

"That's true," she said. "And the flute?"

"Accompaniment." He playfully mimicked impassioned play, before lowering it to ask, "Don't you believe in me?"

She soaped the collar of his uniform and giggled.

"I think I'm quite a good musician now," he said. "Try me."

"Okay." She sang the first verse while she fanned out his shirt, unintentionally spraying his face. She extracted the pants from the milky rinse water. Her voice softened as she wrung them out.

He expected her to glide into the second verse. Instead she repeated the first verse. She sang and fanned out the pants also. Sang and fanned. "Got it?" she asked.

"I think so."

She piled the small mound of laundry into her arms and carried it to the clothesline. One after the other, she slung the garments over the rope.

"Three, two, one," she instructed, then picked up anew. His instrument's sweet notes fit her singing seamlessly. Eyes closed, he sailed through the song. At the end of the first verse she paused and he opened his eyes for instruction.

"Play it the same way for the next verse," she said.

More confident in his ability, her voice soared and he followed her. They embraced after the fourth verse. The flute dug into her groin. She moved it. "I prefer another hardness," she said coyly.

The remainder of the afternoon became one of lovemaking, adopting the uninhibited nature of nighttime. If there was any good to Constable's notification of the imminent American bombing, for Wilder it was that it had muted everyone in daylight as well, giving way to exceptional sex.

Vatsana wondered about Wilder's hat: where it might end up, since he foresaw his own body being pitched a great distance. "You think it will stay on your head?" she asked.

"No," he said. "I will probably lose it. My hope is that my clothes will stay on."

Weariness came with the wait. By the ninth day, boredom took hold and he began to help with washing his clothes himself, sinking his hands into the soapy water as he gripped the end of his pants while Vatsana scoured the waist in rapid swish-swishes. In that near blank state of mind he heard a noise.

"Hear that?" he asked.

"What?"

"Listen."

Even as he spoke, they both heard it: the low zoom of airplane engines. She yanked the fabric out of his hand and he stumbled into the pan. She did not wait for him to pull himself out of the water, seizing him and with surprising force dragging him to the front of the hut. She let go of him and scaled the ladder. At the doorway, she stretched out a hand and screamed, "Come. Please. Come."

The planes were still out of view. His idea had been to run after them but he was unprepared, his army clothes wet in the pan, his boots in some dark corner of Vatsana's hut. He'd removed his hat because of the heat.

"Wilder!" Water dripped from the tips of Vatsana's fingers. "Come!"

All around them villagers were dashing for cover. Together they hurried indoors. She tried to shut every crevice that would reveal existence from outside the hut but she could not suppress the planes' roar. The hut wobbled on its stilts as the planes came closer. A basket of pots and pans tipped over; others shook.

The quaking grew, rocking them where they lay. "I didn't lie about nighttime," she screamed.

"I know you didn't lie. They are probably going with a new strategy. A surprise attack."

She spoke a response into his neck, the words silenced by the pummeling of the ground outside. The floor jolted, blowing them against a wall; Vatsana moaned. A great pain had thumped into his own rear, but he couldn't moan in either solidarity or injury as they were thrown a second time. They fell in different places but close enough that he could reach for her and pull her close. "You all right?" he asked.

Her fast breaths singed. Death was supposed to fear her. She was not the one supposed to fear death. Before he could wrap his mind around what was happening, they were flung apart again.

He was crawling for Vatsana when he felt another quake, which this time caused kitchen items to be flung at him. He swatted aside two pots and a wooden ladle before he could crawl to her. Two more knives fell a few feet away. Baskets tumbled.

The quaking suddenly stopped. But they were not yet in the clear. The racket of the planes had faded but had not completely abated. Wilder shut his eyes hard and tried to muffle the engines inside him.

In Vatsana's voice, he heard, "They're gone."

He opened his eyes. The black of her pupils engulfed his. He blinked, getting a whiff of the soapy water. "Fuck," he said, flipping onto his back.

Something poked through the drapes to Vatsana's bench room. Wilder crawled across the room on his forearms and shook it free. It was Hillard's candle.

"Bombs are supposed to sound like a million guns," he said. "Nothing sounded like that."

"I heard the planes," Vatsana said. "Be furious at me."

"Why?"

"I was selfish. And that's why you are still alive." She sat up. "I dreamed of this. The two of us. We both burned and it made me hopeful. I thought death was possible for me after all. I wasn't going to sit back and lose you, Wilder. What life is there after the loss of two great loves within the span of three months?"

Vatsana trembled to her feet. She tipped a basket upright with her foot. "I didn't need Constable to know that the Americans would soon show because in my dream they came through the brightest sun. How many days of bright sun have we had?" He did not answer. "How many times have I laundered your uniform?" she added. "At least six. Six? Six continuous days of sunlight? On this mountain? Without a whiff of rain? It was the clearest sign."

"You knew they were planning on shifting to daylight."

"I did," she said. "And I kept that from you. In case you tried to stop me from dying with you." She picked up one of the baskets and filled it with two cooking pans that had fallen on the floor. "I challenged the spirits and they won. I am still here. And you are still here."

"Let me," he said, reaching for the basket in her hands.

He carried it to the kitchen. There he gathered a small mound of scattered spoons and forks and dropped them into the basket. "You are one hell of a miracle worker, Vatsana," he said. "If what you are saying is true, it means you foiled American might. A little woman like you. Stopping their bombs from exploding."

They picked up everything that had fallen, delaying the more exacting process of piecing themselves back together. He had imagined that one of the American planes landed on the roof, the raffia disintegrating and descending like shaken hay. Then a monumental crack. Then the metal of the plane's underside.

He heard a fierce shriek. Had his imagination come to life? Vatsana was at the door.

"What's going on?" he asked.

"People are running."

"Where?"

"I can't tell."

He grabbed her and they dove into the crowd, arriving at the

nearest rice paddy. Weeks from harvesting and burned by sunlight, the field was husk colored. The ground heated the soles of
his feet. Along with Vatsana and the others, he stood several feet
back, fearful of the gargantuan metallic pods that clustered on the
land.

"Stay here," Wilder said to Vatsana. He took a few steps, getting close enough to appraise the pods more carefully but clear of
the danger he knew they posed. Each of the three silver pods was
about eight feet long and fifteen inches in diameter, and clearly
weighed hundreds of pounds. There was some writing on them
but he could not make it out.

"It's a warning," he yelled to the crowd. "A warning."

Vatsana translated, as well the ensuing chatter. She told Wilder
that an old man was suggesting that they live the rest of their lives
in the caves. Another man thought the suggestion ludicrous; someone agreed, another disagreed. Two boys almost came to blows.
They settled down after Vatsana talked to them. As people began
to leave, Vatsana said, "They have decided to move into the caves
for good."

She reached out and took Wilder's hands. "What are they?"
she asked about the metallic pods.

"I'm not sure. But I'm starting to think that they are not as
dangerous as I thought."

"They didn't teach you about them in soldier school?"

"We were only trained in what we needed to know."

Now she was looking at him, not the pods. "Do you think it's
kind of them?" she asked. "The warning?"

"You don't think they're past kindness?"

"Maybe it has to do with you," she said. "Maybe Constable told them that you are here."

"You think it's me they are being kind to?"

"Yes," she said. "You are one of them. Aren't you?"

"Vatsana, what did Hillard tell you about Mississippi?"

She didn't respond directly. Instead she said glumly, "The Americans won't be kind to you."

"No, Vatsana, they won't," Wilder said.

On their way back to the hut they moved with careful steps. One or two birds began to sing. He let go of her hand. "We should join the others," he said.

"Is that what you want?" she asked. "The planes will be back. And you will be ready for them. I will stay out of your way. I don't know how I am going to manage. But I will." They were steps from the hut. "You have my word, I will stay out of your way."

Wilder wondered if perhaps she hadn't been listening carefully. Seeking shelter equaled an eagerness to be with her a lifetime. He pulled her toward him and held her tight. "You are what I want, Vatsana," he said. "Both of us, in fact. Alive and well."

They packed two cloth sacks for the caves, distributing between them clothing, chewing sticks, all of Constable's canned foods—mostly peas and beans—that they had. One of the families had offered to leave them a canoe at the river's mouth. When they got to the canoe, Vatsana arranged the weight of the sacks evenly, adding their rolled-up sleeping mat and lantern. She situated herself for paddling on a crosspiece by the stern. With a bag constructed from three flower-patterned napkins slung over his chest that contained little bottles of Constable's mouthwash and deodorant, two plates, and two spoons, Wilder perched on the center crosspiece.

He closed his eyes to stay blind to the river that riled his long-suffering distress. Relying on Vatsana, he opened his eyes only when the canoe ran aground.

Nothing but thick forest greeted him. "Where's the cave?" he asked.

"There," she replied, waving her paddle at the forest. "In there."

They got out of the canoe and hid it in the reeds, then trudged along a muddy path into the jungle. She wore the slinging bag around her back and carried the mat in one hand and the lantern in the other, while he lugged the two sacks. They worked together to use their bodies to push branches out of their way. When the path steepened, he hoisted the sacks onto his shoulders.

A long decline took them to the mouth of the cave. It swarmed with bats. He swung at them several times with a branch and stopped to see if they had been noticed. Vatsana obliged him, each time waiting patiently as he listened, but eventually she grew tired of his caution. When he stopped again, she said, "Wilder. Keep going. These bats are vicious."

"I'm sorry. I've been inside a place like this before." He wanted to make sure that this wasn't the tunnel.

The cave had two reassuring features: its floor did not resonate with a crunch and he could walk upright in it. It was also much cooler. However, he still inspected the ground carefully, in case it soon swept with dry foliage or worse. His gaze steadied when the bats' sounds waned. In the quiet he heard the *plop-plopping* of water and up ahead the voices of human settlement.

The water was the river meeting them as a stream. It ran between two flat-topped stone banks, where camps had been set up. Campfires snapped, around which families huddled and passed food to share. He searched for a place they could claim for themselves, but Vatsana made the decision, pointing to a distant spot.

The gloom of their new confines begged for light. It was so dark that Wilder could not make her out. "Vatsana," he said. "Can you see me?"

He heard her snicker, then felt her tickling fingers around his neck.

"There you are," he said.

He had the unnerving feeling that only now had they rematerialized into being. He went with her to ask the others for firewood, having decided that they should save the lantern for an emergency—the kerosene inside it was all they had left.

Nobody had extra firewood to give, though eventually two boys—the boys Vatsana had kept from fighting—approached with a basket of wood chips, one of whom declared in English, "For Vatsana. And you."

The two boys had quit their meals to gather the wood. They followed Vatsana and Wilder to the spot they were going to make their home and poured the chips at Vatsana's feet. She stepped back and one of the boys lit the wood. After the light soared, she got to work unpacking, as did Wilder. For dinner, they roasted a whole fish the boys had speared for them, plating it with a can of beans.

Within five days, many people's lanterns, now useless, were discarded in a heap. Everyone roamed aided by beguiling torch fires. Their refuge began to suffer damage from the frequent bombings, which broke off boulders that tumbled into the water. When one night a boulder crushed two people in their sleep, Vatsana recalibrated her burials, letting the water carry away the bodies covered with reeds and saying a simple prayer as people wailed. With these deaths, each household switched to sleeping in turns: Wilder never slept while Vatsana did; nor she, he. Time flattened.

Once, left to his own devices after Vatsana dozed off, Wilder went down to the water. Everyone but he rinsed off there and Vatsana had been bringing him a wet rag to wipe his arms and legs, making a second run for his groin. Witnessing the funeral where water carried away human bodies had not helped to change his mind. Now, standing the closest that he'd ever stood over it, Wilder laughed heartily as someone's floating shit moved by. He pulled down his pants and squatted—a difficult release, as sustenance was paltry—then entered the water completely naked to bathe alongside his own feces, which the water was slowly taking away. The water was comforting, flowing around him with a slow, smooth inexorability. It felt natural, inevitable, nothing worthy of fear. He realized that now. After that, he went in every day.

His bath once went red. He did not even flinch at the blood; instead he went underwater and stayed there for as long as he could. When he shot up for air a girl stood over him, her legs streaked. She was young, maybe ten or eleven, in the throes of first menstruation. He swam to the edge and helped her into the water. When she submerged herself, he reached for his clothes and got out of the water and slipped them on. A rope lay steps from him, which for a moment he believed to be a mirage because his pants fit loose and he'd started to ponder all that had been lost, from the grand to the practical: a belt. No mirage, the rope slipped through his belt loops with ease, the knot he tied coming out roselike.

THEIR CAVE COMMUNITY marked a year—people had been keeping track—by collecting both banks' remaining stock of Constable's canned foods. Together they cooked the contents for a celebration. While most of the food was happily consumed, nobody had a taste for the last cans of cranberry sauce—certainly not Vatsana, who watched Wilder gorge on spoonfuls of the three lumps of what looked like plated red gelatin.

Once, during one of Wilder's swims, he came across a woman at the side of the stream giving birth. She was aided by two other women, who softened her agony by massaging her back and stomach. He knew he was impolite for watching, but he could not bring himself to look away; he had never seen a baby being born before. The helping women paid him no mind, focused as they were on bringing the light of new life into the darkness of the water and cave. Lying low in the water watching, Wilder saw the woman's vulva flex and one of the helping women pull her deeper into the water. Many moans, bawls, and cries finally released the infant, whom the midwife raised seemingly from the water's depths. Wilder was still dripping with river water when he found Vatsana and informed her of the wonder that he'd seen. He stammered about the possibility of their own children.

"Maybe when we return to real life," she said quietly.

But months eased into another year. The bombs endured. Boulders fell from the darkness above them. And Vatsana's stomach grumbled from lack of proper nourishment. Mai, the girl

Wilder had watched come into the world, grew, her existence a satisfying reminder of the endurance of real life. Through her Wilder kept track of advancing time.

Mai was in his care once a week, her parents appreciating the time they could have to themselves. Often, he and Vatsana also set off on their own into the hidden parts of the cave. When they chanced on indisputable seclusion, he tethered the torch fire behind him and they proceeded to make love, the light hearkening back to the candles of their early days. Unlike the candles, this fire was close enough to welt his rear. Pain was love. Or was it that love was pain? Childlessness, an unexpected pain, had stricken him. The moment always arrived when Mai's parents came for her, after which his arms felt heavier than ever, though they were empty. Emptiness had to be the heaviest of all the world's emotions, Wilder thought, made worse by the fact that Vatsana was withering away, getting thinner and thinner.

"Imagine how much more a child inside me would take," she said. "What milk could I provide once a child was born?"

He never told her what he wondered in response: Hadn't Mai's mother and other women managed? He never uttered those words because they had not brought Vatsana's bench here with them, and it seemed to him that he had his answer. Not having heard from Vatsana in a while, her spirits were sucking life from her.

The next time he watched Mai, she fell asleep. As she slept, he glimpsed around her head a crown of autumn leaves. He was reminded of the framed sepia photograph of his parents and their wedding party that hung on the wall of the main dining room of their house in Mexia. One of their flower girls, whom he guessed to have been the same age as Mai, three, had worn a crown of leaves.

When Mai awoke, she stood on Wilder's thighs and held his face, her palms warm against his cheeks.

"Mai?" he said. "Are you my flower girl?"

She heaved joyfully with her arms aimed above her head.

"Are you, Mai?" he asked again. "Are you my flower girl?"

VATSANA HAD BEEN officiating makeshift funerals. What made a makeshift wedding more objectionable?

"Death is permanent," she said. "Whatever the situation, you have to find a way to do what has to be done."

"Isn't marriage permanent?" Wilder asked.

"If you want it to be, yes."

"Well, I want ours to be, Vatsana. So let's find a way to do what has to be done. Do you need an engagement ring?"

"We are not like your people," she said. "Just something to show me you want to marry me."

It could be as elementary as the stones scattered about, chipped from the limestone and corroded into brilliance. He scooped up a few on the sly and wrapped them in one of the flower-patterned napkins. He tied a bow of wood strings around the twist. When he presented it to her, she exaggerated her surprise, her lips widening into a smile. She unwrapped the pouch and poured the limestone fragments into her hand.

"What about you?" she said. "Do I have to do anything?"

"Say yes."

"I thought that was clear."

"Still you have to say it."

"Yes, then," she said. "Yes."

He wanted nothing from his own tradition but a flower girl. Vatsana assiduously scratched strings from the napkin, joining them in knots, using the resulting thread to create a small crown ornamented with some of the stones Wilder had given her.

On the wedding day, it sat on top of Mai's head. As though the marriage were a longed-for yearning, Mai beamed. She was a cherub, a butterfly holding court with the river as background. Here was her territory, this water child, and she happily ceded it to them.

The ceremony was simple. The oldest woman of their cave community joined his hand with Vatsana's in a spool of different threads. She fed him a roasted rat leg, from which he gnawed off a shred of crispy flesh. She drew the meat to Vatsana's lips and Vatsana bit off her piece with her front teeth. Together they chewed and looked at each other with a mixture of love and wonder. The meat made intense work of their jaws. Believing that they were readying their mouths for a serious kiss, people giggled.

"Should we say something?" Wilder whispered.

"No."

"Nothing like vows?"

It had just occurred to him. From the way she mulled it over, he knew that the exchange of vows was a ritual unfamiliar to her.

"Something small. About our love."

Her bemusement did not diminish.

"Okay. We can just thank everyone for coming," he said. "But first, a kiss."

———

MARRIED LIFE, it turned out, had no special ring to it. The bombs persisted, and perhaps the only change was that Vatsana exercised a closer watch on him. Perhaps he exercised a closer watch on her as well, dividing his watch with the one he kept on Mai.

Twice, Vatsana protested his attentiveness to Mai. She emphasized that she did not like that he was abandoning her for the child. "This is your way of punishing me for not having one?"

"No," Wilder said, and he meant it. "But even if I wanted to stop, I wouldn't be able to. She prefers me to her parents. Know what her father said? That because of me she speaks such good English that he might just give up on his broken English and have her translate."

In the days that followed, Wilder sensed a change within him he couldn't put a finger on. They had gone a week without hearing the bombs, he realized only after people started to discuss the possibility of returning to the village. Mai's father and three other men volunteered themselves for reconnaissance. After three days away they came back with word that Constable had shown up to confirm that the Americans had stopped bombing. In addition, they announced, some of the huts—including Vatsana's—were wondrously intact.

Mai seized Wilder's waist. She was tall for being only four now. Though Wilder was short, there was something to be said for Mai coming up to his waist. "Papa Wilder," she said joyfully. "The fighting is over."

"It is over, Mai," he underscored.

Mai wanted to be at his side on the day of return, two steps behind her parents. He walked jerkily with her hanging on to him. He held the lantern, the only item Vatsana and he had decided to salvage from the years in the cave.

When they reached the river, the men got to work pulling canoes out of the reeds. There was not enough room to carry everyone back to the village at once, so they agreed to cross the river in turns. Wilder and Vatsana were among the first batch, sharing a canoe with Mai, her parents, and her two older sisters. Their number in the small canoe would have worried Wilder before the cave, but he no longer feared the water and paddled calmly with Mai's father.

On land, Wilder saw that the ground was more upturned now, more unsettled. He couldn't believe what the war had done. They rounded one crater after another and Mai asked their names. Many were filled to the brim with water. "Ponds," he said, not wanting to destroy Mai's innocence with the truth.

Almost at the village, thunder broke and rain began to pellet the trees. Mai began to tremble and squeezed him tight.

He passed the lantern to Vatsana through the dense curtain of water, then picked up Mai. "I'm going to go ahead," he said to Vatsana.

He sprinted with Mai through the marsh. A few feet from Vatsana's hut he saw that the door was open. He bolted for it, and when he went in he tripped on a surviving candle lying on the wet floor. He staggered but quickly found his footing so as not to fall with Mai. Rain was dripping in through holes in the roof. He stood looking over the rancid place, gagging at the sight of the green, mildewed corners. Two cooking pans were filled with water, their surfaces covered in cloudy mold. Mai squirmed to be let down, but not knowing what other hazards had been growing here, Wilder held her more tightly. She squirmed some more—"I want to stand, Papa Wilder," she pled—before she gave in and stayed put.

When Vatsana arrived she stopped, stunned by the reek. She groaned at the disorder around her. When she could no longer stand her despair she wrapped her arms around Wilder and Mai, asking, "How do we begin to fix this?" Wilder did not have an answer for her.

It took Wilder and Vatsana three days to make the place livable again. During respites from the rain, she scrubbed off the mildew, washed the pans, and burned several sheets and clothing items. On a clothesline she rehung out back, she aired out the clothes they could still use, humming all the while, which Wilder took as a sign of her embracing renewal.

Behind one of her trunks, she found Wilder's flute. She raised it above her head, toward the ceiling, where Wilder was thatching the roof and could see her through an opening.

"Resilient little thing, isn't it?" he said about the flute.

For three nights they'd slept outside under the cover of trees. Falling to sleep now under an actual roof felt unseemly, especially in the face of the rampant homelessness that others faced. Forced to extend their cave dwelling, several of the villagers set up campfires at night, with some going to sleep by the fires while others ventured back into the jungle. Vatsana had already dozed off next to Wilder on the new raffia mat she'd woven, and he could hear their neighbors' crackling fires outside. His feelings of uneasiness increased, for what resonated from the crackling were not memories of the life they'd come out of only a few days prior but the times he and the Fists had gathered around fires. He wondered what had happened to all of the men he'd left in Vietnam. Had they survived? Were they back in America?

The next day Wilder woke up later than he'd intended. The men of the village had grouped themselves into six construction teams that began work at first light in order to meet their quotas of building five huts per team within a week. With his and Vatsana's hut repaired, Wilder planned to join Mai's father and the other men who made up his team.

When Wilder arrived, the teams were already at work. He seized the other end of a heavy bamboo log that Mai's father was struggling to hoist, and in the days that followed they raised bamboo stilts, constructed walls from flimsy wood panels, laid raffia roofing. Mai's father was magnanimous; he'd chosen his hut to be the one they built last. Wilder in turn took in Mai and he went home nightly to Vatsana and Mai, like a real family. Sometimes they ate their dinner inside, other times they came out for the communal dinners that had become the temporary norm in the village.

Their team got to Mai's family's hut after eight days. Because three other teams had already met their quotas, some of the other men came to help. With the extra hands they finished in a day.

When Wilder returned Mai to her parents she cried and threw herself on the ground. He promised he would spend time with her every day, which got her to wipe her tears.

But Vatsana stood in his way. Now that she had him to herself she kept him indoors to make up for the nights Mai slept between them on the mat. The raging storms of the rainy season helped Vatsana's cause: there was nowhere for Wilder to go. Constable was yet to show. Without kerosene or candles, night was truly night, with daylight hardly bright.

"I bet I can figure out a way to bring us light," Wilder said to her on his fifth day of confinement.

"How?"

"I never told you. That was my work in New York. Energy."

When the storms let up, he suggested they go out. After seven days of satisfaction, Vatsana was happy to again share him with Mai, whom she knew Wilder wanted to see. She handed him his flute and said goodbye.

"She might never let me come back," he joked, tossing the flute back and forth in his hands.

"I'm not giving you up without a fight," she teased.

Sunshine that day was fiery enough that moisture could be seen roiling in waves. Wilder played the flute and the village children followed. Closest to him, Mai was irritated by the other children's prancing after Wilder's lively melody. She stopped them cold with her stares and snarls. She did look kindly on one girl, Lani, whom Wilder reminded Mai was her cousin. But the furthest Mai went was temporarily putting aside her jealousy to promise that Lani could dance with them next time.

Clear of Lani, Wilder asked Mai, "Are you really going to let her join us next time?"

She hung her head. "No."

He chuckled and Mai smiled.

"I knew it," Wilder said. "I knew you didn't mean it."

She laughed and ran out onto the desolate plain. Pocketing the flute, Wilder hardly recognized this arid land before him, which, even after recent storms, baked in the sun.

Mai had run too far from him. Making a visor with both of his hands, he called out for her, "Mai." She stopped. "Wait. Wait." He stamped the whites of his palms at her. "Wait right there."

But she did not. Instead she ran farther away and he chased after her. He wasn't quick enough—she laughed and was soon out of sight. He stopped to catch his breath at a section of the land with natural low hills that now were pockmarked with craters. He wished he'd brought some drinking water.

Crickets and large ants were scattered across the stones he came across in the natural depressions in the land. Inside the craters, where he expected Mai was most likely to hide, there was nothing but water that was evaporating. After a while he stood on top of one of the craters and scoped out the expanse around him. He cried out, "Mai! Mai!"

Suddenly, a small shadow covered his left arm from behind. He knew it was her before she giggled breezily in victory. When he turned, he saw she was standing about twenty feet from him, her arms raised in celebration. She was holding a small, rusty globe the size of an apple.

"What's that?" he asked, thinking it was likely one of Constable's goods.

"A ball," she said. "It's heavy. But see"—she tossed it, then caught it—"I'm strong."

He cheered without meaning to encourage her. Hearing in his excitement a plea for an encore, she tossed the ball higher. It was a perfect, round sphere bathed in sunlight, so that when it exploded, he experienced it as something cosmic. The truth set in only after he found himself flattened on the ground, earth and patches of grass spuming over him.

A bomb—the metal ball she'd tossed in the air—had gone off. Through the smoke, he saw Mai on the ground.

He rushed to her on his hands and knees. When he got to her body some of the smoke had faded. Half of her face was torn flesh, and rivulets of blood were pouring into the ground. She wasn't breathing.

A jolt of anguish reminded him that his trembling legs and arms still worked. He scooped up Mai, letting her head dangle from his forearm to allow the blood to draw away from him and to hide the face he couldn't bear to see.

He ran to the only place he knew to go, stumbling and running across the unsteady ground. When he got to the foot of Vatsana's hut, his mind froze. He laid Mai on the ground and wept, his anger and grief exploding out of him in strangled sobs. He heard something pop inside the hut, like a starting pistol. He took off. He heard a familiar voice calling out his name but he did not look back.

IT WOULD REQUIRE another two years for Wilder to bring himself to address a common curiosity about war that Rutherford and others had: How many men did you kill, Wilder?

His reply: Even one is one too many, Rutherford.

Wilder's imprecise answer to Rutherford's interest was all he would ever reveal to Rutherford about his five years away from America. It was all he would ever give anybody. He reserved the parts about the Fists, Vatsana and Mai, and the cave for himself. Even after he came back from Southeast Asia and resumed what had been his life, he couldn't accept any of it as real. How was he supposed to tell a story about himself that was inconceivable even to him? Finding Vatsana in the first place was unbelievable, an extraordinary stroke of good fortune. How much more his journey back to the States. Leaving Vatsana and the village to head back to Vietnam, at one point flinging the flute that had been in his pocket the whole time, at another tossing aside his heavy army boots because they were slowing him down. He'd traveled barefoot on sun-scorched ground, so out of his mind with pain and grief that he registered no pain or distress from his blistered feet.

And the Good Samaritans. A Vietnamese van driver who'd picked him up from the side of the road near the Laotian border and passed him a needle to puncture his blisters. The driver's wife, who treated the blisters with a sticky ointment and cotton wool, after which she'd fed him and shown him a place to bathe and given him a change of clothes. A pair of shoes waited for him inside their house.

A succession of handoffs followed, from one Good Samaritan to another, until the most consequential of them all, and the most incredible: a real-life colored American lieutenant who believed Wilder after only two questions and prepared the necessary documents to get him back to America. It was the same colored lieutenant who managed to reach Rutherford on the phone. Minutes before the military transport plane was about to take off from Saigon, the lieutenant found Wilder on the tarmac to announce that he would have someone waiting when he got off the airplane in Newark, New Jersey.

Yet Rutherford missed Wilder in the crowd at the Newark airport. When Wilder approached him, Rutherford was searching the crowds looking for a face he didn't recognize. Wilder had been among the last to exit the plane, and soon he was the only one left by the baggage carousel. With Rutherford's options dwindling to one, he finally copped to the truth. He stared at Wilder, his discomfort turning to amazement.

"Hell," Rutherford said. "Hell."

He pulled his pal to him, then held him by the shoulders for a second examination.

"Look at you, Wilder, looking like one of those bearded prophets."

Telepathy

One

Belinda was screaming for him. Cell phone in hand, she found Wilder in his library.

On speaker was Jacob, sharing the details of their mother's passing, asking about the chances of her returning to Ghana for the funeral.

"We are yet to make funeral arrangements," Jacob said. His silence was clearly meant for her to speak. She did not. Giving up on her, he continued, "It will probably be in a month. You have some time."

At last she spoke. "I cannot come, Jacob. I'm not going to fuck things up for myself."

She held herself together until the end of the call. When it was over she dropped the phone as she collapsed to the floor. Wilder caught her and held her close. "I'm so sorry, Belinda. When was it you last saw her?"

"I was sixteen."

"Nineteen years," Wilder said. "I'm so sorry."

It was an apology about what was not in the cards for her, not sympathy for her loss. Despite her perfectly curated steps down the correct path—her performance of deep love at city hall as she and Wilder signed marriage papers, the efforts she'd made to erase vestiges of her maiden name, their expensive immigration lawyer—her American legality still stagnated. She'd even gone as far as to sometimes wear a wedding ring, although she hated the constricting feeling of it on her finger.

Together with Wilder, she'd submitted her application for a green card on September 1, 2001. Two years later, they'd heard nothing, and Wilder casually offered to return to Ghana with her. Together they could run his company from there. He had already appointed her the company's business manager, with a stipend they both understood to be extravagant but appropriate because she'd proven to be a brilliant business partner. Belinda's response to his offer of returning to Ghana was the first time she spoke the answer that would endure: "No."

On the phone with Jacob, she'd been abrupt, even offensive. After Wilder released her from their tight embrace she tried to get him to talk about Vietnam. Her mother was dead, and with both of them feeling the hollowness of loss, Belinda hoped that she could get him to let down his guard. "I can handle it. Whatever trauma you experienced during the war," she told him.

But he deflected. "Yes, Belinda, the truth is a kind of trauma."

He could see on her face the torment his response inflicted. "You're a hypocrite, Wilder," she said. "You go on and on about the wickedness of this country, but you are just as wicked, keeping things to yourself."

She left him in the library by himself. She did not speak to him for days. When she finally did, he focused on talking to her about business, reviving the idea of a return to Ghana, noting that his company boiled down to the two of them; its small staff could remain in Houston. From Ghana the two of them could run the company together, plot strategy, follow developments, agree on decisions. It was the same case he'd made last year, in 2007, when it was announced that Ghana had discovered oil. They could make a play in a new industry that was in his blood, he'd said then. How sensible the idea was. How it felt like victory.

"I could even diversify there, spread out my investments," he found him- self now adding for emphasis, stunned that he still had to advocate for leaving even in the wake of Belinda's mother's passing.

"What about my investment here?" Belinda said. "What about my chance to reap what I've sown in this country?"

Wilder could not comprehend her love for a place that had, for nearly twenty years, refused her. And even if it ultimately did accept her, it was a charade—he and his kind the perfect examples of that.

"I'm not mad about America, Wilder," Belinda said. "But being American means a great deal."

"What does being American mean?" he asked.

"It means being *able*," she said. "Look how starting on the green card process made me able. I'm able to send money home. Able to help fund a house for my family."

"That was me," he said.

"And for that I'm very grateful," she said. "But you have to admit, Wilder, that you are able because of America."

"You mean able *in spite* of America."

"Your grandfather, Wilder. You were able because of him. He was able because of America."

"No, Belinda. He was able *in spite* of America. Do you know how many obstacles he had to overcome to keep this money going?"

"And that makes you feel good, doesn't it? To overcome every obstacle. To win in spite of the deck stacked against you. Maybe I want to know what that feels like. Maybe I want to know how it feels to win at America in spite of the deck stacked against me."

Wilder had never heard her speak that way before. By this point in their relationship, he believed their minds were in sync, that they understood the world the same way. Now he wondered if that was true.

But he wouldn't give up. He had reason to trust in his ability to read her. It had begun early on when he was able to tell what would bring her pleasure in bed. For two months after she arrived in Houston, he had slept in a room downstairs, agonizing over whether he'd be able to satisfy her at his age. Belinda was still the flirtatious girl she had been in Oak Bluffs, and he could fret for only so long before desire overwhelmed him. So one night he did go upstairs with her. And again the evening that followed. Without her having to tell him, he understood how she wanted to be pleasured. Her response was effusive. For this exhilaration he started sharing a bed with her.

This switch from solitude to passion startled him into recognizing how lonely he had been. He'd had lovers since Vatsana and his return to America, but none of them had ever felt right. Eventually, they would part ways without either of them attempting to fix the problems they never acknowledged in the first place. He'd had no regrets.

He hadn't been miserable. But true companionship was an

unexpected joy. That he was experiencing it with Belinda as old age came toward him was the kind of luck that he was grateful for and pledged to reciprocate.

Instead Belinda was mirroring his joy with an annoying smudge across its center. He'd expected to wipe away the smudge within a year of their marriage—one year, his lawyer had told him, was the average time between a spouse's application for a green card and its delivery. One year turned into two, then into three. Losing patience, he called his lawyer in for a consult.

"How much will it take to get to the bottom of what's going on?" Wilder asked.

"How much you have?"

Wilder overnighted a registered check for fifty thousand dollars, ten thousand more than the lawyer's estimate. In two weeks the lawyer called with the information Wilder's money had bought.

"Something with the FBI," said the lawyer. "FBI's where the snag is. My contact says it has to do with your time in Vietnam."

This was a surprise. "What about it?"

"You went missing," he said. "Then from out of nowhere you showed up. Is that true?"

Wilder swallowed the truth. "No. Where are they getting that from? I've been running my business for over thirty years. My time in Vietnam was back in the twentieth century."

"Beats me," said the lawyer. "In any case, that's what's happening. They're probably gathering intelligence on your connections to the Vietcong."

"That was decades ago," Wilder said. "Those scores have already been settled."

"Settled?" asked the lawyer. "Don't forget that America lost that war, Mr. Thomas. Old wounds die hard. And you put in your application days before nine-eleven. High alert."

THE MESSAGE ABOUT THE FBI set Wilder thinking. He took to strolling back and forth alongside the hedges that surrounded his property. Sometimes, he went riding by himself. After several days a solution to the problem came to him, its obviousness making him question his acuity. Why hadn't he come to it more quickly?

The answer was simple enough: he would explain himself. He'd spend a day outlining logically and persuasively the harmlessness of his time in Laos. The FBI agent would nod his head, put a finger up for Wilder to wait while he opened the door to call in one of his men. A conversation would ensue, interspersed with quick glances at Wilder. It would at most be a five-minute tête-à-tête, after which the promise of the swift delivery of Belinda's green card would be assured.

He knew that he would see this through successfully; he had triumphed over more difficult adversaries than the FBI. The next morning, as he came downstairs to tell Belinda that he had figured out the way to deliver her win, his legs turned to custard. It had been fifteen years since his time on the beach with Belinda, when he'd run from her after she'd started to hum "Four Women." That was the last time he'd felt Vatsana's cord jerk on his leg. And as it had been at the beach, his legs weakened at the hands of memory. Weakness that led him to grip the staircase's balustrade tighter than he ever had before.

Before he left Vatsana to spend time with Mai on that fateful afternoon, Vatsana had warned him that she wouldn't give him up without a fight. He'd laughed off the threat and given it no more thought. But Vatsana was a woman of her word, and for two years after Wilder's return to America, he could feel that she was waging in him a convalescence that had nothing to do with recovery. It was healing without healing. In the efficiency apartment that Rutherford had helped him to secure in Brooklyn when he returned, Wilder cocooned in sedated isolation. In his haze of memory, which was half self-imposed, half prompted by the drink and drugs routinely delivered by the dealer one tenant had pointed Wilder's way, he listened to Vatsana.

"Why?" she asked.

"The fruits," he replied. "I should have known."

"Your not knowing shouldn't have been my suffering."

Most days Rutherford left brown grocery bags of food behind Wilder's door. Wilder would drag the food inside after Rutherford left. A heap of bags accumulated in the apartment by the door. Soon the landlord thudded on it, grumbling that the food Wilder wasn't eating was rotting, the stench of which he knew was coming from Wilder's apartment and was attracting mice and roaches and ruining the building.

Wilder tired of the complaints and the intrusion. He started stuffing the brown bags into black trash bags that Rutherford started to drop off, tying each one securely after filling it.

On the day that he decided he would reenter the world, Wilder listened as Rutherford dropped off the food. After the sound of Rutherford's footsteps disappeared, Wilder opened the door and made several trips to the dumpster downstairs. He had to hold the trash bags as far away from himself as he could manage to avoid the rancid odor that engulfed his senses. He couldn't understand how he'd survived the stink inside the apartment. But he had. Just as he'd survived in the tunnel and the cave.

He was returning after two years of talk with Vatsana. They had reached a compromise: he would bury her and Mai in the basement of his heart while she strung a cord around his ankle, which she would tug on when she thought he needed to be reminded of their love.

When Rutherford next returned to the apartment, Wilder let him in. "Four Women" was playing on the stereo.

"Shit, Wilder, if I'd known that all it took was some Nina Simone to get you up and smiling, I would have played her long ago," Rutherford said.

Vatsana had pushed for the compromise. There was work to be done, she'd stressed. His work.

Wilder began with recent history: In Laos, starting in 1964, America had started dropping pods of grenades across the country, some of which had failed to detonate. The grenades had spilled out of their pods and covered the land like playthings that drew children close. The round things were detonating in the middle of the children's games. Killing and maiming them. Mai.

He also uncovered past histories: The two hundred acres in Mexia had once been plantation land. Meaning that F. R. Stones's son, the first Wilder Thomas, had bought plantation land and converted much of the acreage into an orchard. What insult! A nigger tearing down the white man's monument for some pretty fruits. In retribution, a magnificent madness was brought upon the son's son, also Wilder Thomas. The madness would send the boy far away, to Princeton, and years later even farther away for war, only for him to return at thirty-six after receiving word that they'd gone through with his order to burn the orchard to ash. Nobody recognized him when he went back to Mexia, older and sadder and bearded as he was.

Finally back home in Mexia, Wilder held his dying father's hand, embittered by the impending loss but comforted by the bare earth outside the window. Soon Wilder would know that setting fire to the orchard was nothing—the madness could not be so easily defeated. After all, coming out of the cave, when he'd supposed the world to be pure and harmless and joyful despite the backdrop of death, the world was shown up as a sham through Mai and the rust-peeled fruit in her hand. That moment imprinted in him a forever truth: that seeming calm was an illusion. The orchard, his father's insult to white people, his father's joy that was in fact an affront to white people, could go. Sure, it could go. But there were always other affronting Black joys.

So on a joyful day for Mexia's Negroes, Juneteenth 1981, white folks struck, arresting three of the Negroes' best boys on a charge of possession of marijuana, and drowning them in Lake Mexia while they were being transported to jail in a boat. The three police officers were acquitted of negligent homicide.

Wilder had come to know the boys well. "Booker and Baker were decent swimmers," he told Vatsana soon after the news of the policemen's acquittals reached him. "Yes, Freeman could not swim. But Booker and Baker would have helped him. I know they would have. Vatsana, those white cops made sure the boys drowned."

He'd shivered for her and she'd come to him.

"You want to leave Mexia," Vatsana observed.

"I should have never come back."

"Where will you go?"

"There's a house I have in Houston."

"Who says it's safe there?"

"Temporary measure. Until I figure out where it's safe."

The Houston home evolved into a permanent one. Whenever he left Houston, it was often for Martha's Vineyard, where many years after he lamented with Vatsana about Mexia he met Belinda.

A few days after they met, they went to the beach, the Inkwell, which they had to themselves because it had been closed after a near drowning. This youthful rule-breaking with Belinda thrilled him. After they settled themselves on the sand, he scooped up a handful of it and let it trickle through his fingers like in an hourglass. The sun eased into twilight, oozing thickly like a blood orange over the horizon. They were awash in pleasant warmth. Even the Atlantic was calm.

During part of their conversation he said to Belinda, "You got to this country by plane. By choice. Some of us were not so lucky."

She frowned.

"Is that something Africans think about?" Wilder asked. "Do you people think about us?"

"Yes."

"In what way?"

"Pop culture, mostly," she said. "Films."

He sighed and wiped the residue of sand from his hands.

"And songs, too," she said.

The sky had begun to take on a foreboding quality. Belinda took off her shorts and shirt and in her two-piece bathing suit ran to the water.

Waist-deep in the water, fanning it with her arms, she called out to Wilder: "You don't swim?"

"I do," he said. "I just hadn't planned on it."

To ensure that he wouldn't have to go in the water—he simply couldn't bear to be in it now having more to do with the pain over losing Mai, his water child—he had worn a button-down collared shirt and cotton pants to the beach.

"I thought maybe you brought shorts," Belinda said.

Wilder smiled and shook his head.

Before long, she started humming "Four Women." She watched him closely, hoping for a response. As Wilder listened, he guessed how she knew: Rutherford had probably shared with Kara, his daughter, that "Four Women" was the song that brought Wilder joy. And Kara, Wilder was sure, had shared this with Belinda, who was hoping for him to let loose.

Instead Wilder got up to leave. As soon as he stood up, his legs felt wobbly. Negotiating the sand was always a challenge for him, but this was worse, as with each step he felt himself sinking deeper.

Later that day Vatsana would come to him. She informed him that it was Mai who had jerked the cord around his ankle, turning his legs to custard. "That girl. Belinda. She was in the water. Mai is *your* water child. Don't you see? Mai won't have it," Vatsana said. "It doesn't matter to Mai that you didn't get in the water with Belinda."

Fifteen years later, the tug on the cord that caused him to cling to the staircase balustrade had brought on a prolonged weakness. What great betrayal of Mai have I committed this time around? Wilder wondered. He only wanted Belinda to secure what was rightly hers—a green card—which had nothing to do with Mai.

He would learn that it wasn't Mai this time around. It was Vatsana herself, which he determined when she came to him enraged. Mai may have set him free to move forward with Belinda after that day at the beach, but the only kindness Vatsana could manage toward Belinda was letting her press cold towels on Wilder's hot forehead and administer the wrong remedies. Vatsana's rage was all-encompassing: better him weakened than the kind of strong that brought Belinda's green card and his being together with her in America forever, which he'd denied Vatsana.

But after a week, Vatsana released him. "I don't have it in me to kill you," she said. "I also don't have it in me to watch you suffer." She gave him one last ultimatum: "You cannot tell anyone about us. Not for any reason. Because that would be you kicking me out of your heart."

So mum Wilder kept, conniving with his lawyer to sustain Belinda's hopes with immigration letters. With cash Wilder convinced the man to resort to all measures he saw fit, and corruptible as the lawyer was, he once went as far as writing one of the letters himself because there'd been an extended silence from immigration and Belinda was asking too many questions. Wilder's *assets*, the doctored letter read, had prolonged the otherwise quick background check.

Pushed into a corner though he felt, Wilder held out that someday soon Belinda would give up on America.

Two

Yesterday, Belinda texted Wilder during Edith's wedding. *Jacob is even stranger than I thought, more when I'm home,* her text read. *Btw, what happened to Laurent? The driver who picked me up from the airport?*

Wilder had immediately called the car service to request—demand, actually—Laurent. This morning, the manager promised him that Laurent was assigned to Belinda for the rest of her stay. When Wilder called her next, she confirmed that the manager had called her as well. Belinda was getting ready to see Patricia. He advised her to be calm and kind, and to show Patricia compassion. "You know better than anyone the obstacles that America put in her way," he said.

He was about to inquire about this newly discovered strangeness of Jacob's but stopped himself. For many years he'd lived with guilt about all that he'd kept from Belinda, and it sounded as if the mention of Jacob's strangeness might be one of her roundabout ways of probing into his time in Vietnam and the source of her decades-long wait for a green card.

Where, he wondered, was the decisive Belinda who'd chosen a

wife for her older brother? Where was the unyielding Belinda who hadn't attended her own mother's funeral? Where was the determined Belinda who'd stood up to Kara over a hissing speakerphone? "I don't give a shit if you think it's gross, Kara, I'm in Houston now. I'm marrying Wilder. Your gross is my delicious, Kara. And you know what, it tastes pretty good. Fucking great, actually."

Yes, it was a resolute Belinda who would not leave America without her green card in hand. A resolute Belinda who would endure all the consequences of that decision, including Wilder. But shouldn't that same Belinda have gone digging for her own answers instead of accepting the empty assurances of an endless string of immigration letters?

That Belinda was still unmovable in 2007 when they had the perfect opportunity to grow richer in Ghana's infant oil industry made a lasting impression on Wilder. So his surprise over her refusal to attend her mother's funeral in Ghana was short-lived; he should have known she wouldn't leave America until she had triumphed. But months later, he was truly disheartened by her glee when it became clear that Obama would win the presidency. Hadn't he told her enough about his life—in Mexia, at Princeton, in New York—to inspire in her a wariness of Black joys?

As soon as Wilder saw the victory confirmed, he smashed the two champagne bottles Belinda had waiting on ice. Pieces of emerald glass spangled the floor of the dining room when Belinda and their chef, Simon, came in from the kitchen, where they'd been following election results on television.

Wilder stood by the credenza. In each of his hands was the severed neck of a bottle. He arranged them on the credenza like a conqueror displaying his kills. On his feet were riding boots, which ground into dust the glass fragments that covered the floor.

That night, as Wilder was clipping his beard, Belinda eyed him through the bathroom mirror.

Noticing her he asked, "Scared?"

"Should I be?"

"Yes, but not of me." The scissors he held snipped like background percussion. "You should be afraid of what this means. Instead of drinking to that Black man, you should be drinking to the end of you and me," he said. "Why are you celebrating? White folks don't give up what they see as rightfully theirs without wickedness. That big house. That was the one thing left that we couldn't have. And now we have it?" He stopped to inspect the shape of his beard, turning from side to side to gaze at his reflection. Unsatisfied, he went back to snipping. "You want to celebrate. But what are you celebrating? The next four years with that Black man in the big house? Maybe the next eight? Fine. Celebrate. But celebrate because you know what's to come and you have accepted it. All that drinkin' you want to do, all the hootin' and hollerin', do it because white folks tellin' you that the next four or eight years 'bout to be your last."

Belinda was still stubborn. Still unshakable. So he turned up the dial, partly out of performance and partly out of his genuine and inbred mistrust of white people. From the head of the conference table at his office, he flung a letter opener at a white man because a firm he'd hired had the nerve to not believe his threat. Belinda witnessed it, but that still was not enough for her to reconsider leaving the country.

From behind the wheel of his Ford truck, Wilder came close to running over a great many white people. This elicited nothing but polite concern from Belinda.

The worst was when he shot a horse and burned its carcass and showed it to her. He thought such a violation would move her, cause her to wonder what might be next—a human being?

But she said nothing. She only ran from him, later acting as if he had never killed the horse.

It was not long after that that Wilder did the unthinkable: he said "Vietnam." "Before leaving for Vietnam I was working on natural gas and power." He'd learned that Ghanaians were increasingly suffering from power outages. His thought: the two of them, with their knowledge and talent, could bring light.

Energized, he collected piles of maps and waded through one after another, circling the locations of known Ghanaian gas deposits. Whenever he asked her to study the maps with him, she was discouraging, always concluding, "It would require too much money, Wilder." As though he were not rich and as though that wasn't the way to make more money.

He feared that Belinda had developed a kind of emotional myopia, that by holding out for her greatest hope she had blinded herself to all other pleasures. They no longer achieved heights in their lovemaking. She brushed aside his beard like it was a nuisance; previously, she'd welcomed its sweep on her body. The most affecting of her coldness led him to entertain the possibility that there was a limit to their union; she'd gone as far as differentiating their color: his Black, she said to him, was nothing like hers.

He wished he could read her as well as he once had. When Belinda talked with him about Edith and her upcoming wedding, he got his wish. Without her saying it, he understood the truth underlying Belinda's confession: she still *felt*; she felt deeply. The demise of her friendship with Edith saddened her, more than she had admitted to herself. And in spite of Belinda's allegiance to America, she pined for home. Edith should have been the constant in her life, the one who would connect her life in Ghana with her life in America. But Edith had rejected her, a betrayal Belinda thought she could overcome because America had opened its arms to her. She had gone to school there, worked there, married there, built a life there. But America had been a cruel trick—every bit of it. Even him.

Belinda, much like Wilder, felt she had no place she could call home. Understanding this comforted him: they were back on the same plane, back on the same wavelength, even more connected than ever before.

So when Belinda decided to go to Edith's wedding, Wilder determined that they would build their own fortresses. More than showing up Edith, the designer clothes, shoes, jewelry, and fur coats were all foundations to build their fortresses on. Oh, and red hair. Militant red! "Show them white folks we onto them. Whatever they preparin' for us after Obama, we meetin' with equal fire," he told her when she called from the salon about a fitting hair color for Edith's wedding.

He should have received a call from Belinda by now. Takeoff from Reagan Airport, according to his phone, was in an hour. He pulled up her name on his phone and pressed the screen. Her phone rang but she did not answer. He tried a second time. Again, she did not answer. He decided to give it another five minutes. She was sure to call or text.

Fifteen minutes elapsed and a nervousness lurked in him. He

texted, then called again. When neither prompted a response, he vacillated about what to do next. At last his screen lit up with a message from her: *Please. Give me a minute.*

He permitted her five before replying: *Waiting...*

When his phone tolled its jingle, he tapped twice and put it to his ear. "Finally," he said.

She was gasping for air. He envisioned a kidnapping. Giant white men with guns to her throat.

"Belinda? Belinda, what's wrong?"

He circled the dining table as he listened to her struggling to breathe. "Please, Bels," he pleaded. "Please. Say something."

He froze when she finally spoke. "Alfred," she cried. "My father called. Alfred died."

He could not find the right words. "What? How? He was just a boy."

She sniveled. She bawled.

"Belinda?" he said. "Where are you? Right now, where are you?"

"I have to go."

"Go? Where? No." He began his frantic pacing again. "Where are you going, Bels? Where are you?"

"I'm at Laurent's. The driver."

He slowed. "Okay. Good. You are not alone," he said. "The airport. That's where you meant. Where you have to go?"

"Yes," she said. "I never even laid eyes on him, Wilder. A boy I loved like my own. And I never laid eyes on him." A new wave of sobbing overtook her and he gave her the time she needed. When she composed herself she said, "I have to go back."

"To Ghana," he said. "You mean to Ghana."

"We don't wait long to bury children," she said. "My family will hold out for my arrival. But I can't keep them waiting for more than a week."

"A week is more than enough time," Wilder said. "A day would be more than enough. I can have arrangements finalized by tomorrow. Be on a plane the day after."

"I'm sorry, Wilder."

"Sorry? For what?"

"I'm sorry I'm leaving."

"Why?" he said. "I'm coming with you."

Belinda did not say anything for a time. Then: "I'm not clear minded right now."

Wilder heard a door open. He looked around and realized that he was not within earshot of one. Inside, across his sternum, he felt a beating—an impulse to flee upon a child's passing. Feet barged across the room.

"No," he thought. "Alfred, and only Alfred, was germane to the moment."

He banged the door beating on his heart and tightened his grip on the phone. "Come home," he said to Belinda. "We'll make arrangements together."

Book 3

One

B lack plastic chairs were arranged in two wings in the front yard. They faced Belinda as she stood on the veranda. Last night she'd stood frozen on the bridge that also now faced her, listening to the rolling stream beneath her. She'd made it as far as the bridge's middle and couldn't go on; Wilder had been unable to persuade her further. Powerless, he walked on with their driver and the driver's cell phone light, heading toward a single fluorescent light on her father's house, which brightened the gable like the North Star. They had been driven for five hours from the Accra airport. When the driver parked by the dusty clearing before the bridge, Belinda commented that she'd always remembered it as a four-hour drive from Accra to Kumasi. Wilder reminded her that they'd stopped so that she could cry in a roadside restroom.

Not long after Belinda had been left on the bridge, she heard her father's worn voice gaining on her. Pinpricks of light seemed to sneak through the bushes as they fringed the voice. When he got to her, he seized her arm and she collapsed into him. He put his arms around her and told her the distance from the bridge to the house wasn't far. Against his chest, she nodded for them to forge on. They proceeded delicately. She stole glances at him.

After twenty-two years, her first thought was to question whether his fragility could sustain hers. He soothed the uneasy quiet between them with conversation. "Daring of you to come by road," he said. "I haven't been able to get into a car since Alfred died in the accident."

"It never crossed my mind to fly here," she said. "We always drove to Accra and back."

When they got to the house, her father guided her into one of the cushioned cane chairs on the veranda beside the one Wilder occupied. Now she could see her father clearly. There were creases around his eyes, and his chin hung lower. Sorrow was written on his face. She also noted his strained shuffle as he headed inside the house.

Once they were left to themselves, Wilder got up and stood behind her, trying to massage out the knots in her shoulders. She stared at the piles of folded black chairs by the gate; tomorrow they would be set up for the gathering following Alfred's internment. She couldn't remember whether she'd told Wilder that there would be a gathering at the house after Alfred's funeral—why the chairs were there. She inclined her head at him to let him know.

Before she could speak, darkness burst over them.

"Light-off!" a voice inside the house exclaimed in a high-pitched alto.

Wilder tapped her shoulders reassuringly: this was part of the reason they were here. She sensed him feeling his way back to his chair. The blackout had capped her distress and exhaustion; she was anxious now only for rest. Her father, however, brought out a lantern and held it up so that for several more minutes Belinda and Wilder accepted welcomes: Yaa's, then Robert's and Martha's, then Kwame Broni's and his wife's.

"Where's Jacob?" asked Belinda.

"He's away," replied her father.

"Where?"

"Oh, not far. He should be back soon."

With the benefit of an outsider's remove, Wilder was able to engage Belinda's family in conversation. To Belinda's surprise, her father was talkative, even chatty. But on second thought she realized that his seemingly effortless banter with Wilder was hardly a surprise: he knew how to be a genial host when it mattered. It mattered now; he owed so much to Wilder.

"Welcome home, son," her father said.

Son sounded about right to Belinda, despite her father and Wilder's similar ages. Wilder invited Robert and Martha to join the conversation. In the ensuing silence, Belinda reached for him. "My brother and his wife are deaf," she whispered.

"Shit," he said under his breath. "How did I forget?"

Although she knew nobody believed an apology necessary, Belinda explained to the others to pardon Wilder's error, that they were exhausted, and excused themselves to bed.

But sleep eluded her. Wilder had fallen asleep quickly, and she couldn't stand being awake by herself. She got out of bed, leaving the dying candle on the nightstand. Outside the bedroom door was resolute darkness. Instead of bringing the candle with her, she forged on, groping her way along the walls with just the light of her phone, which was sorely insufficient.

Her foot knocked a chair. She reached to steady herself and squeezed a thigh. "Oh," she said.

The owner moaned, his speechlessness causing her to think it was Robert. She signed "Sorry" into his thigh.

"Weesh."

She thought the thigh had spoken. She stepped back. "Pa?" she said.

"I'm not Pa."

"Jacob," she said. "You're back."

She found a place in the living room to sit down. "I don't know why I never thought to send a generator."

Jacob's cushions sounded like he was making himself more comfortable for sleep.

"Why are you sleeping out here?" she asked.

"Robert and Martha are in my room. You and your husband are in their room."

"Thank you," she said.

He did not answer.

"How are you?" she asked.

"Desperate to sleep."

"Me, too," she said. "I was thinking I wouldn't like to go into tomorrow not having spoken to you. It seems the universe agrees."

"Does it?"

"Please, Jacob. I only want to put an end to the Patricia business."

"They talk about liquid courage. You've found sightless courage."

"I'm happy to wait until tomorrow and look you dead in the eye," she said. "But it seems wrong."

"What seems wrong?"

"Coming together to bury Alfred with our own unfinished business."

"Our business is finished," he said. "Patricia is finished. I'm finished."

"You ever get the ring?"

"I have it."

"Oh, good," she said in genuine relief. "She wasn't lying."

"You knew she wasn't lying."

"You're right. I did."

"I know what you are trying to do," Jacob said. "But you are mistaken if you think trying to criticize her is the way to put us on common ground."

"What is, then?"

"Sleep."

"Fine, but one more thing," Belinda said. "You mentioned sightless courage. What do I have to be so ashamed of that I would find it difficult to look you in the eye?"

He kept still. She could no longer hear him exhaling.

"You're projecting onto me, Jacob," she said. "It's you who couldn't get on the phone with me. How much more to look me in the eye?"

When he groaned, she sat up straighter.

"Belinda."

"Still here."

"I've been trying to decide. When was it your mind went? Before the old man or after the old man?" Jacob asked.

"I don't understand." But she did. She only wanted to keep her temper.

"Of course you don't; your mind is no more."

"So enlighten me," Belinda said.

"It was long before the old man. That's how I see it. When things have always gone right for you then suddenly they don't, something happens to your mind," he said. "Everything is up-turned. And even a bearded old man sets your loins on fire."

Belinda had heard enough. "Or whips and chains for some people," she said.

"Oh," Jacob said. "I see. You know. Yes, or whips and chains."

"I'm not ashamed, Jacob," Belinda said. "You are."

"Long before whips and chains."

"When?"

"Come on, Belinda. I think you can use whatever is left of your mind to figure that one out."

She nodded into the darkness.

That was it. Not a proper reunion. Now standing on the ve-randa the morning after and wondering who had arranged the chairs so neatly spread out before her, she realized that Jacob had not seen her empathic nod. She'd left it there, confounded by the darkness and the conversation's intensity, believing that Jacob had seen and understood her meaning: her many successes in the face of his failures had compounded his shame and she understood why he'd taken it out on her. Over the years she had evolved for the better, which she wished she had gone on to say to Jacob. She could now acknowledge that she had never shown him empathy—or indeed had much of it herself. Lacking empathy, she'd foisted a wife on him without asking even the simple question of what he wanted in a woman. In fact, it was more than a lack of empathy—it was arrogance. She'd always felt superior to Jacob. She'd always thought she knew better than he did. For that, she hoped he could forgive her.

She would pull him aside at some point today and apologize to him face-to-face. She'd been first to rise, first to get ready in head-to-toe black: a silk turban, a floor-length capped-sleeve cotton dress, thong slippers, and sunglasses. She was waiting on the others in a morning nipping with chill.

On the clearing ahead, a vibrant soccer game had just ended. During the game, the players had appeared to her like gladiators, some shirtless, some jerseyed, dueling for ownership of a measly soccer ball and unfazed by the dust storms they were making. All was still now, the collapsible goalposts carted away. A jungle of colorful rooftops spread out at her fore, though there was hardly a sign of the homes' inhabitants. Indeed, birds tweeted as though in their natural habitat, but even they were out of sight.

She descended the small steps from the veranda and walked around the house. She appreciated the accents of beauty that had been artfully arranged—the flowerpots of red hibiscus and purple bougainvillea, the rose-colored motif that zigzagged through the outdoor tiles. She saw that her entire family had joined forces to build an actual home. While it physically paled in comparison with the Houston house, it nevertheless felt more hers and made her proud.

How much she had missed over the years. Never getting to witness Alfred in his element here. Together with Wilder, she had covered the cost for Alfred's three-piece burial suit, a splendid coffin, a full-blown limousine hearse (not the usual pickup truck or ambulance). Still, she should have arrived back in Ghana sooner to help with the preparations. When Wilder promised to make their travel plans quickly, he hadn't considered the time that was required to uncoil his business interests long enough for him to be away. While she waited, she used the time to dye her hair from bloodred back to black. There was no need to give her conventional father a fright.

Had it just been her, she could have been on a plane within a day of hearing the news, instead of arriving the evening before the funeral. She could have simply packed her bags and left. It was that easy for someone with no entanglements. In a country that had deceived her into believing herself valuable, she'd been unable to build anything for herself. What she'd built, she'd built for Wilder. And although he'd spoken of the need to unpack, divest, and liquidate *their* interests—*our* stake in this, *our* stake in that, *our* properties—she did not think of his money as hers. She couldn't. On the surface she was his wife. An American wife. But how reliable was that title when it had not earned her a benefit as basic as legal permission to live and work in the country?

The day brightened as she stood by the small vegetable garden. Alfred's viewing would begin at nine, and she did not need a watch to apprise her of the moment. She rounded the corner to the front of the house, where Wilder and her father stood in the aisle separating the clusters of chairs into two wings. Wilder held up a pair of white tennis shoes at her. "You almost forgot these," he said.

"Thank God you didn't."

Her father strained forward with little steps. "If you want to get those shoes on Alfred's feet, we have to leave now."

"Is Jacob here?"

"I believe he already left."

"Robert and Martha?"

"They left."

"How about Yaa?"

"She went with them."

Belinda stuck to Wilder, shadowing him with her hand on his bare shoulder. He was draped in an extra brisi that her father had dug up so that Wilder, who was now part of their family, would not stick out among the men by wearing a sober American business suit. At least not as a result of his attire, which he'd been taught to seam with a firm hand on the hems congregated at his right. It was the other shoulder that was bared, where her hand lay and where Wilder's light complexion reddened like a foreign stain under the African sun.

People witnessed the three of them walking up the road to the church and bolstered their progress with encouraging wails about Alfred's angelic turn. Some said they were almost ready and would see them at the church; some joined them. What had been a small legion grew. By the time they reached their destination, Belinda had lost count of the mourners in tow.

Her father had led them to four churches that stood in a circle, each with crosses for steeples. In front of them were squat wooden signs announcing the Christian denomination of each: Lutheran, Presbyterian, Catholic, Apostolic. For a moment Belinda was confused. Which of the four was going to be the venue? Then she noticed people gathering on the benches and chairs that had been set up in the center. In death, Alfred had galvanized the town in an ecumenical worship.

A teenage girl guarding a white canopy walked up to her with a determined stare. "Aunty Belinda," said the girl, "they are waiting for you."

The voice established the girl as Yaa. "Waiting for me?" Belinda said.

"The people dressing Alfred." She nodded toward the canopy. "They've finished with everything. They just need the shoes."

Belinda held out the pair. "Here," she said.

"But they said you wanted to do it yourself."

Behind the dark ovals of her sunglasses, Belinda felt her eyes sting. "I thought I could but I can't."

Yaa cradled the shoes and scurried toward the structure, slipping through the tarpaulin. Wilder's hand caressed the small of Belinda's back, easing her out of her stupefaction.

Before long, the tarpaulin opened, revealing Alfred burgeoned in a bed of flowers. Wreaths girded his head. This was Belinda's first sighting of death—at thirty-eight and for death to be a boy swindled of the lifetime he deserved. Guilt engulfed her as she considered the fact that she'd spent years of her life abroad for nothing. She'd been self-serving, one-track-minded. She had no right to claim Alfred as like her own. If she insisted on believing him hers, she had to concede that she'd been a wicked mother and had left her child for dead.

"I'm a dreadful person, aren't I?" she whispered, more to herself than anyone.

"Belinda," Wilder said, "nobody is expecting you to get any closer. You don't have to if you don't want to."

"I don't want to."

They took places on a long bench set behind Robert and

Martha. In high, cushioned chairs, her brother and his wife posed like statues. Nothing of the commotion of the moment moved them. Deaf to the fast and shallow screams for the salvation of their son's soul, they remained still. Yet what their ears missed, their eyes must have seen. Positioned in full view, they witnessed more than anyone the hobbles exacted on the brave who filed close; the sagging women and children who had to be picked up from the sand and carted away; the steely manliness that disintegrated.

Belinda saw through the space between Robert's and Martha's necks, but her sunglasses' lenses were moist and fogging over. She wiped the lenses on her dress and kept her head down.

"Where's Jacob?" Wilder asked. "I've yet to lay eyes on him."

"He's supposed to be here," she said, searching the crowd for him.

"Why are they in white?" Wilder asked under his breath.

"Robert and Martha?"

"Yes."

"*Sodoɔ.*"

"Meaning?"

"Twi," Belinda said. "It refers to the type of funeral. You want to discourage this kind of death from happening again, so you deviate from norms. Wearing white to ward off death. The common instinct is to think of white as celebratory. But black gives death its moment. White doesn't. It's counterintuitive."

"Shouldn't we all be in white, then?"

"Not necessarily," Belinda said. "And remember you don't have to whisper around them." She aborted her search for Jacob. She lowered her head for closer inspection of the smudges on her lenses. "It affects Robert and Martha the most," she said. "It's more meaningful if they are the ones not giving death its moment." She looked at him.

"You don't see the sense in it," she asked after a while.

"Oh, no. I do. Very much. I just need a minute," he said.

This minute stretched an eternity. Wilder was noticeably inattentive during the homily that was delivered by Alfred's preacher over a loudspeaker, and throughout the children's choir's rendition of a song introduced as Alfred's favorite, about Christ and light. An interpreter signed with a showman's panache, and when Belinda tapped at Wilder's rib to call his attention to the drama— because he was staring into space with an unnerving remove—he did not budge. After the ceremony, he did not notice her offering her hand as they filed closer to the road. He agreed with a vague nod when she proposed that he join the car carrying her father, behind the hearse and second among the motorcade assembling for the cemetery. She was sitting out the burial and instead would go with Robert and Martha to receive guests at the house. "See you later?" she said, and again he nodded in apparent accord.

She made it a considerable distance with Robert and Martha before she turned to find Wilder standing alone in the same spot, bare-chested in just his shorts, the black cloth he'd been wearing lumped on the ground. He appeared smaller, as though he'd shrunk. Past him, the last car in the motorcade was slowly moving out of view.

Belinda signed for Robert and Martha to take the lead; she also signed, when they responded with concern about Wilder, that he would be fine. She hiked her dress above her ankles and picked up her feet. Sand grated between her toes.

She slowed down as she got closer to Wilder and noticed that his eyes were as flushed as his sun-drenched skin. Without speaking, she tried to drape the cloth around him again. Out of practice, she fixed the material on him in many knots, after which she watched him carefully and tried to come up with a consoling message. "He's in a better place, Wilder."

Timidly she clutched his hand and tried to prompt him to walk, getting him to take one difficult step. After another she realized it was too much and she flagged down a honking taxi. The driver assisted with seating Wilder. When they arrived back at the house, he helped to get Wilder from the car onto the bridge and then into bed.

As Belinda paid him, the driver asked, "Madam, will he be fine? Doesn't he need hospital?"

"Jet lag. That's all it is," Belinda assured him.

She went back into the bedroom and found Wilder curled into a deep sleep, sweating within a dense sheet swaddle. This was not merely jet lag—Wilder had turned to sludge. Yet she heard herself repeating Wilder's certainty from years ago, when he fell sick and she thought he might die: "It will pass."

Two

You've done it now, Vatsana. You and Mai, I suppose. Since I walked through the door of that Brooklyn studio, you'd gone easy with the cord. The two times you yanked on it—you, Vatsana, both times, and not Mai—you eventually set me free. Not this time, though. Not when it had to do with the bench. You watched me see it. Isn't that right, Vatsana? The one thing I was supposed to steer clear of, you saw me pondering. When Belinda made her move, before I made mine, you started with your warning of a special custard in my toes. But I kept on. Which drove you mad. What was I supposed to do, Vatsana? Stop her? Tell her that I couldn't sit on the bench because the custard was starting up in my toes? How would I have explained that? The bench. And right there at Alfred's funeral? It would have been unseemly for me to bring out my own commotion. There was no other place for us to have sat but there. Behind Robert and Martha. On that bench. You saw that it had been reserved for family, no? Saw that Pa soon joined at my left? Uncle Kwame Broni and his wife at Belinda's right? There and only there. No place but there. I don't know how I made it onto the bench in the first place. My legs turning more quickly to custard with every step. But I made it anyhow. And I confess that making it there, and having the sense to talk with Belinda, made me believe you'd let go, as you'd done before. And why not this time? Especially when the bench was not a replica of yours. Yours was a lot shorter, Vatsana. A whole lot shorter, my dear Vatsana. Yes, the brown of the wood reflected the brown of yours, the top slab's curvature reflected the curvature of yours. But damn it, Vatsana, it was a lot longer. It could have fit three of you floating on it. Yours had barely fit you, dainty thing that you are. And despite your own daintiness, atop it you were long and grand. I sneaked a peek at you once. Who was I fooling thinking you'd missed me looking? You never brought it up, but you'd seen me with your eyes closed. Of course you'd seen me. Oh, Vatsana, please believe me. I wasn't defying you when I followed Belinda. Simply, Vatsana, it was not the bench I knew to be yours. And in any case the special custard became like the other custards: it came, it went. I sat solid. Everyone sat solid. But the solidity was merely a test, wasn't it? You were giving me one more chance, waiting to see whether I would come to my senses and get off my ass, tell the others to get off their asses, too, in remembrance and recognition of you. But I made no such efforts. So you did what you had to do. You snatched Belinda's voice. I heard the echo of your own talk of adapted funerals as loud as a scream. No, you couldn't keep quiet. I had taken it far enough. Sitting on your bench with strangers, in spite of the signs of your opposition. But Vatsana. Oh, Vatsana. I thought we had come to an understanding after those two years in the Brooklyn studio. You'd assured me that you and Mai forgave me. You said you loved me too much not to see me put an end to the fruits, even though it meant sacrificing yourself. You loved me too much, you said, to keep me in bed, languishing for you, languishing for Mai. I heard Hillard then, which I know was your doing. I heard him: *The fruits, they got somethin' to do with white folks, ain't they?* So I buried you and Mai deep in my heart and got to work making sense of what you summoned Hillard to share with me. You. Me. Hillard. Together the three of us sang the song. How high we'd gone on the part that was ours: *Saffronia, Saffronia, Saffronia.* We were over. You and I were finished.

Not so finished, though. You'd sensed Belinda creep onto your territory the very day I met her. The other women you didn't mind, but Belinda reflected Mai. I should have remembered how covetous you'd been after the cave, not letting me see Mai for a week. How threatened by her you felt. Your jealousy is a hell of a thing, Vatsana. I should have anticipated it. Hell, you'd once flouted your own spirits for me. Ready to die with me. It is only now, Vatsana, that I understand your manipulation. At least you and Belinda were equals, both marriages makeshift. And if yours hadn't succeeded, hers was also not going to. So you made her green card dependent on you; you would never let it happen. Got your way all these years. Thought you'd won. But one thing you'd overlooked was our talk of home. No one knows better than you what it's like for me to be filled with the softness of home. Because no one but you has ever filled me with that. You can't stand that I've found it here, too. All these years since leaving you, and I've found it again. A special custard it would be. A very special custard. But to what end, Vatsana? You have me here, curled up like a bud. To what end?

I—

Listen, Vatsana. Listen. You listenin'? This ain't love. Got

Lieutenant here sweatin' like he stole your last dollar. Misthinkin' it to be love. Leave him be. He did you wrong. Ain't no denyin'. He did you wrong. But he tryna do you right. I say leave him be. Ain't you wanna see your name in lights, Vatsana? *Saffronia Power*. Ain't that a nice name for an enterprise? Saffronia Power. Ever dream your name in lights all the way in Africa, Vatsana? Come. Come. Come see. There. Way up there. You see it, don't you? Saffronia Power. I know you see it. Twinklin'. Ain't it nice? When last you seen a yellow so bright?

Three

When the mourners at the house shrank to stragglers, Belinda excused herself to check on Wilder. He looked the same. To her relief, he seemed to be breathing easier. She jigged him out of his swaddle, and rolled the sheets down to his legs so she could wipe the perspiration from his belly with the hem of her dress.

She could hear the muted roar of the rented generator outside. The standing fan she'd asked Yaa to bring to the room stood unplugged by the door. She plugged it in and turned it on, waiting until Wilder's forehead cooled before going to find Jacob.

He hadn't appeared at the funeral or at the gathering at the house. She'd had to thank the well-wishers on her own, muddling Twi and English, her American intonation heightening people's fascination with her. Some people had seen her bringing in Wilder. They asked about him—thoughtfulness that quickly grated on her. To avoid further conversation, she sank into an armchair in the living room, donning her sunglasses as repellent. People walked by and assumed, she presumed, that she'd become like Wilder, sick from the heat. A litter of children waved their palms in her face and gently backed away from her. Their fear amused her, her first bit of amusement since arriving back in Ghana.

She was able to be by herself for a while, until her father summoned her. People were leaving and as was custom they needed to be seated as a family so that those exiting could properly say their farewells. By the gate, Belinda took up a chair next to Martha, and the four of them—her father, Robert, Martha, and she—shook so many hands that she found herself working her hand to rush blood back into it. She couldn't wait to get back inside. Checking on Wilder, which she really wanted to do, was the perfect excuse when the coast cleared.

Wilder, thankfully, was fine. What about Jacob?

Out in the front yard, Robert was assisting the audio-rental man with putting away the speakers. Martha and Yaa were folding the chairs. Four girls had stayed behind to help.

"How is Wilder?" Mr. Nti asked. He was in the middle of coiling a microphone cable around the stem. Over the veranda wall, he handed it to one of the girls.

"He'll be fine," Belinda said. "Jacob back yet?"

"I don't know that he will be back."

Belinda frowned in surprise. "Ever?"

"Oh, not ever," her father said. "This is how he grieves. He heads off. You were not here for the divorce."

"But not to show for the funeral? I have so much to say to him."

Mr. Nti sat down and then motioned for her to sit, but she refused.

"He'll be back," he said. He noticed Martha. "She's brave. Still able to keep going."

"Robert is still going, no?"

"Should we expect anything less?"

"No," she said. "I guess not."

He stared at her. "Won't you sit?"

"I was going to help them."

"No need. They'll take care of it," he said. "Yaa corralled those girls for a reason."

Belinda settled down, leaving a chair between them.

"It's because he's a man. Right?" he said.

"What?"

"Because Robert is a man, you think I don't expect him to grieve. But I expect Martha to grieve."

"More or less," Belinda said.

"You weren't here for your mother's funeral. So I forgive you for that line of thinking," he said. "In any case, I'm no hypocrite. How could I have cried as much as I did over your mother and not expect Robert to do the same for his son?"

Belinda didn't know what to say.

"Robert is wickedly resilient. It probably has to do with his pastoring. You have to be able to weather a lot to help others weather their own storms," he said. "Martha has surprised me. That's all."

"Fine."

"All right, darling," he said. "Am I not permitting Jacob his grief? He's a man, no?"

"Jacob is different."

"Exactly," he said. "Jacob is different. He's built differently. Grief has nothing to do with what's between a person's legs."

"Listen to you, Pa."

"Listen to me?"

"Vulgar."

"You have something on your mind," he said. "What is it you have to tell me?"

"You're fond of Wilder," she said.

"Shouldn't I be?"

"You should. So many reasons why you should," she said. "I just think you were too quick to be fond of him. Too quick to discard me and give him credit."

"I know you think that."

"But you haven't stopped. Even though I'm sure you also know that it hurts me."

"Know why, Belinda?" he said. "I came to realize the errors of my ways. Robert had his problem so I never expected much from him. Jacob never showed promise. You, on the other hand, were something else. I kept reminding you of how special you were. To a fault, maybe. I made you self-absorbed. Made you think you didn't need people."

"I know I need people, Pa."

"Not as much as you should," he said. "Your friend Kara. That was terrible. Someone who had been so generous to you. And for you to be so quick to get rid of her."

"She disapproved of me and Wilder."

"Can you blame her?" he asked. "Her best friend and her uncle. Can you blame her?"

"Not by blood."

"But by something. Enough for you to have been able to make Wilder family," he said. "What's done is done. But I need you to understand that I don't have a need to give credit to a man when a woman deserves the credit more. I'm not that bad. What I do have is a deep need to right my wrongs. To help you realize that as brilliant as you are, you've been remarkably lucky."

"I know I've been lucky."

"You know it up to a point," he said. "Your whole life has been one long walk with luck, in the form of people. Then as soon as luck takes a break from you, you want me to look badly on someone who's been good to you."

"I'm not asking for you to look badly on Wilder," she said. "I just want some credit. I don't think you've ever thanked me for this house. As if I had nothing to do with it."

"Maybe I haven't. And I'm sorry about that," he said. "But you shouldn't need that. Because nobody needs to tell you that I have always cherished you." Mr. Nti leaned toward her. He said, "Belinda, even without that green card look at all that you have achieved. How decorated you are with all of your degrees, which you got all on your own. Wilder looks like one hell of a smart man. He's not keeping you around because you look good on his arm."

"He does love me."

"And you love him," he said. "And that is good, Belinda. Well and good. Napoleon had his army. He had help."

"He's Napoleon?"

"Well, I must be honest, he's pretty short," her father said, winking. "That came as a surprise."

Belinda giggled, and in a rapid shift that did not shock her because she'd been mending her sorrow, she actually began to cry.

She accepted the handkerchief her father held out.

"In all seriousness, he's done what Napoleon could not do. All that he has accomplished. And you. All that you have accomplished," her father said.

She looked up at him. "Pa, he literally could not do." She gulped one word after the other. "He could not get me a green card."

"The green card was based on your marriage. On your partnership. At the end of the day, it was the partnership that failed." With both of his hands, he held her hand, the one without the handkerchief Belinda was using to dab her eyes. "But it will succeed on other fronts. I imagine you two are not here to be idle."

She shook her head.

"Whatever it is you achieve in this country, I may look at Wilder and say, 'You have done what Napoleon could not do.' I want you to know that you are part of that credit. And who knows . . . I may even say it to you first."

She glanced at the front yard. The girls had dispersed, the chairs perfectly tiered. "I have a lot to say to Jacob."

"He'll be back." He sighed. "Belinda, I confess that I don't know or understand your husband."

"I confess I don't, either."

"That so," he said. Whispering, he asked, "The gag order lifted?"

"What do you mean?"

"What's the Vietnam story?"

She grimaced. "Your guess is as good as mine," she said. "But I doubt it matters anymore."

He pulled away. "If you are well with that, then so am I," he said. "One more thing. Are you sure he's ready to live his life here?"

She smiled. "Pa, that's probably the only thing I'm sure of when it comes to Wilder Thomas."

At that moment Robert appeared and came up the three steps toward them.

"All right?" he signed.

Belinda shook her hand from her father's. "No. Not me," she signed. "You. You all right?"

"Better than yesterday."

He asked about their father and she signaled behind her to express her primary concern for Martha, who'd just entered the house.

"Better than yesterday," he repeated.

"Where's Jacob?" she asked. "I'd like to see him."

"He's where he always is."

"The café?" she signed. "I thought that has been closed down since Benjamin died."

Before Robert could answer, Mr. Nti waved his hand in Belinda's face. "Ask him, Belinda," he said. "Maybe he knows where Jacob is."

Before Belinda could, Yaa rapped on the glass of the living room door.

"Come. Somebody. Please. Come," cried Yaa. "Mama Martha is causing commotion. She is breaking all the plates."

Belinda squeezed Robert's biceps and they ran inside. They stood back as Martha shattered two plates in the sink before Robert dove to catch the third in midair. He quickly handed the plate to Yaa before swooping Martha up, her face in his neck. Against Robert's arm she marched her right fingers. It was the highest decibel of emphasis—Belinda thought she could actually hear her. *No more life. No more life. No more life for me to live.*

Four

High above Wilder's feet at the end of the bed, soot-colored waves hung in the air. He blinked to quiet them. Belinda was asleep in a desk chair, her mouth open, her black turban unlaced and veiling her cheeks as if she were a mourning bride.

He shed his sheets and got out of bed. He was alive—a truth that made him want to leap in elation.

But Belinda's sleep was deep, exhausted. He tempered his boisterous joy and, with his toes, tested the wheels of the chair Belinda was in. Her neck rubbed the headrest that cushioned it, which made her writhe like an infant: hands fisted, rubbing her eyes. Her eyes opened and she sat up.

"Why didn't you join me on the bed?" Wilder asked.

"You looked like you'd caught something." She looked him over as he bounced lightly on his feet. "Obviously it was a lot less serious than I thought."

He grasped her chair's armrests, moving the chair gently. "I've caught something, all right."

"What?"

"Africanitis."

She was not taken by his comic turn. "Hardly," she said.

Her solemn disregard reminded him unexpectedly of Alfred. "I missed the rest of the funeral."

"You got through the church service. That was enough."

"You missed the burial."

"I never planned on going," she said. "And how do you know?"

"Know what?"

"That I missed the burial," she said. "Last I remember, you left this world sometime during the sermon."

"Blame grief."

"Some grief."

"I have some years on you, Belinda," he said. "Grief weighs harder on me."

It was that old excuse of age, which Wilder knew she could have challenged by mentioning her father's sprightliness in grief. She would ease off, however.

"I was worried," Belinda said. "You were breathing normally. Sweating. But no fever. Had I known that you'd be back like a spring chicken I would have at least changed out of my clothes."

"Oh, so that's the rank I smell."

"No, Wilder," she said, "that's your breath."

He retreated. She stood to disrobe, holding off at the halfway point of her zip. "On second thought, why don't you shower first."

"Why?"

"Jacob is somewhere," she said. "Robert knows where. He will take you."

"Where?"

"I haven't gotten the chance to find out where exactly," she said. "At this point, it really doesn't matter. And I'm pretty sure Jacob would prefer that I don't know."

"Hm."

"I think it's important that you find him. You. Not me."

"Why not you?"

"Jacob sees me and all he sees is luck. Very good luck. I'm an aggravation. Under the circumstances, an aggravating sight might send him over the edge." She brought him a towel from the wardrobe. "When you do see him, tell him about your intentions here. Make it seem like he's the first person you've told."

"Why?"

"He will take it that you value his mind more than mine."

Wilder smirked. "You can't help yourself, can you?"

"Help myself with what?"

"With meddling in your brother's life."

"My brother is desperate, Wilder. The internet café—where that chair came from—was supposed to be his big breakthrough. He was planning on turning it into a computer school and Benjamin was supposed to be his partner. Benjamin had just gone for new chairs for the school when . . . what happened to him and Alfred happened." She zipped up her dress. "Jacob hurled the old chairs onto the street." She pointed at the chair she'd been sleeping on. "Yaa salvaged this one. Apparently, he doesn't know it's in here."

"So his desperation excuses your meddling?"

"Wilder, you are looking to harness natural gas for electricity. Here. In Ghana. I'm looking to harness my brother's resentment of me. Here. In the end, we all win."

"You want to bring him on board?"

Belinda nodded. "Yes."

Wilder showered and got dressed. When he was finished,

Belinda handed him a pen and paper to pass between himself and Robert. The church van driver, who would be driving them to wherever they were going, could sign satisfactorily, but his hands would be occupied. Were his hands to be free, too much time would be wasted with him trying to understand Wilder's American pitch for Robert's benefit. They may never get through a question.

First, Wilder wrote, "Where are we headed?"

Robert wrote, "A construction site."

"Why?"

"I'm confident that's where he went to clear his mind."

"He always has a lot on his mind?"

"Easy with the tensions of our household."

"You, too? Always a lot on your mind?"

"I am unhearing. A benefit."

"What was Belinda like when she was younger?"

"Sharper than the splendor of our present midday light."

"That can be its own burden."

"Very much."

With a small grin, Robert motioned for the paper he'd just passed to Wilder. Robert wrote, "Ain't that the truth!"

Wilder beamed. He could see Hillard in Robert's grin. He wrote, "Ain't it tho?"

"Sho is." The way Robert held this up for Wilder to read was also all Hillard, playfully covering his own face. Robert turned to continue writing and soon let Wilder have the paper, which read, "You and Belinda plannin on some kids?"

"Now that we here, anythin mighty possible."

"Sound to me like just the right possible to bring joy."

Something about who Robert was had made room for Hillard. Was it because Robert was a pastor? Wilder wanted to know. "Know folks like me?"

"Met many of y'all in y'all's books. Ain't no better way to be with long lost kin."

The rest of what Robert wrote was all him. He wanted to talk of Jacob. "Under most circumstances there are no traits in life more disagreeable for a man to exhibit than fecklessness. But there are circumstances in which fecklessness seems what is to be begotten, what must be accepted. Jacob was begotten feckless."

He wrote on: "On news broadcasts a corner box displays an interpreter for the deaf's benefit. Your country employs people more adept at the skill. Here, our interpreters leave much to be desired. How do I know? The chyrons. Every broadcast floods one chyron after another. It is a shame the way the interpreters misrepresent the news. It is infuriating how ill-considered my kind is here."

Wilder had nothing to write in response. He passed the paper back.

"I am an unwitting expert on reading chyrons. They are synopses, in essence. Not even the briefest chyrons escape me. The loss of one sense sharpens another, Wilder. I am unhearing, but I can see chyrons that others are blind to."

"What do you mean?"

"I read Jacob's chyron long ago: innate hopelessness, as if a curse."

"And Belinda's?" Wilder quickly scribbled.

"I'm sure she continues to be sharper than the splendor of our midday light. She's tenacious. But to a fault. America is supposed to reward tenacity. The fact that it didn't reward hers is a stain on it. But it doesn't hurt, Wilder. It doesn't hurt that Belinda's tenacity did not pay off. It will make her less self-centered."

Wilder thought that Robert was being harsh. But Robert had lost his only child. If this was how he expressed his grief, he was entitled to it.

What might Robert say about his own life? Robert's omniscience astonished Wilder. "We still new to each other, Wilder," Robert wrote, "but it ain't take no genius to see all them bombs markin you."

The driver took them along dirt roads before stopping at a gate.

Robert wrote, "Go. I'll wait."

"Just me?"

"It's you searchin for talk."

Wilder got out of the van and went through the gate. To his left sat a powder-blue structure: a small home. Ahead was a concrete structure nobody needed to tell him was the beginnings of a much larger home.

Jacob appeared barefoot through the concrete columns. His muscularity was effortless, arms and shoulders stretching the fibers of his T-shirt. It was the same muscularity that Robert had. The brothers were giants.

The quiet here was deafening. Wilder closed in on him, stopping at the bottom of the flight of small steps to the front porch.

"Robert's not coming out?" asked Jacob.

Wilder wondered how Jacob knew who he was. Then he remembered the wedding picture of himself and Belinda that was part of the family portraits in the living room.

"They're driving around." Wilder surveyed his surroundings. "Yours?" he asked, indicating the house. He wondered whether Belinda knew.

"Not mine. Postwoman."

"Who?"

"She no longer matters. Coming here has confirmed that for me." Jacob stroked an invisible beard and said, "Tell me about it."

Wilder stroked his beard. "You like?"

"You keep it fine," he said. "How long have you been growing it?"

"I don't know," Wilder admitted. "And that's not because it's been so long that I have forgotten. It wasn't intentional. I went away. And when I returned a friend drew my attention to the fact that I had a beard going."

"And you kept it."

"Yes."

"Come up," Jacob said, stretching out his hand. But Wilder did not take it as he walked up the steps. Side by side, they both looked forward like land inspectors. "You are really here for good?" Jacob asked.

"That's the plan."

"For good?" he repeated.

"For good."

Jacob's eyelids flitted like flies. He sucked on a forefinger. Then, violently, he pinched its skin with his front teeth and bit off a piece he spat out. "I read in the newspaper about oil. Well, not oil as such. Gas flaring. I hear it's a waste."

Jacob's pronouncement did not alarm Wilder. His omniscience was just as it should be on a day that felt porous to the divine.

What, Wilder thought, was in store from Belinda when he returned home to her?

"Instead of just letting the gas into the atmosphere, it can be trapped and turned into electricity," Jacob continued. "I understand you are an oilman."

"I am."

"When my father told me that you were thinking of coming for good, I didn't believe it. Why leave America?" Jacob asked. "All the nonsense we have to go through here just to get something as small as an appointment at the American embassy. And you have America already. You just want to leave it?"

Wilder wouldn't call Jacob hopeless, he decided. Perhaps misguided, at least on this point of America's desirability.

"I know you love her, but to leave a whole America just for Belinda?" Jacob said. "And then it came to me. You are a businessman. An oilman. Why not leave America for Ghana when we now have oil? Here we are thinking that America is the prize. It's about what's possible. For you, maybe Ghana is the prize."

"What you are talking about is no small investment," Wilder said. He would do as Belinda had directed: make Jacob think that the idea rested with him. "A smart idea, though," he said. "Smart."

They locked eyes. Jacob looked away first. "It's smart for someone like you to make a play for the industry here while it's still young," he said.

The ploy had worked; Jacob believed he was enlightening him. "The power situation here is that bad?" Wilder asked.

"A serious problem. I don't remember the last time the power was on for six hours straight." Jacob dropped his voice to ask, "Did it stay on yesterday? For the program at the house?"

"I don't know. I was not feeling well."

"Neither was I," Jacob said. "Did the children sing Alfred's song at the funeral?"

"I don't know."

"It has the line—*When he comes, darkness will turn to light*?" Jacob said. "Wilder, if that isn't some higher power speaking, I don't know what is."

"So you're a spiritual man," Wilder said.

"Far from it."

"Then you believe in the power of song."

"Alfred has made me a believer." Jacob paused. Then, "Benjamin, too. I don't know what kind of believer he's made me yet. But Benjamin, too."

"You will know with time," Wilder said. "I lost a friend myself. It changed me." He wanted to give Jacob his hand. Yet he held back, interlocking his fingers in front of him. "I couldn't ask Robert; I thought it might be too much for him to take," Wilder said. "So I'll ask you. What was Alfred like?"

Jacob was quiet for a long moment. His eyelids fluttered rapidly. When finally he spoke, he said, "Believe it or not, Wilder, Robert would have had an easier time telling you.

"My father is fond of saying, 'You have done what Napoleon could not do.' That's his way of saying, *Congratulations!* Maybe Belinda has told you." Jacob walked to the edge of the construction site, where a wooden slab sloped down to the ground. Wilder followed him there. Jacob brought his feet together and stretched his arms out as wings. "If bringing light to an entire nation is not what Napoleon could not do, I don't know what is." Then he started down the slab. Right bare foot after left bare foot, like a playing boy. "Tell Belinda she's right. Tell her I can't look her in the eye."

Before Wilder could ask for clarification, Jacob ran through the gate. Wilder did not move; there was no mistaking this kind of flight. Yet he knew why he had bolted out of Laos: he'd had a direct hand in his child's death. Why was Jacob running? What direct hand had Jacob had in Alfred's? There was no chance of asking now. Jacob had shrunk to a speck.

Acknowledgments

In 2019, Margot Livesey, nurturer that she is, giver that she is, asked for the five-hundred-plus pages I was meekly cradling through the halls of the Iowa Writers' Workshop. After the embarrassing number of drafts Margot endured, we find ourselves here. Tameka Cage Conley, kin that she is, giver she too is, endured the same embarrassing number of drafts, and yet it was my withstanding the endurance she worried about most, feeding my soul with oxtails that slid off the bone, keeping me on with words of encouragement—"Kingly," the propelling moniker she gave me, was balm.

There is kindness so grand and so particular that one must eventually abandon the desperation to reciprocate and commit to not failing at love. Margot, Tameka, please forgive me if ever my being human and fallible causes me to fail.

Sam Chang, dear mentor, dear friend, dear revolutionary at the helm of the Iowa Writers' Workshop made way for Margot and Tameka to be just so in my life. Of course, there was that phone call in 2014, but mattering more is the environment Sam has fostered at the Workshop, where I instantly felt at home.

Before the Workshop, there was Tristan Davies, who at Johns Hopkins helped me recognize that, indeed, writing was in the cards for me.

I am grateful to teachers like T. Geronimo Johnson and Benjamin Hale who also saw promise early on. And to friends like Novuyo Rosa Tshuma and Adam Haslett who go the extra mile.

Thank you to Connie Brothers, Deb West, Janice Zenisek, and Sasha Khmelnik for holding me down. To Kate Christensen and Claire Lombardo for their generosity. And to Frank Amling, Elizabeth Menninger Wallace, Joshua Siefken, Steve Erickson, and Edmund Gaisie for coming to my rescue repeatedly. The Meg Walsh Leadership Award (Second Decade Society, Johns Hopkins University), Meta Rosenberg Graduate Fellowship (University of Iowa), Robert J. Schulze Memorial Fellowship (University of Iowa), and Ragdale in Schools Fellowship (Ragdale Foundation) made all the difference.

Jake Morrissey's magic and belief saw me to the finish line. He is a gem among other gems I am grateful to at Riverhead: Bianca Flores, Jynne Dilling Martin, Ashley Sutton, Ashley Garland, Helen Yentus, and Jackie Shost. And to Richard Abate and Rachel Kim, who took a chance, thank you. Thank you, too, to Martha Stevens.

Eskor David Johnson, Nana Nkweti, Mgbechi Erondu, De'Shawn Charles Winslow, and William Pei Shih are family. As are Aaron Adusei, Lily Paemka (Lilykins), Shawn Fu, Monique Francis, Boris Tokpley, Joanna Owusu, Chanel Sencherey, Kojo

Annan Ampofo, and Richmond Tandoh. To my loving siblings, cousins, aunts, uncles—and there many!—I owe so much to you.

Finally, to my loving and supportive wife, Maame Amma (MA) Nnuro, whose patience is the stuff of legend, having you in my life means that I can never question my luck.

Praise for What Napoleon Could Not Do

"DK Nnuro's striking first novel offers its readers a highly nuanced portrait of how the shadow of American hegemony shapes the lives of two Ghanian siblings, one who immigrates and one who doesn't. In Nnuro's deft hands, these particulars rise into a vision, panoramic in scope, of the global trade not in goods and services but in fantasy, desire, and regret. Jacob and Belinda are characters you will not soon forget, and the ache of their lives caught between Ghana and the United States is at the heart of this subtle, surprising, and captivating novel."

—Adam Haslettt, author of *Imagine Me Gone*

"*What Napoleon Could Not Do* is a multifaceted drama of familial relationships, duty, loss, and dreams deferred. Nnuro creates beautiful symmetry between America and Ghana, juxtaposing the physically draining disappointments of the Ghanaian government with the emotionally draining letdowns of the US bureaucracy. He boldly explores discrimination across and within race and culture and intricately crafts characters readers will feel intimately connected with. In this deeply thoughtful tale, Nnuro establishes himself as a powerful storyteller."   —*Booklist*

"What a majestic, poignant debut. So often I wanted to pull these characters to the side, as one would a friend, and hug them and ask, 'What are you doing?' The storytelling is exquisite. It delights in its intellect, its precision, and its keen, surprising insights. Nnuro is a writer of supreme powers. Here is a storyteller of the ages."

—Novuyo Rosa Tshuma, author of *House of Stone* and *I Dream America*